FOX'S EARTH

ANNE RIVERS SIDDONS

BALLANTINE BOOKS • NEW YORK

The author wishes to thank Houghton-Mifflin Company for permission to reprint three lines from the poem "Epistle to Be Left in the Earth" by Archibald MacLeish, which appears in *New and Collected Poems, 1917–1976*, © 1976 by Archibald MacLeish.

Library of Congress Catalog Card Number: 81-1920

ISBN 0-345-30461-6

This edition published by arrangement with Simon and Schuster, Inc.

Manufactured in the United States of America

First Ballantine Books Edition: September 1982

20 19 18 17 16 15

For my friend Jim Townsend,
who has made all the difference

I pray you
          you (if any open this writing)
Make in your mouths the words that were our names.

Archibald MacLeish
"Epistle to Be Left in the Earth"

Prologue

THERE ARE TWO WAYS to get from Atlanta to Sparta, and the one that is chosen will say not a little about the chooser. The first consists of the interstate, which veers north about twenty miles out of Atlanta toward the middle-sized cities of the Carolinas and, ultimately, the glittering conurbation of the East. Here, mown rights of way, rolling farms, neat suburbs, prosperous towns, and expensive federal road signs show the traveler what this land can be, given care and responsible tending. The South at its best, it is, or so many people think. The Sunbelt waits for *you*. Passers-through take this way, and urbanites visiting, for one reason or another, the state university, which lies in Sparta, and students and parents of students. People in a hurry, and with a purpose. It is a pretty way to go to Sparta.

The other way is a leprous two-lane blacktop, first clawed out of the pine forest of the Piedmont Plateau in the late 1830s to afford tiny, savage Atlanta access to the mellower world of the university. This road is patched and shored up annually, after each macadam-buckling Georgia winter, but the last time anyone remembers its being totally resurfaced was in 1937, when Harry Hopkins's young WPA got hold of it.

The old road lies in another country, in an older South. Broom sedge and seedling pines chew voraciously at the roadside ditches. Malignant green kudzu masks toppling tenant shanties, rusted barbed-wire fences, brittle old telephone poles, whole sweeping miles of lunar roadside landscape. Cotton fields here are smaller, scantily tended, leached much of the year to blowing pink dust; 1930s iron bridges span tea-colored creeks with names like One Stump,

1

Hellpeckish, Booger's Water, Coosaula. They are tributaries of the deep-running Oconee River, which powers the textile mill in Sparta and a dozen towns like it, on its leaping journey to join the Ocmulgee and create the Altamaha at the fall line. The creek names are the harsh and homely place music of the Piedmont.

The naked earth is seldom visible along this old road, thatched as it is with sedge, pine, and kudzu. The pale dust of the fields and ditches is not the true color of the earth but the color of fatigue and decay. The earth is littered crazily here: with cement-block houses and grocery stores; with one-pump filling stations attached to wailing roadhouses and evil-smelling rest rooms; with ancient, gap-toothed family graveyards; with sagging power lines and county road signs bleached by decades and pitted by the showered gravel of pickup trucks and tossed Pabst and Nehi bottles. Along this road only Jesus saves, only Coke adds life.

Not even an errant spectre from the South's splendid, sad and silly Civil War walks the matted earth here, for, lacking a significant railroad or munitions factory, Sparta held little allure for the main body of William Tecumseh Sherman's troops on their way through Atlanta to Savannah and the sea. Only sullen and sporadic skirmishes between Fightin' Joe Wheeler's Confederate cavalry and a bored division or two of the Union's best broke the quiet of that time-lost and terrible red July. In any case, Fightin' Joe undoubtedly did as much damage to the land as did the strayed bluecoats, since his pale-eyed, hookwormed southerners lived off the land wherever they could.

So at first or, indeed, at any glance the land along the old road from Atlanta to Sparta does not look to be the sort of bountiful and savage red earth that men across the South fought their kinsmen for, bled into, died for. But men did die for this land, and women too, and even more lived and died for the land in Sparta proper, upon which stood the neoclassical buildings of the university and a handful of old white houses as beautiful as anything that rose in the damned and beautiful South of those last quiet years before apocalypse.

The people who take this old way to Sparta are rarely in a hurry, and their only purpose for doing so is that they belong to the town and the land, though not necessarily to one of the old houses in it.

But the two women in the blue Volvo who drove along the old road on a fitful May morning did belong, and as they drove, many old deaths and one new one reached out to them from a great white house at 15 Church Street in Sparta, called Fox's Earth.

Part One

RUTH

1

By two p.m. they had walked for half an hour, the man and his family, and the sweat of that sun-blanched September Saturday in 1903 lay sour in waistbands and collars and dampened pale hair and ran rank down thin necks and backs and legs. Pink dust puffed and flew from beneath the wheels of passing wagons and buggies, coating wet skin miserably and mingling with residual traces of cotton lint and waste to catch in the creases of elbows and neck and in hair. The dust was the effluvia of the great brick mill behind them to the south, where they all worked . . . all except the small girl and the woman. It had not rained for nearly six weeks, and the small town lay in a near-coma of drought and unrelenting heat.

In the town, in back yards and browning gardens and over fences, the wives of the small merchants and liverymen and smiths and draymen paused over their black-iron washpots, their chicken coops and their clotheslines. Steaming in close-buttoned, high-collared shirtwaists and long, swathing skirts, viciously bound in viselike, back-laced corsets, they pushed back straggling hair and mopped red faces and sighed to one another.

"Cruel hot ain't it?" "Will it ever rain?" "Have you got summer sickness at your house? Two of mine are down with it." "Dear Lord, we need rain."

Downtown, their husbands struggled against the relentless pall of dust that lay over their stores and wagons and wares and hauled water for their stock and scanned the white-bronze sky a dozen times a day. The bell on the volunteer fire wagon rang frequently and old Dr Hopkins's buggy and young Dr Hopkins's phaeton were seen often on the choking streets. Voices dropped faces stilled heads turned slowly when the bell rang and the buggy rolled. With the murderous heat and drought came the threat of the summer murderers: Fire. Typhoid, in stagnant and

7

diminished wells and rain barrels and reservoirs. Infantile paralysis, from no one knew where.

But outside the town, in the rolling pink and green fields, the farmers sweated and stank and stumbled and drank more often from the water wagon . . . and smiled.

"Good for the cotton, though, ain't it?" "Cotton looks real good this year. Real good." "Heard in town that cotton might go as high as twelve this fall, maybe higher."

Cotton! In Sparta, and all over the Deep South in that malignant third September of the new century, cotton was once more the lifeblood of the red land. For the first time since the guns of Sumter, in Charleston, tolled the death knell of the great plantations and the slave nation that supported them, southern agriculture was reversing its sickening downward spiral . . . or, at least, the descent was becoming markedly less precipitous. And once again it was cotton that fueled the march back to prosperity and former glory. Not cotton in the role it had played before the war, when black backs broke in endless red fields to send the white tide surging north to mills and manufacturers. But cotton in a new role: grown by small farmers on small, poor farms, hauled in their own homemade, iron-wheeled wagons by lean-honed mules into the nearest town, to be sold on marketing day and fed into the maws of the great, forbidding mills that had sprung up across the southern earth like ravenous mushrooms.

After the Civil War there had been only a scant handful of crude mills operating in the South; by 1900, four hundred mills bulked dark against the sky. And across the South, more than a quarter of a million of the white tenant farmers and sharecroppers, reduced by poverty of land, purse, and spirit to subsisting at the level of the blacks they despised and, worse, to working side by side with them, had flown for refuge into the mills. Cotton. What was good for cotton was good for the South, and those who damned the heat and drought of early autumn did so in small voices.

Around Sparta, on this late summer afternoon, the roads into town billowed and thundered with a steady stream of mules and white-laden wagons. Farm families sat decorously in large wagons and a few newer buggies, their cotton on the way to market and their purses filled with coins to buy household supplies and a small luxury or two in the shops of town. Saturday. Cotton-market day.

8

In all the crowd streaming into Sparta that Saturday, only Negroes walked in the dust of the roadside. Negroes and the family of Cater Yancey. None of the families from the rotting, rectilinear mill village owned buggies or wagons, let alone mules to pull them, but there were no other mill families afoot on the road into town that day. They all did their meager shopping at the company commissary, where thin-strung credit could be spun even tauter against the hopelessly small wages that never were enough. The Yanceys alone walked the streets of Sparta, with Cater at their head, his back straight and rigid in the dusty black clawhammer coat he wore, summer and winter, for Sunday preaching and weddings and funerals and town, his blue eyes far-focused and flat with hating. He did not break the long, rolling stride that he had learned on the blue mountains of North Georgia when he took his first steps. Seventy-two hours a week for twenty-six years as a spinner in the roaring, radiant hells of two cotton mills had not crushed the long hill stride from his legs nor dimmed the mad blue of his eyes. The cruel, stern God of his Presbyterian ancestry thundered in his head day and night, and the Celtic gods of his ancestral Scotland chanted and howled silently to him of blood and red, sweet pleasures and wild rites in the thin blue air of the Highlands, and both took his tongue in turn on Sundays when he sometimes preached at the unpainted little church in the mill village, when the regular Baptist preacher from town had fatter and sleeker fish to fry.

The silent, dull-eyed congregation understood little of his garbled litany, but his yellow and beautiful head and long white hands stirred and fed them, and his terrible fervor frightened and excited them as little else in their deadened days did. On the Sundays he did not preach, he herded his cowed family into the bare little front room of the mill house, and cried aloud from the Old Testament to them for hours, and harangued and exhorted them in a voice of ringing brass until the smaller children wept with fear, and all trembled. Cater's family knew that he could not read, that his prodigious store of biblical knowledge had been learned at the knee of the mad old grandmother who had raised him on her wild mountaintop; but no one else knew, and his repertoire was much admired in the mill village.

After the sessions in the church and the front room, he

was white and drained and silent, gone away somewhere within himself; he remembered nothing of what he had said. Most who heard him agreed that it was the Holy Spirit who spoke through Brother Yancey, but some, Ruth and Pearl Yancey among them, knew that it was something or someone else, and feared and hated the sessions, recognizing without being able to name it the thing that truly spoke on those mornings: his amorphous and immutable madness. They did not protest, for Cater Yancey was a violent and dangerous man. He beat his family frequently —long, savage beatings with the heavy length of mule harness he kept for the purpose on a peg on the kitchen wall. They stifled their cries as best they could, with fists and sometimes wads of skirt pressed to their mouths, for all knew that to cry out was to fuel his efforts. Even sly, proud Pearl Steed Yancey sometimes broke and cried aloud under the harness. But small Ruth never did. She had been sustained since her earliest memory by a bright, hard, and perfect hatred of her father.

It burned steadily and purely on this afternoon as she followed him, matching his stride step for step, not lifting her hand to wipe away the perspiration that ran from her own white-blond hair and blinded her blue eyes, or to claw the choking dust from her mouth. There were whimpers from eight-year-old Sarah and nine-year-old Hagar, and mutinous mutters and whispered oaths from twelve-year-old Lot, and Isaac, who was thirteen. But Ruth, aged ten and a miniature replica of Cater Yancey, was silent in her hate. If she were silent enough, still enough, except for her bare feet in the whispering dust, if she kept her blue eyes fixed steadily enough on his back, if she concentrated hard enough on the flame of her hatred for him, she could shut out the sights and sounds of the people on the road beside her, get through their scalding mission in the stores of Sparta and back out on the road toward home again without ever once meeting a pair of searing, scornful town eyes or hearing a single hissed epithet of "linthead" or "mill rat."

It seemed to her on those hated one-a-month Saturday trips that the town eyes bit into her like rodents, and in a sense she was right; eyes did rest more often on her than on the other children of Pearl and Cater Yancey, and lingered longer. For Ruth Steed Yancey was an extraordinarily, startlingly beautiful child, and the promise of a

10

womanhood so spectacular as to stop breath hung about her, even at ten. Pearl whispered often to her daughter that she was pretty, and a special child, marked for a special destiny, but since any Yancey child who gazed longer into the crazed shard of Cater's shaving mirror than it took to straighten hair into seemliness would quickly feel the wrath of the mule harness, Ruth did not know the extent of her physical comeliness, and would not for yet a little while longer.

Cater Yancey's mission on those Saturdays was three-fold. One, he took his family among the Philistines of Sparta to show them the sins of the flesh and the evils of affluence, intoning loudly before the glittering array of goods in Dorrance's Mercantile and Mabry's Drugstore and pressing their faces ruthlessly to the glass windows of the Sparta Cafe and Wright's glorious barbershop. He stopped them before the alien mystery of the Sparta tele-phone exchange, to chant of the evils of mindless progress against the Old Ways, and herded them, stiff-faced and inwardly cringing, through the cold and gamy plenty of the butcher shop and the marble and wrought-iron mag-nificence of the Sparta Railroad Savings Bank. He howled imprecations at the town's two stuttering automobiles as they jumped harelike through the dust of the street, and raised his fist like a prophet of the Old Testament at the upholstered carriages of the comfortable and at the smart liveried coaches and broughams from the great old white houses on the edge of the university campus. It was for these houses, and the university itself, that he saved his bitterest imprecations. In Cater Yancey's twilit mind, Satan himself dwelled in those houses, and walked the shade-dappled hills of the mellow old brick university.

Cater's second purpose on the Saturday missions was to shame and instruct, by example, the townspeople of Sparta, and to this end he bade his family dress in their cleanest but shabbiest scraps of clothing, and assume their most modest demeanor, and cast down their eyes and close their lips in the face of even the cruelest taunts. He would, from somewhere, lay by a few pennies with which to buy a scrap or two of salt pork and a bag of dried beans and a small bag of flour, and these he selected after long and ostentatious examination of each single item in Lapham's Grocery, all the while railing at the folly and wastefulness of Lapham's bounty of fresh meats, cheeses, produce, coffee waiting to be ground, and, above all, the temptations of the long glass-and-mahogany case full of candies. Ruth, whose flashing, if untutored, intelligence led her to teach herself reading and sums at an early age, aided by Pearl's scanty store of knowledge, assumed the task of toting up the family's purchase and doling out the coins that Cater grudgingly handed her. The sight of the small, beautiful child, grave and pale in her rags and possessed of a powerful adult dignity, silently adding up the price of the pitiful objects while the starveling man howled his outrage and the wasted woman and her razor-shanked children shrank mutely away from him in shame wrung more than one good Spartan heart. But when Marcus Lapham once slipped Ruth a red jawbreaker, Cater wrenched the godless candy from her fist and flung it on the counter beneath the grocer's nose, and his rantings were so terrible and caused his family to quail in such obvious humiliation that Lapham never did it again, nor did any of the townspeople who witnessed the incident again offer aid or succor to the family of Cater Yancey.

His third mission in town was simpler. As the humbled band stole out of town on their way home to the mill village, he would station them under a giant magnolia that hung over the railroad trestle and, bidding them not move from their tracks nor speak to passersby, slip away down a well-worn path through the kudzu thickets into the shadows of the ravine. Through and beyond the ravine lay Suches, or niggertown, as it was called by the impoverished whites of the mill village, and in a grease-smelling house propped anonymously among the other unpainted, stilted houses of Suches, Titterbaby Calhoun dispensed fruit jars of his malignant homemade whiskey at prices that were, to say the least, fiercely competitive with those at Carnes's saloon in Sparta proper.

The blue-green shadows on the kudzu in the ravine would be deepening into solid darkness by the time Cater returned. Pearl and the children would hear him singing and mumbling his way up through the kudzu, and wait silently to see how bad it would be this time. Often he would have had only a taste of Titterbaby's whiskey in Titterbaby's kitchen. If this was the case, and the croker sack he carried was still full of sealed fruit jars chinking softly together in newspaper cocoons, Cater would be expansive and mildly indulgent, patting Ruth and the smaller

12

girls roughly on their heads and poking awkwardly at the sullen boys and laying light, crablike hands on Pearl's flanks and buttocks. He would sing oddly cadenced, silvery ballads with the sounds of pipes and fiddles in them, and once or twice he stopped on these trips home and caught Pearl around the waist and swept her, protesting, into a light-footed, jigging dance. At these times the children would look at their father with flat and unknowing eyes, with no ken in them for this stranger capering in the dust.

But at other times the croker sack would be only half full, and the shadows in the ravine would have turned to black, and at these times Cater would be lost and deep in that strange, terrible country behind his eyes, and they knew that when they got home there would be shouting and singing, and then the beatings, and the breath-strangling moment when he would catch their mother by her sharp-knobbed shoulders and jerk her into the tiny, windowless room where they slept and slam the warped door. Then the children would creep into the other room, where their stale pallets were, and lie in the darkness, and hear their mother's screams, and the howls and singing rising, and then the last great howl, and then a thumping, squeaking silence that faded at last into Pearl's soft, snuffling sobs and Cater's great gargling snores.

In the morning Pearl would be windbroke and lame, with bruises and scratches on her sallow flesh, and often her injuries were more severe. Blackened and swollen eyes were not unusual on the Sunday after cotton-market Saturday, and one morning three teeth were gone from her mouth that decay had not claimed.

Once Ruth had asked her mother, after one of those nights, "What does he do to you in there?"

"Well, he beats me. You know. He's a beatin' man when the likker takes him."

"No'm, I mean when he hollers funny like that. I know it's a long time after he's quit beatin' you, because you've quit yellin' way before then. What does he do then?"

Pearl looked at her daughter, a long, measuring look. The child looked back at her, the slanted blue eyes aware and old, with nothing of childhood in them.

"He has this old thing between his legs . . . you know, like Lot and Isaac have, only lots bigger . . . and it gets all swole up and fat and long and red-like, and he pushes

13

me down on my back and pulls my legs apart and he rams it way up between them."

"Mama! He don't! Oh, Lord! You mean where you tee-tee?" Ruth began to cry with fright.

"Right there. And he leaves it there and jams it up and down till he gits real excited, and then he hollers like that, and he shoots this nasty old white stuff all up me, and it runs down all over my legs, and sometimes there's blood, too. That's what he does."

"He must be awful mad at you, Mama, to do a thing like that to you," Ruth snuffled.

Pearl smiled, a crippled smile. "He ain't mad. It's what he likes, he wants to do that. All men want to do that to all women. They'll be wantin' to do that to you pretty soon, an' some probably already do, seein' what a pretty thing you are. But you listen to me, Ruth, and listen good. You don't let no man put that old thing up you until you've got what you want from him, startin' with a gold wedding ring. If you remember that, you can get a lot of good things by keepin' your legs together. A man's a fool when it comes to his big ol' thing."

"No man is ever gon' do that to me," Ruth sobbed between clenched teeth. "No man in shoe leather on this earth is goin' to put that thing in me. I'll kill the man that does that."

Pearl crouched down on her heels beside her daughter and took Ruth's slender shoulders in her hands. She looked into the small, furious face with her dead eyes. She dropped her voice.

"Ruth, listen. Men are devils, and a man'll hurt you and half-kill you 'fore he'll look at you. He'll use you up and wear you out and take what's yours and never give you what ought to be yours. A man has all the power, a man is strong, a man will win every time . . . but a man is a fool. A woman is weak, a woman don't have nothing, a woman is a man's toy and a man's slave . . . but a woman has one thing that can git anything a man has, if she uses it right. And that's what's between her legs. You can use that to git anything in this world that you want, if you do the right things, if you know what to do. . . ."

"What do you do, Mama?"

"Well, you just pick out the man you want something from, and you git around him an' make sure he notices you good, an' has time to think about it, and then you

14

sorta let him see what you got, and you rub up against him like, and when you see that thing start swellin' up, you just lay back and take your hands and put it in you slow-like, and you pet him, and you wiggle, and you whisper to him, 'That's right, honey. That's good, honey. You got a real fine one, honey, just what a woman wants,' and on and on like that, and pretty soon that ol' fool will give you anything he's got that you want. You just make sure you pick you out a man that has somethin' worth gittin'. You, now, there ain't nothing you can't git, lookin' like you do, if you take your best chance and pick out the right man. But you got to be ready, Ruth. All the time you got to be lookin' for that chance, and when it comes, you got to take it an' never look back. Not ever, not for nothin'. You remember what I'm sayin' to you."

Ruth looked at her mother. Saffron bruises were fading at her throat; fresh, dark ones mottled her upper arms, so thin that the skin hung slackly from them like wet, dimpled cloth, with no cushioning fat beneath them. The long hair, wound into an untidy bun at her nape, had been thick and glossy and a vivid chestnut once, but it was thin now, and dull and dry, like the mane of an old horse. The three missing teeth gave Pearl's mouth the sunken appearance of a very old woman, and the stark lunar ridge of the collarbone, notched where an old break had healed unevenly, moved up and down under the faint, persistent hacking that was the beginning of white lung.

"What did all that ever git you from Pa?" she said.

Pearl was silent so long that Ruth thought she was not going to answer. She looked beyond and over the child's head, her eyes full of time and distance, seeing into a long-ago time that seemed, now, so remote and fabled as to be myth. She looked back at Ruth.

"You ain't never worked in the mill, have you? That's what I got from your pa. That's all he had to give me, and that's what I got. And that's how I got it. You ain't never knowed the inside of that mill nor any other, and you never will. You can thank that place between my legs for that."

Ruth had been nine then. It was the last time in her life she remembered crying.

They passed over the railroad trestle, shimmering miragelike in the heat over the fathomless green of the kudzu

15

ravine, and turned onto a tree-shaded street that narrowed
tunnel-like through dim, cool green, straight into the heart
of the town. Parallel to the street proper, set far back on
smooth lawns vaulted with soaring old oaks, stretched a
long line of great white-columned houses. Ornamental
ironwork, hanging balconies, ranks of Doric and Corinthian colonnades, Grecian pediments and friezes shimmered
remotely, like the tombs of Atlantis, behind formal box
and rose gardens, magnolias and cedars of Lebanon, arbors
of wisteria and Virginia creeper. To the left of the street
were other streets like it, if not quite so sepulchrally white
and grand; to the right, behind it, lay the complex of the
university. Sounds on this street were strangely muffled,
even in winter, when the enshrouding trees were bare; it
was a quiet that seemed to breathe on the street like a
benediction from an enchanted past. A slammed door, the
cries and laughter of a children's party in a cloistered
back garden, the rich laughter of Negro servants, the
chink of harness and the light tattoo of delicate and expensive hooves, a dinner bell, a woman's low laugh, a
spinet's splash . . . the great quiet drew them all into itself
and drowned them. Church Street.

Of all the streets of the town, Ruth Yancey loved this
one best of all. Her small, knotted body relaxed on Church
Street; her stiff, set little face lifted to the great houses and
trees and, of itself, smoothed and softened into something
tender and misted, only then young. The houses on Church
Street had voices; they spoke and sang to Ruth Yancey. It
was the only sound she heard.

There was one house. . . . The voice of this house rose
to an anthem so pure and drowning that Ruth, when she
first saw it and heard its song, turned involuntarily to the
others. When she saw that they did not hear it, she was
surprised, but later she came to accept it. The house spoke
just to her; its song was hers alone.

The house was larger than its neighbors on Church
Street, though not by far. Like its neighbors, it was three-
storied and flat-roofed, in the Classical Revival style for
which the small town was renowned. Fourteen tall, dazzling white Corinthian columns extended in a colonnade
around the front and two sides, and a fan of shallow steps
swept in a graceful curve up to the Italian-tile veranda.
The steps were flanked by dignified Medici lions, and there
was another lion, a fine, militant head, on the bronze door

16

knocker. Tall green-shuttered windows marched symmetrically around the house on the ground floor, reaching from the veranda ceiling to the tiles, and more shuttered windows girdled the second floor. Ruth counted sixteen windows on the front of the house, eight on the first floor and eight on the second; the windows marched on around the house and were lost in the towering Cape jessamine hedges that shielded the back garden from the street. She did not know how many rooms there were but thought there were a great many.

Between the windows on the second floor, floating in space like a small boat under sail, hung a white-railed balcony. Once Ruth saw a beautiful woman in a cloud of starched white standing on the balcony, her hand resting lightly on the railing, staring out over the street. In the leaf-dappled light and silence of early afternoon, she looked inconstant, incorporeal. Ruth thought she might be a ghost. It seemed fitting that such a house would have a beautiful ghost. She said nothing about seeing the woman.

And once, in the front garden, which was a formal box garden planted with clipped box, magnolias, and cedars of Lebanon, cherry laurel, gardenia, tea olive, sweet syringa, and flowering quince, she saw a boy on the path of flat marble squares that led from the hollowed carriage block at the street up to the steps. He was older than she by about three years—eleven, maybe, at the time—and wore white, like the woman on the balcony. His was a starched sailor suit, with a square collar that hung down his back, and a black sateen tie, and short pants. His legs were encased in black stockings, and his high-topped shoes were magnificently mirror-shiny. He wore a round, upbrimmed straw sailor hat on his hair, which was a clear, ashen brown, and he had a hoop and a stick in his hand. He was a pudgy boy, somehow soft and unformed in his fine clothes, and his face was round and pale and small-featured, with great brown eyes.

The boy stood very still on the path, pinned motionless under the stolid eyes of the passing children. They stared at his clothes, fabled garments which they could not imagine, for they knew no clothes but their own thin-worn cutoff overalls and long-tailed shirts made from the feed sacks which the mill produced; they stared at the hoop, which they had seen before only in Olcott's dry-goods store, never in the living hand of a child. There was no glint of

17

surprise in the five pairs of children's eyes; like white sailor suits and hoops, surprise was not a part of their world. The boy might have been a phantom.

The boy's brown eyes met Ruth's blue ones, and widened slightly, and then Cater, bringing up the rear, spied him, and he paused on the sidewalk and motioned his flock to a halt, and lifted his long face to heaven.

"Spawn of Hell," he began, pointing a long white finger at the frozen boy. "Imp of Satan . . ."

The boy fled up the walk and into the house as soundlessly as a fawn in a forest, leaving the flickering light on the lawn as still and untouched as if he had never been there. The Yancey family moved on.

That night, before Cater jerked Pearl into the closed room and the shouting and screaming began, while he still nodded and mumbled on the damp-rotted back porch with his croker sack of fruit jars, Ruth went to Pearl Yancey in the tiny, evil-smelling kitchen, where Pearl was frying salt pork.

"Who was the boy, Mama?" Ruth asked. She did not say which boy she meant, but Pearl knew.

"That's the Fox boy. Po'-lookin' soul, ain't he? Comes from bein' the only one. Spoiled, I reckon, with all that money and them schoolin' him at home an' all. No 'count, most likely, and'll never be."

"Are they the people that live in the house? The Foxes? Tell me about the Foxes, Mama."

"Why do you care about them people? They ain't no mind of yourn."

"I want to know. I want to know about who lives in that house."

Pearl shot her a keen look. "You like that house?"

"It's the most beautiful house in the world. I'm going to have one just like it some day."

Pearl snorted, but she set down her fork and leaned against the rickety kitchen table that stood, covered with stained oilcloth, in the middle of the room, and crossed her arms.

"Well, the daddy, Mr. Fox, he's president of the school. And the mama, Mrs. Fox, she's a rich Yankee schoolmarm that he met while he was up North at that fancy rich man's college. And the boy is their only chick. He don't go to the school; they have a schoolteacher come to the house to teach him."

18

"How do you know about 'em, Mama? Have you met 'em?"

"Of course I ain't met 'em. I've just heard about 'em. Where would I be meetin' the great Foxes of Fox's Earth?"

"Fox's Earth . . ." Ruth breathed softly. The words rang with portent, sang like the voice of the house.

"It's what they call the house, what they named it. Did you ever hear such nonsense? A house with a name?"

"Fox's Earth. What does it mean, Mama?"

"*I* don't know, Ruth. Nothing good, sure as gun's iron."

"Could you find out?"

"No, and you don't need to know, neither. Why are you carryin' on so about that house? You'd think you was gon' go live in it tomorrow, the way you're takin' on about it."

"Mama," said Ruth slowly, knowing with a faraway, unsurprised certainty that came from somewhere far outside herself that what she said was true, "Mama, I might. I could."

Pearl did not chide her daughter. She turned back to the hissing meat in the skillet, and her thin back stiffened under the sweat-soiled everyday dress that had come out of the poor box at the mill church.

"Well, it ain't like you warn't born to it," she said, but she said no more.

Ruth had heard it before, this legend of her aristocratic birthright, intoned to her like a rosary in the nights when she was sick with colic or earache or summer fever; repeated, like a catechism, as she and her mother worked together over the iron washpot in the scanty back yard, or scrubbed futilely at the whitening, buckled boards of the floors with lye soap and a stiff brush, or labored over the heavy sadirons that sat in the ashes of the fire that burned, winter and summer, in the kitchen fireplace.

For it was as Pearl had said. From the moment her first daughter was born, Pearl had set her sloping jaw in the face of Cater Yancey's incandescent wrath and refused to go back into the mill, and no amount of beating and roaring and exhorting of God could budge her. Moreover, when Ruth reached the age of six, the time when most children went into the mills to climb upon their wooden boxes and tend their bobbins for twelve or fourteen hours a day, Pearl had once again defied Cater and refused to let her daughter join the boys, Lot and Isaac, in the eternally lighted, booming caldron of the Dixie Bag and Cotton Manufacturing Company. The other little girls who came along after Ruth, sallow Hagar and weaseled, squinting Sarah, she surrendered to the mill without a qualm, for it was true that as many of them as possible must work if Cater was to receive a subsistence family wage. None of the other children of Cater Yancey was curious or energetic enough to question the fact that Ruth stayed home with their mother. There was about Ruth, from the day she was born, a bright and preternaturally focused aura, a nimbus of gold, that set her apart from the dull-eyed, lank-haired, worm-and-pellagra-riddled mill children and silenced resentful questioning. If it was a reflection from the furnace of Cater's own madness, no one saw it. On Ruth's flesh it seemed a promise, a patina, like the bloom on a grape.

Looking on her new daughter, beautiful even in the first hour after the birth that almost killed her mother, the exhausted and white-bled Pearl performed her first act of defiance of her husband in Ruth's behalf. Sister Martha Flaherty, the obese, mustached midwife who had jerked the child into the world, paused over the Yancey family Bible to record the newborn's name, and looked to Cater.

"She will be called Esther," mumbled Cater, drunk and in a rage because his third child was a girl, and a fragile, small one at that.

"No," Pearl said clearly from the bed. "She will be called Ruth. For whither I goeth she will go, and whither I lodgeth, she will lodge. And my people will be her people."

The midwife looked upon Pearl Yancey's rapt face and wrote down, "Ruth Steed Yancey." For weeks afterward, although the midwife denied it indignantly, Pearl insisted that the child must have been born with a caul, and implored the woman to give it back to her.

"Because anybody can plainly see that she ain't no mill baby, not this one," Pearl said, and even the coarse old woman was forced to agree that there was something unique about little Ruth Yancey, something luminous and more finely wrought than in other children.

The story of how she acquired her name was one of the first Ruth heard from Pearl when she was old enough to understand her mother's talk.

20

"Tell again about my name, Mama," Ruth would say, and Pearl would repeat again the story of Ruth, who said to her mother-in-law, "Thy people shall be my people."

"Because, Ruth," Pearl would say, "our people wasn't born to the mill, no matter if we have come on hard times, and you wasn't, neither. I cain't hardly remember a time when things was different, but I know they was. My mama was born on a great big plantation the year the war started, and even if things was real bad by the time she was old enough to remember 'em, she used to tell me the stories her mama told her, about the house they lived in, and the clothes they wore, and the food they ate, and the parties and balls and barbecues. The ground was white like snow as far as the eye could see at pickin' time, white with cotton an' black with niggers pickin' it, an' all of it was ourn. So you just remember, you wasn't born to no mill, an' you ain't gon' end up in no mill. We was the cream of the county in them days, an' you will be again."

There was a grain of truth in the story, but only a grain. The Steeds had been mildly prosperous small upland planters in the red-hill country to the north of Sparta, clinging to the fringes of the rich cotton land that began at the fall line and lay like a fecund mantle over middle Georgia. But with the defeat of the Confederacy had come grinding poverty and illness, and Pearl Steed's grandparents and, later, the elderly farmer who married her mother and begat Pearl died struggling to claw a living out of the ruined earth. The day after her husband's funeral, Pearl's mother sold the unpainted house with its two peeling columns and its crazily canted chimneys, the puny livestock, and the flinty acres to her prosperous adjoining neighbor, sewed the money into the last remaining machine-made corset cover from her scanty trousseau, took tiny Pearl and her clothing and a basket of eggs down the red-dirt road and into town to the mill village, to the house of a woman with whom she had become friendly at church, and vanished on foot toward the seductive silver ribbon of the railroad track that stretched shimmering in the heat haze toward Atlanta. Pearl never saw her again.

The woman who took her in was husbandless herself; her man had simply left a line scrawled on a feed-store receipt some years before, "Gone to West," and vanished, leaving her with eight children between the ages of two and thirteen. The woman could neither read nor write and, without her husband, could not expect to stay on in the tenant farmhouse they occupied. She had no choice. She took her children and went into town and the new mill that had risen nearby on the banks of a mountain river. She was, in the main, rather glad to have small Pearl Steed with her. The child did not take up much room, nor eat much, nor require any clothing, and she was so silent as to give no trouble at all. She did as she was bidden, trudging into the mill before daybreak and coming home with the other children after sunset in the winter months; and it was soon obvious that her small, quick hands were destined to become the hands of a weaver. Considering Pearl's contribution to the family wage and the fact that, by age fourteen, she was already an apprentice weaver, the woman got a real bargain in Pearl Steed.

Pearl grew into a slight, silent girl with a sly face, downcast eyes, and an erect back in spite of the hours and years of work at the loom. The only color about her was in the heavy, silken mass of hair that burned a living red on her small head and slender neck. She said little, even when spoken to; she had said little since the day her mother went away. When she did speak, her voice was the texture and color of tepid water, with nothing in it of her grandfather's rich Irish brogue or her mother's fluting trill, and her speech soon lapsed back into the laconic illiteracy of the mill people she lived among. She was meek, biddable, and almost totally unremarkable. It would have been impossible to guess that inside her inconsequential small body there stretched an entire, vast country of burning rage at the people around her, and at the mill, towering grief and yearning for her vanished mother and for the refuge of that other life that had never been, her legacy that never was, the great white ghost house that had, in reality, been an unpainted frame house with two pitted columns, surrounded by dead earth.

The land. The actual, palpable red earth, the fertile clay of North Georgia, the land of the South, the bearer of the great white houses, the nurturer of the sacred white surf of cotton. In the clamorous mill, in the stifling church, in the fetid little mill house, or on the baked, treeless streets of the mill village, the land called and called to

Pearl Steed, slipped into body and being to become bone of her spine, fiber of her heart. The slow rhythms of the days and the majestic turning of the years upon the land became the rhythm and pulse of her blood; the void where the land was not howled in her soul, the loss of the phantom land of her people was her life force.

Something had been born in Pearl's grandmother after the war, something that she had passed on to her girl child, who had in turn planted it in the willing heart and mind of her daughter Pearl before the child could remember; there was not a time that Pearl had not been aware of that thing. It was a knowing, a certainty, an unspoken tenet, an immutable constant, a gift from woman to woman to woman down a web of days that stretched from that rending time of folly and loss into a future that could not even be imagined. It was an absolute surety, as basic as the world-old knowledge of love and evil and death, that only the land and its gifts mattered, and with that surety came an accompanying cool and ruthless determination that never again would the winning and tending of the land be left in the hands of men, who had so cavalierly tossed it away for the sake of a foolish and nebulous ideal, a Glorious Cause made more stingingly ludicrous because it was not a cause at all, but the crowing hatred of thwarted children masquerading in clouds of chauvinistic idealism.

They were pragmatists of the highest order, those defeated southern women, and they realized that, while they could not control their men and their land and their destinies by strength and force, they could control them through wiles and graces and the very femininity that rendered them overtly helpless. They taught their daughters well, and those daughters taught their daughters, and whether or not the earliest of those women to whom the knowing came were, in their lifetimes, able to regain the lands and the lives they had lost, they never ceased their instruction.

And so Pearl Steed, fingers flying at her loom, heart and soul walking in the cool green-and-white grace of her imagined birthright, pregnant with the bitter knowing that was her mother's only legacy to her, met Cater Yancey on a Sunday in June when she was sixteen years old and as supple and sweetly wrought as she would ever be, when the only promise in her life was the promise that sang secretly in blood and viscera, for in her foreseeable tomorrows in the house of the woman and the mill, there was no promise. And she married him five months later.

Cater was then in his mid-twenties, and had been in the mills since he was eighteen years old. He had come out of the high mountains of northernmost Georgia almost literally a starveling; the intrepid revenue officers of the United States were, by the close of the century, well on the way to closing off the southern mountaineers' chief source of revenue, the production of corn whiskey. The Yancey clan had devoted its carefully husbanded energies to the making of shine, hunting, and a very little crop tending in the narrow valleys between their crags, since time out of the clan's collective mind. Like many of the people of the Southern Appalachians, the family of Cater Yancey were a strange, insular lot, half pagan-wild, half sternly Presbyterian, both traits legacies from the Scots who had first found refuge in those hills after the defeat of Bonnie Prince Charlie at Culloden.

The Yanceys, like most of the other mountain men living in the hidden clefts and under the great shoulders of the mountains, kept to themselves, often speaking to no outsider for the space of a year or more, speaking little enough to each other. Locked away from other men by weather and topography and preference, and often by the necessity of keeping blood crimes hidden, these mountain men got their children on their own silent women, and their children in turn on theirs, so that whole mountain communities and outposts were filled with people who looked startlingly the one like the other.

In Cater Yancey's case, the generations that were got on each other in those inhospitable hills were a handsome people, long and slender of bone, light of hair and eye, narrow of head and hands and feet, heirs to a strain of marauding Viking blood that overwrestled the blood of the squat black Celt and culminated, in young Cater, in a beauty that was fine-honed and almost princely, though he was illiterate, ill-clad, and eerily aberrant by the time he reached puberty. His madness, at least in those early years, seemed more a sheen, a bloom sprung from the blood, so that he walked in a vivid luminosity that drew eyes as naturally as a wild animal, or wildfire.

He had, in addition, from his half-crazed grandmother, who took him in early childhood after his uncle killed his

24

father with an ax and took his mother to earth in his hidden cabin across the mountain, a ringing gift of tongue and a worshipful terror of a strange and privately perceived God of the Old Testament. When the old woman died and left him alone in the bare cabin, he had already preached for three or four years, sporadically, to congregations of perhaps a dozen people in tiny churches huddled meanly in the valleys, and he went down out of the mountains with the thought of working in the mills only until he could establish himself as a preacher and choose a regular church. He buried his grandmother in a shallow grave clawed from the shale a way up the mountain, left her there unmarked but covered with large stones against animals, packed his few tatters of clothes and put on his shoes and removed the small store of money from the prized Staffordshire cow creamer in the tin pie safe, set fire to the cabin and watched it until it burned itself out, raked out and sanded the embers, and strode off down the mountain to the hill town to the south, where, in the mill for which he was bound, Pearl Steed dreamed and hungered.

Pearl Steed walked straight up to Cater Yancey after his first sermon in the little mill church, straight as an arrow, as if in a trance . . . as indeed she was, seeing in the slender, long figure and the crown of bright hair the plantation aristocrat she thought her grandfather to have been, and hearing in the sweet, thundering tongue a song that, for the first time in her life, seemed sung to her alone . . . and asked him to come to supper. Cater watched as Pearl's slender figure moved around the kitchen preparing the spare dinner. From her guardian's prattle he deduced that Pearl was already a weaver and capable of earning top money in the mills. She had a neat, narrow waist and a ripe swell of hip and buttock and heavy, plummy breasts that called out to the cups of his hands; and her hair was living fire on her shoulders, for she had let it down for the evening. Out of the old knowing, quickening for the first time somewhere in her loins and lights, she hung on to his words and complimented his sermon shyly and blushed from her delicate collarbone when he admired her cooking.

He could feel her warmth and moisture reaching out to him, feel it palpably against his face and the backs of

25

his hands, and he burned with it, and since the Bible clearly stated that it is better to marry than to burn, marry her he did, five months later, and burn with her and in her each night in the company house that was let to him for a dollar a week, until the children began to come and she slowed and thickened and drooped with the unrelenting toil and privation, and began to grow querulous and bitter, wriggling away from under him in the nights, so that the red rage that had been seeded in him in the womb budded and bloomed, and he would beat her until she lay down for him once more.

Under her increasing scorn his sermons grew more terrible and vague, and the madness that had seemed a skin of light was now a fire on him, consuming him and frightening the congregation. The deacons of the church finally told him that he could preach there no more, and, souring with the rejection and simmering in the juices of the madness in his blood, he brought his family down out of the hills to the older mill and more worldly church and congregation in the beautiful white town of Sparta. Here Ruth Yancey was born, and here, after she had won from him his promise that he would not send the child into the mill, Pearl Steed Yancey closed her legs to him forever, except when he beat and raped her on market Saturdays.

And here the child Ruth grew, and toiled ceaselessly and futilely beside Pearl (but never in that mill, or any other), and was petted and groomed and doted upon by her mother, and was regaled with stories of the phantom many-columned house on that long-ago lost hill, and was catechized by Pearl in the knowing, so that once again, anew, it was whole and perfect, waiting, waiting.

2

THEY CAME OUT of the green tunnel of Church Street and crossed the courthouse square. It was clogged with people; they spilled out of their wagons and down the streets of Sparta, in and out of the brick-fronted stores, and overflowed onto the benches in the square and under the tin awnings along the sidewalks, a molten lava of people, as intransigent as heat phantoms in the pall of dust that hung as high as the second-story windows of the stores. Ruth quailed inwardly at the sight of the people, though she knew that Sparta on cotton-market Saturday was the commercial Mecca for the entire county. That was the point of their Saturday mission. Cater had long since, through seniority and a dogged diligence, secured this third Saturday of the month for his monthly half-day off. The ceaseless, dawn-to-dusk torrent of buying and selling both goaded and drew him, and he was never more terribly eloquent than on these Saturdays in his furious ravings against mammon.

The haranguing oratory was worse than usual today; it had been growing worse, Ruth thought, since the beginning of the summer. In fact, the general disintegration of Cater Yancey had been marked and rapid this year. He had begun to drink even more than usual, depleting his store of Titterbaby Calhoun's fruit jars midway through the month and going out into the hot night for more. The beatings of Pearl Yancey grew more frequent and more severe, too. Once they had occurred only on market Saturday nights. But during this summer the door to his and Pearl's room had slammed and the screams and howls had rent the air at least once a week.

There was, too, in the thick, swaddling air of this summer something new and dangerous, something Ruth could not name but that hung in the air like a pestilence. Cater's eyes, on those nights when he returned from Titterbaby's

27

did not burn only on the flaccid, used flesh of Pearl. More than once Ruth felt their blue fingers on her own body. When she felt her father's eyes upon her, she would drop whatever she was doing and run into the children's sleeping room, or out the door and into the darkness, or wherever he would not follow. She would find herself outdoors or in another room without knowing how she had gotten there, heart pounding in her mouth, blood storming at her wrists and temples, rage gagging her.

Pearl noticed the eyes on Ruth, too. Ruth saw her, more than once, take in the eyes of her husband on her daughter, and looked into her mother's face for some sign of illumination or protest. Pearl would look back at her impassively, and there was no flicker of sympathy or answering rage. But there was something, a magnification of import, a sharpening of attention that Ruth thought that her mother was imparting to her with those looks, some information of great value. She could not understand the message, and something in her mother's still face forbade her to ask. For the first time in their lives, Ruth and Pearl did not speak of a thing that lay powerful and enormous between them.

They went into Tierney's Meat Market. Pearl and the children stood before the counter on the damp sawdust, the icy bloodbreath from Tierney's cold room numbing their feet. Whenever the massive doors swung open they could glimpse the slowly twirling headless corpses of cattle and pigs hanging from great hooks. Lot and Isaac shuffled their cold feet and slid sullen, oblique glances at the hulking farm children who jostled and chattered in sociable groups as their parents did their trading. Sarah and Hagar whimpered. But Ruth was still, waiting.

Pearl quieted the boys and the whining smaller girls with a sharp hiss and a cuff on their pink-red heads, but Ruth stood as silent and still as a stone child as her father roared of the heathen who ate the flesh of sacrificial animals. Weary Tierney did not even bother to chase him away, and the crowd broke and flowed around the knot of Yanceys beside the meat counter and came together again as heedlessly and surely as a river around a rock. Finally Cater pointed to his selection of side meat, and Tierney deftly hacked it off with his great cleaver and gave it to his fat wife to wrap, and Ruth moved forward as if by rote to receive the raveling Bull Durham pouch which Cater produced ostentatiously from his overalls pocket. Impassively she took the package from Mrs. Tierney, counted out a few coins from the sack, and gave over both into Cater's outstretched hands. They moved on down the street to Lapham's.

The crowd was usually thicker here, for Lapham's was a palace among grocery stores, catering as it did to the cooks and butlers from the great houses of Church Street and other like streets and to the northern and eastern tastes of the university faculty, as well as to the middle-class townspeople and the surrounding farm families. Side by side with Lapham's tin bins of staples and shelves of canned goods and baskets of produce brought in from the farms that morning were rows of fancy groceries and spices and teas and coffees with exotic names and splendid, strange scents, and the great glass confectioners' counter for which Lapham was known far and wide. In Lapham's, Cater Yancey was at his grandest and most terrible.

Today he ranged his straggling band along the mahogany confectioner's counter and stood before them, howling to the crowd pressing close around him, rising on their tiptoes and craning their necks to peer over the red and tow Yancey heads blocking their view of the counter's contents. Pearl and the boys and the two younger girls dropped their chins and looked fixedly at the dark, oiled boards of Lapham's floor, but Ruth raised her head and stared levelly and unseeing out at the crowd over her father's shoulder, her eyes pure and still.

"The sword of the Lord is sated with blood; it is gorged with flesh as though used for slaying lambs and goats for sacrifice," Cater shrieked. "For the Lord will slay a great sacrifice in Sparta and make a mighty slaughter there. The strongest will perish, young boys and veterans, too. The land will be soaked with blood, and the soil made rich with fat. For it is the day of vengeance, the year of recompense for what Sparta has done to Israel. The streams of Sparta will be filled with burning pitch and the ground will be covered with fire. This judgment on Sparta will never end. Its smoke will rise up forever. The land will lie deserted . . ."

"You mean Edom, don't you, Brother Yancey?" a voice called from the crowd. "Edom, over there in Holland with the tulips and windmills? The Lord sho' ain't goin' fool

29

with po' little ol' Sparta when he can smite him a mess of windmills every day before breakfast."

There was laughter, and Cater's howling rose higher and higher, until the words were lost in an ululating scream of meaningless sound, and the vacant eyes began to roll back into their sockets. The laughter faltered and died; in its dying, Ruth heard a high, clear, precise voice say, "Mother, that's the man I told you about, with the very poor family, who goes by on Saturdays. Is he ill, do you think?"

"Hush, Paul," said a woman's voice, clearer and cooler than the boy's but essentially the same.

Ruth focused her eyes and turned them toward the voices. She looked into the large, melted-chocolate eyes of the fat boy she had seen with the hoop on the walk of the great white house, and, above his head, into the eyes of the beautiful woman she had seen there on the balcony long ago. They were as large as the boy's, but thick-lashed and hazel, and full of a naked, terrible pity. The store's dimness turned slowly to dark, buzzing red; the outraged blood receded from her hands and forearms. Only Pearl's fingers, biting deep into her daughter's shoulders, kept her from slipping to the floor in a faint.

At last Cater was done with his tirade and began his royal progress through the store, inspecting the goods. The crystal remoteness slipped once more into place around Ruth, and she was able to take her place in the ranks behind her father with firm steps and straight back. He pointed, finally, with his abnormally long, blue-white index finger, to the flour barrel and the bin of dried peas. Lapham's clerk did not have to ask him how much of either he wanted. Ruth, a small gilded doll in a faded-to-white shift hanging unevenly around bare ankles from a ragged yoke, stepped forward and received the Bull Durham pouch. She scanned the figures on the chalkboard the clerk presented to each customer in the interest of clarity, toted them up in her head, lips moving silently, and reached into the pouch. She laid the coins on the counter smartly and took in exchange the bags of flour and beans which the clerk handed down to her. When nothing more appeared, she cleared her throat and spoke. Her words sounded loud in her ears, like shouts above the monotonous hubbub of background voices.

"I make it four cents you owe me," she said. "It was a dime and nickel I give you, not a dime and a penny."

"It was a penny, miss," the clerk said firmly. "I have it right here, see?" He held up a coin.

"Nossir, because I didn't have no penny, else I would have give it to you," Ruth said.

"It was this penny right here," said the clerk.

Cater began to mutter again, more and more loudly, and to jig up and down in place in front of the counter. Ruth set her jaw.

"I give you a nickel," she said.

"It was a nickel. I was watching. I saw her give it to you," said a voice, and the ghost woman from the Fox house stood suddenly beside Ruth. Her skirts whispered as she moved; a scent of lemon verbena rose from them and bathed Ruth's face and nose, and cooled the stinging red that was flooding up from her collarbone again.

"If you say so, Miz Fox," the clerk said sullenly, and slapped four pennies down on the counter.

"I believe it would be a bit nicer if you handed them to the young lady, along with an apology," the woman said sweetly; her voice sounded, in Ruth's burning ears, like the song of the wood thrush that sang in the late afternoons sometimes from the upper branches of the magnolia, as they waited by the kudzu ravine for Cater to come up out of it.

The clerk held the pennies out and down over the counter to Ruth and mumbled, "Sorry for the mistake, miss."

Ruth took the pennies. She did not look at the woman. The presence of the fat boy behind her bulked huge on the periphery of her vision, like a statue or a mountain. The store seemed to have fallen silent; Cater was quiet again, and the Yancey children were as still as rabbits when the red-tailed hawk is overhead. Ruth could not sense the presence of Pearl. A pulse, crazily out of control, leaped in her neck.

"You're very clever with sums and money," the woman said, leaning down to Ruth. A fold of her skirt drifted over Ruth's bare foot. It was white, of some silky-crisp stuff, and sprigged with tiny raised designs of roses and leaves. The slender toe of a white glazed-kid boot glimmered briefly beneath it and was gone. Ruth did not raise her head.

"You're really far better at it than I was at your age," the cool, liquid voice went on. "I think you must be a very smart girl. Will you tell me your name? Mine is Fox. Alicia Fox. I live on Church Street, near the university."

Ruth was rooted, deafened with the tumult in her blood. She did not move, did not look up. Silence spun out. The woman's scent fingered her face and neck like a lover's hands.

She felt a sharp prod in her back, between her shoulder blades. Instinctively she resisted; another prod followed, so insistent that she took an inadvertent step forward. In her blazing ears Pearl's hissed whisper rang like a klaxon: "Take your chance!"

Ruth raised her face to the woman and smiled, a radiant, tremulous smile. She bobbed her bright head in the brief, graceful curtsy Pearl had taught her.

"My name is Ruth Steed Yancey," she said clearly to the woman. "I'm real proud to meet you."

3

"SOMETHING must be done about that child, Claudius. There is too much there to waste."

Alicia Fox bent slightly from her supple waist with urgency, almost but not quite resting her white forearms on the dining-room table. At the other end of the table, far down a polished length of Honduran mahogany, Claudius Fox made a tent of his small, plump white hands and regarded them gravely. Then he looked up at his wife, framed in candlelight. His eyes, the same liquid brown that looked out of his son's face, softened and lighted up behind his thick round spectacles. Light from the candles and the gaslit gilt and crystal sconces on the silken walls arrowed off the wire frames.

He smiled at her vehemence and the sheer wonder of her, there in the candlelight at his table. They had been married fifteen years, and he was still breathless and humble at the miracle of this lovely, gentle, cultivated creature in his life and his home. She did not seem to him a woman of blood and humors and odors and passions, though he had lain with her tremulously in the nights, in the tester bed upstairs, and his son Paul had come wet and red with her blood from her white loins. She was to him a concept, a perfection. When he had first seen her naked, her head turned with the embarrassment of it but her arms held out to him, he had wept.

"I have looked on beauty bare," he sobbed to her in a transport of shy passion.

He had met her in the home of his New Testament professor in New Haven, when he was a senior at Yale. Unable to go home to Sparta for the Christmas holidays because of an examination to be made up, he gratefully accepted Dr. Chambliss's invitation to Christmas dinner in the minister's fine old brick Federal home. He would remember always his first glimpse of her, standing on the stair landing in her Sunday dress of cranberry velvet, reaching up to refasten a slipping festoon of spruce around a gas jet. He came in out of the brilliant, diamond-edged cold of that Christmas noon, stamping his feet to restore feeling in them, shrouded and muffled to his small nose against the alien cold of the Northeast, and raised his head, and there she was, Hester Alicia Chambliss, nineteen years old and home from Vassar for the holidays, laughing down at him with glorious hazel eyes set obliquely in the face of a young Diana.

"Good afternoon, Mr. Fox," she said, in a voice that was the music of bells compared to the staccato twangs of most of the Yankee girls he had met. "Papa said you had been set adrift on an ice floe, and that we must rescue you. Let me take your coat and come and toast yourself by the fire."

Always a shy and earnest young man, Claudius Fox, southern aristocrat to his core and classical scholar by nature and education, felt his tongue cleave to the roof of his mouth. He cleared his throat several times, goggled at the glowing girl and trod upon her foot, stumbled over the family spaniel, and fetched up in a heap on the drawing-room hearth rug under the amused and compassionate eyes of the family of Matthew Chambliss, who had observed Alicia's effect on young men before. The tall minister, a worldly and practical man who saw in the dreaming young southerner in his Bible class something fine, if unformed, raised Claudius up from the rug and brushed him off and

33

teased him gravely and gently, and congratulated himself again on his acuity. Alicia did not know it yet, but Claudius would make her a fine husband and cherish her all her days, as her father intended.

Matthew Chambliss knew that there was money in the Fox family, and enough breeding and cultivation to keep Alicia's glinting steel mind honed without encouraging the radical and unwomanly ideas she had acquired from somewhere about teaching the appallingly ignorant and desperately poor children of the New England cotton-mill towns. A worthy enough aspiration, he thought dryly, and a cause which, God knew, could use the attention of more good men. But Alicia proposed to go and live among the mill people, and even to work in the mills for six months or a year, so that she could win their trust and truly understand their plight, and Matthew had no intention of allowing that to come about. He admired his daughter's lofty ideals, but he did not think she was strong enough to live them. He thought that the slow, symmetrical, sheltered life that she would lead in the small southern university town would be a rich and good one for her, and that Claudius Fox would keep her content and secure all her life. He thought that she would soon find sufficient outlet for her ardent altruism in a family of her own. He was correct on the first two counts, and wrong on the third.

As her father had hoped, Alicia Chambliss's unsullied heart was won by the patrician young southerner. There was a real and powerful goodness about Claudius Fox, a bright simplicity of soul that burned with a pure fire at times and slid over into astounding naïveté at others. The ardor that this strong-principled, high-minded New England girl, so unlike the prattling, dimpling, frivolous young women of his class back in Sparta, roused in him had heretofore flamed only for his studies. Claudius laid siege to Alicia during the hot New Haven summer and captured her consent in the autumn.

They married in September of the following year, when Claudius followed his father and grandfather into the classical-studies classroom of the university in Sparta. They moved into large, airy rooms in the big white house on Church Street, built by Claudius's grandfather Wade Howell Fox in 1817, and shared the orderly, slightly fusty life that Claudius's father, Horatio, a longtime widower, had contrived for himself with the help of the doting,

34

elderly black servants when his wife died. Horatio Fox was president of the austere little state university, and his entire life consisted of his none-too-rigorous duties, his classical studies, his comfortable lair of a den on the first floor of the great white house, and the near-Grecian order and symmetry of his household and his daily routine. He was absently fond of his pale, sweet-tempered son, who had his mother's small, delicate features and hands and feet and his own passion for the culture of the Greeks. Horatio thought the young wife pretty and agreeable, though a Yankee, and quick of mind and admirably educated, and she had the wit not to disrupt his household routine and rile up the servants. He admitted vaguely to himself, when he thought of it, that it was pleasant to have a pretty young woman in the house again, and submerged himself once more in the office of the president and Pindar's odes and came up, nodding and blinking affably, only for such occasions as the birth of his grandson, Horatio Paul, a delicate pink infant who bore his own name and gurgled quietly in his cradle upstairs, troubling no one with night-rending or dawn-splitting cries or worrisome illnesses.

The baby required almost no tending, and his grandfather lived the few short years left to him and went quietly to his grave in, fittingly, a miniature Greek temple in the Confederate cemetery in Sparta without ever having cause to worry or fret over his grandson. Infant Paul was the delight of Claudius's heart, and he dandled his bathed and powdered and fragrant child on his knee when he came in from his classroom, and remarked on his resemblance to Alicia—who, as the baby was a tiny carbon of Claudius, smiled indulgently—and wondered at his obvious intelligence.

"A classical scholar in his cradle," he would coo fatuously as little Paul reached to tweak the marble nose of the bust of Homer or reflectively dampened the leather bindings of Plutarch or Pliny with his toothless gums. And then Paul's cushiony black nurse would bear him back to the nursery, and Claudius and Alicia would move sedately in to dinner, and afterward settle into the library for an evening of reading. If Alicia Chambliss Fox often stared absently into the shadows beyond her reading lamp, or sighed over her book, or stirred impatiently and in indignation over the newspaper on those evenings, Claudius

35

Fox was too far away in ancient Greece to notice. He would raise his head at her movements, and smile fondly and absently at her, and murmur, "You're a picture in the lamplight tonight, my dear," and go down again into Attica, there to drown.

But the truth was Alicia was restless and near boredom, though she struggled ceaselessly to banish the ennui, considering it a self-indulgence. She genuinely loved her husband, if in a somewhat less thunderous manner than she had envisioned when she accepted his proposal, and she was still, these years later, soothed and beguiled by the grace and sweetness of life in this beautiful old town and house. Small Paul she adored with the fullness of passion that she had thought to bend on Claudius had the unconsciously wielded and impenetrable Greek shield not deflected it, but in truth, his care as an infant in this house where servants came and went like silent-footed clockwork figures required little of her time and less of her imagination.

Later, when he was six, she began to tutor him at home, using at last the fruits of her education, which had for so long lain fallow in that slow-spinning world. The new century had brought public education to Sparta, but Alicia agreed with Claudius that Paul would follow his forebears into the classics if he so desired, and the clamorous public school, bursting with the rude and healthy children of the townspeople and a few prosperous farmers, was not especially fertile soil for a classical scholar. So Paul was taught at home, by Alicia for three or four years, and then by the promising and impecunious young man Claudius chose from his one remaining classical-studies class, who came daily to teach Paul Greek and Latin. The supervision of Paul's studies, as well as the ever increasing social obligations that fell to a young wife whose husband was moving up in the hierarchy of the university, occupied more and more of Alicia's time and talents, and when Claudius was named president of the university, when Paul was eleven, her duties multiplied and she was busier than ever.

But it was not enough. Her New England heritage of altruism had been reinforced in her father's house by the coolly implacable Protestant tenets of duty and service, and at Vassar she had been drawn to the modern teachings of social reform like a strong young moth to a flame. Bank

36

her zeal though she might under the sweet weight of family and social duties, channel such of it as was needed into the teaching and shaping of young Paul, she was still the natural and spiritual heiress of those crusading Yankee schoolteachers who came south in the wake of the carpet-baggers during Reconstruction to educate the black man and teach the near-heathen whites the principles of Christian love and philanthropy. The fact that she had missed the cause of Emancipation by almost thirty years and knew or saw none of Sparta's true poor, cloistered away as they were by the fortress of the mill and mill village, only served to swell the torrent of zeal that boiled under her serene façade. By the time she met small Ruth Yancey in Lapham's Grocery that burning September of 1903, Alicia Chambliss Fox was thrilling like a tuning fork with undischarged altruism. A trembling smile and the shy dip of a small white-gilt head were all it took to set it raging free.

"She sounds like an extraordinary child, my dear," said Claudius that evening in the Fox dining room. He had been admiring the play of candlelight on Alicia's serious face and had scarcely heard what she said about Ruth.

"She's more than that, Claudius. She is . . . luminous. A lovely child, with the face of a Renaissance angel and a delicacy of manner that is simply a triumph over her environment. So quick with her figures, and so modest, and such a sweet smile . . . but her clothes, Claudius! Rags, simply rags, though clean enough. And that dreadful, terrible man. . . . Henry told me about the family driving home. He drinks terribly, they say, and beats that poor, spiritless creature and the children cruelly, and spends their precious bits of money on homemade liquor that one of the Negroes makes in his home, in Suches. Did you know that the Negroes were making spirits?"

Claudius shook his head; he had not known.

"But what's worse is the humiliation he makes his family suffer in the town. He preaches on the street corners, and shames and berates anyone passing by, and drags his wife and children through the stores with him. Everyone in town seems to know him; Brother Yancey, they call him. Even the servants laugh at him. I suppose I would have seen him before if I'd ever gone into town on market Saturday, but there's such a press I'm afraid I've fallen into the habit of sending Violet and Henry, only Violet

37

has cut her finger badly, and is lying down. . . . Paul says they pass the house sometimes on Saturdays."

Claudius looked at his son, who sat quietly in his place, turning his pale, velvety head from his mother to his father and back again. At thirteen, he was no taller than he had been at eleven, and a good bit plumper. Alicia regretfully concluded that he was going to have his father's physique as well as his pale, fragile features and great nearsighted eyes. But he was sweet-tempered and affectionate, and she decided that, after all, he could do worse than take after Claudius.

"And what did you think of our little paragon, my boy?" Claudius asked. "Do you agree with your mother that she is rarer than pearls, more priceless than rubies?"

"I think she is most awfully pretty, Papa," Paul Fox said. "And she does seem good at sums. Her speech is awful, though." He did not mention that he had seen her before, and had been stricken to helpless stone under her crystal-blue eyes.

"Of course it's awful," Alicia said heatedly. "What must she hear all day but the speech of ignorant, crude people? I know they can't help it, but you can hardly expect that she would speak like a lady. Although I think she could learn to do so quickly enough. I think she could learn anything she set her mind to. Really, when you think of the chances she will never have, the waste of all that natural fineness . . ."

"Does she not go to the school, then?" Claudius asked.

"Claudius, dear, for the president of a state university, you really do wonder at your innocence sometimes. Henry says none of the mill children go to the school. They go to work in the mills along with their parents when they are as young as six years old. Six years old, Claudius! I was not aware, I did not know . . . and to think of *that* child working in a cotton mill . . . I am so ashamed, Claudius. We have so much. Paul has so much. We have not been generous in sharing it."

Claudius Fox sighed. He admired and loved the nobility of his wife's spirit, but he also had the southern aristocrat's bone-deep sense of his own natural superiority and dominance; his forebears had been spoilt by generations of women, and Claudius himself had been made supremely, blissfully comfortable by his wife since the day he brought her home to Fox's Earth. His sigh was the sigh of a man

38

who foresees the death of his well-worn-and-loved status quo.

"Do you have in mind to arrange for her education, my dear?" he ventured.

"I have in mind rather more than that, Claudius. I would like to bring the child here to live and study with Paul. I would like to give her clothes and music lessons, and teach her deportment and gentle manners, and see to her speech. She could make so much of the opportunities we could give her, Claudius, and she could go away to school later, maybe even to college. With an education, she would not be condemned to the mill village for the rest of her life. She could . . . oh, marry well, or even have a career . . . Claudius, you really must meet her, you'll see what I mean."

"Do you think she would want to come, dear? I mean, leave her family, her friends, all she has ever known? Would her parents allow it?" Claudius said hopefully, but under the hope was the knowledge that he was bested.

"I've wanted another child in the house for so long, Claudius," Alicia said softly. It was true. Try as they might, no other baby had followed Paul. Though she had in no way suggested such a thing, he assumed that the fault lay somehow with him, and it saddened and shamed him. She was, in his eyes, simply too well-wrought a creature, too near perfection, to be unable to conceive another child.

"We have enough room, you know we do. We have a shameful amount of room, and money, too," she went on. "And, oh, Claudius, of *course* she would want to come, how could she not? After the rags she wears, the beatings? And she's so thin, I know there's not enough to eat. . . . And her mother would be overjoyed for her to have the chance, any mother would. As for the father, well, he can scarcely care for her if he beats her, can he? Besides, it would be one less mouth for him to feed. Please, Claudius. Let me just go and talk to her, and see."

"I do not want you going into the mill village alone, Alicia," he said firmly. On this point he was not prepared to argue.

"Well, Henry will drive me, of course, you old worrywart, and I'll take Paul with me. Really, Claudius, I would be a poor-spirited thing indeed if I let silly, ungrounded fears for my personal safety keep me from doing what I know to be right. We have never believed that, my dear. We have not taught Paul that."

He bowed to the victor.

"Whatever you think, Alicia. I suspect you're right on all counts, as usual. What do you think, Paul? Will you share your precious Mr. Carruthers with our lovely little unfortunate?"

"She'll need a powerful lot of English before she can tackle Greek and Latin," Paul said offhandedly. "But sure, I don't care if she comes."

He excused himself and sauntered carelessly out of the dining room before they could hear the great anthem that had soared up in his heart.

4

AT TWO O'CLOCK the following Sunday afternoon, the smart black Fox carriage, drawn by Alicia's own dancing roan, came to a halt in front of the Yancey cabin in the mill village. Henry maneuvered the carriage as far over to the side of the rutted, dust-palled road as he could, but it still loomed in the road like a monstrous black insect, its mellow leather and gleaming brass powdered to ashy pink-white by its progress through Sparta and into the mill village proper. Henry stared straight ahead, his back rigid with disapproval, his shoulders eloquent with disdain at the bleached faces of the children who swarmed out of the mill cabins to stare at the carriage and the scarlet-faced, sailor-suited boy in it.

A few adults, thin, corded men mostly, stared impassively at the carriage from rotting front porches, not moving except to lift jars to their lips and drink deeply. But in those cabins that had curtains hanging in the front-room windows, women drew aside the tatters to peer out at the carriage and the boy and the Negro, and to follow with their dead eyes the tall, slim woman in a drift of white, crystal-pleated lawn and a pale straw hat, its brim weighted with white daisies, who swung lightly down from the carriage, said a word over her shoulder to the boy, and walked with her head held very high up the two sagging brick and board steps of Cater Yancey's house and across the ruined porch.

Alicia Fox had never felt such heat before. Inside Fox's Earth, foot-thick brick walls and fifteen-foot ceilings held the cool of the nights all day, and heavy curtains were drawn against the invading heat by ten in the morning. The sheltering trees of the lawns and gardens on Church Street took the brunt of the savage sun, filtering only green-gold coin-dapples down to the old white houses and sidewalks. Long, tepid baths and afternoon naps in dim-shaded bedrooms, their French windows opened to second-floor balconies hanging virtually in the highest branches of the trees, kept the women and children of Church Street crisp in the inferno of the Georgia summers. At dinner on the heaviest and hottest of the September evenings, the children of servants could usually be cajoled with a sweet to stand behind the chairs in the shadowy dining rooms and wield long-handled palmetto fans, creating small pools of breeze and banishing errant flies at the same time. If a Church Street lady had to venture outside during the worst of the heat, a parasol and a ribbon-and-flower-decked hat kept face and neck and bosom white. The ice wagon came twice a day to Church Street, and the ladies and children had iced tea and lemonade in the slow bronze afternoons, and ice cream for dessert at dinner and on Sunday afternoons. In the time it took for her to walk from her carriage to the front porch of Cater Yancey's house, Alicia Fox realized that never in her fifteen years in the South had she felt the full and terrible weight of a Georgia heat wave.

"I would die in three days here," Alicia thought, and knew, humbly, that she did not exaggerate. As it was, she was afraid she would faint on this canted platform of rotted boards, and fall backward into the dust of the minuscule yard, where chips and shards of flint, fragments of the great spine of Georgia, pushed up through the iron-hard ruts and fissures. There was no one in the yard or on the porch, and no sound from the house.

But from the dark, hot box of the front room, where she had been sitting with her mother on the backless wooden bench since they returned from church at noon, Ruth

Yancey saw Alicia's carriage draw up in front of the house.

It was a strange Sunday. Cater had not returned home with them from church, mumbling and intoning, for the session in the front room before dinner that usually followed market Saturday nights. Instead, Pearl had pressed a few coins from the worn purse that only Ruth knew she kept hidden in the clothes bag into his hand and asked in a low voice if he would mind going into Suches and getting her a little jar of the pennyroyal mixture old Aunty Calhoun made up, that was so good for women's complaints. Ruth had stared at her mother: send her father back to the house of Titterbaby Calhoun, with money in his hand, when on her cheekbone and neck last night's bruises lay fresh and livid? But her mother's eyes, turned to her husband, were only humble and mild, and he had taken the money and stumped off, grumbling. Ruth had looked after him, and then again at her mother, but said nothing.

Even more strange, she had not removed her Sunday dress, as she usually did when she returned home from church, and put on one of her three feed-sack shifts and gone into the kitchen to help Pearl prepare the midday meal. Instead, Pearl had said, "Leave on your good clothes and come set in the front room with me for a spell," and Ruth had done so. The dress was a winter one, a heavy smock of stout, dark-blue serge that went over matching blue woolen stockings; it had a sailor collar and was inches too short for Ruth. Like most of her clothes, it had come from the church poor barrel, and it was, on this September day, agony to wear. But Ruth did not question her mother's bidding.

Nor did she feel excitement or curiosity when she saw the big black carriage stop before the house, though it was a sight that had never before been seen in the mill village. But something inexorable opened its fist inside her, and spread tingling fingers from her stomach out to the ends of her arms and legs. She lifted her head to her mother. Pearl looked down at her, and her face was still and without surprise.

"That's Miz Fox," Ruth said.

"Reckon it is," said Pearl.

"Looks like she's stopping."

"When she knocks, I want you to go to the door," Pearl

said. "You smile at her nice, and curtsy for her like you did yesterday. And then you bid her come in and set."

Ruth stared in genuine astonishment.

"What's she want to come in here for?"

"You remember what I said about keepin' your ears open? Well, when I send you out of the room, you stand out there in the kitchen and you listen, and you'll find out what she wants in here."

"How do you know what she wants? Why do I have to leave?"

"I just know."

"Is that ol' fat boy comin' in here?"

"I don't think so. Reckon this is between her and me."

"But it's about me. Ain't it? Ain't it, Ma?"

Pearl looked down at Ruth and, incredulous, Ruth saw a sheen of wetness in the pale eyes, where before there had always been only the fierce brightness of drought. It was an unsettling sight, frightening, disorienting. Ruth reached out to touch her arm.

"Mama?"

"Yes, it's about you. Go on, now. And pull your skirt down in back."

Ruth opened the door and looked up at Alicia Fox. Tall, tall and white, silver-dazzling in the light of the sun from behind her, shimmering in the heat. Alicia's cool smell this afternoon was that of violets. Her voice drifted down out of that huge radiance of hot white, as cool as splashing mountain water.

"Ruth? It's Mrs. Fox. Alicia Fox. We met yesterday in Lapham's Grocery. Do you think I might come in for a moment? I'd like to talk to your mother, if she isn't busy. I won't take much of her time."

Ruth smiled up at the towering, featureless, silver whiteness.

"Yes'm, I remember. Mama ain't busy. She says for you to come in and set."

She turned to lead the way, then remembered, turned, and bobbed the curtsy. Alicia Fox smiled.

"You have lovely manners, my dear, but you mustn't curtsy to me anymore. I'm not royalty," she said, resting her lace-gloved hand on Ruth's shoulder. Ruth's face burned. She could feel each separate, slender bone in Alicia's hand through the thick serge. Her flesh shrank away from them, but she held her shoulder steady.

"Yes, ma'am," she said.

Pearl Yancey was on her feet to receive Alicia, standing straight and still before the wooden bench. Her yellow face was deferential and unsurprised, and she wore an ingratiating smile. It was an oddly and unpleasantly sly look; she seemed almost to fawn on the woman in white, who went toward her with her hand outstretched, seeming determined not to look around her at the bare, blighted little room. Ruth had not seen such a look on her mother's face before. She felt shame at the sight of it, and shame at the shame. But above the sunken mouth, stretched tight with the humble, alien smile, Pearl's eyes blazed with . . . what? Anger? Resentment? Fear? Ruth, goggling at her mother, could not tell. Pearl said, "Come in an' set, Miz Fox." And to Ruth, "Ruth, go out and git us some of that lemonade in the kitchen there."

Ruth stood still. Had her mother lost her senses? There was no lemonade; there had never been lemons in the Yancey house. Ruth had never tasted lemonade.

"Lemonade?" she said stupidly.

Quickly Alicia Fox said, "I'm afraid I've just finished luncheon, Mrs. Yancey. I couldn't take a thing, really. But thank you for offering. I just wanted to talk with you a moment about . . . about Ruth. . . ." She fell silent under the blaze of Pearl's eyes.

Pearl dropped them. "Please set," she said. She jerked her head emphatically at Ruth, rooted in the middle of the room. Ruth turned and fled into the kitchen. She leaned against the wooden table, bending toward the open door into the front room. She heard the scrape of the single wooden straight chair, and the heavier sound of the bench, as the women sat down. She listened.

When the voices in the front room, one a cool silver flute, one a midge's diminished whine, stopped for a moment, Ruth straightened up. She stared sightlessly at the kitchen, feeling rather than seeing the rotting floorboards, the broken faucet, the rusting bucket that she took each morning to the pump at the foot of the street. A fierce, hot joy started up in her bowels, flooded upward, curled her fingers and slammed her eyes closed. In all her life she had felt nothing like it before.

Alicia Fox wanted her to come and live at Fox's Earth and study with the fat child Paul, and have opportunities and advantages.

Pearl had consented.

"I will kill anyone who tries to stop me," Ruth thought to herself, as matter-of-factly as she had thought that the morning was hot and there was dinner to get. "Anybody tries to keep me out of that house, I'll lay low and look and listen and think, and I'll find a way, and I'll kill 'em. I don't care how long it takes me to do it, neither."

There was a further flurry of talk in the front room, but in a desultory, finishing-up tone. Ruth knew that the transaction had been completed and agreement reached. She heard again the scraping of Alicia's chair, and the noise of the wooden bench on which Pearl sat, and the rustle of Alicia's skirts, and then footsteps as the women moved toward the door. She heard Pearl say, "I'll ask him directly he comes in, Miz Fox, but I know he'll see like I do that it's God's business you're doing, and he'll bless you for it like I do. She's a right smart young'un an' she won't bring no shame to your house."

"Oh, Mrs. Yancey, of *course* she won't!" Alicia said warmly. "We're all so very pleased you'll let her come. We'll try to make her very happy, and, of course, you're welcome to visit her . . . us . . . any time at all, and she you. It's not as if she was going away from you. You must come every day, if you want to."

"That wouldn't be fittin', Miz Fox," Pearl said simply, and Ruth's heart gave a great, clumsy lurch. "But I 'spect we'll see plenty of her without that."

There was a pause, and then Alicia Fox said, "Well, I'll send Henry down tomorrow for Mr. Yancey's answer, then, shall I? And then we'll plan from there. Good afternoon, Mrs. Yancey. And thank you. Thank you so much."

"Good afternoon to you, Miz Fox," Pearl said.

Ruth waited, the savage joy pinwheeling behind her eyes, for her mother to come into the kitchen or call her into the front room. When she did not, she went into the room that Alicia had left so recently. After the hot brightness of the kitchen, the dark room seemed still burnt with the vivid white after-image of Alicia Fox. Pearl Yancey sat once more on the wooden bench, and her face was buried in her hands. She made no sound and she sat perfectly still.

"Mama?"

Pearl did not move.

"Mama, are you all right?"

Pearl did move then; she lifted her head and turned to look at Ruth. Her face was eroded, torn, collapsed under the weight of a terrible sorrow. Then she smiled, her dry, sour smile, and the desolation fled, and she was Pearl again, Mama.

"I'm all right," she said. "It's just so powerful hot, is all. Well, Ruth. I reckon you heard what she wanted."

"Yes'm."

"You think you can do that? You think you can go live in that great big ol' house and act like quality and learn stuff out of books? You think you can live like them Foxes and not carry on like a Yancey anymore?"

"I . . . yes'm. But, Mama, I don't want to leave you here, I can't do that."

"YES, YOU CAN DO THAT!"

Her mother's voice was so angry that Ruth flinched back and stared. Once again, Pearl was no woman she knew, but a white-faced menacing stranger.

"YOU CAN DO THAT AND YOU WILL DO IT! DO YOU THINK I'D LET GO OF YOU FOR AUGHT LESS THAN THAT? DON'T YOU NEVER LET ME HEAR YOU SAY YOU CAN'T DO THAT NO MORE! YOU LITTLE FOOL! That woman with all them fancy clothes and that la-di-da talk and them airs is your ticket out of this stinkin' hellhole of a mill town, and if you have to call her Mama an' suck up to her an' carry on over her all your life and never see me no more on this earth . . . if that's what she wants you to do . . . you'll do it. This is the biggest chance you're gon' git, Ruth; there ain't gon' be another one like this. You remember what I said to you once, that you got to all the time be lookin' for your chance, and when it comes, you got to take it an' not ever look back? Not for nothin' an' nobody? Well, now, here it is your turn, an' if you don't do like I say, you're lookin' at what the rest of your life's gon' be like. Look at me good, Ruth. Is this how you want to be in twenty years? Or thirty?"

Ruth looked and dropped her eyes. Tears stood in them but did not spill.

"I'll do it, Mama. I told you I was gon' live in that house some day, an' I will. I know that. But I ain't gon' just leave you and not see you no more. I ain't gon' do that, Mama, an' you can't make me."

"I can make you, all right, do it come to that," Pearl said, her voice and face calm and closed once again. "Now git in there an' help me git some dinner on the table, before your daddy comes home. He ain't gon' take to this at all, as it is. You don't want to rile him no more."

"He's not gon' say no, is he, Mama?" This had not occurred to Ruth; suddenly the singing, barbarian joy and the child's woe at the prospect of estrangement from Pearl were overflooded with a cold, still weight. She could scarcely breathe under it.

"Oh, I 'spect he will, at first," Pearl said. "But he'll change his mind terreckly. There's more than one way to skin a cat. Don't you worry none."

But Cater did not change his mind. He howled his fury and his forbiddance, and when Pearl tried to argue and to reason with him, he beat her so savagely that, for the first time, Ruth left the pallet where she and Sarah and Hagar huddled in the hot night and jerked open the door to her parents' room, and landed on her father's naked back like a lean little cat, clawing and scratching and spitting. For this she received a beating that paled all the others he had given her into insignificance, a beating that went on and on, beyond the sound of his mad, singing voice, beyond Pearl's renewed screams, beyond pain. Ruth fainted, and when she came to she was lying with her mother on the narrow, shored-up bed in her parents' room, and Cater had gone howling into the night, out into the woodshed, where he prayed and shouted and sang to his dancing, light-showered visions until dawn.

Ruth did not yet feel the pain of the welts and cuts and bruises that the mule harness had made, and she felt warm and emptied out and faraway in the circle of her mother's arms. Once she looked down on the coarse gray sheet between her own body and her mother's, and saw the thin red threads of their blood, mingled and pooled on the sheet. Somehow the sight made her feel even warmer, even more secure and not-yet-born. Pearl's breath came in short, soft gasps that caught, now and then, in rusty, unwilling sobs, and Ruth moved her head slightly against her mother's arm.

"Hush, Mama," she said dreamily. "I'm gon' go. You wait an' see."

"I reckon you will," Pearl said. "I just figured to help you more, is all. But I ain't gon' be able to help you with this, Ruth. You're gon' have to find your own way."

"Well, I will, then," Ruth said. "I ain't afraid of him." She realized without surprise that she wasn't; all fear had died in Ruth under that night's beating. "He can't do no more than beat me, and I reckon he's already done that. It don't even hurt, Mama. There ain't nothin' to cry about."

Pearl's sobs subsided, and Ruth drifted toward sleep in the circle of her mother's arms.

Just before sleep took her, she heard her mother half-moan, half-whisper, "Lord, God, you ain't but ten years old."

"That's old enough." The words came fully formed and from nowhere into Ruth's drifting head, but before she could examine them to see what it was that she was old enough for, she slept.

Cater did not mention it the next morning when he came in, white-faced and hollow-eyed, from the wood-shed to eat his breakfast and go to his shift at the mill. He washed perfunctorily at the chipped white enamel basin on the back porch, which Ruth had filled that morning, and slicked back his hair until the water darkened it to tallow-colored spikes. He looked bluely, emptily past Pearl and Ruth and the other silent children around the table, and ate steadily, and said nothing. Once in a while he nodded vigorously, as if agreeing with himself on some point of considerable import, and a thin trickle of watery grits made its way out of the corner of his mouth and petered out in the white stubble of his narrow chin. No one spoke, and the only sound was the tink of the tin mugs and plates on the table and the soft hiss-crash of the kindling in the wood stove as it grayed into ash from red ember and caved in upon itself. Ruth chewed carefully, and lifted mild, still eyes to her father's face, and lowered them back to her plate. Her face was as calm and still and empty as a summer sea at dawn.

She was still quiet-faced and silent when the Fox carriage rolled to a stop in the dust in front of the cabin again, and black Henry got out and picked his way with vast distaste to the front door and knocked. She did not look up from the kitchen floor, where she was scrubbing on her hands and knees in a sheen of cold, soapy water, as she heard Pearl saying in an uninflected whine, "Tell

Miz Fox my husband ain't gon' let the child come, an' say thank her very much just the same."

She and Pearl did not speak of the night before, or much else, during the day; their involuntary grunts of pain as they knelt and scrubbed and emptied out pails and knelt again were almost the only sounds in the kitchen. It was very hot and quiet, and seemed no time at all. Ruth scarcely heard the knock at the screen door in midafternoon that was Alicia Fox again, and she did not strain to hear what the two women said when Pearl rose stiffly and went to the door.

She heard her mother's voice rise, once, and heard her say, "No'm, Miz Fox, please don't do that. I know you mean well, but it'll go bad for the child if Mr. Fox comes down here. It'll go bad for all of us." There was an answering murmur from Alicia Fox, indistinct, but distress was evident in the low, cool tones, and then her mother's voice again, sharp and high, with nothing in it of the fawning drone she had used before with Alicia.

"No! If you got to know, he beat us both till we was almost dead last night, and he'll beat her again till she *is* dead! I thank you for what you tried to do, but don't mess with it no more. You have shamed me, makin' me tell you that. Ruth cain't come, and that's an end to it. Go back to your big ol' house, Miz Fox; you got no truck with us down here."

Alicia went. Ruth heard the squeak of springs as Henry maneuvered the carriage around in the road, heard the dancing clop of hooves as they started back toward Sparta and Church Street and Fox's Earth.

Cater did not come home for supper that evening, and he did not come home by late dusk, and by the time Ruth and Pearl had cleared away the supper dishes and Ruth had slopped the cold dishwater out into the night, he still had not come home. Ruth knew that he had gone directly from the mill to the house of Titterbaby Calhoun in Suches. It was his third night of steady drinking, and he would be bad when he came lurching and chanting home. He would not know any of them; the faces he saw with his wild blue eyes would be the faces of his demons and, perhaps, the terrible face of his God. On such a night it would be best if they were all quiet and, if not actually asleep, very still in the dark. If he found no one about, he might, as he did sometimes, go straight to the shed, there to rage and weep and plead and sing to his invisible host. They would be safe for a time; he had never kept up his drinking into a fourth day. Tomorrow would be a day of trembling and sweating sobriety, of remoteness and silence. He would be gone away inside himself.

Tomorrow would be too late.

For a long time Ruth lay awake in the darkness, still and quiet on the pallet with Sarah and Hagar. She saw the moon come sliding into the clean black square of night where the smeared pane was gone, saw the night bleach from dark into silver. She heard a fly buzz and whine through the room, felt it walk with sticky-spurred feet across her chin and mouth; she did not lift her hand to brush it away. She lay still, she thought of nothing, she felt nothing. She listened.

She heard him while he was still far away, heard him singing and cursing and floundering in the road, heard him cry aloud, "Yaweh, Yaweh!" She sat up on the pallet and looked at the sleeping forms of the younger girls, and then at the bodies of her brothers. She rose to her feet and reached for her thin, too-short undershift, and slipped it over her head. She stole out of the room into the dog-trot hall.

The hall was silvered with the same light that lay over the world outside. She could see well enough to move noiselessly to the screen door. She paused with one hand on the door and looked back. Pearl Steed Yancey stood in the open doorway of her own room looking at her. Her face shone with the strange silver light, but her eyes were great mirror pools of darkness. Ruth could not see into them. Pearl did not move; Ruth, frozen under her mother's ungiving eyes, could not. Pearl might have been an apparition, a sleepwalker, but she was awake, and Ruth knew without knowing how that she saw.

They stood in the silver hallway, mother and daughter, looking steadily and silently at each other for the space of a hundred heartbeats, and then Pearl turned and went back into her room on noiseless feet, and pulled the door closed behind her.

Ruth slipped through the screen door and out onto the porch.

She met him on the top step, her arms outstretched and shining in the moonlight, her hair blazing with the trapped moon. The muscles of her mouth moved, independently and as if drilled, into a smile. Her neck, obeying something sly and earth-old, tossed her head so that her unplaited heaviness of hair moved pale and silk-whispering on her bare shoulders. He stopped; the thin chanting stopped. His arms fell to his sides, hands trembling, slow fire starting out to the ends of his fingers. The fire reached down into his belly, low and insinuating, tightening, stiffening. He raised his hand and put it into the hand of the strange child-woman who stood, miraculously, on his doorstep. He did not know what she was . . . unripened angel? . . . older creature of air and wildness, from his ancient Highlands? . . . but his blood knew.

She drew him around the house and into the woodshed. She slipped the shift from her body and drew him down to her, and sank with him onto the pile of soiled croker sacks he kept there for the nights when he did not come in to bed. That her body was cold, and vertebraed like the body of a slim young snake just come out of a deep well, did not strike him as odd even on this night of great ravenous heat, for he was beyond thought. He did not see, and felt and heard only dimly, and what he felt was cold, sure, small hands on him at the root and base of his focused blood, gathering the heat of him into a great shout that swelled into his throat, and what he heard was a high, pure, singsong voice chanting, "That's right, honey. That's good, honey. You got a real fine one, honey, just what a woman wants."

And as the blood and the shout burst, he heard a great, full woman's wail of despair and desolation and pure horror, but an instant later he was past all hearing, and in any case, there was only the one cry.

5

HE WAS DEAD in five months' time. He died strangled on his own vomit in the middle of a black-iced February freeze, on his way home from Titterbaby Calhoun's house in Suches. An old laundress on her way up through the railroad ravine with a basket of starch-slicked linens found him in the brittle black kudzu vines beside the ice-bristling path; the spittle and vomit had frozen in the stubble on his face and shirt. He wore no collar and no coat. His eyes were open, as gray-white and opaque as the ice in the old laundress's rinse tub when she had gone out to her wash house that morning. He was dead, as Ruth had known he would be, of guilt and his terrible, helpless lusting and of the drink, and after that there was nothing to do but wait. Ruth did not chafe. Waiting was the thing she did best.

In early March, Alicia Fox came again.

"Ruth will be ready tomorrow afternoon," Pearl said.

Alicia did not exclaim and flutter. She and Pearl stood straight and still, looking into each other's eyes. They seemed to Ruth, for a moment, to be almost the same woman, facing profiles on two identical coins. Unsaid things flowed between them. Hazel-green and nearly-white eyes leaped for a moment with the same intelligence. Silence spun out, and then agreement sparked in both pairs of eyes.

"Thank you," Alicia said simply. She left soon after that.

That night, they worked long in the kitchen over the sadirons, getting Ruth's scanty wardrobe ready. Pearl brought out a worn bag that seemed to Ruth to be made from some faded, malodorous carpet, not unlike the one in the mean little study of the mill parsonage.

"It was a rug," Pearl said. "My mama said it was called a carpetbag. It was her mama's. It used to belong to some

Yankee that came down here after the war along with all them others that wanted to give the vote to the niggers and git rich off'n the miseries of respectable folks. Sorry scoundrels. I don't know what happened to the one who owned this one. Died, probably. Well. That's it, I guess. Don't look like much, does it? But you'll have finer clothes than you ever seen in two shakes of a sheep's tail. What's the matter, Ruth, cat got your tongue? Ain't you excited?"

"Yes'm," Ruth said, but she wasn't. The afternoon's exultation had given way to a great, fierce impatience, and to something else. Sadness? Ruth didn't know; she had never felt true sadness. But a dull ache swelled in her throat, stung in her nose and behind her eyes. It made a cold, sick pool around her heart.

"Mama, can I come home whenever I want to?" she said.

"Now why on earth would you want to do that?" Pearl said. "You been dreamin' about livin' in that house since you was a little thing, and now here you are, gon' do it, and you're talking already about comin' home. At least give yourself a chance to get used to it. Don't fret none, you will, 'fore you know it. You were born to a house like that, remember. You don't never forget that, Ruth. It ain't like you was trash, or country come to town. You got as much right in that house as they have. I want you to stay right there until you feel at home. Then we'll see about visitin'."

"I want to come home for a little while every day."

"Well, you can't. Not at first. So don't even think about it. She didn't ask you up there to come runnin' down here every two minutes, you can bet on that, missy. You put everything out of your head right now but pleasin' her."

"I don't care about her. I don't want to please anybody but you." Ruth's lower lip began to tremble mutinously, and her brows drew together.

Pearl put her two hands on Ruth's shoulder and sat her down on the kitchen stool.

"Ruth, there's something else I want you to remember just as hard as what I said about taking your chance. And that's this. You can git most ever'thing you want from a man; you already know about that. I'm right proud of you about that. No, that's all. We'll speak of it no more.

53

You did no more than what I told you, what you had to do.

"But now listen good, Ruth. A woman's different. A woman can know your mind like no man ever can. You be careful around a woman, especially a woman like that one. Because you're beholden to her, Ruth, and you got to stay beholden to her for a long spell yet. The only safe woman to have around is a woman who's beholden to you. Don't you never forget that. You got to see right quick who's got the reins an' git on the seat beside 'em, even if it means pushin' off the top hen in the henhouse. Better if *you*'re the top hen, and best thing of all is if you're the only hen. But till you are, lay low. For you that means suckin' up to Mrs. Godalmighty Gotrocks Fox till her eyes bug clean outen her head, an' it means stayin' there till she clean forgets you come from the mill village at all. You hear me?"

"You said I'd see you all the time; you said so back last summer when she come the first time. I ain't gon' stay there an' not never see you no more! I'll run away; I just won't be here tomorrow when they come for me! You cain't stop me; you know I'll do it! You know I can do it!" Ruth's voice rose shrilly with fear and loss and fury.

Pearl looked at her in silence, and her eyes softened and filled with pale water. She looked down and blinked it away and raised her head again and gave Ruth a conciliatory smile. Ruth knew swiftly and clearly that it was false.

"All right, then. You always could get around me. I promise that if you'll stay there till Sunday, you can come stay all day with me, and then you can come for a little spell every day after that. All right? Is that all right?"

"That's all right," Ruth said sullenly.

"Well, then. Go on an' git in bed now. It's past midnight. You'll look like the hind end of hard times if you don't git some sleep."

The next evening, after traveling in the Fox carriage for a distance that was measured in more than miles, Ruth Yancey turned a flower face up to Claudius Fox, who was waiting, smiling and magisterial and thrumming with misgivings, to greet her when Alicia brought her into the foyer of Fox's Earth, out of a flurry of late sleet. She smiled shyly.

"What does 'Fox's Earth' mean, Dr. Fox?" she said. "It's a real pretty name."

"Why . . . a fox's earth is his den, my dear," Claudius said, thinking that she was as quick a child as Alicia had said, and really quite enchantingly pretty, even in her appalling clothes. "It's the place where he goes to hide, where he's safe. It's his own earth."

"The place where he's safe, his own earth," she repeated to herself that night, lying between lavender-smelling sheets in a little painted French bed in a room between Paul's and Alicia and Claudius's, in this most unimaginable and yet, somehow, most familiar of houses.

"Yes."

She fell asleep for the first of the more than twenty-seven thousand nights she would spend under the flat roof of Fox's Earth.

On Sunday, when Henry drove Ruth back to the house in the mill village for the visit Pearl had promised, the house was locked and dark. Ruth looked into all the windows she could reach; each one showed rooms already beginning to be furred with dust. The sparse furniture was still in place, but Ruth knew it was not now a house where anyone lived. Neighbors on one side knew nothing except that the Yancey children had not been at their shifts for the past three mornings. The woman on the other side, though, told Ruth that she had seen Pearl and the children set out on foot, shouldering bundles, in the predawn darkness the morning after Ruth herself had gone away in the big black carriage. Ruth said nothing, but climbed back into the carriage and told Henry that she wanted to go home. She did not say "Fox's Earth" or "the Foxes' house," but "home." Her face was white and still and her eyes large and very dark, the pupils dilated to black. She shivered violently, until her teeth rattled. She did not speak; it seemed to Alicia, who met her in alarm at the front door when she heard the carriage returning so early from what was planned to be an all-day visit, that she could not speak.

Henry told Alicia that the Yanceys had gone. Claudius drove that afternoon to the home of the mill superintendent, who promised to look into the matter and report back in the morning. Ruth was ill in the night, and feverish; the fever became a virulent cold, and then influenza, and then pneumonia. For a long, ringing, floating time she knew nothing; when she regained her senses Alicia sat on the side of her bed and told her, gently and sweetly, that her mother had taken the children and gone farther south, where better cotton land meant better cotton-goods prices and higher mill salaries, and she would undoubtedly be getting in touch with them as soon as she was settled.

But she did not. Pearl Steed Yancey was seen no more in the mill village, nor the children of Cater Yancey in the Dixie Bag and Cotton Manufacturing Company, and Ruth slowly recovered in the rose-sprigged room next to Alicia's, and was fed by her on silver spoons from trays, and sponged in Alicia's own toilet water, and dressed in fresh, ruffled lawn nightgowns. On the first day she was able to get up and come downstairs for luncheon, she heard them talking about it. She heard Claudius say a trifle petulantly, "Well, after all, it really is just like those mill people when you get right down to it, isn't it? Pure irresponsibility. What on earth will we tell the poor little mite when she asks?"

But even in her grief Ruth knew that the disappearance of Pearl Steed Yancey was the highest act of love that her mother would ever perform, and she did not ask.

Part Two

RIP

6

IT WAS NOT just the bother and fuss of a new baby in the house. In her sixteen years Rip had dealt with many new babies. One of them, an exquisitely formed caramel girl of seven months who was cared for by Rip's capable old laundress grandmother at home in Suches, was her own child. Rip saw the baby almost every weekend and sometimes, briefly, on weekday mornings, when the old woman brought the Foxes' hand laundry to the kitchen door of the big white house on Church Street. If the weather was fine and the flat wicker basket she used was less full than usual, the old woman would wrap the child in a bit of clean toweling and lay her on top of the fragrant, newly ironed laundry and bring her along to Fox's Earth, so that Rip might see her daughter. Unlike the other Fox servants, who lived in Suches, Rip had a tiny room under the flat roof of the great house, with a small round window that would not open, a narrow iron bed, a washstand and bowl and pitcher, and her own hand-painted slop jar. She did not find the room oppressive; it was better by far than what she left behind in Suches. There she had shared a bed with her grandmother while the infant slept in a basket on the floor beside her.

Rip's heart was always gladdened at the sight of the handsome baby, who was thriving so under the old woman's care that she changed literally from weekend to weekend. If it was early enough and Pinky had not come in yet to light the fire in the huge, shining black stove for the other servants' breakfast, Rip would light it herself, and set the coffee to boil, and rock her daughter in her thin arms while she and the old woman talked in monosyllables over Alicia Fox's special coffee with chicory, ordered by Lapham the grocer from New Orleans. Rip's high-planed face, just assembling itself out of the blank, polished-chestnut oval of childhood, did not change or soften as she held her child, but her heart moved with love for her.

On her placid surface Rip seemed a simple girl. She moved silently through her small world, an obedient and hard-working ward to her grandmother, seemingly content, smiling her splendid smile seldom and laughing her low, rich laugh even more seldom, concealing the deep well of untouched complexity and unengaged intelligence that her straight, fine bones cradled like a sculptor's armature.

The mother on whom she might have lavished much of her unused affection had vanished early in Rip's infancy; the old grandmother who took her in thought that her daughter was probably in Atlanta, and wished her well. The errant daughter herself did not know for certain who Rip's father was. The father of her own baby was known to Rip, but she had had, at fifteen, no wish to marry him, though she saw him frequently and amiably when he came to her grandmother's house to see his daughter and plead once more with Rip to marry him. The child was the prized fruit of that union; miracle enough for Rip. There was always a new baby somewhere close by in Suches, and she learned early to be deft-handed and sure with them.

So Rip knew that it wasn't the new baby upstairs in the big white corner bedroom of Fox's Earth who was the source of the unease, the sense of something unquiet in the great house. The other servants did not feel the strangeness, Rip knew. Henry's duties were less rigorous than usual, since Miss Alicia and young Miss Ruth were not going out these days, and he had only to drive Mr. Paul to his law office and that less frequently than ever, since Paul had, the previous Christmas, astounded his family by leapfrogging wildly home in a terrifying silver Pierce Arrow. Red and Rusky, the housemaids, were temporarily banished from the upstairs because of their feckless penchants for clanging slop jars and bumping furniture and singing aloud. Rip and Miss Alicia herself did what cleaning was done while the baby was still in danger. Pinky, in her huge white kitchen, grumbled only that the trained nurse who had come to see to the child and help Miss Alicia nurse young Miss Ruth was a common and high-handed baggage who made extra work with her endless trays and cups of tea and coffee. "Po' white trash is all she is," Pinky muttered. "Not fo' years outen de mill; I knows who her fo'kses was."

Pinky did know. All the Negroes in the big white houses knew all there was to know about their employers. It was not that they lurked at doors to listen and windows to watch, though some did. It was rather that, in the eyes of the white men and women who paid them, they were as much a part of the substructures and furniture of the houses they served as actual beam and joist and mortar, sideboard and highboy, and tongues were seldom guarded around them. Then, too, it was the black servants of the great white houses who were entrusted with the enormous task of tending their day-to-day ongoings. The servants of Sparta knew to a man and woman what the Cobbs paid their gardener, how often and in what condition Mr. Phinizy Heard came home late from his lodge meeting, just what it was old Mrs. Ellerslie was dying of in her upstairs bedroom, how long it had been since pretty young Mrs. Powell Frazier had shared her husband's bed, how many months had elapsed since Colonel Lefferty McNeill had paid Lapham's, what it was the Varnadoes' maiden great-aunt Lucy, in spectral white, raved about in her stoutly barred upstairs suite, and what little piece of trashy mill tail the second-oldest Courtland boy had night after night in his room at the Chi Phi house over on University Hill. White Sparta may have speculated on these things; black Sparta knew.

But they did not feel what Rip felt, nor know what she knew: that there were currents and crosscurrents of strangeness and unnamed trouble eddying and massing in Fox's Earth, currents that seemed to Rip to emanate from the young woman who lay in the big canopied bed upstairs . . . Ruth Yancey Fox, daughter-in-law of Alicia and the late Claudius Fox, wife of Paul, new mother of shriveled infant Hebe.

Rip knew this in her own blood and long bones, even though she had been in the house only ten weeks. She had come up from Suches then, from her grandmother's cabin, to become young Mrs. Fox's personal maid. Rip knew, without rancor, that she was a gift to Miss Ruth from Miss Alicia on the occasion of baby Hebe's birth, and she gave to the wrinkled blue baby the bountiful overflow of love that spilled off her own daughter.

To Ruth Fox she gave an unspoken covenant of loyalty

that sprang from perfect knowing. She would never speak of this knowing to Ruth Yancey Fox; they would become old women together, and Ruth's origins would, for the most part, long since have been buried in the graves of the few remaining people who knew them, but those origins would live in Rip's mind until she went to her own grave. It was Rip's grandmother, the old laundress, who had found Cater Yancey dead in his own frozen bile beside the path in Suches.

Rip knew who Ruth Yancey Fox was.

Ruth would never know that she did.

It was inevitable that they would marry, Ruth and young Paul Fox. It had been inevitable from the moment Ruth walked into the foyer of Fox's Earth out of a March sleet and turned her face up to Claudius Fox and asked, "What does 'Fox's Earth' mean, Dr. Fox?"

Claudius, who had had his reservations at the outset, capitulated in that instant; shy, fat Paul, hiding his white bulk behind the velvet draperies in the arch of the foyer, had lost his heart to her long before, on the front walk of Fox's Earth. Ruth's eyes were fixed on the fatuously beaming face of Claudius, but she saw with other than her eyes the fat boy behind the curtain, knowing him even then to be both captor and deliverer, and she turned her head and smiled at the spot where he was hidden until he forgot himself and came out to stand silently before her, staring.

"Paul," said Alicia rather sharply, for he looked singularly sheeplike and stupid even to her, and she knew that he was not stupid, "do stop goggling and say hello to Ruth. She'll think we raised you to be the wild man from Borneo if you don't say *something*."

Paul tried, but his voice, which had for two or three months been a respectable tenor if not the resonant, satisfying bass he lusted after, shot dizzyingly up into a silver soprano, and he stopped, miserable vermilion staining his taut, smooth cheeks. Ruth's viscera surged with contempt, but she said, "My mama said you had a pony. I never seen no pony. I wisht you would show him to me sometime."

In his mind the elderly, choleric pony became a radiant, silver-white unicorn; he led the fabled beast to her and it knelt and laid its horn in her lap.

"It's just an old pony," he heard himself saying carelessly, his voice restored to him. "You can have him if you want him. I'm too old for him. I'm getting a real horse for my birthday, a hunter. He's nineteen hands high."

Claudius and Alicia Fox exchanged glances over the two heads, one gold, the other the pale, clear brown of creek water. To her son Alicia said, "Take Ruth upstairs and show her her room, Paul, and wait for her in the hall while she freshens up for dinner, and then bring her back down. Henry will take your things up, my dear," she added to the child, who was staring around the vast black-and-white-marble foyer as if to memorize each item in it. She was pale and quiet and large-eyed in the light from the great chandelier, but, on the whole, not so awed or intimidated as Alicia would have thought, for a child of ten who had just been catapulted from a stark and stunted world into one infinitely brighter and larger, leaving behind all her family and associations. Alicia turned her head to follow the two children out of sight with her eyes as they climbed the curving stairs. She marveled again at Ruth's unchildlike self-possession, and saw ahead the bright advantages to which it might be turned. But a tiny part of her noted and recorded the flat absence of fear and childish clinging, of face-lighting gratitude and vulnerable wonder. She shook her head briskly.

"Am I to demand subservience and gratitude as payment from this child?" she thought in disgust. "Was it for that that I brought her here? I thought better of myself than that."

She turned to her husband, who said, "Well, my dear. She's all you said, and more. She's quite bowled poor old Paul off his feet, hasn't she? But I see what you mean. Her clothes are frightful, and she's thin as a poor chicken. We must make her very welcome indeed, and see that she's happy here, and lacks for nothing. I cannot imagine what her life has been like up to now."

"Nor can I," Alicia answered warmly. "Don't worry, Claudius. She shall lack for nothing at all, if I can help it. From now on I intend to see that she has whatever her heart desires."

From then on, Ruth did.

In the beginning, she did not study with Paul and his tutor, for her deficiencies were in basic English, in grammar and elementary reading and writing, and the gap between their levels of achievement was too great. Alicia thought to send her to school in the town, but after her pneumonia she appeared so fragile that light seemed to spill from her flesh, throwing thin blue veins and bones into stark relief, and a dry, hacking cough clung far into the wet spring, and Alicia kept her at home.

She lavished on the child all the attention and intensity that she had held in check on her own son for fear of spoiling him. Her good heart wrung itself in pain when Ruth's mother vanished, and she dressed the child in lace-and-ruffled frocks and underclothes and fitted coats and capes, made by her own dressmaker, who came and stayed for nearly a month to sew for Ruth. She sent away for toys and baubles of a splendor unattainable in Sparta; to New York and England for wonderful dolls and real carriages and wardrobes, and hoops, and a velocipede, and a smart, gleaming miniature trap that fit behind the baleful pony, who did indeed become Ruth's property. A complete and correct riding habit arrived from London, too, with shining boots and a miniature whip, but Ruth hated and feared the fat, yellow-eyed pony, and was afraid to ride astride, preferring the trap and the whip.

Alicia set aside a regular time in the afternoons, after her rest and Ruth's nap, and during this time she brought Ruth into the big room she shared with Claudius and drilled her gently and relentlessly in deportment and social skills.

"A curtsy is lovely in a formal situation, my dear, but when it's just old friends for a simple supper or an afternoon call, I think a little nod of the head . . . like this . . . and a big smile is ever so much more charming. Now you try it. A little slower, maybe, and with your eyes cast down . . . it really is rather rude to stare directly into an older person's eyes . . . and a real smile. Yes, lovely, darling! Your own smile is just wonderful!"

Or, "You must try to say a little quiet something to each person when you're handing 'round the cakes and the teacups, lovey. To simply thrust it into their faces is so abrupt. Say something like, 'I believe you'll like these cakes, Mrs. Cobb. I helped cook make them just this morning.' Or, 'I remembered from last time that you like lemon instead of milk, Mrs. Varnadoe.' "

"I believe you'll like these cakes, Mrs. Cobb," Ruth parroted obediently, hating the woman who sought so im-

64

placably to remold her. But still, she went dutifully through her paces for Alicia on those endless afternoons in the sweet-smelling room, bobbing, nodding, crossing and recrossing her slender ankles, handling thin cups and saucers and teapots and heavy silver trays and bonbon dishes, gliding with heavy, leatherbound books balanced on her shining head, sinking gracefully into chairs and spreading her skirts around her and rising again, stabbing her impatient fingers over and over with fine silver needles as she tried to push them through taut fabric over embroidery hoops, and repeating, over and over, alien and choking vowels and consonants.

"Is not. Is not. Isn't, isn't, isn't. Not 'ain't.' Now, again."

"His, hers, ours, theirs. *Not* 'hisn, hern, ourn.' Now remember, Ruth. Say them again for me.

"Ruth! Do *not* say 'so-an-so like to had a hissy.' It's almost a foreign language, dear; no one would know what you were talking about. Say 'so-and-so was very upset,' or 'seemed agitated,' or even 'let his temper get out of hand.' Now. Suppose you are at a birthday party and a young gentleman spills ice cream on your frock. What would a lady say to him, to put him at his ease? What would *you* say?"

"Please don't trouble yourself on my account. Rusky can sponge it right out for me when I get home. Mama says organdy washes and irons beautifully," murmured Ruth, to whom ice cream and organdy and laundresses had been unknown two months before. She kept her face still and her eyes cast down so that Alicia could not see the dislike leaping in them, and Alicia, seeing only the quiet, demure face, would hug Ruth to her in pleasure at her willingness to learn.

The result was that, in all too short a time, Ruth was, to the casual eye at least, virtually indistinguishable from a graceful, small Fox of Fox's Earth, and the drilling and coaching in Alicia's bedroom gave way to lessons: reading; writing; arithmetic, which she took to with an adult's relish and skill from the very beginning; piano, singing, drawing, elocution, dancing. Ruth had her lessons in the same enormous second-floor room that Paul and his tutor used for a schoolroom, and though the room was large enough so that his lessons did not intrude upon hers, nor hers upon his, she felt his eyes on her at intervals throughout the day, and would flinch under them as she had long ago, under her father's. She threw herself into these lessons, too—though she loathed them all except reading and writing and sums—and by dint of constant practice and repetition became adequate as a player of simple melodies on the piano and a singer of small, pleasant songs in the drawing room after company dinners.

She toiled at her studies. She did all her assignments immediately and asked for more. She let nothing go until she was as good at it as she knew she would ever be. She absorbed knowledge like a sponge in a pool, through every sense and every pore: she watched, she listened, she smelt and tasted and touched and emulated and remembered. Her tutors were amazed and delighted with her; Alicia and Claudius had all they could do to be modest in their pride. She stayed in her bower of a room every possible minute, learning and practicing and committing to memory. They had to urge her to come down for meals, to get to bed and to sleep in the evenings. Once they tried to make her put her studies aside for a week or two; they were sure that such concentrated effort was not healthy for her; but she was so stricken that after that they let her alone to work and study.

When she was studying she was safe from the adoring eyes of Paul, eyes that gouged and tugged at her until she felt that, should she look down suddenly, there would be little ragged, smoking holes in her flesh. She flinched away from them as she had from the eyes of the town upon her on those hated Saturday trips to town with Cater and Pearl and the other children. But she knew that, unlike the eyes of the town, the pits and craters left by Paul's eyes were essential to her continued existence at Fox's Earth, and that she must learn to bear and even cultivate them. Their absence would be a mortal danger. She must learn even better how to draw the lucent brown eyes of Horatio Paul Fox to her flesh, and keep them fastened there. But not yet. Not yet. First there was Alicia.

Even without the memory of her mother's words on the night before Ruth came to live at Fox's Earth, her own fine-honed, intuitive sense of power and dominance would have told her that the first priority at hand was the winning of Alicia Fox. For although it was Claudius Fox who held the reins and the overt power in Fox's Earth, Ruth knew that it was Alicia who sat on the seat beside him and guided his hands on the reins. Hadn't Pearl told her that early on? Hadn't she said that a wise woman could have whatever she wanted if she got it through a man? There was no doubt in Ruth's mind that Fox's Earth was the essential property and preserve of Alicia Fox, and no doubt at all how she had come by that ownership. Alicia must be won, finally and forever, before she could be discarded.

Alicia first, then Claudius, and then . . . and only then . . . would come Paul.

So the winning of Alicia Fox spun on, through the slow spring and summer days of 1904, and through the searing autumn of red dust and white cotton and shrinking brown creeks and reddening sumac, through the sharp, silver-fogged winter, past the glittering pageant of Christmas at Fox's Earth, through the traditional Fox New Year's Day Open House, when half of Sparta filed through the drawing room and dining room.

The Open House marked Ruth's first public presentation to Sparta's small society, though most of the people who came to file past Alicia and Claudius as they stood receiving in the foyer knew of her presence at Fox's Earth, and a few . . . Alicia's two or three intimates . . . had met her when they called during the fall and winter.

Alicia had felt that those autumn visits would be good practice occasions for Ruth, and Ruth had, dutifully and with a heart full of lashing snakes, passed cups and saucers and cake plates, and smiled sunnily, and flawlessly enunciated the charming little phrases Alicia had taught her. The visiting women were delighted, and full of praise for her beauty and graces, and for Alicia's generosity of heart in rescuing the child from the prison of the mill village, and said so, charmingly and in Ruth's presence.

Ruth said nothing, and gave no indication that she had heard, but when Alicia sent her back into the kitchen to replenish the plates of Pinky's lace cookies and Lane cake, she stood for a moment and leaned her flaming cheek against the cool, silky paneling of the door into the drawing room. That Alicia should be praised for bringing her to this house, where she so obviously belonged, which she was so obviously born to . . . that Alicia should be praised, when it was she who had toiled and slaved through three endless seasons, as she had never slaved in the house of her father, to be ready to meet the terrible women from

67

whose mouths such words had dropped, toadlike . . . Ruth thought that she would die of rage, there in the dim, wax-scented front hall of Fox's Earth.

Her breathing slowed gradually, and the roaring in her ears subsided, and over it she could hear Alicia's cool voice, raised in unaccustomed sharpness.

"For heaven's *sake*, LaBelle, the child has ears; she can hear as well as an adult! How *could* you, to praise me in front of her for saving her from the gutter like some horrible Lady Bountiful with a stray kitten! Ruth has spirit and pride; she has earned her place here with us over and over again, she gives us more joy than we can ever repay her for, and I will not have her humiliated, nor made to feel that she must be forever in our debt. We've gone out of our *way* to avoid any such implications. . . ."

"Well, Alicia, I'm just as sorry as I can be, I sure am, and you are a lesson to us all, you really are," came the answering drawl, languid and unrepentent, and Ruth knew that the woman would recount the little scene to half a dozen of her friends the next day, in one of the drawing rooms of one of the vast white houses on Church Street, and that they would agree among themselves that Alicia Fox really was a sight, wasn't she? Just too good. But then, you know how those Yankees are, and one had to remember that Alicia *was* a Yankee, no matter how long she'd been at Fox's Earth. Small wonder, really, that she had taken some little no-'count mill chit in and made a regular little lady out of her; the more wonder that there weren't a dozen little raggedy shirttail shikeposts in residence at Fox's Earth. What on earth *would* old Dr. Fox have said? But you had to admit that the little thing was pretty as a june bug, and smart and cunning, too. . . .

After those initial autumn afternoons, Ruth did not again fear the scrutiny of strangers, and she stood between Claudius and Paul in the candlelit, pine-garlanded hall on New Year's afternoon clothed in jade-green velvet and lace and tiny pearls and shining invulnerability, and held her hand up to half of Sparta as they bent toward her, smiling and exclaiming. To a soul, they capitulated to her there in the foyer, as Claudius Fox had the previous spring, and it was all so easy, so easy. The day was a great success, and her presentation a total triumph; she read it in the lilt of Alicia's voice as she said, to first one person and then another, "And you must meet Ruth, who is staying with us and is the light of our eyes."

She read it in the warmth of Claudius's embrace after the last guest had left, as he drew her clumsily onto his knee and jiggled her up and down awkwardly, as he fancied one did with children until they were old enough so that their feet danced on the floor. He pressed her against the hard, tight mound of his waistcoated stomach, which spilled over to rest upon his thighs, and proclaimed that she was a regular little Circe, and he would have to take a buggy whip to a veritable army of moonstruck calves before he knew it, and she controlled her flinching disgust at the intrusive pressing of his stomach and the fruity smell of claret cup and candied cherries on his breath, and snuggled winsomely into the moist, soft folds of his neck.

She read it in the brown eyes of Paul, which sucked at her like tides from the gentle, yearning white moon of his face.

Her heart rang with triumph like struck bronze, even while it shrank in contempt at them all. She knew then, as she ran lightly up the stairs to bed and darkness to examine and probe and assess the knowledge, that the time had come for Paul now, that the days of her respite were over, that she must move to meet the devouring eyes and let him read in her own, not assent, but the ghost of the beginning of hope that there might be assent there one day.

From the next morning onward, she turned her face toward Paul, and moved to meet him, and gave him back glance for glance, and there was scarcely an hour of the day that they were not together, either in their studies in the upstairs schoolroom, or at meals, or after dinner in the fire and lamplight of the little parlor that served as Alicia's morning room during the daylight hours, or in the waning afternoons and early evenings.

At these times Paul would, with the peremptory boldness of the formerly shy, escort her on his horse as she took the pony trap out, or appear at her side, silent and scowling, at the parties for the younger children of the town to which she was invited, or loll stubbornly at her side as she tried to read or swing in the hammock or play the piano in the music room off the drawing room. He became a squat, permanent shadow to her quicksilver form, and the townspeople would smile to see them together, the lissome girl-becoming-woman and the flaccid, large-eyed, determined boy hulking stubbornly over her. The servants smiled and nodded, too, though there was less indulgence than arcane knowing in their smiles; and Claudius also smiled, vaguely and sentimentally, from the flickering depths of his Aegean; and sometimes Alicia, too, would smile to see them pass on some absorbing errand, or at their two heads bent together over one of Paul's well-thumbed and beloved classical texts or picture books of antiquities. But she did not smile so often as the year of Ruth's stay became two, and then three, and four and five, and there still had been shed on her no ray of the warmth and companionship that she had fancied would rise between the child and her, no daughterly confidences, no womanly alliance or quick, spontaneous sunflares of love, gaiety, or even temper.

Ruth was, at fifteen, a petite and astonishingly pretty girl, delicate and rounded of figure, small of bone and hand and foot, brilliant of hair and truly startlingly blue of eyes, light as a dandelion in her step, perfectly modulated of voice, and grave and sweet of speech . . . and as entrenchedly distant in manner as she had been on the day Alicia had swept her thin little body up into the carriage and driven her away from the cold house of Cater Yancey. The odd radiance that wrapped her, seeming to lie like a palpable light about her and shine through and from her white flesh, that drew eyes to her with a click as of magnets coming together, remained just that . . . a cloak of light that shielded like pure and invisible ice, and did not part to admit anyone through to the core that was Ruth. Alicia knew that Claudius fancied himself close to Ruth, but knew also that he was only as close as the shell of light, and no closer, and she felt in bewildered distress that, despite the hours she spent in his company, Ruth held Paul in a kind of enchanted stasis, keeping him at the length of one blue-white arm while drawing him inexorably toward her with the other. There was a falseness about their relationship, she thought, that boded future pain for the son that she so loved, as if Ruth's upturned smile at him was a prettily disguised rictus of . . . what? Fear? Distaste? Or something deeper, more primal?

Or was the falseness there at all?

"Sometimes," Alicia said to herself, pressing fingers to her temples, which ached often these days, "sometimes I think I am still subconsciously punishing that child for not becoming the perfect daughter that I wished to make of her, and if I am, I am ashamed. I will not allow such thoughts houseroom in my head. She is still only a child, and so is Paul."

(And, said a cooler, dryer voice below the voice of her conscience, she will be going away to school next fall, and Paul will be leaving for New Haven, and so the matter can be set aside for quite a long time. Maybe forever. A lot can happen in four years.)

But Paul did not leave for New Haven. He did not leave for anywhere. He stayed at home, in his room at Fox's Earth, and left only for classes in prelaw at the university three streets over from Church Street, where his father was now president, and came home again at the end of each day. His heavy books of classical studies and antiquities and Greek and Latin were put away in a trunk in the attic of Fox's Earth, and books with the dry breath of the law about them took their place in untidy heaps and slithering piles on his bed and desk and armchair in his room, and beside the leather armchair that was the twin to Claudius's own in the downstairs library. And all his mother's soft, bewildered questions and reluctant tears could not move him back into the classics and into Yale; nor could the stiff, formal remonstrances and the rambling tirades and the bewildered anguish of Claudius. Paul tossed away the classical mantle of the Greeks and the black gown of the university presidents that had flopped about Fox calves since 1830 without so much as a backward glance, and laid the dusty baggage of the law at the feet of Ruth like a trophy . . . which, indeed, it was.

She had demanded the trophy the previous Christmas, after weeks of thought. In the daytime she endured the omnipresence of Paul with as much grace as she could muster, and considerable was required of her, for the holidays meant far more leisure time for both of them, and many parties and balls and hayrides and caroling evenings. She was nevertheless frequently overcome with loathing and rage at his constant, clumsy-footed devotion, and would plead a headache and flee upstairs to her bedroom, to lie in the dusk and literally shake with anger and hopelessness. But even then, and most often in the night, a coldly pragmatic inner voice would whisper to her, "The time is now. The chance is here. Take it. Cement this relationship. Bind him. Don't think about it; think about the house. Don't look back. Do it."

71

And she knew on those nights that she must not allow this devotion to wane, not even for a moment, nor to abate, not even a millimeter. She thought of the fall, when he would go away to New Haven, to Yale, to the North, to walk for four long years under old trees in an unknown and unknowable part of the world, in orderly, alien eastern quadrangles. Anything could happen there, Ruth knew, in that seductive world of her people's ancient enemy. That she herself would be going away to school did not worry her; she knew instinctively that those left behind in the mire of the familiar were the piners and the grievers, not the ones who left. She welcomed the time away from him.

But he must not go away from this house.

"I'll miss you, all the way up there at Yale College," she said to him on Christmas Eve of 1908. They were sitting beneath the lowest boughs of the great Christmas pine that glowed in front of the French windows between the two fireplaces in the drawing room. She had lit the tiny candles on the tree earlier, so that their white firefly light would fall on her hair and shower flickering coins on her cheeks, and she had put on her new white brocade frock with the drift of maribou feathers at the neckline that left her arms and shoulders bare. She breathed deeply and held the breath, so that the beginning slopes of her smooth, young breasts trembled with it, and looked upward at him through the sheltering golden eyelashes. Dinner was over, and people were coming for carols that she would play on the Steinway, but for the moment they were alone.

"I'll come home as often as I can," he breathed adenoidally into her ear. "And you'll come up for dances and weekends and things, won't you?"

"I don't think so," she said, looking down at her hands. She took another breath, and the feathers quivered as if in flight, or pain. "I don't believe I could bear to see you like that, just a weekend every so often, when you'll be gone so long."

"But you promised you'd come! You said you would last fall, when we talked about it."

"Well, I didn't know last fall how I'd feel now . . . I didn't know it was going to hurt so to have you go."

"Fool," she thought savagely, seeing the perspiration start on his forehead, the wetness rise in his eyes.

"I don't have to go," he breathed; the evening's grilled

calves' liver washed over her face, damply, and she averted it, raising her hand as if to brush away nonexistent tears.

"Of course you do, it's all set, and your mama and papa would skin you alive if you didn't," she said.

"They don't own me," he said, a note of bright bravado bugling in his voice, which had been threatening to break.

"But you're supposed to come back and be the college president, and spend all your time playing school and having all those dull old professors and their wives to silly tea parties and things. The men in your family have always done that. You can't just not do it," she said.

"Well, I'd like to know who's to stop me," he said belligerently, looking around as if someone was making to do so.

"Your mama would stop you," she said teasingly.

"Darned if she would." He looked at her curiously. "Do you really think it's so silly, being a college president? Is it like playing school to you? I never knew you felt that way. You never said."

"Well, of course I never said so. I wouldn't insult your sweet daddy for anything in the world, and besides, I thought you had your heart set on it. But yes, I used to feel so sorry for your mama, all those teas and parties and dinners, and you just knew she hated every one of them, but of course she couldn't say so. And I'd think, 'Just look at Daddy Claudius, such a fine, *dignified* man, so good-looking and . . . and, oh, powerful, somehow, playing school when he could be something like a lawyer.' You're just like him, you know. I'd think about you doing the same thing all your life, and I'd just go up to my room and cry."

"Would you really?" His voice skidded back into the soprano of his childhood; he did not seem to notice.

"I really would."

"Would you like it if I was a lawyer, then?"

"Oh, yes! You just look like a lawyer, Paul, so dignified, and then, of course, you could go to school right here, couldn't you, and I could see you real often, because I'm only going over to Madison, to the academy, and that's just a little way away. But I mustn't carry on so, and you mustn't listen to me. You'd just break your mama's heart, you would. You're her boy, you know."

"I'm not anybody's boy, except maybe yours," he said loudly and boldly, and reached over and kissed her on the cheek, and when she raised starry, quasi-startled eyes to his, and breathed, "Why, Paul Fox," he gave her a great caricature of a wink and kissed her again.

When, the next September, they hugged her good-bye on the platform of the Sparta passenger depot, while the train for Madison chuffed on the tracks and the porter handed her smart new leather baggage into the baggage car, Alicia said in bewilderment and with a trace of sorrow, "I never thought that I'd be waving you off while Paul stayed at home. I just don't understand how it happened. Have you any idea at all what's gotten into him, Ruth?"

"No, ma'am," Ruth said. "Just none at all."

7

"WHUT SHE DOIN' up there? Fo'kses say she done kilt her papa and Mr. Claudius, and now she after Miss Alicia."

Jester's mouth was muffled against the ebony pear of Rip's breast, but she understood his words, and turned lazily in his arms to cuff him lightly on the side of his face. It felt carved and pure and solid under her palm, satisfying; marble stretched over with supple palomino leather.

"What you talking 'bout, nigger? Ain't nobody kilt nobody. You crazy as a june bug, an' so is fo'kses what say such trash. Ain't nothin' wrong with Miss 'Licia. I'd know it, wouldn't I, in and out up there all day and night?"

He stretched mightily, his long, corded limbs heavy with languor. His thighs flexed against her stomach; she ground her hips against them in drowsy pleasure. In all their couplings, he filled and overflowed her, flooding all the tiny hollow places inside her and pumping her tight and smooth and eased. Only he had been able to soothe the empty, whistling pain of the last few months, since her baby had been gone.

They lay under a thin-worn quilt on a pallet of straw in the shed behind her grandmother's cabin in Suches, where

the Jersey milk cow spent the nights. An April rain
thrummed on the rusted tin roof of the shed, and the
small, dim earth-floored enclosure smelt of sweat, damp
hay, dried dung, molding earth and cobwebs, and the
rank, fecund humors of their coming together. It was their
place; all of Suches knew it and respected it. No one would
come hoo-hooing for Rip or Jester near the shed; no small
black children would dart in and out at their play. The
old grandmother turned the taciturn Jersey out for the
summer a little earlier than usual, and even the scruffling
Domineckers avoided the shed until twilight, when they
flapped heavily to the fishing poles crisscrossing the ceiling
at shoulder height that were their roosting perches.

They met at the shed most afternoons around four,
when year-old Hebe and Ruth and Alicia Fox were napping, and Rip was free until the baby's six-o'clock supper.
She would lay aside her apron and wrap her small, ob-
long head in a bright cotton scarf and hurry silently across
the back lawn of Fox's Earth, and through the box hedge,
and down the path that led to the railroad ravine and
Suches, and melt quietly into the low, doorless opening of
the shed. He would be waiting for her, his massive napped
head and great golden shoulders bare and glistening with
droplets from the pump in the middle of the dusty open
space that served Suches as a common. He always washed
away the sweat of his days in the gardens of the white
houses on Church Street before he came to Rip. It was
one of the first things that had drawn her, his fastidious
cleanliness. Suches marveled at it, such fussiness in a man,
and teased him about it.

"Jes' 'cause I lives with pigs don't mean I got to stink
like 'em," he would say, grinning his fierce white grin.

From the very first time, they came together silently
and quietly, with no words and no ritual foreplay. It was
as if their union were an act of absoluteness and primitive
dignity that would have been demeaned by the rote gestures of coyness and courtship. He covered and penetrated
her violently and wholly, engulfed her, swallowed her,
reamed and scourged her, emptied himself without restraint into the bucketing cup her pumping hips cradled,
until all pain and sorrow and heaviness were drowned and
gone. She would hear herself shouting aloud, strange,
hoarse, atonal cries, she who had never cried aloud beneath
the father of her child, who seldom spoke and never sang

75

in the great white house of the Foxes. She cried aloud and, afterward, she smiled and laughed with greedy, animal delight, and on the way back to the big white house she sang as she adjusted her clothes and patted smooth her kerchief. She knew that he would save her.

She was seventeen when she became aware of him as a man, though she had known him all her life. He had been born and grown up in Suches, as she had, one of a brood of golden boy children raised, as she had been raised, by an elderly relative, while his mother worked in the kitchen of a Church Street house. Like many of the children of Suches, he was fatherless; he knew who his father was, but the man had long since vanished, as Rip's mother had done, and no one knew or cared very much where he was. Jester was older than Rip by some five years, though, and by the time she was beginning to notice boys as separate, sexual beings, he had long since been working from dawn until past her bedtime as an apprentice gardener.

So she first met his man's eyes with the eyes of a woman when she came to be nurse and maid for Ruth Fox, only seven years older than she was; and even then, though she saw that he was tall and carved and lustrous of skin and fine of face, and somehow different from other men she knew, with his silences and cool economy of motion, she did not really see him. Her eyes and heart were full of the small girl child at home, and her arms were full of the dismal scrap of a child in the nursery of Fox's Earth, and her womb, not a year emptied of her child, still turned and leaped at the cry of a child and not the need of a man.

She thought, when she did think of it at all, that this business of lying with a man was not at all what had been whispered to her by the older girls in the slow twilights of summer. She had felt nothing beneath the handsome young man who had cut her out of the herd of giggling woman children in her fourteenth year and taken her off into the darkness of the woods behind Suches, nothing but fear, and then rapid, blinding pain between her slim thighs, and an overwhelming sense of suffocation at being pinned beneath him, and surprise at her own hips and thighs that began a strange and rhythmic churning of themselves, a motion she had not known she knew. When he shouted and lunged atop her, she thought that she had somehow hurt him, and when he began to pet and caress her and mumble in her ear, she wriggled away from under him like a snake from

76

beneath a rock, and ran away home. She did not so much as speak to him again, avoiding him when he approached her on the rutted streets and refusing to come out when he appeared on her grandmother's front porch. The great, bursting pleasure she had been told she would feel in her loins she did not feel until she learned that she was going to have her baby.

The baby, both in prospect and in fact, had filled her heart and soul and mind, so that she had not thought nor vision to spare for its father or any other man, though the boy haunted her grandmother's cabin ceaselessly, cajoling and then pleading, near tears, and finally blustering and threatening in the way of thwarted men children. He begged her to marry him; he would, he said, give their child a good home; but she scarcely heard him, and sensed that he did not care for the child. In any event, she ignored him until finally he appeared less and less frequently, and by the time she left the baby with her grandmother and went to live under the eaves of Fox's Earth, he had stopped coming around at all.

Until the night that he came in the cold, early dusk of January, and waited in the shadows outside the cabin until the old woman went out to the shed to take a pail of cottonseed mash to the Jersey cow, and he slipped into the back door and swept up the baby, quilt and basket and all, and disappeared with her down the darkening road toward the ravine. The old woman saw him going, with the child in his arms, and her screams brought people spilling from their suppers into the night, but the boy had a good start, and had evidently planned his route, for they never found him or the baby, and no one had heard from him since.

Rip went limp and collapsed into her grandmother's arms when they told her. They put her into the musty bed she had once shared with the old woman, and told Alicia Fox that she had come down with chest misery and shouldn't be around infant Hebe, and for two days she lay rigid and still and silent as a stone, her eyes fixed on the ceiling. When she arose at last, it was with a face that was thinned to elegant bone with misery, and mouth that was silent, and eyes that were, suddenly, great in her face and old as the world with loss. They assured her that he was a good boy at heart, only gone off his head with the wanting of her, and surely would not harm the baby, and had probably only taken it to distant relatives until he thought

77

she had learned her lesson, and would soon bring it back. But her howling heart and empty, pulsing womb knew that this was not true, and she feared that the child was dead. She bowed her thin neck and shoulders under the freight of her helplessness . . . for it was unthinkable that a resident of Suches would go to the sheriff in Sparta for a non-life-threatening occurrence such as the kidnaping of a child, especially since the kidnaper was its own father. "If I've told you all oncet," Sheriff Gaither Floyd had told various Suches citizens time and again, "I've told you a thousand times. I ain't got the manpower nor the taxpayers' money to waste on some nigger squabble that you can settle just as well among yourselves."

And she went back to the frail, pansy-eyed eight-month-old in the white nursery at Fox's Earth, who still was not thriving, and picked her up, and was shaken to the depths of her numbed and desolate young being at the great surge of savage, absolute, earth-old love that swept over her. In that moment, and forever, Hebe Fox became more the daughter of black Rip than she would ever be to Ruth Yancey Fox.

After that, it was as if the grief that filled her . . . for she never ceased to grieve for her own child . . . somehow welled up high enough to push the scales from her eyes, and one mild, bud-swelling morning in February, when she went out into the back garden to cut an armful of early forsythia for the nursery, she raised her head and looked full into the black eyes of Jester Tully, and knew him as a man, and knew him as more: the man. Her man. She knew then that what they had told her was true, those giggling girls so many and so few months ago in the hot dusk: that the sweetest and hottest pleasure a woman would know on this earth she would know under a man, and that she . . . Rip . . . would have that pleasure for her own. And so she did have it, not a week later, in the first of those meetings in her grandmother's cowshed. People who lived in Suches did not habitually use such terms as "love," or even think in them, but Rip thought that she loved Jester Tully, and though her lost daughter hurt her heart sorely and constantly, the love of Jester and small Hebe Fox overlay the hurt like a poultice, so that she found that there was room in her, after all, for all of it. Astonishingly, Rip found that she was happy.

On this April day, she knew that it was Ruth Fox that

he was talking about, and this did not trouble her. All of Suches talked about Ruth Fox. All of Suches talked about all of Church Street, for that matter, but the black men of Suches talked more of Ruth Yancey Fox than they did of anything else. Shudderingly female, spectacularly beautiful, almost ridiculously, Nordically white, and born in circumstances even direr than his own, Ruth Fox was a natural target for Jester's casual enmity.

"They says she a conjure wife," he teased Rip, rolling over and tumbling her off him, so that the broken straw stabbed her buttocks and she flinched away. "They say she got a conjure eye. They say Miss 'Licia jus' drying up like a li'l ol' frog whut a wagon wheel done run over. They say she lookin' to have that big ol' house all to herself, Miss Ruth is."

Rip stood up, an eloquent young awkwardness of long leg, small, high rump, small, thrusting breasts, long neck, high, small head. He looked at her, smiling slowly. She snorted at him.

"They say, they say! What does *you* say? You sees Miss 'Licia 'bout every day of the world, just like I do, an' Miss Ruth, too. Do Miss 'Licia look like arry squashed frog to you? Do Miss Ruth look at you with arry conjure eye?"

"She look at me with another kind of eye, to be sure," he said, leering at her, and she giggled.

"Miss Ruth ain't studyin' you. She don't see nothin' but a big ol' yaller mule in her garden when she *do* see you. What you reckon you gon' do with her if you did git holt of her?"

"Lay yo' black ass back down here an' I'll show you." He lunged at her and she darted away, squealing. A person standing outside the cowshed and listening to the sounds coming from it through the snickering rain might have thought he was listening to two children at play.

But Rip was silent as she climbed the long path up the ravine through the wet green April shadows of Fox's Earth, silent and troubled. The strangeness that had been there when she arrived almost a year ago had piled upon itself like storm waves against a barrier reef, emanating from the enigmatic, chill-eyed, beautiful young woman who had so come to dominate the big house. Always before it had lacked focus, definition, a shape. But now there was talk inside Fox's Earth itself, and a shadowy form shaping itself out of the talk, and it was this talk that knit Rip's brow, not the cheerfully obscene and idle gossip of Jester Tully.

"Whut she doin'?" Pinky had said the day before as they were singeing chickens in the kitchen preparatory to plucking them. She had been a fixture in the kitchen at Fox's Earth ever since she could barely totter after her mother, who had cooked for old Horatio when he brought Claudius Fox's mother there as a bride. "That Miss Ruth, I means, and you knows I does, girl. What she got in that yaller head of hern? Look like she done push Miss 'Licia clean outen her own room. The heart must have gone clean outen Miss 'Licia, to let that li'l ol' gal take her own room, what she an' Mr. Claudius done sleep in all them years. Look like ain't nothin' been right in this house since she marry Mr. Paul."

Rip nodded solemnly, in deference to Pinky's superior rank and tenure.

"Unh, *unh*," she crooned, the wordless black Greek-chorus response or agreement and chagrin from time immemorial. Pinky peered at her more closely, as if to determine whether Rip's sympathy was real, decided it was, and continued.

"Do you ask me, that gal done put a conjure on Miss 'Licia. I sees her lookin' at her, an' Mr. Claudius, too, before he died, all long an' funny an' kinda white in them blue eyes, like this here dead chicken."

She flapped a chicken head across the table at Rip, who jumped and flinched. Its eyes regarded her with milky solemnity, a blue-white scrim seeping over the once-malicious bright-black eye.

"Where you reckon she learn to conjure?" Rip asked doubtfully. She had dismissed Jester's words as social chatter, but Pinky's could not be ignored. She was serious, Rip knew. Rip herself did not believe that Ruth had a conjure eye; she knew by now that the girl's very real power lay within her and had not been learned or given. But she was willing to listen to all good arguments. If Ruth had another power, had *the* power . . . if she was a conjure wife . . . she needed to know it. The guarding of small Hebe would have to be rethought.

"She ain't learn it nowhere," Pinky said with certainty. "She git it from her daddy. Ever'body know he a conjure man; all you got to do was listen to him an' look at them eyes. She got them same eyes. Didn't yo' granny tell you that? She know he a conjure man; she the one that find

80

him dead by the road there. Fo'kses say he open them crazy ol' blue eyes of his an' look right at her when she lean over him, even though a fool could see he dead as a doornail. Look at her an' wink. Ain't she tell you that?"

"No'm," Rip said, impressed in spite of herself. Her own granny! But then she thought, "That's not true. Miss Ruth ain't no conjure wife, an' her daddy ain't no conjure man. My granny ain't gon' let me come up here an' work for her if she be, or even if she be the chile of one. No, she strong, strong an' bound to make somethin' of herself. An' she cold, an' she mean. Lordy-lord, don't I know that now, though! I wonder do she really be mean enough to flat-out hurt somebody? I got to watch that young'un better."

Rip wished that she could tell stouthearted, motherly Pinky what she had learned of Ruth Fox in the year she had been in the house. Though she lacked wit and guile, Pinky's strength was as the strength of ten, because her heart was pure. She would make a devoted and tenacious ally. But Rip knew she dared not tell; would never dare.

"Unh, unh," she crooned. "Unh, unh, *unh*." But that was all she said.

There were deeps and deeps, she knew, tier upon tier of things that she sensed about Alicia's fading health and nerves, about Paul's increasing silences and knit brow, about how Ruth and the child had come to be ensconced in the room that had been Claudius and Alicia Fox's own. But there was much that she did not know and knew she did not.

She did not know, for instance, that a full three years after the elaborate wedding in 1911, with all of Sparta in attendance and guests come from as far away as New Haven, Connecticut; with so many white candles glowing in the sweet-scented gloom of Fox's Earth that half the little boys of Suches had been hired for a nickel to stand out of sight with pails of sand and watch for fire; that three years after this glorious event Ruth Yancey Fox made her first overt move into the seat on the buggy that had been Alicia's.

She allowed herself to get pregnant.

For the three years after the marriage, Ruth had bided her time, practicing the skills that she had perfected within the decorous, fading, and hated walls of the Madison Female Academy, playing the role of Young Miss at Fox's

Earth, gracious young wife to Paul, dutiful apprentice to Alicia in the role of vice-chatelaine of Fox's Earth. Her industry in learning the role impressed even Alicia, who knew her capacity for application and her quickness to sense and grasp. Where before her marriage to Paul she had been drilled in the catechism of ladyhood, now she applied her cold, pure intelligence and her steel will to acquiring the skills of mistress of a great house. Alicia and Claudius and Paul himself assumed that that house would be one the young couple built themselves after Paul was settled in his law practice; ancestral money and land were ample for the purpose of building. He would, Paul told Ruth, build her a home even finer than Fox's Earth when the time came, and she smiled.

Only she knew that the house of which she meant to become mistress was Fox's Earth.

And so she toiled ceaselessly at Alicia's side and at her heels for the three years that Paul read the law. She rose in the dawns before Paul awoke to lay out and brush his clothes, as Alicia did for Claudius. She was downstairs in the kitchen when Pinky came in to light the fire in the wood stove for breakfast, and hung over her shoulder, silently absorbing the making of biscuits and waffles and spoon bread and cheese grits, the proper frying of crisp bacon and salty pink ham and eye-watering sausage, the precise alchemy of eggs. Pinky grumbled to Henry and Red and Rusky that she couldn't take a step in her own kitchen without stumbling over Miss Ruth, but she did not complain to Alicia or Ruth herself. Something in Ruth's still, unblinking eyes froze even Pinky's tongue to the roof of her mouth.

After breakfast, when Alicia settled herself at the little French escritoire in her morning room to deal with her correspondence and the household accounts, Ruth was at her elbow. She watched and listened as Alicia planned the day's menu, conferred with Pinky, sorted household bills, entered figures in the huge, leatherbound ledger on her desk. With her clever natural head for figures, she was often able to point out to Alicia . . . deferentially, even apologetically . . . a small error or a shortcut, and soon Alicia was allowing Ruth to handle routine bookkeeping chores alone while she dealt with her personal correspondence. She was pleased that this allowed her more time for reading and playing her piano. Ruth was pleased to have her hands on the heavy, leatherbound, living heart of Fox's Earth.

After luncheon, with Claudius and Paul gone back to their respective offices, Alicia napped in her room, and assumed that Ruth did the same in the room she shared with Paul. But Ruth seldom slept on those dim, shuttered afternoons. Often she talked with Pearl, who seemed to wait in the shadows by the French windows to the balcony for her daily accounting of Ruth's progress.

"How am I doing, Mama?" Ruth would say.

"You're doin' just fine, honey. Just fine," vanished Pearl Steed Yancey would answer. "But you cain't let up. You got a lot more to do yet. Pretty soon you got to do somethin' big."

"I'm so *tired* of just piddling along like this. I learned all I need to know about running this house a year ago. I want something to happen; I want to *make* something happen."

"Won't be long now."

"How will I know when it's time?"

"Ain't you learned nothin' from me, Ruth? You'll know when the chance comes. An' you'll know what to do. An' you'll do it."

"Mama, what if, one day, something comes along that I have to do that I just can't do? What if it's something so awful that I just can't, just can*not* do it?"

"You already done the worst thing, Ruth. Don't you remember? The worst is behind you. Ain't nothing left that you cain't do now."

"Will you help me?"

"I'll help you."

"Mama? Wait a minute, don't go . . . Mama?"

"What you want, Ruth?"

"Mama . . . was it worth it? To go away like that, to just leave, so I could be here . . . was it worth it?"

"It was worth it."

And Ruth would rise from the mahogany bed and dress for an afternoon round of calls with Alicia.

Ruth's diligence should have delighted Alicia Fox and won the servants to her, but somehow it did not. There was a relentlessness to her as she went about the house behind Alicia, an implacability to her progress through her days, a sucking, tidelike pull in her great blue eyes as they fastened themselves on the people who kept Fox's

Earth running. Hands went unconsciously and nervously to straighten aprons or bandanas in the presence of young Mrs. Fox; heads snapped around to face her; conversations and underbreath humming and snatches of song faltered and died under the level blue stare.

More and more in Ruth's presence, Alicia Fox was aware of a hard, bright, celluloid quality to Ruth's deference, an elaborate patience that edged past caricature and flirted with out-and-out impatience. There was, she thought, a carefully concealed contempt in Ruth's fluting voice . . . the voice she herself had so carefully wrought out of base, nasal clay . . . a trivial contempt of the sort that an adult might try to conceal from a boring child. But if she stole a look at Ruth's face when she detected . . . or thought she did . . . that note of contempt, she saw nothing but interest and openness and a fond desire to please in the face that still had the power to stop her breath with its perfection.

"I *am* imagining things; I do not know what is wrong with me these days," Alicia would think with growing distress. "I must be starting the change. She is everything I hoped she would become; she is as capable of running this great barn of a house as I am; she is popular with both our friends and the young set; she and Paul have invitations almost every night. I have never once heard her say an unkind word about anyone; Claudius adores her, and she has certainly been a perfect daughter-in-law to me. I have no reason to feel this way about her, to think that she is . . . patronizing me, dealing falsely with me. I dishonor her. I do hope I'm not going to turn into one of those horrible, possessive, sniping mothers-in-law."

But the shifting, sliding feeling she got under Ruth's blue eyes that things were not as they should be—and not as they seemed to be—continued to dog her, and she began to waken in the nights with the feeling that something unimaginable and savage sat just outside the far edges of her perception, waiting patiently for her vision to reach it, like a wild beast just beyond the light of a campfire.

On the day that Judge Thaddeus Hill formally asked Paul to enter the firm as a junior partner, holding out the promise that the white frosted glass of the dignified door off the second-floor corridor of the Sparta Bank and Trust Building would one day read, "Hurlburt, Hill and Fox," he came home for lunch and announced the glad tidings to Ruth and Alicia and Claudius, adding almost casually, "so I've decided to accept your offer of a little loan, Papa, seeing as how I'll soon be in a position to pay you back, and Ruth and I will start the new house."

"Well, son . . ." Claudius Fox began, beaming, but Ruth cut him off.

"When?" she said; her voice seemed to come out with very little breath behind it; small but commanding.

"Soon, my dear. Sooner than you think, in fact. I've already got plans; Hamilton Hunt has been working on them for me since Christmas. And that land I showed you, out by the river, just north of the mill? You remember?"

She nodded, wordless, eyes very large and blue in the dimness of the dining room.

"Well, I put a down payment on it after you made such a fuss over it. So we can break ground as soon as you've said you love the house, because you will love it, darling. It's the very last word in modern design; Ham is nothing if not avant-garde. It's nothing like this one, of course . . . there could never be another Fox's Earth, could there? . . . but it's just as spectacular in its way, I think. You want to see? I have the plans right out in the . . ."

"Ruth dear, whatever is the matter?"

Alicia Fox's eyes had turned to Ruth's face at the odd, breathless quality of her voice when she first spoke, and something in the stillness of Ruth's head and the straightness of her shoulders kept them there. She half rose from her seat as Ruth pressed her hand to her forehead and leaned back in her chair.

"I . . . the heat, I think, Mother Fox. I just feel a bit faint, I'll be quite all right . . ."

Alicia and Paul bore her upstairs, protesting weakly, and put her into bed with cool compresses for her forehead and Alicia's violet cologne to dab on her temples. Alicia looked closely at her after she shooed Paul, still chattering fussily, from the room. She *was* rather whiter than usual, and her hands and pointed chin were shaking noticeably. But then it *was* a stifling day, the hottest they'd had yet, and Ruth had been out all morning with Pinky at the shops, insisting gaily that the only thing she had left to learn was how to market properly, and this was as good a time as any.

"She'll be just fine; it's only that she got too hot this morning, and came in too late to rest before she changed for lunch. It's really my fault; I should never have let her go out in this sun with Pinky, but I didn't realize . . . But she must rest this afternoon and this evening, and have a tray in bed. Don't *dither* so, Paul. Go on back to work, to your new office . . . darling, I'm so proud! She'll be as good as new in the morning."

So Paul Fox was profoundly and happily shocked that night when, after tiptoeing in from work and seeing her asleep and going back downstairs to his dinner, he entered his bedroom and found his young wife naked in his bed, her gilt hair tumbling down over her breasts, her white arms outstretched to him.

He had seen her naked only once before, on their wedding night, when he had found her, not timid and trembling, as he had thought, but wild and thrashing and warm and slippery-wet and abandoned as he had not dreamed a good woman could ever be, murmuring and then shouting aloud things he still blushed to remember, doing things to him and with him that made him buck like a mule and bellow aloud like a steer when they were happening, but that he put out of his mind afterward, because he could not and would not imagine how she could have known them. He had fallen that night into a stunned and blissful sleep, never once wondering that she had not had the terrible pain and bleeding his married cronies had warned him of, and wakened tumescent again, already reaching for the warm, snake-whipping body of his bride, only to find her fully dressed and cowering in a wing chair across the room, sobbing her heart out into her cupped hands. She cried even harder when he approached her in his dismay, hiccuping that she had never known she had such a streak of wantonness. in her, and that he must never let her behave like a common slut again in his marriage bed; she would never forgive herself. When he attempted to tell her that she had behaved more magnificently than any man alive deserved, and, hoping to tease her out of her tears and support his point, boldly took her breasts in his hands and suggested a repeat performance "just to make sure it wasn't a wonderful fluke," she went dead white and rigid and gasped for breath, such shudders racking her that he thought she would burst her heart.

86

After the one in his arms the night before, it was the greatest performance of her marriage.

From that day on, they coupled, when they did, under cover of darkness, starched linen sheets, and a nightgown that came up to her chin and down to her toes. She never refused him when he asked, and she did not lie supine and let herself be performed upon, as some of his longer-married friends complained bitterly that their wives did. Somehow she had the ability to make him frantic with her hips and thighs in a remarkably short time, even when he thought to be slow and gentle and employ some new technique he had read about, in hopes of recapturing that first glorious night, when she had enslaved him forever. But he knew that her essential self was not engaged in their acts of lovemaking, and he finally came to believe, miserably, that he had somehow so hurt and disappointed her in that first violent night that he had killed all her natural young ardor. Indeed, when he asked her if this was so, near tears with guilt and horror at his own clumsiness, she had not denied it, but she took his face in her hands and jiggled his softening cheeks affectionately, and said, "Don't fret, my sweet, funny, fat Paul. It's only the way men are; they can't help it, and women soon get used to it. I get enough pleasure just knowing I give it to you. We're going to have to be far more sparing of it, though, sweetheart. You are, you know . . . well, you really are very *big.*"

So that even though they made love less and less frequently after that, and he felt a profound loss and sorrow at the thought of the long-vanished wild thing who had shrieked and flailed under him that first night, the loss and sorrow was soothed and diluted with a rakish, goaty surge of masculine pride.

"You really are very *big,*" he repeated to himself.

Later, after they had been in his room for three or four months, he had told her of his father's plans for the house, and of his own plans to build a dream home for them somewhere in the country around Sparta, "where we can raise our own earth of little foxes." And they had stopped having intercourse almost entirely.

"Because, of course," she had said, sweetly and sadly, "we must wait until then before we can even think of having children, and I simply can't take the chance. Some women could probably get away from it, but the women in my family are just notorious about it . . . we get preg-

87

nant if a man *touches* us, practically. It's always been that way."

"You haven't up to now," he said, seeing even the few scanty, far-apart, sheeted and darkened gropings left to him flying out the window on the treacherous wings of his own tongue.

"Well, of course not, silly." She laughed. "Did you know that a woman almost never gets pregnant for three months after she's married? Mother Nature takes care of us until then, but after that we're on our own. Did you really not know that?"

He shook his head; he had not known. Until his marriage Horatio Paul Fox had known very little about the arcane territory of womanhood. It would no more have occurred to him to question her on this astonishing fact than it would have to question his textbooks about the date of the fall of Troy. And he would never, she well knew, mention it . . . or anything else about their relationship . . . to anyone else. He approached his marriage to her as a devout prince might his own private chapel. It was his in which to worship, but not to share.

So it was not only because he had thought her ill and prostrate that he was astounded and unbelieving when he found her naked under bright lamplight in their bed that night. And only when he had come near to her, and she had silently, and with the same strange smile playing like lightning around her mouth, unbuttoned his trousers, did he begin to believe what was going to happen to him.

And while it was happening, and while he was bucking like a mule and bellowing like a steer for the second time in his life, and she was heaving under him, shouting her own shrill, sad shouts, he was not sure he heard her correctly when her cries and moans became a thin, high chant: "That's right, honey. That's good, honey. You got a real fine one, honey, just what a woman wants. . . ."

And in the morning he did not even remember it.

8

FROM THE OUTSET Ruth's pregnancy was difficult. Just as she had not doubted, when she lay down for the joyously befuddled Paul that night, that pregnancy would come of it, so she did not doubt that that pregnancy would be miserable and even dangerous. Ruth was accustomed to paying in hard-struck coin for what she got, and would have feared and distrusted a boon not won in travail. She meant to have Fox's Earth, and she meant to pay well for every inch of it. Something earned and bought was yours forever; gifts floated on the whims of the giver. Ruth had had few gifts in her life.

She knew she was pregnant the week after that night. A brassy queasiness flooded her throat and woke her early in the mornings, progressing inexorably to violent, helpless vomiting if she so much as lifted her head from her pillow and grinding its way through continuous, strangling retching and heaving that shook her whole body before it subsided, leaving her limp and sweating and white. It came every morning without fail, despite the ministrations of Alicia and Dr. Hopkins and the trays of sweet tea and soda crackers sent up by Pinky. It did not go away after the third or fourth month, as Dr. Hopkins had said it would; Ruth vomited and sweated and heaved until six weeks before the birth of her daughter, and when she stopped, the vomiting was replaced by a less painful but potentially far more dangerous edema, which caused Dr. Hopkins to put her to bed until the baby came, fearing toxemia. Her blood pressure soared, too; until the medication that he gave her began to take effect, her nose bled frequently, and she grew dizzy if she stirred out of bed, and her head ached blindingly at the base of her skull. She could have little to eat but unsalted soups and broths and rice and stewed fruit, but in any case she was not hungry after the months of nausea; and by the beginning

89

of her sixth month, despite the small, hard bulge of the baby, she was frail to the point of emaciation. Her fine bones stood out like twigs under her bleached white skin; her eyes sank into her skull and were ringed with soiled yellow shadows; her blond hair became whiter and dryer until it resembled excelsior hanging about her thin face; her narrow pelvic bones bracketed the mound of the baby like croquet wickets. These bones caused Dr. Hopkins to chirr fussily like a chipmunk each time he examined her. To Ruth he spoke soothingly and patted her bloated hands reassuringly, wrongly reading in her fixed, white-ringed, glittering stare the fear of a very young woman during a hard first pregnancy, but to Paul and Alicia and Claudius he voiced his worry that she might easily slip into toxemia, and spoke more and more often of a Caesarean section.

"She is very narrow, and her physical strength is at a low ebb," he said. "I don't like her mental state, either. I wish she had come to me before starting this child. We could have built her up a bit, perhaps. It was not a good time to get pregnant."

He looked severely at Paul, who whitened wretchedly under the doctor's stare.

"I . . . we hadn't exactly planned it," he stammered. "We meant to wait until we were in our own house; I had just told her we'd be starting building the day we . . . the night she . . ."

He reddened over the white, and dropped his eyes. Alicia's heart was wrung with pain for him. He had been overjoyed at the pregnancy, but the joy soon faded in the face of Ruth's sickness and was replaced by a miserable, guilt-stricken hovering and a suffering silence that was more troubling than any voiced trepidation, and hurt her as much as Ruth's own illness.

He raised his eyes to the doctor's. Hope leaped in them.

"Maybe if I had Hamilton Hunt go ahead with the house? She seemed so set on it, and a change of scene . . . by the time the baby is a few months old, it would be ready, and she'd have her own house to move into . . . and it would give her something to look forward to. . . ."

"Maybe," said the doctor doubtfully. "If you think it would make her happy, by all means go ahead with your new house. But on no account must she feel under any strain to cope with it. She'll have to be in bed a long time after the birth, and will have to take it easy for a year after that . . . no more pregnancies until I say so, hear me, Paul? . . . and she'll have to have help with the house. That won't be any problem, I assume. If having the house waiting for her will perk her up, I'm all for it. But she must not be upset or excited in any way. That blood pressure is already dangerous."

After the doctor left, Paul hastened upstairs to tell Ruth that he intended to go ahead with the building of her dream house. And Ruth, who had not complained during all the bitter months of nausea and vomiting and dizziness and bloating, who had set her teeth against the loathing that threatened to swamp her at the thickening rebellion of her own body and the thought of the greedy, parasitical infant who was the author of it, who had kept her eyes steady and her gaunt face serene by clinging to the cool, remote white vision of Fox's Earth, began to scream like a small teakettle when her husband told her, and promptly fainted.

Late that night, after Dr. Hopkins had left for the second time that day, having given Paul a tongue-lashing that started the sweat glistening on his pale face and tears welling in his myopic eyes, Paul and Alicia sat in the little parlor behind the drawing room, talking.

"I never meant to upset her, Mama," Paul said, wiping his glasses and looking bleakly at his mother, whose face in the small pool of light from the desk lamp was tired and lined and almost as thin as Ruth's, but gentle with pity for her son.

"Of course not, darling. I thought she'd like to be thinking about the house, too. But I suppose the idea of moving the baby, and all the bustle and work that goes into setting up a new house, was just too much even to be thinking about right now. Women are like that sometimes when they're waiting for their babies. They need their own familiar surroundings around them; it makes them feel secure and safe, somehow. Don't fret, darling. She'll be just fine, and we won't mention the house again until your baby is here all safe and sound. You'll see . . . by then she'll be feeling strong and happy, and she'll look forward to that glorious new house."

"Do you think I ought to have Ham start on it, Mama? It could be a surprise for her when she's well again."

Alicia's mind moved, unbidden but as sure and swift as

a swallow's flight, back to the day he had come in from his office to lunch and told Ruth about the house. He had been just on the point of showing her the plans when she had been taken by the dizzy spell. And it was that night, apparently, that the baby had been conceived . . . Without knowing why, she jerked her mind abruptly away from the memory. But a small, cold hollow pulsed where it had been.

"I wouldn't, darling, really. It's not the kind of surprise a woman likes. And we mustn't take even the tiniest chance of upsetting her either now or after the baby has come. Not after tonight."

"I feel terrible about that, Mama. What if she had . . . what if it had *hurt* her?"

"Well, it didn't, my darling, and from now on we're going to take such good care of her as you never saw. Listen, darling, what do you think of this? There really isn't all that much longer to go, and you're losing sleep . . . I can tell by looking at your eyes in the morning . . . what would you say if I had a cot moved into your room and slept there until the baby comes and you took the yellow bedroom? I'd be so happy to do it, you know, and I think she needs the kind of supervision and light nursing that I can give her, and you really must start getting your sleep at night. You can't let your health go; you're no good to her ill yourself. And you mustn't let your work slide. What do you think? Would you let me do it? It's for her own good and yours, too, really it is. And I would truly love it."

"I have been sort of tired lately," he said gratefully.

"I know you have. We'll ask her in the morning. Surely she'll see that it's best for everybody."

But Ruth didn't see. Tears sprang to her eyes, and her hands and head shook, and her slight breast rose and fell so fast that she could scarcely get her breath.

"Paul, please, *please* don't leave me at night, I have such awful dreams about the baby dying, and me dying. . . . I get so scared, and I want my mama, and I don't even know where she is . . . Paul, *please, please*. . . ."

And so he continued to sleep beside her in the big double bed, jerking awake five or six times during the night when she cried out, getting up to stumble downstairs for warm milk to tempt her back to sleep, putting cool wet cloths on her forehead and neck to ease the spiraling pains of the headaches, growing daily heavier of step and more shadowed of eye and stooping with deepening worry for her. And Alicia continued to hover anxiously at the doorway of the room and the fringes of their lives, seeing less and less of her son and growing more and more tentative in the big house as her feelings of helplessness and uselessness to her son and Ruth grew, tiptoeing past the door and around the place on the staircase where the old boards creaked, lifting her finger to her lips whenever Pinky exploded at Henry in the kitchen, or Red or Rusky sang on the stairs. Thinking that Ruth might need her, she curtailed and then abandoned her daytime calls and activities, and kept to the house. Fearing to disturb Ruth by looking into her room . . . for the girl really got so upset at the thought that she was taking Alicia away from her duties that it was not worth it to insist on keeping her company . . . and ultimately fearing to disturb her by moving around too much upstairs, Alicia spent most of her days closeted in her morning room, reading or resting uncomfortably against the straight-backed chairs. In the evenings after dinner she sat alone in the drawing room or in her bedroom, a magazine or book open on her lap, one ear unconsciously cocked for a call from Ruth or Paul that never came. She did not realize it, but for the first time in her life under the flat Grecian roof of Fox's Earth, with her husband and son and daughter-in-law and servants around her, Alicia Fox was desperately and profoundly lonely.

And she was worried about Claudius, who daily grew more corpulent, abstracted, and vague, and even more about Paul. For the past three years Alicia had watched as her only child slogged his way through the viscid quagmire of the law, coming home from the judge's office later and later in the evenings with fatigue-bleared eyes, only to return upstairs to the room he shared with Ruth after dinner and bury himself once again in the volumes that seemed somehow heavier, more turgid, than even his heavy classical volumes had. These latter stood idle in piles in the corners of the pretty room, newly poufed and curtained and ruffled by Ruth, that had been Paul's room all his life, until finally Ruth had Red and Rusky crate them up and Henry bore them to the attic. Paul had asked about them that evening at dinner; Ruth had wrinkled her small, straight nose at him and said, "Well, darling, they were so terribly dusty, and took up so much room. . . . I stumbled over them every time I took a step. And then you really don't have time to read them right now, do you? It's been months since you've read anything but your law books. We'll have a place for them one day . . . room for shelves, maybe a whole wall of them. . . ."

She let her voice trail off wistfully, and Paul, thinking she was longing for a home of her own, hastened to assure her that she had done the right thing. Alicia's heart turned; it *was* a smallish room they shared, though with the finest view in the house, and hers and Claudius's room was so vast, so sweetly proportioned, for just the two of them.

"And we have the whole house to live in besides," she thought guiltily. "But they and all their belongings are crammed into that one room. No wonder Paul is so quiet. . . ."

For he was quiet, quieter than she had ever known him before, and growing daily more silent. Like his father before him, he ate when he was troubled and unhappy; ate as if to fill the deepening crater inside him that the silent unhappiness was leaving. By the time Ruth's pregnancy was evident, Paul, who had been a plump but taut young bridegroom, had become a slack, pink-jowled, puffing small figure from atop a wedding cake, with a middle-aged paunch over which his great-grandfather's gold watch fob danced fussily. Hunched in his leather chair in the evening, absorbed in his law books, his thumb and forefinger unconsciously massaging the red imprints left by his glasses on the bridge of his nose, he looked poignantly and ludicrously like his father, downstairs in his leather chair in his own study.

"He's a true Spartan boy," Alicia thought to herself more than once, attempting to josh herself out of her anxiety. "A little fox eats at his vitals, but he smiles and has another piece of pie."

But it really was not funny, and by the time the child's birth drew near, and Ruth lay ill and exhausted in the massive oak bed upstairs, the frail, inexorable focal point of all the eyes, ears, and energies of Fox's Earth, Alicia knew in her heart of hearts what it was that was troubling her son. It was more than the natural, almost comic adjustment of a bookish, solitary young man to marriage with a dazzling point of light like Ruth; more than the

94

curbed restlessness and longing for a home of his own and children; more than continued overwork and painful worry about Ruth and his unborn child.

Alicia knew, without knowing how she did, that Paul was deeply unhappy in the law. She also knew with equal certainty that he would never in his life speak of it to her or anyone else, and that he would spend his life at it. She wept for him, her gallant, stubborn, bewildered, unhappy child, during the long evenings she sat alone in her bedroom or in the drawing room, and sometimes she wept for all of them . . . herself, Claudius, Ruth, Paul . . . and wondered helplessly and for the thousandth time what had happened to them in three short years that she should weep hopelessly alone in dim rooms.

"This was such a happy house. It always was," she thought. "I don't know how to be unhappy in it. I don't know what the rules are for being unhappy at Fox's Earth."

And then she would think, "What a spoiled, whimpering woman you are. For the first time in your fortunate life there is trouble in your house, and instead of meeting it and riding it out with dignity and courage you sit in the dark and snivel like a baby. Everybody has trouble these days; this dreadful war, and those poor, suffering people overseas . . . Everything will be better when the baby comes and the war is over. We'll all be able to get back to normal then. Meanwhile, see if you can't get some grit in your craw, as Pinky says, and see what you can do for the others, instead of feeling sorry for yourself."

She would feel better after these times, and was able to mine the necessary rock from somewhere deep within her to combat the loneliness and worry and the other ephemeral, more troubling uneasiness that plagued her night and day.

But when Claudius died in April of 1915, died suddenly and in cawing, gargling terror, hand to head and eyes staring whitely from their blood-flooded sockets as he sat with her in his study after dinner on a quiet night of sighing rain and sweet little winds from beyond the French windows, the lode of New England granite that had served Alicia Chambliss Fox well through the days of her life in this slow, hot, alien land gave out, and she buckled under the grief and emptiness of his loss; and when she stood again it was tentatively, and with a frail stoop, and never again altogether upright, but assisted by the arms of others.

People said that Claudius was a war casualty, as surely as if he had fought with the *poilus* against the Hun or flown with the Lafayette Escadrille. On the floor beside him at his death was his beloved Bulfinch, worn limp and fine with repeated thumbing, but at his feet, tumbled where it had fallen when he had half risen in his death throes, was the front page of the Sparta *Sentinel*, with a black-bannered headline atop its account of the Germans' treacherous use of poison gas at Ypres. Angered and saddened by the worsening war news, he did not usually read the newspapers by this time, but Paul, outraged at this new evidence of Teutonic atrocity, had brought the paper home from the office and laid it in his father's chair, thinking to have a discussion with him after dinner, as they had done in the happier times of his adolescence.

Forever after Paul carried the burden of his father's death lashed atop the pack of guilts and regrets he wore on his back, and no heartbroken denials from Alicia or assurances from Dr. Hopkins could assuage the pain. But he buried it deeply, under concern for the frail, elderly stranger who was, incredibly, his beautiful mother, and worry for Ruth, who was so distraught when she was told that Dr. Hopkins was forced to give her an injection from which she did not wake until the following morning. It was Paul who pulled the covers up over her swollen stomach and thin shoulders, and Paul who put his mother to bed in a narrow, stark little room at the end of an upstairs back corridor . . . for she would not sleep in the room that had been hers and Claudius's . . . and it was Paul who, finally, sat alone with his father in the quiet den, throughout the longest night of his life, until dour Angus Cromartie came in the morning with his new motorized hearse, and Claudius Fox went out from Fox's Earth for the last time into the soft, wet mother-of-pearl of an April morning.

Two days later he was buried in the old Confederate cemetery. That night, at eleven o'clock, Ruth went into labor with Hebe, and after that nothing was ever the same again.

9

It was a savage labor and delivery, a two-day tunnel of red agony that rose from small gripings in the pit of Ruth's stomach steadily upward in grinding anguish to peak in an unspeakable intensity of pain, hung there endlessly, while far away, in some back region, a woman screamed weak, high, piping screams, and then tumbled her back down into a pool of bitter sweat before beginning the upward spiral again. The light seemed to change in the tunnel . . . black swelled into red-black and bled to gray and lit to hot rose-gray and then faded into black again . . . but there appeared at the end of it no opening door, no cessation, no point beyond which she could look and think, "Once I get past that, it will be over and I will have lived through it." The pain simply was; it existed as an element like light and air, flooding and surrounding her. Ruth did not think she would live past the pain.

People came and went in the red-black tunnel; at the times when the pain dropped low, she recognized Dr. Hopkins, grim-faced and stubble-chinned and waxen with fatigue; and Paul, paper-white and terrified, his tongue tangling with fright whenever he bent over her to talk to her, his hands cold and wet as the hands of the drowned dead when they clasped hers. Each time he leaned over her in the night lamplight or the bars of blinding white daylight that crept at noon through the drawn curtains, the silver tracks of tears shone on his fat cheeks, and she would think in faint peevishness, "What has that silly fool got to cry about? It's me that's being torn apart, not him." The tunnel was stifling hot and wet with oppressive dampness, for an April hot spell hammered Sparta under a fist as punishing as any of August's, and Ruth's monstrously bloated body writhed and arched and jackknifed amid tangled sheets that went wet and gray as fast as Pinky could change them. Someone—not Alicia, but a massive, stolid black presence—stood silently and endlessly beside the bed, alternately wiping Ruth's face and neck and hands with a linen dish towel wrung out in cool water and fanning her with a long-handled palmetto fan. She was grateful for it when she struggled up out of the pain as if out of water, to draw great, gulping breaths of air, but she did not come up often.

Ruth was aware of very little except the howling red pain, but she was aware to the tips of her clawing fingers and arching feet that she lay in the great tester bed in the room that had been Alicia and Claudius's. Paul had carried her into the big room when her labor began, because she had wept and sobbed and begged so to be taken there that he dared not refuse her.

"It's so hot here, Paul," she had whimpered, rolling her yellow head fretfully back and forth on her piled pillows in the room they shared. "The big room will be so cool, and so nice and dim . . . and I feel like Daddy Claudius will be there, that somehow he'll stay there long enough to know that he's got a grandbaby. Oh, please, Paul . . ."

And Paul, who had only that afternoon buried the gentle, pompous little man who had been his adored father, was rent to his marrow with fresh grief for Claudius and love for Ruth, that in her pain and fright she would still think of Claudius. Alicia, too, who hovered like a bewildered shade in the doorway of Ruth and Paul's room when the labor first began, brightened infinitesimally when she heard those words. Since Claudius's death she had been so fragile and fragmented and grief-blurred that they had thought she did not fully comprehend what was happening, and Paul and the servants and Dr. Hopkins noted with joy and hope the focusing of her eyes on Ruth's face, the frail smile that curved her cracked lips, and the faint stain of color that crept into her thin cheeks.

"Oh, yes, darling, what a splendid idea," she breathed. "Of course you must go there; I'm sorry I didn't think of it myself. It's the master suite for Fox's Earth, you know, and that's exactly where your son must be born. Claudius would be so pleased."

"Mama," Paul said, wavering unhappily between the two polestars of his life, "we can't ask you to leave your room, not now. All your things are there . . . all Papa's things, too. It's too much; you must have your room to rest and . . . get your strength back. Ruth wasn't thinking, and besides, Dr. Hopkins will probably be taking her to the hospital before long. . . ."

"*NO!*" shrieked Ruth. "*NO*, no, no, no, no, no. . . ."

Blue veins stood out in her neck and temples and her face flooded with scalding vermilion. Her eyes seemed to start from her head; the corner of one filled with blood. Dr. Hopkins was beside her in an instant, shouting for his bag.

"No hospital! No hospital! I will not go to a hospital; I want to go to Daddy Claudius's room! I want to go there *now!*"

Despite the hypodermic, they could not quiet her until the doctor murmured reluctantly, "All right, then, Ruth, no hospital. No hospital." Then her screams faded, and her head drooped, and her eyes feathered shut, and they carried her swiftly into Alicia and Claudius's room and slipped her between the fresh, lavender-scented linen sheets that Rusky hastily put on the bed.

Downstairs, over scalding chickory coffee, Dr. Hopkins talked somberly to Paul.

"She should be in the hospital. She's two months early. Her blood pressure is alarming. She's been flirting with pre-eclampsia right along. And, of course, there's that narrow pelvis. It's going to be touch and go with the baby at best. Ideally she should be in the hospital at this moment, and we should be prepping her for a Caesarean."

"Well, can't you tell her that? Surely you can convince her; you're a doctor."

Paul was staring with fright and fatigue. This talk of pre-eclampsia and Caesarean sections meant nothing to him but a terrifying arcana from which he was barred; realities to him now were a new red grave, a mumbling stranger in his mother's place, and a wife upstairs who had moved away from him and into the very valley of the shadow. Always before when he had talked with the doctor about Ruth's pregnancy, Alicia's cool common sense and sparing grace had been a buffer for him. But Alicia now lay far out of his sight and hearing in the austere little back bedroom she had chosen, sleeping heavily under the weight of sorrow and confusion and the sedative Dr. Hopkins had given her.

"Your mother's had too much," the doctor had said briefly. "She can't take any more today. I've given her a shot; she'll sleep until morning, and, God willing, by then that baby will be here, or almost. I don't want her anywhere near all this, as disoriented and frail as she is. I'll be here right along, and one of the women can stay. Alicia can't help Ruth now, and all this could do her a great deal of harm. You'll be here too, of course."

"Of course," Paul mumbled, but he hadn't planned on being there at all. He'd planned all along, he realized, to ride out the night of Ruth's labor . . . for somehow, in his mind's eye, he had seen it taking place at night . . . in his father's study, drinking brandy with Claudius and receiving comfort from his pedantic, unworldly presence. He had foreseen the two of them allied together in the lamplight, walled in with books and ringed about with the tokens of civility: brandy, cigars, newspapers, men's talk, amulets against the ancient, mystic female barbarism going on upstairs. Paul had, in his fervid, romantic mind's eye, seen, at last, Alicia, pale and disheveled but smiling a misty, world-encompassing smile, appearing in the study door as the dawn broke over Fox's Earth, holding the small, fragrant bundle that was his son, and had heard the thin, spiraling cry of the son rising up and up in the joyful morning until it broke over the very roof of Fox's Earth like an anthem.

In the darkened kitchen, Paul felt fresh tears sting his tired eyes. In all his life he would never again feel so despairingly alone. He looked drearily at the doctor.

"I just don't know," the doctor said distractedly, thinking that he would be lucky if he got Paul through the birth of his child without having to put him, too, to bed with a hypodermic. "It's a matter, really, of which is worse for her: to be here with her blood pressure ready to blow any minute and a long, hard labor to go through, or to take her to the hospital against her will and have her go into hysterics again and almost surely blow that pressure through the top of her skull. And then I don't know if she could physically stand major abdominal surgery right now. On the whole, I think we're better off keeping her here, and waiting to see . . ."

And so Ruth writhed and screamed and sweated and ground her way through that night, and the next morning and afternoon, and the next night, and still the baby did not come.

Toward dawn on the second day of the labor, Pearl

Steed Yancey came into the room and stood beside the bed where her daughter lay.

"Mama," Ruth rasped through flayed and swollen lips, and Paul and Rusky, who had been dozing in chairs at her side, snapped awake and came to hover over her.

"What is it, precious?" Paul said, taking her hands in his.

"Get out of my light; I can't see Mama with you in the light," Ruth said impatiently, and struggled to raise herself on her pillows.

"Wait, let me help you," he said, putting an arm around her shoulders.

"Leave me alone, you fool, I want to talk to my mama!" she snapped, and he stepped back, looking involuntarily around in the shadows. He met Rusky's eyes, white-ringed in the dim turning of the night, goggling apprehensively toward where Ruth was looking.

"She's seein' ghos'ses, Mr. Paul," Rusky moaned. "Maw say that mean sick fo'kses gon' die fo' sure, when they talks to ghos'es."

"Get down there and wake up Dr. Hopkins and bring him up here, and hurry," Paul said sharply, tears thick in his throat.

"Yassuh." She was gone. He turned back to Ruth. She sat bolt upright in the bed, staring at a point just beyond the edge of the bed, where a pool of light from an averted bridge lamp fell on an empty stretch of Aubusson. She was talking to the empty space, head cocked to one side, talking earnestly and in simple fright, like a small child. He started to reach for her, to draw her back down onto the pillows, and then let his arms fall back to his sides.

"Mama, I think I'm going to die," Ruth said.

"Not yet you ain't," Pearl Steed said. "Not till you done what you got to do. Quit lollygaggin', Ruth, an' git on with it now. You ain't got much time."

"What have I got to do, Mama? I forget," Ruth said dreamily.

"Why, you got to birth that girl of yourn. Don't you know what you're doin', you silly chit? Don't you know what's happenin' to you?"

"I forgot. Mama, it hurts so much. You never said it would hurt like this, you never told me . . . Mama, I be-believe I *will* die. I believe I'd like that. It would be so easy; all I'd have to do is just sort of let go, and then it wouldn't hurt anymore. . . ."

"You ain't no daughter of mine, then, Ruth Yancey, and I ain't gon' have no more truck with you. I thought you had good stuff in you; I thought you'd learned oncet and for all, I thought, oncet you'd done did the worst thing, you could do it all . . . shoot, Ruth, this ain't *nothin'* to what you already done done, don't you remember? You went and done all that for this house, and now you say you cain't go on an' have this here young'un what's gon' make it yours oncet and for all. Huh! Any fool can prop her legs apart an' let a young'un shoot out! You ain't no Yancey if you cain't do a little thing like that!"

"Why? Why do I have to, Mama? Why can't I just go on and die and be done with it? I know, I *know* it wouldn't be any different from just going to sleep. Just going to sleep . . ."

Pearl came closer to the bed and glared down at Ruth. Somewhere behind her, Ruth could hear Paul sobbing over and over, "She's talking to her mother, and there's nobody there! She says she wants to die, that she's going to die. . . ."

Ruth closed her ears to him and concentrated on keeping her mother's wolfish face from wavering on the tide of weariness and coldness that was creeping up her legs.

"I'll tell you why," Pearl said. "I'll tell you why, and don't you *never* forget it, Ruth. You got to have that baby because there's always got to be a Yancey woman at Fox's Earth. You hear me? You listen good. There must *always* be a Yancey woman at Fox's Earth. Elseways warn't nothin' worth it. Now you lay back there an' you have that girl all healthy and proper like a girl ought to be."

"A girl?"

"Of course. You ain't gon' have no more Fox men aroun' here if you 'n' me can help it. Git you a little gal here, so's there's always a Fox woman at Fox's Earth, and then go on an' die on me if you got to. Like as not you're just pawky enough to do it, too."

"In a pig's ass I will," said Ruth strongly. Color flamed into her face, and she took a great breath, and, as an enormous contraction took her, she cried a great, ringing cry as of a Valkyrie going into battle.

Ruth's daughter was born less than an hour later, a waxen, shriveled little thing with the mewling cry of a half-drowned kitten and a dangerously low birth weight. Her underformed little lungs rattled and her skin was blue and did not bloom, and she fit easily into the palms of Paul's hands when the bloody-armed doctor laid her there. Paul sobbed aloud when he saw her, and was still sobbing when he leaned over Ruth, so white and flattened that she looked melted into her pillows.

"We have a little girl, dearest, and she's just a perfect little girl, but the doctor says you mustn't get too attached to her. You see, she's just so very little, and she's had such a long, hard fight . . . please don't set your heart on her, dearest. She could so easily just slip away from us."

He dropped his head onto his arms, folded on her bed. She studied him dispassionately.

"He's going to be bald as an egg before he's thirty," she thought to herself.

Aloud she said, "She's not going to slip away anywhere. She's going to live to be a hundred, right here at Fox's Earth. Her name is Hebe Pearl Fox . . . Hebe because Daddy Claudius picked it out; Hebe the Cupbearer, he said . . . and Pearl because my mama came and got her here safe and sound. And if you say one more word about her slipping away from us, Paul Fox, I'll leave you, just as soon as I can get up out of this bed."

And for the first time in seven months, Ruth Yancey Fox went to sleep and slept the deep, sweet sleep that is usually given only to childhood, when all the world's fears are yet to be learned, and the body is borne up on a mattress of certainties.

Three weeks later, Rip came to Fox's Earth, and scrawny, ailing little Hebe Fox lay for the first time in the thin young arms of her life's protector. Pinky and Red and Rusky jealously ignored the exotic mahogany girl who slipped like a shadow into the sacrosanct upstairs, or spoke shortly and sullenly to her when they were forced to speak at all. Paul scarcely saw her, or at best saw only a thin black teenager who looked too young to be handling his baby; Alicia, who was still vague and listless, though brighter, and tremendously absorbed in the small, miraculous fact of her granddaughter and the comforting, bustling ritual that surrounded her, was kind but abstracted with Rip. Ruth had noticed no Negroes, except to measure their performances, in all the time she had been living at Fox's

Earth, so she paid Rip no particular attention when she came into the room to pick up Hebe and take her downstairs where the wet nurse waited for her, or sat with the baby in the newly decorated nursery beside her own tiny cubicle under the back eaves, rocking her and singing to her:

> " 'Bye-bye, baby bunting,
> Daddy's gone ahunting,
> Git a little rabbit skin
> To wrap his baby bunting in.' "

She did not mind that she was largely ignored in the great white house. The forlorn scrap of infant in the beribboned cradle at Fox's Earth and the shining, crowing black infant in the laundry basket back in Suches were, for the moment, enough and more than enough for Rip. The million and one new scents and sights and sounds of the huge white house, and the unfathomable complexities of the white people in it, intrigued and occupied her waking hours. Miss Alicia was unfailingly kind, and young Miss Ruth was so beautiful that Rip thought that she must look like the angels in the white people's heaven. If her temper was a trifle sharp and her eyes, when they fell on Rip, were unseeing and cold, well, that was nothing to Rip, so long as all was well with infant Hebe. It did strike Rip as odd that Ruth did not seem to care much for the child, did not wish to spend her time holding and cuddling Hebe, did not respond at all to her fretful wails except to ring for Rip and say petulantly, "Can't you hear anything, Rip? She's been squalling for half an hour. Take her to the nursery and rock her or something. She hurts my head." Miss Ruth had been very sick herself, and had had a very bad time; she obviously wasn't herself yet. She would love the baby as much as Rip did when she was fully recovered. And anyway, Rip suspected that it was not the way of the white people, especially the grand ones in the big white houses of Church Street, to carry on about their babies like the women of Suches did.

"That wouldn't be fittin'," Rip thought. All in all, she was quite content at Fox's Earth, as content as she had ever been in her short and straitened life.

Six weeks after Hebe's birth, Paul came up to Ruth's bedside after his solitary dinner with Alicia in the too-big, too-silent dining room, his pallid forehead knit with trouble and resolution. Rip, rocking quietly with the sleeping infant in the Boston rocker in the corner of the room, rose dutifully to bring Hebe to her father as she usually did when he visited in the evenings, but Ruth looked intently into Paul's face and motioned for Rip to take the baby away. Rip did, silently and quickly, the felt slippers she wore in the upstairs of the house noiseless on the Aubusson.

Paul sat down on the edge of Ruth's bed and took her hands in his. She looked enchanting to him in the flush of light from Alicia's rose-shaded crystal lamp; still too sharp-faced and shadowed and hollowed by half, but with a returning sheen of silk to her gilt hair, and a renascence of the peculiar gold light that always seemed to emanate from her flesh. She was wearing a bed jacket he had ordered for her from New York in the first days after Hebe's birth, when it had first become apparent that the child would live and Ruth herself would recover. It had just come the day before, an expensive and ludicrous breath of cornflower-blue georgette and maribou, and in it she looked suddenly and overwhelmingly uncanny, like a fabulous apparition superimposing itself over a familiar and mundane landscape. It was as if, for a moment, he did not know who or what she was, and he blinked. Ruth smiled up at him, enjoying the effect she created there in the lamplight, misted around with her blue.

"I'm worried about Mama," he said abruptly, and she realized that his rapt preoccupation was not wrought by her mariboued countenance after all, but by concern for Alicia. Her silken gold brows drew together ever so faintly.

"What's the matter with her? I thought she seemed fine this afternoon," she said.

"I don't think she's fine at all," Paul said. "She's getting thinner and thinner, and most of the time she doesn't even seem . . . I don't know, in the same world with the rest of us . . . she doesn't hear you when you speak to her, and she hardly ever smiles anymore."

"Well, Paul, after all, Daddy Claudius has only been gone six weeks. She's bound to be grieving for him. I know I still do."

"It's more than that. She hasn't said, but I think she feels like she isn't needed here much anymore, like we
105

can do just fine without her . . . and of course we can't. I never could. But we've all tried so hard to protect her, and spare her, and let her rest, that she just hasn't been a part of the household since Papa died. And I think it's slowly killing her. I know Mama; that's the one thing that would finish her off; thinking she wasn't useful anymore."

"Yes, I guess it would at that."

Ruth's eyes were shadowed by her lashes, and her face was still.

"You've got Rip now, and Pinky's been doing just fine in the kitchen without her, and I've been doing the accounts, and I know she hasn't been out of the house, or had visitors, since you were pregnant, practically. I think we've got to change that. I think we've got to get ourselves back to normal as soon as possible, and her with us. She needs to get back to running her house, just like she always has."

Ruth was silent; she looked at him.

"I think we'll start by moving you back to our own room. You're looking much better, really, darling, and Dr. Hopkins says you're perfectly able to move, provided we don't . . . you know. I've told Henry to set up the cot in there for me, until you're perfectly well again, and the baby will be just fine with Rip in the nursery now. What do you say, precious? Mama's been more than good about it, but I know she misses her own room. The . . . whole history of her marriage to Papa is here, in a way. And I've missed you terribly."

He smiled down at her in the lamplight. She did not move or reply for a long while, and then she said, "Of course, Paul, if you think it will help Mama Alicia. I'll have Rip get the baby ready in the morning, and Rusky can help her move my things. I only have a few."

"Thank you, darling," he said, and kissed her forehead and went out of the room. Rip, coming back with the baby, heard . . . or thought she did . . . Ruth's clear, cold, sweet voice saying, "I won't do it, Mama. I'll die first. It's my room now; it's mine by right. He can just think again."

"Was you callin' me, Miss Ruth?" Rip said, for there was clearly no one else in the room, and no one could have left it without her seeing them from the hallway.

"No. I didn't say anything. I don't like eavesdropping,

106

Rip. Take the baby and put her to sleep in the nursery. I don't need you any more tonight."

"Yas'm," Rip said. She cut her long eyes around at the shadowy corners of the big bedroom as she left with the baby. So Rusky was right . . . Ruth did talk to her mother, who wasn't there. Rip did not care for the idea. Her arms tightened protectively around the baby, who whimpered in her sleep.

In the morning, when Rip was moving the crib where Hebe spent several hours each day from the big bedroom to Paul and Ruth's room down the hall, she heard the baby give a sharp, thin scream and settle into the shrill, engine-like crying that always lasted for hours. She hurried into the bedroom where Ruth sat propped up against the pillows, rocking the swaddled baby back and forth in her arms and staring at her in distress. Paul, just leaving for his office, heard the screams and came upstairs to investigate.

"I don't know what's the matter," Ruth said worriedly. "She isn't hungry or wet, and I know she isn't sick. It all started when Rip moved her crib out, to take it down to our room. She just started this screaming, and she won't stop. No, Rip . . ." and Rip, reaching automatically for the baby, stepped back . . . "let me see if I can soothe her. It's as if she knows, somehow, that she's being moved out of the room where she was born. She needs her mommy now."

So they did not move Ruth and the baby that day, and gradually the helpless crying subsided, and Hebe drifted into an exhausted sleep. Ruth did not give her over to Rip, as she usually did, but kept her beside her in the big bed all day, wrapped snugly in her summer blanket or cradled in her mother's arms. For the next several days, in fact, Hebe did not leave Ruth's side, for whenever they attempted to take her up, sleeping, and lay her softly in her crib in the bedroom down the hall, she burst into fresh shrieks, and Ruth took her consolingly back into her arms.

Rip had far more time to spend with Jester Tully in the cowshed during those sweet June days, and could not have said why she was not happier, but all during their times together, it was as if her inner ear listened for a call . . . something . . . from the upstairs bedroom at Fox's Earth, a call that did not come. She was restless and preoccupied, and when she told Jester she was worried about Hebe, he grew sullen and then angry, and finally took himself off to do a job for old Colonel Coulter at the other end of Church Street, a three-day planting project he had been postponing so he could spend the time with Rip. Rip did not fret; she knew Jester's proud, impatient ways by now, and knew he would be back, without apology but with renewed and loving vigor.

But still the unease lay heavy on her, and the ear listened.

So it was almost a week later that Rip, undressing Hebe to give her her bath, saw the faint, purplish-yellow half-moon marks on the thin, pearled skin of her legs . . . seven or eight sets of symmetrical twin marks down the baby's legs . . . and knew with absolute certainty that Hebe had been cruelly pinched.

That evening Paul came again to his parents' bedroom and broached the subject of moving Ruth to their own room.

"But, Paul, the baby . . ." Ruth began.

"The baby hasn't cried for several days now," he said firmly. "And besides, I do not believe that we can afford to indulge the baby in this, Ruth. Mama's well-being is more important than the whim of a seven-week-old child. Now here, I've brought your robe and slippers, and Rusky has made up the bed with your Swiss embroidered sheets, and I sprinkled them with lavender water myself. Lean on my arm while you get into your robe, and let's get you back in our own bed, where you belong."

"Of course, darling," Ruth said, her eyes veiled, and slipped out of bed, and fainted into a crumpled heap on the Aubusson before he could catch her.

In the ensuing melee, while Paul ran downstairs shouting for Henry to call Dr. Hopkins, and Alicia, hearing the furor, hovered uncertainly at the door to her own bedroom, wringing her thin hands, Rip caught up sleeping Hebe from her nursery crib and ran down the stairs to the room where Ruth lay on the rug. In her carpet slippers she moved as silently as a ghost, and so it was that Ruth, thinking herself alone, raised her head and looked about her with a cool, assessing glance and found herself staring full into the impassive face of the young black girl, who stared back at her over the form of her baby.

They measured each other, white woman and black, for the space of perhaps thirty seconds, and then, with Paul's footsteps pounding back up the stairs, Ruth closed her eyes once more and slumped back onto the carpet, and Rip took Hebe away, down the hall and into the nursery. Presently the doctor came and was closeted with Ruth for a brief time, and then, after conferring with Paul in his study, drove away again. Paul returned to stay for a while with Ruth, and sat beside her bed patting her hands until she closed her eyes and her head drooped on Alicia's pillows, and then he went wearily back to his own room. Ruth did not leave the room of Alicia and Claudius Fox that evening, and she did not leave it ever again. Alicia herself would not have it otherwise, and Paul finally acceded.

The morning after her faint, Ruth rang the little silver bell on the table by her bed. The bell had, by custom, become Rip's summons, and in due time Rip appeared at Ruth's bedside, with Hebe dressed for the day in ruffled lawn and ready to be put into her mother's arms.

Ruth waved the baby away and stared at Rip with the great blue-violet eyes that seemed to both manufacture and give back light. She was silent for a long time, while she looked, and Rip was quiet, too. She did not fidget, or drop her eyes, but looked levelly back at Ruth over Hebe's head.

"If you tell anybody what you saw last night, I'll fire you," Ruth said.

"Yas'm," Rip said serenely. She did not move to go. Ruth frowned.

"Do you understand what I'm saying? I'll fire you, and I'll see that you never get work in Sparta again. I can do it, too; I'll tell people that you . . . hurt the baby, somehow. Nobody would hire you then. I mean that, Rip."

"Yas'm," Rip said, still not moving, but involuntarily tucking Hebe closer to her breast. The gesture did not escape Ruth. She looked more closely at the black girl, seeing as if for the first time the elegance of bone, the substance and intelligence in the narrow face, the grace in the slight, long body. She saw something more, too; her brow knit with the perplexity of it. This girl loved . . . really, deeply loved . . . the white baby that she held. It was a new idea for Ruth, and it troubled her. She was even more perplexed at Rip's serenity; it appeared to be genuine. The girl was untouched, unfrightened. She would not be intimidated, and she would not be adversary. What

109

manner of woman was this, this insignificant black chit of a girl? Ruth had not met her like before.

"I will need a woman," Ruth thought suddenly and clearly. "I will need a woman to be my ally for all the years to come, if I am to get what I want, what I need. If Fox's Earth is truly to be mine, I will need help from a woman who knows what I am doing and will help me do it. She does not have to like it, or me, but she must comply. It must be a woman I can control, and I can control this woman through my child . . . and I will. Yes. I need a woman, and it will be Rip."

Aloud she said, "You love the baby, don't you? You love my baby. You would take good care of her always, wouldn't you?"

"Yas'm," Rip said, and her face softened; it was the face of one woman equal before another woman. "I aim to take good care of Hebe."

"Well, if you'll keep your mouth shut, I won't fire you, then. There's just no telling what might happen to Hebe if you weren't here, and we don't want anything to happen to Hebe. Do we, Rip?"

"No'm. Ain't nothin' gon' happen to Hebe."

They looked at each other once more, a long look that bridged deeps, gulfs, worlds, generations, unimaginable spaces. A tacit understanding passed between them; it would stand and serve, they both knew, for as long as they both lived.

"Then you won't say anything, and you won't be leaving. That's right, isn't it, Rip?"

Rip nodded.

She wouldn't have left anyway.

10

ON A DAZZLING, wind-booming morning in mid-March of 1917, Rip went into Alicia's sickroom with whining Hebe in tow, and saw, in the sudden flare of light that burst through the door with them, that Alicia was dying.

She looked no different from the way she had looked for many months, since she had taken to her bed the previous summer with a virulent bout of food poisoning and simply failed to rise again; but Rip, seeing her plain in that first wind of light that blew ahead of the coming spring, saw also the cold death crouching at her head on the flattened pillows, and heard its slow, silent hissing, and knew that Alicia would not see the full flood of the new spring.

She was not frightened or even astonished to see that Alicia Fox lay with her head next to death on the pillow. Had she not, herself, felt death waiting for someone at Fox's Earth from the time she arrived there all through the ensuing weeks and months? She had not been able to sense for whom it waited and had, for a long time, feared it was for tiny Hebe, who was as frailly unfinished as a baby possum before it crawls into the pouch to complete its maturing. But Hebe was nearly two years old now, a spindrift dandelion of a child, prattling in a voice as mothy and breathless as a midge's whine; so pale as to be almost translucent, and for all of it, as tough and enduring as spun-steel filament. Ruth Fox slowly regained her strength, and still death waited in the house; Rip's own baby was gone and death did not go with her; Alicia sickened in the stifling days of the previous August and grew a bit stronger again, and still death did not show its face in Fox's Earth, only breathed its long, hollow breaths.

But here it was now, as plain and palpable in the fetid air of the room as Alicia herself, and it was all Rip could do to keep from jerking Hebe from the room by her matchstick arm and slamming the door in the face of death. She did not want that eyeless great face to turn itself upon the child, even though she knew that its arms were already about Alicia Fox, and its face firmly fixed on hers. Instead, she gave Hebe a little push into the room and followed her briskly, leaving the door into the hall to swing back upon itself and let in the fresh, streaming air and light of normalcy and life.

"Miss Hebe want to say hello to her grandma," she said, guiding the child by her shoulders to Alicia's bedside. "She been out diggin' in the dirt this mornin', and she got some daffydillys for her grandma."

Alicia's face, the color of dirty tallow on the pillows, lighted faintly at the sight of the child, and she smiled. The smile was a caricature, a ghastly joke; illness and sorrow and fear had eaten away the substance of Alicia's strong, carved face until only the armature remained. She looked, in the merciless morning light, like a Hallowe'en jack-o'-lantern, with gaping, burnt holes for eyes, a beaky nose with the flesh shrunken away around it, a stretched, great-gummed grin. She held out her arms to the balking child and gave a small, glad cry.

"Hebe, darling! Grandma is so *glad* to see you! Come and tell me how you are; it's been so long since I've seen you. My, just look at you; when did you go and get all grown up? You're practically a proper lady, isn't she, Rip? And the prettiest one I've ever seen."

Alicia propped herself up on her pillows and pulled the bedside lamp closer, and light fell across her face and over the bed. Hebe, who had sidled up to the bed, crushed daffodils drooping from one grubby fist and the index finger of the other hand firmly entrenched in her tiny Fox nose, stopped in her tracks, stared, gave a startling great howl, and flew to bury her face in Rip's apron. No amount of scolding or coaxing would dislodge her; the shrieks flew up and up in the quiet upper air of the great house, and Rip was just turning to take her back to the nursey when Ruth appeared in the doorway. She was holding her silk kimono together with one white hand; under the parted petals of the kimono, her peach-colored crepe de Chine underwear shone against her pearly, blue-white limbs. Ruth was fully recovered from Hebe's birth, and was as delicately and sweetly molded of limb and sheened of skin as she had ever been in her life.

"Rip! What on earth! I could hear that child screeching all the way into my bathroom, with the door closed. Is she hurt? No, I see not. Hebe, do stop right now, or Mama will have Daddy spank you when he comes home tonight, and you won't like that one bit, will you?"

Hebe stopped the shrieking and raised her flushed face to her mother's. Ruth looked at Rip, and then at Alicia, huddled miserably in the bed, her thin hand lifted helplessly to her mouth. She sighed, a great, patient sigh.

"Rip, I know you meant well, but I've told you not once but a thousand times that you're not to disturb Mama Alicia by bringing Hebe here." Alicia shook her head to protest, and murmured imploringly to Ruth something that Rip could not hear.

"No, Mama Alicia," Ruth said firmly. "You know you aren't strong enough to deal with her yet. Don't you remember what happened last time she came here by herself? And I told you what Dr. Hopkins said on Monday, don't you remember? I told you then, and I told you again yesterday. He said you must absolutely rest until every trace of that awful cold you got Christmas is gone for good, else you'd have a relapse and get pleurisy again, and he'd have to take you to the hospital. Now you remember, don't you? And he said that it would be better if we waited until you were feeling better and . . . well, you know, more in control of yourself . . . before we brought Hebe to see you again. She's too young to understand about sick people, and I'm afraid she still remembers last time."

Tears started weakly in Alicia's eyes, and her collapsed mouth trembled. She averted her head, and Ruth sighed again, and thrust Hebe back into Rip's grasp, and went to the narrow bed and sat down on the side.

"Mama Alicia, don't cry. I'm not criticizing you. It's just that you don't realize how sick you've been, and how worried we are, and how weak you are still. When you insist on doing things Dr. Hopkins has forbidden you to do, we all suffer, don't you see? Now you'll be much better soon if you'll do as you're told, but meanwhile, you can see how you would frighten Hebe while you're still so easily upset and sensitive, can't you? Don't you think it would be better to wait until you're your old self, the granny she knows, before she visits you again? I've told Rip; I don't know what got into her . . ."

113

She glared at Rip, who looked back at her serenely and said nothing.

Alicia tried to speak, strangled on a sob and tried again.

"It's not Rip's fault . . . I told her to bring Hebe here. It's been so long, and I've missed her . . . I hear her footsteps sometimes, and her voice, but I never see her, and I felt better this morning . . . Don't be mad at me, please, Ruth. I feel such a foolish old woman, and you know how I hate to cause bother. I wouldn't frighten Hebe for the world. I didn't realize I had . . . done anything."

She stopped; her voice broke and the tears welled over her lids once again. She buried her face in her hands.

Ruth touched her shoulder, rising as she did so. "I'm going to take her back to the nursery now, Mama Alicia. You've gotten yourself all upset again, and it's not good for you. Rip will stay with you until I leave for lunch, and then Red or Rusky can sit with you. I think I'll call Dr. Hopkins and see if he'll look in on you this afternoon, too. I can hear that rattle in your lungs again, as plain as day. Stop crying, now. You know what a headache it gives you. Hebe can come back again soon."

". . . better off if I was dead," Alicia sobbed into her hands, weakly and hopelessly. "Now you won't let her come back, and Paul never comes . . ."

"Paul comes all the time. Paul was here last night just before you went to sleep. Really, Mama Alicia, don't tell me you've forgotten that too? Now hush. You'll make yourself really sick. I'll send Rusky up on my way out. Hebe, run give Grandma a kiss and let's go play with old Teddy bear, would you like that?"

The child flew on tiptoes across the floor, gave the air around Alicia's hidden face a loud smack, and darted out the door ahead of her mother. Ruth turned back on the threshold, to meet Rip's eyes.

"Do what you can for her, Rip," she said. "Maybe next time you'll believe me when I say Hebe isn't to visit here until I say so. You see how she is."

"Yes'm," Rip said, her eyes unwavering on Ruth's face. "I sees."

She held the look until Ruth dropped her own eyes and turned and followed Hebe from the room. Rip went to Alicia's bedside, drew up the Boston rocker, and sat down. She reached out and took Alicia's rigid hands in her own and drew them gently away from her face. Alicia raised

114

brimming, sunken eyes to Rip's young face; something
there spoke softly and quietly to her, and her thin shoulders relaxed, and she lay back on her pillows with a small,
ragged sigh.

"Ain't nothin' ever so bad but it don't get better, Miss
Alicia," Rip said.

"Will I get better, Rip?"

"You gittin' better every day, look lak to me."

"No. I'm not getting better. I don't care what Dr.
Hopkins says: I know what he's up to. Rip, you must tell
me the truth now. It's my mind, isn't it? My mind is playing tricks on me. That's why Ruth won't let Hebe come
here . . . I've hurt or frightened Hebe somehow, haven't I,
and I don't remember? And everyone is afraid I'll do it
again? And that's why I can't remember when Paul comes
to see me . . . because I can't, you know, I could swear I
haven't seen my son in . . . oh, in months. And all those
things I've lost, and broken, and the things I've . . . taken
. . . I no more remember them than I can remember before I was born, and yet there they were, right where Ruth
or someone found them . . . broken, or hidden right here
in my room . . . Oh, Rip! I never wanted to be like this!
What use is a sick, crazy old woman to anybody? A crazy
old woman who frightens her only grandchild in the
world . . . ?"

Rip was silent, looking into Alicia's anguished face. How
to ease this unwarranted pain without placing in jeopardy
the small girl she was sworn in her soul to guard? It was
within her power to ease and free Alicia Fox; Rip, alone of
everyone at Fox's Earth, knew the truth, that Alicia was
not, in fact, dangerously ill; that she had never once
frightened or harmed small Hebe; that it was not she who
lost or hid household objects, only to have them turn up
days later in unexpected places; that Paul did not, in fact,
visit his mother, having been told by Ruth that Alicia did
not want him to see her as she was. It was within Rip's
power to make these things known to Alicia, but in doing
so she would forfeit her ability to keep safe the precious
small person of Hebe Fox. There was no choice; Rip's
capacious heart ached even as it lifted to the task. Even if
she died in terror and heartbreak, Alicia had had a life.
Hebe's life-to-be lay, still unexposed to the quickening air,
in the cup of Rip's strong black hands.

"You be spry as Job's turkey afore long, Miss 'Licia, an'

115

then you'll see; Miss Hebe be all over you then. You min'
Miss Ruth an' rest, an' don't worry 'bout them little ol'
things she fin' in yo' room. They ain't worth spittin' on,
nohow; don't nobody pay 'em no min'."

"Rip, can't you just tell me what it was I did to Hebe,
to frighten her so? Please, so I'll know not to do it again."

Rip's soul shriveled in anguish and outrage, but she said
only, "Miss Ruth ain't tell me, Miss 'Licia. I 'spect it don't
'mount to hardly nothin' at all. Don't you fret none about
it. Li'l ol' babies like Miss Hebe, they forgets real quick."

Alicia did not reply. She turned her head on the pillow
away from Rip, and sighed a soft, accepting sigh, and
dozed.

"Miss Ruth wicked, she wicked," Rip would have intoned in sorrow and impotent rage to Jester Tully as she
lay in his arms that evening, for she had done so many
times in her past few months at Fox's Earth. But she could
not do that now. Jester was gone.

Looking back on it later, Rip could see that it was inevitable that he should go; he was gone from her in all
but the fact of his leave-taking when she looked into Ruth
Yancey Fox's blue eyes over the sleeping form of Hebe
and pledged herself to stay at Fox's Earth. Jester wanted
for himself what Rip could give to no man: all of herself.
He did not understand about Hebe, and she could not explain it.

"What you needs is another young'un," he said more
than once as they lay together in the cowshed in Suches
in the dim afternoons when Rip could leave Fox's Earth
for a little while.

"I don't need no other young'un," Rip would say. "I got
my hands full lookin' after Miss Hebe. She mighty po',
Jester. She gon' need all the lookin' after I can give her."

He frowned and raised himself on one elbow to look
down on her. She thought again how beautiful he was in
the winter light seeping through the unchinked walls of the
shed. He was naked in the clean, deep straw, leaving her
to huddle in the blanket the old woman had left in the
shed for their winter meetings. The flame of Jester's great
body burned higher than hers; he was seldom cold in the
shed, even in the bitterest weather.

"I mean a young'un of your own. *My* young'un. Don't
you want that, gal? Git yo' mind offen yo' baby *an'* that
li'l white baby."

"Well, I might like another young'un, truly, Jester. But right now I got to think about Miss Hebe. Who gon' look after her if I has another young'un?"

"Somebody else, I reckon. Somebody else goin' to sooner or later, anyway, 'cause I ain' gon' have you raisin' no white baby after we's married an' has chirrun of our own."

"Who says I gon' marry you, nigger?" She cuffed his great head playfully, and he ducked and grinned down at her.

"I says, that's who says."

"I ain't noticed you askin' me."

"I ain't noticed you keepin' yo' legs together, neither. What you doin' in here every day if you ain't aimin' to marry me?"

"Huh. What you think you got so good that I'm gon' marry you for it, anyhow?"

"Lay back down here and I'll show you."

He did.

Afterward, she said seriously, "Jester. You really aim to marry me?"

"Said I did, didn't I?"

"But you didn't mean right now, did you?"

"What's wrong with right now? I'm making good money, steady money. With what Miss 'Licia pays me, I got enough so we can get us a little ol' house come spring, an' you wouldn't have to stay up there all the time and nurse no white baby. You could go in the kitchen ha'f a day, maybe, or he'p yo' granny with the washin', wouldn't have to live with white fo'kses."

"But what's wrong with like it is now? I sees you every day. I sees more of you than if I was workin' in some kitchen an' takin' care of your young'un. You probably gits more in bed now than you would then."

"But it ain't my bed."

She sighed and squirmed away from him, and sat up. She reached for the dark woolen street dress Ruth had bought her that winter; it was Rip's one small rebellion that she would not wear a uniform. She looked intently at Jester. His huge jaw was outthrust, his brows drawn together.

"I cain't leave Miss Hebe right now, Jester. I just cain't do that. Later, maybe, when she old enough to look out for herself. . . ."

"Goda'mighty, gal, she got a mama! What you think,

she some kind of orphan cain't nobody but you take care of? Why cain't you leave her? They git somebody else to nurse her in two shakes of a sheep's tail . . .''

"I just cain't leave her. I cain't tell you why. I wants to marry you, an' I wants to have yo' young'uns, but I cain't do neither one right now. If you goes to pressin' me, I'm gon' say no. We talk about it later.''

"Not much later, Rip. I ain't gon' play second fiddle to no white baby much longer. You don' want to lay in my bed, they's lots of gals that does.''

He had leaped up from the straw and dressed hastily and in bullish silence, and flung himself out into the lowering dusk, and she had followed him slowly, heavy in her heart, feeling already the wrenching, inexorable loosening of ties.

So it was, perhaps, inevitable that he would leave her, though not so soon nor so abruptly if Ruth Fox had not fired him.

This she did in September, a month after Alicia had been stricken with food poisoning from an egg-custard pie inexplicably left to sit in the August heat without being put into the icebox, and then taken by Ruth to her mother-in-law for a late-night treat. Ruth had gone out into the back garden of Fox's Earth in search of Rip, who had been told she was not needed while Hebe napped, and, walking soft-footed in her small kid house slippers on the thick grass, came upon Rip and Jester Tully as they stood at the fringe of the rioting rose garden where Jester toiled most of these late-summer days.

There was nothing untoward in the meeting. Jester and Rip were not touching. They stood side by side, backs to Ruth, looking across the fervent, bloody-velvet heads of the roses to the gap in the box hedge beyond that showed a snatch of the gently decaying two-room wooden shanty that was all that remained of the old slave quarters of Fox's Earth.

On this still afternoon Jester was remarking to Rip, as he had done before, that with a little fixing up the house could be made quite livable, and that he felt sure that Mr. Paul would be so happy to have someone undertake the task that he might let them live in it rent-free. Ruth did not overhear this; there was nothing in their young backs to suggest anything more to her than her child's nurse chatting idly with the sullen yellow gardener on a hot autumn day. Still, skin prickling, the air around her face as thick with buzzing portent as though an earthquake impended, she stopped still and, silent, watched them.

In a moment, Rip turned to face Jester so that her profile presented itself to Ruth, and she smiled. It was a brief, flickering smile, but Ruth had never seen Rip smile, and in that smile she read threatened defection, the weakening of her hold upon Rip, the loss of her reluctant accessory, the passing of her power into the great golden hands of the yellow Negro.

"Rip," she said sharply, and the girl turned and looked at her impassively. The man did, too.

"I need you in the house. Hebe is awake. I think she has some temperature."

Ruth turned and went back into the house, not looking back. In a moment she heard the dry scuffling of Rip's feet in her soft slippers as she followed across the grass. She did not hear the big yellow Negro move among his roses, but she knew that he looked after her. She could feel the precise point on her back where his eyes were fastened, as implacably rooted in her flesh as the eyes of those hated, long-ago town children on the hot Saturday streets of Sparta.

She fired him the next morning.

His rage knew no bounds. For the first time in their relationship, Rip felt fear in Jester's presence. But she understood. Jester had been wronged. He had done nothing. The excuse Ruth had given him . . . that until Alicia recovered she wanted to keep the house and grounds as quiet and free of outsiders as possible, and that his work in the gardens of Fox's Earth was noisy and troubling to the sick woman . . . was patent invention, delivered to Jester with insolent carelessness. When he started to protest, she had cut him off with cold whips of words that stung his flesh like an actual lash.

He waited for Rip in the cowshed that afternoon. Pacing the narrow, mote-dancing little space that had been so totally theirs, swinging his great head from side to side like a tethered and tormented bull, Jester roared his fury and hammered his ivory palms with his darker, golden fist, and several times struck the flimsy wall of the cowshed, so that rotted wood and bark showered down onto the spread hay. Rip, huddled on the straw at his feet, rocked herself gently to and fro in the sweetly gamy dimness and followed him

119

with her eyes, her throat choked with sorrow and hurt for him, and fear, and the same passive, abstracted anger with which she daily watched Ruth systematically destroying Alicia Fox. Tears of loss stood unshed in her eyes; they had not been there even for her vanished baby. So long as there was a vestige of hope, Rip did not weep.

Presently, when dusk was settling over Suches, Jester whirled on Rip.

"I be goin' tonight. You come with me."

"Oh, Jester, where you gon' go? Stay here; you git another job any place on Church Street. Any of them white fo'kses he glad to have you. You the best gardener in town."

"I goin'. I be gone by sunup. I wants you with me, Rip. Ain't nothin' for you in that house; that mothuh-fuckin' white bitch, she cut yo' heart out same as mine, an' laugh while she do it. You don' need that white baby of hern; I fill you up with young'uns; we git us a place down to Atlanta, an' I'll git me a job in one of them big houses down there, an' you can nuss white chirrun jus' as well as here, an' git more money for it, too. Titterbaby tell me all the time what fo'kses payin' in Atlanta, what with all the white men goin' off to the war 'fo' long. We make out jus' fine. Go git yo' stuff, Rip. You my gal, you know in yo' heart you is. Always my gal."

The tears ached in her throat and stung her nose but did not spill.

"I cain't go with you, Jester. I done tol' you. I cain't leave. Please God, don't you go, not yet. You ain't got no call to up an' leave; what Miss Ruth to you? Jester, you stay here an' git you another job, an' we git married. I marry you any time you say. I marry you tomorrow; don't nothin' have to change. I do anything you says, 'cept I cain't leave that young'un up there by herself. 'Afore God, Jester, I cain't do that."

"Then God damn yo' soul to burn in hell always, you white woman's nigger. White nigger is all you is. I hope she do cut the livin' heart right outen you, an' eat it an' throw it away, an' her alaughin' all the time."

He rounded on her, face blind and terrible, fists clenched. Rip ran. She ran, the unshed tears a tumor in her throat, loss and wailing, endless sorrow running with her, the blackness of unimaginable time spread before her, with no lights anywhere. She did not see him leave the cowshed, and she did not see him again in her lifetime.

In the morning at first light, before the baby began to stir in the gray-cool nursery next door, Rip slipped out of her narrow iron bed and into the dark dress and went, barefoot and silent in the warm, foggy dawn, down the ravine path to Suches. She moved through the sleeping, tumbledown community of huts, around the shanty of her grandmother, and into the dark rectangle of the cowshed door. The warm-breathing, bony cow looked at her unsurprised, and then closed her great brown eyes again and dozed, hip-hung. Rip bent down and picked up her grandmother's blanket, thinking to fold it and take it away to Fox's Earth, where she would wash it during her empty hour that afternoon and hang it to dry before returning it to her grandmother. This seemed a very important thing to do. The abandoned blanket had nagged and tugged her out of sleep time after time during the long night, as the thought of Jester moving, aflame, through the dark toward Atlanta did not.

Something fell from the folds of the blanket with a soft thud, into the hay. She reached for it. It was Jester's buckeye, his lucky piece, his amulet against the larger world that had howled and spat at him since his birth. The buckeye was polished to a soft, satin sheen by generations of black hands and decade upon decade of overalls pockets, and it was set into a crude filigree of heavy, soft rose-gold, with a rough ring attached to it. Jester did not know for sure how old it was, but his great-grandmother had told him that she always heard that *her* grandfather had melted down a tribal ornament to make the filigree that held it, back in the forests of equatorial Africa where he had been born, and had set the buckeye into it. It was thought to have potent powers of protection, Jester had told Rip. He was never without the buckeye in his pocket.

He had not lost it, Rip knew. He had left it there on the blanket where she would find it, and gone away into that vast, inhospitable world beyond Sparta without it, leaving her, along with his curses, the only legacy he had to give. She put the buckeye into her own pocket, folded the blanket, and went back up the path to Fox's Earth.

That evening after supper, as Hebe slept, Rip took the buckeye out again, and rummaged in the old wicker laundry basket that held her treasures, and drew out a scrap of candlelight-colored satin that the old grandmother had given her as a child, simply because it was pretty. Rip had kept it for many years. Now she swiftly and skillfully whipped it into a sturdy little pouch with her needle, and held the buckeye briefly to her lips, and slipped it into the pouch. She strung the pouch on a length of light silken cord, also from her grandmother, and made a knot in it, and sat for a long time in the yellow light from her kerosene lamp, looking at it. Then she tiptoed into the nursery and drew Hebe's light coverlet back, and slipped the pouch around her neck and covered her again.

And then, finally Rip put on her nightgown and slid between the clean, rough feed-sack sheets of her narrow bed, and turned down the lamp's wick until the little room sank into shadows, and wept.

11

ON A BLUSTERY NIGHT in late March of 1917, Alicia Fox waited until her household was asleep, all except for her son Paul, whom she could hear stirring restlessly downstairs in the study that had been his father's, and then crept, lightheaded and weak and frightened, out of her bed and down the stairs that had not been trodden since the previous August. In her severely tailored nightrobe of blue silk, Alicia looked little more than a starved twelve-year-old; the traitorous step on the left stair of the curving staircase scarcely whimpered under her tentative weight, but she stopped there anyway, and hung against the polished banister, heart pounding high and light and sickly in her throat, pepperings of pure light pinwheeling before her eyes. She thought for a moment that she would faint, but she did not, and presently she began her journey downstairs again.

Paul sat slumped into the chair that had cradled Claudius Fox for so long that Paul's greater girth was still hard put to squeeze itself into the niche his father's hips and buttocks had made in the cracked old leather. Lamplight showered down onto his balding head and the newspaper that was open on his lap. Paul, like his father before him, hated and despaired of the war in Europe, recoiling from both the barbarity and mindlessness of it and the spurious, ignorant, and self-righteous pacifist mouthings with which his own country kept its sleek, fat corpus separate from the conflict. He was captivated, though, unwillingly and guiltily, by the sheer glorious panache of the half-mad, near-Bedouin Englishman T. E. Lawrence, and his glancing, flamboyant campaign in the desert of Arabia under the direction of (and often to the despair of) Allenby. On this day the front page of the Sparta *Sentinel* was black and vehement with the fall of Baghdad, and Paul Fox was thinking that here, by God, was a hero out of Thermopylae, a figure worthy of the very steel of Alexander, no matter that he was more than a little aberrant and engaged in a sad and shabby war on the same blowing soil that the son of Macedon had unified so gloriously all those golden centuries ago. The same vivid, lifelong romance with the past that had so enthralled Claudius burned unrequited in Paul's gentle heart, an old love left unengaged by the law that he practiced grimly during his working days, and it was with the flush of this love in his mild, dazzled eyes that he lifted his head and saw in the doorway of his den the figure of his mother.

"Let me come in," she said, and her voice was trembling. "Let me come in and sit with you for a minute. Please, Paul. Please, just let me sit here for a minute. I just wanted to sit in my old chair and talk to you a while. Darling, it's been so long . . ."

He saw that she was crying, though she made no noise as she wept, only looked humbly, glancingly up at him, as a habitually abused child might. He had known, had been told, that she had aged and failed, but he was profoundly shocked at this metamorphosis. She might have been his grandmother.

"Sit down, Mama, sit down here by me. Here. Let me put the afghan around you . . . now. Are you sick, dearest? Did something frighten you; did you have a bad dream? Let me just slip up and get Ruth; she'll make you all comfortable again . . ."

"No!" Alicia's voice was strong, almost crisp; he looked

123

at her in surprise and the beginning of relief. She sounded almost like her old self . . .

"Don't call Ruth, not just yet," she said, and her voice was small and singing again, the fey child's voice. "Please don't. She'll make me go back to my room, and I'm so terribly lonely, Paul. I've missed you so much. I know I've been sick, and a bother to everybody, and I know I've done . . . bad things and then forgotten them . . . but if you'll let me stay, I'll try not to do them anymore. I'm sorry I've been bad, Paul."

"Mama, what are you talking about? How could you be bad?" He leaned toward her, anguished, and took her thin hands in his own. "Of course you can stay; I've missed you too."

"But you've seen me, haven't you? Haven't you come to see me every night? Ruth said you had. She said you and Hebe come to see me every night just before I go to sleep, and that when I'm well, I'll remember. But it feels like I haven't seen you in so long, even if I have, and so I thought I would come down here just for a minute and see you. How are you, my darling? Tell me how you are. Tell me what you've been doing with yourself."

He stared at her. There seemed, in the face of her strangeness, nothing to say. What was she talking about? Did she really think that he visited her each night, and she could not remember the visits? Did she not even remember telling Ruth she did not wish to see him until she was herself again? What bad things did she think, in her poor, broken mind, that she had done? Why had they not known she was living like this, trapped in the hell inside her own head, meekly accepting her "punishment"?

Ruth came into the den then. Her light jade silk robe was in disarray; she had slipped into it so hastily that it was inside out, and her quicksilver hair leapt from her narrow skull in a radiant disorder. Her face was very white in the low lamplight, and her blue eyes looked almost black. Where had he seen that rapt, swollen, dark-pupiled look before?

"Oh, Mama Alicia," Ruth breathed, and came into the room lightly and swiftly. She took Alicia's shoulders in her hands,. and the older woman's head drooped onto her breast, and her eyes closed. She sat very still in Ruth's grasp, in the chair that had stood beside Claudius's and been her own.

Ruth looked up at Paul.

"How long has she been here? Why didn't you call me? She's not strong enough; she's not well enough . . ."

"She just came. I just looked up from the paper and . . . there she was."

"Oh, poor thing! Poor Mama Alicia, to think she had to slip away by herself to see you. I'd have brought you to her whenever she was ready to see you; she knows that. What's bothering her, did she say? What did she tell you?"

"Well, she didn't make much sense, actually. Just . . . things about being punished for being bad, and not remembering all the times I'd come to see her . . ."

"Oh, how awful. I had no idea she was this bad, darling. I'd have put Red or Rusky or Rip in with her on a cot if I had. I can't imagine why she thought you came to see her, when she's told me over and over she didn't want you to see her like this . . . Well, don't worry about her any more than you can help. I'll just take her back on up to bed, and Rip can sit up with her till she falls asleep, and I'll come back down and make us some coffee. Would you like that? Pinky's made an apple cobbler, too. How about it, darling?"

He looked at her unseeingly, then nodded slowly. "That would be fine, dear. Just fine. I'd help you with her, but I hardly know . . . she seems so . . . Ruth, she seemed so very sure that there are . . . all those terrible things . . . that she can't remember. That we were punishing her. Why on earth would she think such things? What would put them into her mind?"

Alicia raised her head and opened her hazel eyes and looked levelly at Paul. She said, very clearly, "I am not demented, Paul. I have been told dreadful things. I may be sick, and old, but I am not insane."

He stared at his mother and, above her head, Ruth shook her own head rapidly from side to side, little, frantic motions: "No. Don't say anything. Be quiet."

He said nothing.

"I'm going to take Mama Alicia back upstairs now, darling. We'll get her all tucked in and comfortable, and I'll give her one of her pills, and she'll be much, much better in the morning. Now come and kiss her good night, and tell her you'll see her soon, and I'll be down directly for that pie. Come on, Mama 'Licia. Up you go."

125

Ruth raised her mother-in-law to her feet. She stood, still and quiet, while Paul came and kissed her cold cheek, her eyes closed once again, her chin resting on the collar of her robe. She made no move to resist Ruth's hands, and let herself be walked obediently out of the room. Presently Paul heard the stair creak, and Alicia's door open and close, and then Ruth's voice, speaking in low whispers to Rip. Paul stared, unseeing now, at the adventures of Lawrence of Arabia until, finally, Ruth came back into the room.

"I'm terribly sorry you had to see her like that, darling," she said over the pie. "I never dreamed she could manage the stairs alone. I should have watched her more closely; from now on, I'll see that she's not alone."

"I . . . just had no idea. I can't believe . . . did you know she was like this? Have you known right along how bad she was?"

His voice trembled.

"Of course I knew, dearest. Why do you think I've been so insistent when you've wanted to visit her? Why do you think Dr. Hopkins is here so often, and I've kept the servants away from her? I wanted so to spare you this, darling; I've so hoped she would get better soon . . . Of course, after this, there's just no question of letting Hebe go to her again, and she must be watched all the time, around the clock . . . Paul. Darling. Have you ever thought that she really might be better off in a . . . an institution of some sort? Just for a little while, until she's better again . . . not so confused. . . ."

"My mother will never spend one night away from Fox's Earth. I do not care what it takes to keep her comfortable. This is not to be discussed again."

He did not raise his voice, but he spoke in tones Ruth had never heard before.

"Of course," she said in a mild voice, "if that's what you wish. I'll think of something else."

He dropped his head into his hands and scoured his eyes tiredly with his fingers.

"She seemed so very sure of what she was saying. Ruth, she really *believes* she's forgetting all these things; she *believes* she does bad things and can't remember; that I come to see her and she can't remember. She honestly thinks that you've *told* her I come every night . . ."

"Well, darling, that's the way of . . . some mental illnesses. Dr. Hopkins said so. He said patients with—her illness—can often be terribly convincing. I promise you, Paul, that I've told her nothing of the sort; of course no one has made her think that she does . . . oh, bad things, frightens Hebe . . . though in fact she *has* done that, but I've never taxed her with it. But if you're worried about that, don't take my word for it. By all means go to Dr. Hopkins and ask him to verify what I've said. I'm sure he'll be glad to set your mind at rest; I'll call him myself in the morning, and ask him to come by and tell you that I'm not lying to you. . . ."

"Oh, sweetheart, of *course* you're not! I never thought *that!*" Paul started up in horrified contrition. "I know you've done your best and more; no one could have been kinder to Mama than you've been; you've done an inhuman amount of work for her, day after day . . . don't cry, darling. I didn't mean to doubt your word. I never would do that. It's just . . . she . . . it was a shock to see her like that, that's all."

She wiped her eyes. "Well, then, Paul darling, please promise me just one thing? Will you do that? Just one thing?"

"Anything. You know."

"Please, please, don't put yourself and her through this again. Don't go in to see her until she's better. I'll tell you when. But promise. It's just too painful for everyone. It hurts me too much, my precious Paul, to see you so confused and miserable. Promise?"

"I promise. I do promise."

"Good."

She vanished from the doorway, and he sat looking into the dimness where her after-image still burned, feeling sad and tired and older—so old—and unable to stay or divert the tides that ran free through Fox's Earth, and thinking nothing at all. Later, his head nodded onto his chest, and he slept.

In the night, the wind that had blown free and blue and yellow all day blackened and clotted with rain, and an electrical storm broke over the flat roof of Fox's Earth. Rip wakened in the small room next to the nursery and crept in to cover Hebe, who turned and whimpered restlessly but did not wake, and returned to her narrow bed, where she lay awake, listening to the first storm of the spring. She heard the rain lift to a crescendo, and the wind strengthen, and presently she heard over it the now familiar voice of Ruth Fox, intoning to the mother who was not there. Rip slid out of her bed and went noiselessly to the door that separated her cubicle from the nursery, and cracked it. She pulled her rocking chair up to the crack, which gave a faint grayish light into her little room, and sat down to listen and to wait.

Before long the door from the hall opened silently, and the figure of Ruth Fox came into her daughter's nursery and stood looking down into the crib at the sleeping baby. Rip, thinking that the phantom of Pearl Steed that she had feared so often had finally come into the child's room, started up, her heart hammering in her throat and her lips drawn unknowingly back from her teeth in a rictus of fear and menace. But then she recognized Ruth, and heard her voice, and she stopped.

"It seems a shame to take her out in this, Mama," Ruth said. Rip grew cold, for Ruth was alone with Hebe.

"Go on, Ruth," Pearl Steed Yancey said from the other side of the baby's crib. "It ain't gon' hurt her none. Just be sure to wrap her up good. She won't even get her head wet. Won't even wake up. Go on, now."

"Mama, why can't I wait till it's warmer? It's coming down cats and dogs out there, and cold, too. Later on, when spring's really here . . ."

Later on gon' be too late, Ruth. You ain't got no more time. You saw how that old woman was tonight. Do she git loose agin, ain't no tellin' who she'll git to, and ain't ever'body as easy to fool as that sorry husband of yourn. You gon' take that chance? Go on, now, 'fore that nigger gal wakes up. She ain't gon' let you take that young'un outen here while she got breath."

"Rip won't tell on me, Mama. I can handle Rip. Rip's too scared I'll fire her to say anything to anybody."

"That nigger ain't scared of nothin' but whut might happen to your young'un, missy. You'd do well to remember that. She ain't no more scared of you than she is a ol' Dominecker hen."

"She knows . . . about me, Mama. I'm not worried about Rip. . . ."

"*Move, Ruth!* Stop this here yaingin' at me an' move. *Take your chance!*"

Ruth moved.

She lifted Hebe out of the crib and wrapped the child, limp and sodden with sleep, in a crib blanket, and then into a vast rubber poncho that Rip recognized as Claudius's old one, which had hung for years on a peg in the garden room at the back of the house. Hebe made snicking sounds with her fat little pursed mouth, and opened her great gray eyes to look, unsurprised, at her mother.

"Mama," she said.

"Hush, sweetheart. Hush, Mama's good bunny rabbit. We're going to go downstairs and . . . play a little game with Grandma. Just for a minute, and then you'll be right back in your warm bed again. Mama promises. Would you like that? Would you like to play a game with Grandma?"

"Grandma," said Hebe, and turned her face into Ruth's neck and closed her eyes once more. Ruth pulled the poncho over the child's head and walked soundlessly out of the room with her, and down the stairs. Rip waited until she heard the sharp complaint of the errant stair midway down the left staircase, and then she slipped out into the hall and looked over the banister to the black-and-white-tile foyer below. She was just in time to see the trailing edge of the poncho and the bottom ruffle of Ruth's white nightgown disappear through the green baize door into the kitchen. She followed silently.

When she reached the kitchen, the door to the back porch was just closing. Rip stood for a moment in the empty room, its great appliances and gleaming fixtures alive and menacing to her on this night of strangeness and whispers and figures, real and not real, moving through Fox's Earth. Then she opened the door onto the back porch and followed them, mother and daughter, into the great sibilant dirge of the rain.

She lost them for a moment in the shouting, tossing maelstrom of the back garden, and stood on the latticed back porch behind one of the supporting columns, peering into the slanting sheets of rain that whitened the garden to a fearful opacity. She could see nothing and hear nothing over the banshee storm. Then a great flower of lightning blued the garden, and she saw Ruth standing in the open space beneath Alicia's little window, with the cocoon of blankets and poncho that was Hebe in her arms. Ruth was black and white and blue in the eerie storm-light, a photographic negative, an elemental spirit limned on the combustible air in strokes of white fire. Rip shrank back against her pillar in atavistic and involuntary terror. In that moment Ruth Yancey Fox seemed not a living, mortal woman. Rip, who had thought to run out into the storm and snatch the child from Ruth's arms and dash with her . . . somewhere, to some small safety . . . was rooted to the porch and could not move. In the next, smaller flare of lightning, she saw that Hebe was well covered against the driving rain and was, after all, dry and warm, though her mother was all running water, and the white body shone through the transparent, flesh-stuck stuff of the nightgown. Rip clutched her pillar and swallowed around her swelling heart, and leaned forward to see and hear into the rain. Thunder boomed and rolled.

"Mama!" called Ruth Fox, and the long word sang and rode over the surf of the storm, and curled away into the boiling sky. "Ma-aa-a-ma! Now!"

The thunder rolled away and slid to a stop, and for a moment there was only the shouting wind and the long sigh of rain. Into the silence Rip heard Ruth say, "Wake up, Hebe. Wake up, now. Are you awake? All right. Now. I want you to call Grandma. Can you do that? Call Grandma, dearest. Good and loud, for Mama. Say, 'Grandma! Grandma! Help me!' "

The little bundle stirred, and Rip heard the familiar frightened whimper. She moved out from behind the pillar, but Ruth spoke again and the whimpering stopped.

"Call Grandma, Hebe, and then we can go back inside and go to bed. Mama will bring you some milk and gingersnaps. Hebe! If you don't do what Mama says, she's going to leave you out here in the rain and the old bird will come and get you. Do you hear me? Now CALL GRANDMA!"

"Grandma!"

The child's voice was a thin, fluting wail, a minor element of the storm. It climbed eerily and rode upon the wind to the upstairs window and beat frailly against it. Rip's flesh crawled.

"Grandma!" Again.

And again, "Grandma! Grandma! Help me, Grandma. . . ."

It was a small, lost, demonic sound, but Rip did not doubt that Alicia would hear it, and she did. The little window flew up, and the white blur of Alicia's face appeared there. Rip heard her voice, cracked and old and fearful, but full of resolution.

"Hebe? Hebe? Darling, is that you?"

A whisper from Ruth, and, "Grandma, let me in! Let me in!"

"Oh, my God, Hebe! I'm coming, darling, Grandma's coming," Alicia's voice cried, fading away into the room, and the window banged shut. Rip slid far back into darkness as Ruth wheeled and ran with Hebe up the steps onto the back porch and into the darkened kitchen. She did not look to her right or left as she passed Rip, and Rip knew that the black-eyed, streaming, blinded face would not have seen her if she had moved directly into its path. Ruth panted as she ran past, and she half sang, "Mama, I did it. I did it, Mama. It's all going to be fixed now. Hush, Hebe; you must be very quiet and not say a word now. Not a word, or the bird will surely get you this very night and fly away with you, and you'll never see your mama or daddy or Rip again, or Teddy, either. Mama, I did it. . . ."

Rip heard her footsteps stop somewhere in the blackness of the kitchen, and the night was silent again. Hebe did not murmur, and only the wind sang outside, and the rain. Rip hugged herself and rocked silently back and forth, and closed her eyes. She did not want to see what happened next, and she did not. But she heard.

Heard Alicia's steps come, rapid and stumbling, down the stairs, straight through the kitchen. Heard the door open again, heard Alicia patter across the back porch and unhesitatingly down the stairs and out into the tomb-cold night, heard her frantic, light voice calling, over and over, "Hebe! Where are you, darling? Grandma's here, where are you? Call out to me again, call Grandma . . ."

Heard the firm, measured step of Ruth Yancey Fox cross the kitchen to the back door and shut it, heard the metallic scratching and then the sharp click as the key slid home in the lock. Heard Ruth walk back through the kitchen and into the foyer and up the stairs. And heard, before she turned and fled, hands over ears, up the dark staircase and into her own room, the voice of Alicia Fox, faint and lost at the back door, calling weakly, "Let me in! Please, Paul, someone, let me in!"

Rip waited until Ruth slipped the already-sleeping Hebe back into her crib and went back to her own bedroom, waited until the singing chant to Pearl had finally died away and the upstairs had been silent for a long time, and then she stole out of bed and went into the nursery. She reached into the crib; Hebe slept soundly and was warm and dry. She drew up the covers about the child's neck and then pushed the door into the hall open a faltering inch. She would take the far staircase, the right one that did not creak, and creep down to the back door and let Alicia in. Perhaps she had not, after all, gotten too soaked; perhaps she had sheltered on the back porch in time, had found an old coat or quilt there in which to wrap herself. Perhaps she could get Alicia up the stairs and to her room and into a hot bath, get her back to bed and to sleep without waking Ruth. She could say that she'd gotten up to go to the bathroom, and heard a noise downstairs, and found Alicia wandering there, wet and confused; she could pretend that the back door had been unlocked when she went down, that Alicia must have, somehow, managed to unlock it herself, from outside. . . . Whimpering with urgency and fright, Rip edged into the dim upstairs hallway.

Ruth Fox stood at the top of the stairs, still in her white nightgown, drying now to fall away from her body, but clinging yet in spots. In the dying flashes of lightning from the storm, she seemed to give off her own light. She stood straight and still, looking down into the black pool of the stairwell: Rip's mouth dried and her head thrummed. She could not move.

Slowly the silver-white figure turned and looked at her, full into her face, as she stood there in the nursery doorway. Neither one of them moved for a long moment, and then Ruth wheeled and resumed her sentinel's post. Rip went back into her own room and sat down in the rocking chair. When she looked out again at dawn, the figure was still there. Outside, the rain had stopped.

It was Pinky, come to light the fire in the stove for breakfast, who found Alicia next morning, found her huddled semiconscious on the back porch beneath an old hunting jacket that Jester had used for gardening in the cool months. A silver March frost had come stealing in after the rain, and Alicia was rimed all over with it, whitened like a statue woman, a marble effigy off her own tomb. Pinky's shrieks brought Paul thumping down the stairs from his bed in his old room, where he slept these nights when he fell asleep in his chair. Ruth, fresh-faced and dewy from deep sleep, followed him, murmuring in distress. Rip picked the stirring Hebe out of her crib and sat with her in the rocking chair, rocking, rocking, but she did not take the child downstairs for her breakfast, and presently, after Hebe had snuffled and whined herself back to sleep, Rip laid her back in the crib and covered her and went to dress for the day. When she finally went out into the upstairs hall, they had gotten Alicia back into her bed, with hot-water bottles and piled blankets, and Ruth and Red were chafing her cold blue hands, and Pinky was trying without success to spoon hot chicken broth laced with Claudius's brandy between her whitened, rigid lips. Paul, his face blanched and streaked with tears, paced the foyer and waited for the crunch of Dr. Hopkins's tires on the gravel of the drive.

But she did not regain consciousness; the cough that had lingered since the previous Christmas hoarsened and deepened, and she was unable to tell them how she came to be locked out of her house in the rain. Forever after Paul Fox thought his mother had strayed into the storm in her madness and inadvertently locked the door behind her, and died of it. She was unable to speak at all, except to call out, over and over, in her painfully cracked whisper, "Hebe! Hebe! Let Hebe in!" She died on April 6, on the day that the United States entered the War to End All Wars, and she died calling out for them to let Hebe in.

On the night of her funeral, Paul Fox left his study, where he had shut himself away upon returning home from the cemetery, and went into the kitchen of Fox's Earth. Henry and Pinky and Red and Rusky, who had stayed until the last guest had eaten the last lace cookie and slice of Lane cake, were gone themselves, tired and grief-shrunken. They had loved Alicia Fox totally and long.

The kitchen was scoured and polished and dark; it was late, and very still. Paul opened the icebox door and pulled out ham, and cold fried chicken, and pies and gelatin desserts molded into fanciful turrets and spires. From beneath a clean white tablecloth he rummaged the remainders of cakes and cookies. He poured milk from Alicia's Waterford pitcher and sat down at the kitchen table. With his fingers he pulled glistening chunks of ham away, and pushed whole slices of pie and cake into his mouth. He ate and ate; crumbs littered Pinky's spotless oilcloth, and grease smeared it and shone. Presently all the food was gone, and Paul drank the last of the milk from the pitcher, and stood up from the kitchen chair. He wavered on his feet, and then went to the kitchen sink and bent over it, and retched, and began to vomit. The vomiting lasted a long time. When it was over he wiped his face with a damp dishcloth, and then he slid down to the floor on legs that would no longer support him, and he sat on the kitchen floor in the dark and wept for his mother, long into the night.

Upstairs, Rip came out of the nursery door and went down the stairs and looked into every room, every corner of Fox's Earth, looked for death. She saw Paul huddled on the kitchen floor, but did not move to rouse him; it was not Paul she sought. She climbed the stairs again to the second floor and moved silently and methodically through all the bedrooms except Ruth's, which she knew to be locked, and the bathrooms, and the big nursery and trunk room. She climbed the twisting, canted stairs up into the attic under the flat roof, where last summer's heat still coiled dustily. The light from her kerosene lantern slid restless yellow fingers into every chink and orifice of Fox's Earth. Death was not there. Death had gone. Rip went back to bed and slept.

In her bedroom, in the graceful room that had been Alicia Fox's and still smelled faintly of her perfume, Ruth Steed Yancey Fox lay curled on the great tester bed, knees drawn up to her stomach, arms wrapping her blond head. She sang to her mother, who stood across the room regarding her, unsurprised.

"No more, Mama," said the child of Pearl Steed Yancey. "No more, no more, no more, no more."

And for a long time, far into the night, into the night and through it and into the tender April dawn, Ruth Fox sang to her mother. She talked, and she laughed, and once or twice she argued, and she sang, and sang, and sang.

12

Two weeks before her sixth birthday, in late March of 1921, Hebe had the first of the terrifying convulsions that led to her being kept home from Sparta's public elementary school and tutored privately for the entirety of her education. She was alone in the back garden of Fox's Earth at the time; Pinky, glancing out the back door, saw her writhing in the black dirt of the rose garden and by the time she had lumbered out to Hebe's aid the child had voided her bladder and bowels, bitten her tongue so that it bled copiously over her organdy pinafore, and fallen limply into unconsciousness. Ruth, who had left her daughter to go upstairs for her sun hat only minutes before the seizure occurred, was pale and distraught and at a loss to explain it.

"She was just fine; she was running around the garden as happy as a little lark," she said to Dr. Hopkins, who questioned her extensively in the wisteria bower on the veranda over iced tea after he had examined the child and left her in Rip's care in her froth of a bedroom next to Ruth and Paul's. The doctor could find no reason for the convulsion, superficially, at least. Hebe had no fever, had suffered no injuries, and had complained of no headaches, dizziness, or nausea in the hours before she was stricken. He was puzzled. He treated her tongue, which was rather severely bitten, as best he could, and painted the web of bloody scratches left by the rosebushes with iodine, and ordered her kept still and quiet until he had observed her for at least twenty-four hours. When Hebe regained consciousness, she was drowsy and docile and remembered nothing of the event.

In subsequent months Hebe was taken to a famed children's neurological hospital in Atlanta and given the most exhaustive series of tests available to medicine in that prosperous and enlightened year of 1921. The physicians

135

found nothing; Hebe did not suffer from brain tumor, hyperinsulinism, hypoparathyroidism, or any of the other malicious neurological puppeteers that made grotesque dancers of the young. She had never in her sheltered life had so much as a fall, and had certainly suffered no major fevers or illnesses, for all her worrisome frailty. Doubtfully the doctors concluded that she had a transitory type of epilepsy due to an undetected head injury during her long and difficult birth, and could hold out little hope for cure, though they said the incidents of convulsion might be so far apart that they would hardly trouble her, and, indeed, might never recur.

But Ruth took no chances. A tutor was found for Hebe, and from then on she learned . . . when she did learn . . . in the schoolroom that had cradled the labors of her father and grandfather before her. It was evident early on that Hebe was not a scholar.

The incidents of hysteria and convulsion did recur, though, at infrequent intervals during Hebe's cloistered childhood, and after each one Ruth kept her daughter closer to her, and curtailed more and more of her physical and social activities. Hebe became a skittish, clinging child, dancing along in the wake of her mother's skirts, with a strange, near-albino face topped by dandelion-white, blowing-fine hair and dominated by enormous, luminous gray eyes with a hairline ring of blue-white around them. In the presence of her mother or Rip she was a tiny, gossamer mosquito, prattling incessantly of strange, elliptical things in her sweet, airy, droning voice. Left long without them she fell silent and became huge-eyed, and the skin around the base of her small nose would whiten, and she would slide from panicky whimperings into piercing, wild shrieks in an eye-blink if she could not find them.

Only Rip, of all the household of Fox's Earth, suspected that Hebe's seizures were not epilepsy. Only Ruth knew they were fear.

On the day of the first seizure, Hebe had been tagging after Ruth as she cut early tulips in the back garden, pattering with her light, erratic steps among the flourishing plants tended now by elderly Ramah Williams from Suches and his little son, Fortune. Hebe was entranced with the idea of her sixth birthday, and excited to incandescence about the party Ruth had promised her for the event, a gala with a bright-striped tent in the side garden, if the weather was fine, and paper hats and favors and balloons and confetti, and games, and ice cream and cake, and pony rides for the privileged small girls and boys of Sparta who would be Hebe's schoolmates in first grade the following September. About school Hebe was an effervescent small parrot: "When I go to school . . ." "When I'm a big girl in the first grade . . ." "When I have a desk in front of Tommy Munro at school, we'll be sweethearts . . ."

"School is hard, you know, and little girls who study all the time grow up to be grinds, and never have any boy friends," Ruth would tell her. To Paul she explained that Hebe was clearly not cut out for scholastic success, and she was trying to prepare her child ahead of time for certain croppers on the paths of academe.

"Is she really dense?" he would say doubtfully, watching the child flit feverishly from one toy to another, one subject of conversation to another. "I thought perhaps she was just . . . oh, you know, high-strung. She seems to me to be very creative."

"Love has blinded your eyes, sweetheart," Ruth said. "Hebe is a sweet and charming child, and I think she's going to be a real beauty, but let's be realistic. She is simply not a terribly intelligent child. And there's no reason why she should be. She will be an ornament to her little world, and a lovely and graceful woman, and what else does she need to be? It's not as if she'll have to earn her way in the world, after all."

"I suppose not," Paul would say wistfully, thinking of the crates of loved classical textbooks gathering dust and neglect in the attic. It was clear that his daughter would never read them, and beginning to look as though no son would, either. At twenty-eight, his delicate and lovely wife had developed painful fibroid tumors on her ovaries that, she said, made her periods sheer torture and negated her chances of becoming pregnant again. Besides, she told him ruefully, if she *should* happen to get pregnant, it would probably kill her. Their infrequent couplings dwindled to almost none, and Paul ceased to sigh for a son to read his beloved books and hang on his knee in the evenings after dinner, and sit in his grandfather's seat at the university and, eventually, at the head of the great mahogany table in the dining room of Fox's Earth.

"Well," he said to himself, "Hebe will stay here with her husband, perhaps, and there'll be a boy from that

137

some day . . . It's not as if there won't ever be another Fox at Fox's Earth."

To Ruth, when she told her daughter that school was perilous and she would have to study hard and have no boy friends, Hebe chortled joyously, a surprising, deep burble that seemed to rise from her slim little body like a belch. Ruth frowned whenever she heard that laugh. It was too masculine, too red of corpuscle, too close to the mill by far. Independence and leave-taking swam in its rich, bawdy depths like tough, muscular minnows. She made a mental note to drill Hebe on the musical, fluting laugh that she herself had emulated from Alicia.

"I'm going to have a hundred boy friends, Mama," Hebe caroled. "And school won't be hard for me, 'cause I'm smart. Rip said so."

Ruth said nothing.

In the garden that day, Hebe suddenly looked up in the midst of her machine-gun prattle about school and her party, and said, "What is a love child, Mama?"

Ruth stopped still and looked at her.

"Who told you that?"

"Rip. She said Pinky's new grandbaby was a love child. She said that's why he has to come to work with Pinky, in a basket, 'cause nobody else will take care of him 'cause he's a love child. But I would, Mama. I'd like to have him. Can I have a love child? I'm gon' get me one as soon as I'm old enough. Rip says they're the best kind of all."

Ruth's eyes darkened to the black-blue of a stormy sea, or a fresh bruise. Hebe stepped back and put her finger into her mouth. It was a look she feared and hated; when her mother's eyes got like that, she was gone away from her, strange and not there at all. Hebe did not know her at those times. She made a small, involuntary sound.

Ruth knelt and took Hebe's shoulders in her hands. Her pink-buffed nails, with their white moons, bit into the soft flesh and met delicate bones.

"You want to know what a love child is? I'll tell you. I'll tell you just how you get yourself a love child. You can have one any time you want to, Hebe."

Ruth's voice lifted into a nasal keen Hebe had never heard before.

"First you got to have a boy," Ruth said. "Any old boy will do. They's plenty of boys all over. Bet you they's a boy right over there now, behind that bush. Just waitin'

138

for you, Hebe; waitin' till I'm gone to come an' give you a love child. And do you know what he'll do when I'm gone, Hebe? Do you know?"

Ruth looked down at her child with sightless eyes.

"No, ma'am," Hebe whispered.

"Why, a boy has this old thing between his legs, and it gets all swole up and fat and long and red-like, and he'll come out from behind that bush and push you down on your back and pull your legs apart and he'll ram that old thing way up between them, right where you tee-tee, and he'll jam it up and down, and pretty soon he'll holler, and then he'll shoot this nasty old white stuff all up you, and it'll run down and all over your legs, and there'll be blood, too. Blood just arunnin' down your legs. And after that, you'll get you a love child. That's how you do it, Hebe."

"Mama, Mama . . ." Hebe began to whimper and then to cry. Her small feet tore themselves loose and danced up and down on the earth, and she clutched at Ruth with frantic hands. Ruth pried them off and looked past the rose garden to the towering box hedge that separated the back lawn of Fox's Earth from the empty slave cabin.

"You gon' get you a love child right now, Hebe," she cried out, and pointed to the hedge. "Because they's a boy right over there behind that hedge, and when I leave he's gon' come right out here in this rose garden and throw you down and give you one. How you gon' like that, Hebe? I hope you like it, because here I go, and here he comes!"

And she whirled and ran out of the rose garden and up the back steps and vanished into the house.

Hebe turned round and round in the rose garden like a mortally injured dog, her small fists flailing empty air, her head jerking oddly. She screamed repeatedly, but no one heard her, for there was no breath in her small lungs, and by the time she was able to draw in enough air to make a sound, the convulsion took her and she spun into blackness.

When Hebe wakened in her own sweet-smelling bed, Ruth's face was the first thing she saw, and she nestled into her mother's arms and buried her face in the lavender-breathing bosom of Ruth's afternoon frock. She did not remember what had happened in the garden, but she remembered the fear, and she strained her small body into Ruth's until it felt as if their very flesh would merge.

139

Ruth's hair, cut short now, and falling over her high white forehead, slipped forward to screen her daughter's face and drift across her tightly shut eyes, and Hebe heard her whisper, "Now, baby. Now, Hebe. Mama's here. Mama won't ever leave you again, not ever. Mama will stay with you always. You need your mama, don't you, precious?"

"Yes," wept Hebe gratefully. "Yes!"

And so the round of tests in the Atlanta hospital began. Rip watched the departure of Ruth and Hebe in silence. Her heart ached dully with futile anger and sorrow, and pain for Hebe, but her dark eyes were unsurprised. There had been other incidents that Rip knew about; since babyhood, Ruth had alternately set her daughter up in small situations in which she was apt to be mildly hurt or frightened, and then rushed to Hebe's side with soothing hugs and kisses and assurances that she would not leave her.

"Little girls need their mamas" was Hebe's first complete, lisping sentence.

Rip would watch from the nursery as Ruth lifted Hebe into a tree and strolled away, seemingly absorbed in a flower or an errant leaf, and then hurried back at the child's first terrified screech. From the veranda she saw Ruth maneuver Hebe into the path of the Carmichaels' monstrous, purple-tongued red Chow dog and then vanish around the side of the house, only to dash back and sweep Hebe up into her arms and bear her, howling, into the house, when the inevitable surprise encounter between child and dog on the marble-blocked front walk of Fox's Earth took place. When Hebe, with three-year-old insouciance, insisted on exploring the jungle of kudzu that rioted a square block beyond the little cabin, Ruth let her go, and followed her into the hellish green morass only when her screams had taken on the desperate, mindless quality of a trapped animal's. Hebe did not stray far from her mother's side again.

Ruth would not, Rip knew, let Hebe come to real physical harm. In her own strange way, Rip thought, Ruth Fox had come to love her child; at least she seemed to have a genuine need for her. This heartened Rip, and she held her silence at most of the incidents in Hebe's early childhood. But the child's abandonment in the kudzu patch tore through her heart like wildfire, and she had started toward the direction of the shrieks when she felt a hand on her arm and turned to meet the serene blue eyes of Ruth.

140

"I was just going to get her, Rip," Ruth said. "I'm trying to teach her to be careful and not stray away. But I appreciate your concern, anyway."

"Miss Ruth, she turnin' into a bad-scairt little gal," Rip said, emboldened by desperation. "Maybe I sees it when you don't, puttin' her to bed an' all like I does. She got where she ain' gon' close her eyes without I puts the night light on, an' she plumb scairt to even go outen the house without you or me's with her. Lord, Miss Ruth, she ain't gon' be fit to live in the world . . ."

"Suppose you let me be the judge of that, Rip," Ruth said, her eyes the cobalt of polar seas. "Who knows better how to raise my little girl, her own mother or a nigger gal who couldn't even keep her own baby from being kidnaped?"

Rip dropped her eyes.

After that the battle for Hebe Fox went underground, but it soon petered out and died. It was a battle Rip could not win, and knew it; Ruth Fox had no scruples and all the cards. Though Rip suspected Ruth of the worst in connection with Hebe's initial convulsion, the child could remember nothing, and Rip did not dare mention it to Ruth. Even to the other servants, who knew nothing of the silent struggle for Hebe that was being waged over their heads, Ruth Yancey Fox in that frenetic year of 1921 was no longer a nascent and half-formed girl but a finished and mature woman in the full flush of her power, and she was formidable indeed.

At twenty-eight, Ruth had a timelessness, an agelessness about her that seemed the antithesis of the flippant, transitory postwar Jazz Age that was unfolding across the country. Except for her uncanny resemblance to Mary Pickford, who was capturing hearts all over America, she belonged to another era entirely, though which one her bemused acquaintances and even doting Paul could not have said. She was supremely beautiful, but one did not get the sense that she was at the fleeting apogee of her beauty; rather it seemed that she had reached a summit of perfection whereupon she would live forever. She moved tranquilly through her days with an immense natural dignity and presence that sprang from steel purpose and a total lack of humor; it was as hard to imagine Ruth Fox as a child as to imagine her as an old woman.

She was admired, if not popular, in the young crowd of Sparta. Together the young Foxes were asked everywhere, and they went, but none of the other southern women in the set ever got close to her. Still, they did not gossip about her, as they did about other women who remained outside their circle. Something in her brilliant, far-focused blue eyes, some essential difference, haunted them and stilled their tongues. The nearest thing to criticism that was ever voiced about Ruth Fox was, "I wouldn't want her for an enemy." None of them had her for such. She spared none of her awesome energy on casual hatings.

Even among the older people, those fifth- and sixth-generation Spartan contemporaries of Alicia and Claudius Fox, there was little of the brightly malicious social gossip permitted to elders in the South about Ruth Yancey Fox. Almost miraculously she was not punished in the drawing rooms and clubs of old Sparta for her origins and background. There was about her straight, slim figure and burning white face something that commanded the Old Guard's respect and, on a deeper level which few of them cared to explore, their fear. No stigmas from that long-ago mill village clung to her shoulders when she visited in the other white houses on Church Street. The spectres of Pearl Steed and Cater Yancey did not accompany her into those drawing rooms. By and large Ruth was, in her twenty-eighth year, as sleek and soothed and self-absorbed as it was possible for her to be, a cat in a creamery; and Fox's Earth was a graceful, smoothly run house of women in all but the physical presence of doting, unworldly Paul Fox.

On the eve of her child's sixth birthday party, Ruth went into Hebe's room and sat down on the side of her little painted French bed. She pushed the flyaway hair back from Hebe's forehead, which was cool and tranquil these two weeks after the convulsion, and looked for a moment into the great gray eyes. They met her own, shallow and unshadowed.

"I have a lovely idea, darling," Ruth said. "Let's have just little girls for your party, shall we? I can call the boys' mothers tonight. Boys are so mean and nasty. They hurt little girls."

"Oh, yes, Mama, let's," piped Hebe. "Boys are nasty!"

Ruth hugged her.

13

For a long time, then, in that restless and graceful time
slung like a precarious hammock between two wars, Fox's
Earth bobbed gently and ripely, a great, solid ship riding
the dancing seas of the twenties, and Ruth Yancey Fox
moved serenely through her thirties toward her forties, all
her early struggles now behind her, and found it all good.

It was a decade of hedonism of the highest order, and
of cruel contrasts, but Sparta, sunk in the secular amber
of the southern Bible Belt, remained essentially unengaged
by the underlying rebellious carnival spirit of the twenties.
Still, Ruth Fox would not have noticed if Scott and Zelda
Fitzgerald themselves had come to town; for her it was a
time in port, a long dreaming, a ten-year hiatus in which
to polish and perfect the great raw gem of a life she had
spent the past eighteen years rough-carving for herself.

She started with Paul. He was, in these seemingly endless days of hiatus and plenitude, as happy a man as he
would ever be in his life. Ruth now turned the full force
of her wiles and graces back upon her husband, and
soothed and bedazzled him into a state of torporous contentment. She sensed, perhaps, that his lingering sorrow over
the death of his parents, his tacit disappointment with the
flighty Hebe, and the eroding unhappiness he had found in
the law would, if allowed to fester unallayed any longer,
make of Paul Fox something at last rebellious and dangerous. Pearl had taught her early and well: Take nothing
for granted. Leave nothing to chance.

So she bought drifts of the beruffled things that he loved
to see her in; sat close to him at luncheon and dinner and
hung on to his every word as he talked of his business,
the comings and goings of the masculine downtown community. She spent hours with thunder-browed old Pinky
each day, planning elaborate meals and treats of the cloying, rich foods that he loved best, and drove muttering

Henry to distraction as he searched the markets and farms for miles around Sparta for the richest cream and butter, the largest eggs, the reddest and most snowily marbled cuts of meat. Sometimes she bade him drive all the way into Atlanta to root out, like a truffle-snuffing hog, some offering of exotica that was unavailable even at Lapham's. Off he would go, a shuffling thunderstorm of outraged dignity, to find the best and richest provender in a sixty-mile radius and, in frosty silence, bear it home for the ballooning stomach and constricting arteries of Paul Fox.

The pleasures of his table were almost the only pleasures of the flesh left to Paul Fox, Ruth having virtually abandoned his bed and succeeded in moving him unobtrusively back into his old bedroom. But as his bulk mushroomed and his parched soul bloomed under the sun of Ruth's fascinated attention, he gradually became a benevolent eunuch, and was content to look upon his wife's supple white flesh and crystal face, as she sat beside him in the evenings or opposite him at the mahogany dinner tables of his boyhood friends, with awe and appreciation instead of lust. Those few wild, transported nights in their early marriage had become fabulous with distance and the refracting patina of memory, and he examined them often in his mind as another man might finger perfect diamonds, feeling a contented, goatish glow that he had once been able to stir so incredible a creature to such shrieking excesses of passion, and faintly grateful that the effort was no longer required of him.

Under Ruth's renewed interest, he had his classical books brought down from the attic, and read aloud from them in the evenings with joy and relish to Ruth and Hebe, never lifting his shining bald head from the seductive pages to see the glaze of boredom and dislike whitening Ruth's blue eyes, or the blank, beautiful gray incomprehension in Hebe's.

The Foxes went out less and less in these days; Ruth did not mind this. Social acceptance had been hers ever since the long-ago New Year's Day in 1905, when she had stood with Alicia and Claudius in the drawing room and felled the walls of Sparta with her grace and manners and hatred-buttressed determination. Over the years her loathing of those prattling, self-assured southern women and later their daughters had abated to an impatient disregard, but Ruth still did not enjoy time spent with them; she was bored. Paul, a loner from childhood, had all he wanted in his wife and daughter and books and perfect meals. During the Jazz Age, while the world around them went out into the streets and speakeasies and stadiums to play, the Foxes of Fox's Earth drew in upon themselves, a charmed circle of three, and it was, for the moment, enough.

There were only a few flies bumbling in his Eden. Dr. Hopkins would snort in disgust and frustration when Paul went reluctantly for his yearly physicals.

"You're going to keel over at the dinner table before you're forty-five if you don't lose some weight and get that blood pressure down," he told Paul. "You saw your father and grandfather die of this damned Fox gluttony; do you want to follow in their footsteps and leave that pretty wife and daughter of yours? I'm serious, Paul. If your heart doesn't get you, a stroke is going to. Get out and play golf, play tennis, walk, ride a horse, do handstands, get a pogo stick . . . I don't care what, but get moving. Now go home and tell Ruth I want her to call me this afternoon, or to come by here and I'll give her a diet sheet for you. I'll bet you never gave her any of those others I sent you home with and you won't give her this one. I want to see you again in two months, and I want to see you twenty pounds lighter by then, and that's just for a start."

Paul would puff home full of unease and resolve; he did not, indeed, want to leave his wife and daughter and shining, symmetrical life. He would embark that day on a low-calorie, salt-free diet. . . . But he had skipped his lunch to keep the appointment, and by three o'clock visions of that evening's dinner were dancing delectably before his eyes. It was sweetbreads in puff pastry and sherry sauce, Ruth had told him with a kiss as she saw him off that morning, and apple charlotte for dessert.

And so, when he dutifully handed the diet sheet over to Ruth and told her what the doctor had said, his resolve melted away like spun sugar upon the tongue when she said, "Oh, pooh. Alex Hopkins is just an old worrywart and a spoilsport. Just look at him; skinny as a rail and sour as vinegar. I'll bet he never enjoyed a meal in his life. Everybody knows a husky man is a healthy man, and I do so love to see you enjoy your meals. I'm making the pastry for the sweetbreads myself; did I tell you?"

And Paul sat down the next night to stuffed pork chops

and mashed potatoes, and life at Fox's Earth spun on. Now Ruth began, slowly and delicately, to carve her own imprint upon his few remaining business and civic and charitable associations. Entering his forties, Paul sat upon a respectable number of boards and committees in town and on the hill at the university; he did not occupy them out of any real merit, but because he was affable and conservative and serious, and because a Fox had always sat upon them. At his law office Paul was reliable and thorough and had a gentle, courtly way about him, especially with the firm's tottering Old Sparta clients, and, in his position of frequent executor and confidant, he had his small, plump fingers on the pulse and fortunes of most of the real powers in the town. Paul talked expansively and often to Ruth about his prowess in estate law, and after each board and committee meeting would bring the evening's business and his own efficient, responsible role in it home and lay it out like a trophy for Ruth's murmuring admiration.

He was constantly amazed at her grasp of business and financial matters, and when she began, hesitantly and modestly, with her gold-brushed lashes dropped upon her cheeks, to offer comments and suggestions, he listened absorbedly and with no trace of husbandly condescension. Some of her ideas were bold and innovative and had the deft, sure kiss of the born businessman on them, and these he would offer in the next meetings, and receive high praise for the originality and effectiveness of his thinking. Some he shamefacedly passed off as his own, but others he was impelled by honor and honest admiration to admit, in tones of fond unctuousness, were his wife's.

"Ruth says" and "My wife pointed out to me" soon became familiar phrases in the gilt-and-paneled meeting rooms of Sparta, and more than one shrewd, laconic country banker or landowner was heard to remark, not quite in Paul's hearing, that it was too bad Miss Ruth couldn't sit on the board, as it was plain as the spots on a red calf who had the money sense in that family, as well as the looks.

And so they began to take her seriously in the board rooms and business offices of Sparta, and soon Ruth moved from a disembodied presence whose words hung in the blue-smoked air to a physical presence of some consequence.

She had long since taken over the entire financial opera-
tion of the Fox family's estate, as well as the household
accounts. Paul was not incapable, but vague, when it came
to the payment of notes and mortgages and the investment
of what cash there was in the family coffers, and Ruth
persuaded him soon after Alicia's death to let her handle
all the business matters relating to the estate.

"Because, darling, you've such a heavy load on you
right now, and I've got all the servants, and Rip to help
with Hebe, and I truly love to manage money, and you
said yourself I'm good with it."

And she was. Using the information she gleaned from
the accounts Paul brought home from his meetings and
his office, Ruth began to buy property. She knew before
anyone else what spendthrift, bourbon-soaked blue blood
was about to lose the old family place for taxes, and made
him an offer on it . . . a low one, but an immediate one
that would educate his sons and keep him in Wild Turkey
and spare him the disgrace of a public auction on the
tobacco-spattered marble steps of the Chilton County
Courthouse. She heard from Paul which stubborn, senile
old widow, who had insisted on clinging to a decaying,
huge old Church Street house when her husband died,
leaving her exasperated children saddled with her soaring
taxes and relay sitting duties in their mother's house, was
near death and could not be expected to last the month.
She went to the oldest of the children quietly; when their
mother died they remembered Ruth's offer with relief, and
pounced upon it. Some of the properties, those with houses
on them, especially, she resold, and invested the money in
more land, and soon most of the property along a forlorn,
wandering red-dirt road that straggled from Sparta to the
county line belonged to the Foxes. Ruth could not have
said what prompted her to buy it, but something implacable
deep within her made her fingers itch until she signed the
papers for it, and she held on to it for years, through re-
cession and the Great Depression, until the day in 1959
that the state made her an offer, nearly obscene in its
munificence, to turn her dirt road into a freeway.

From the boards of the bank and the mill she had early
and privileged information on stock splits and new offerings, but Ruth bought little stock. The thing that had
sprung like sacred fire into the hearts and brains of those
frail, indomitable women of the South after the Civil War

147

dictated that the land . . . the land, the earth, the red clay, and the houses that stood upon it . . . that only this was important, only this counted, only this would endure. Ruth obeyed.

So that even when the Great Depression that smashed the South along with the rest of the country came, borne along on frantic cries from the New York Stock Exchange of "More margin! More margin!" the household of Ruth and Paul Fox did not suffer materially. Ruth sold some of her land to pay taxes, bought more at public auction, cut her household expenses to the bone, gritted her teeth, and held fast. When World War II came crashing down upon the heads of Americans, and booming war production spread prosperity once again across the land, Paul Fox blinked and nodded and looked about to find himself a wealthy man. And Ruth was, once and for all, a power in her own right in Sparta. And she was more: in essence, in some obscure way, she *was* Sparta. It was just where she had meant to be.

14

FOR MUCH of the despairing country 1933 was the darkest year in a decade sodden with hardship and hopelessness. In Atlanta, only sixty miles to the west of Sparta, privation was bitter and visible. Businessmen and shoppers returning to Sparta told horrific tales of soup lines, dead-eyed men on every street corner with small hoards of carefully polished apples for sale, hobo jungles and wind-whistling Hoovervilles flung together of packing boxes and scrap metal, where entire families lived in the shadows of the tall civic towers.

"Men and women all together in one little shoebox of a room; there must have been seven or eight of them," red-haired Fancy Cobb told Ruth Fox over Country Captain at the Sparta Country Club on one of the Foxes' rare evenings out. "I know they're poor, and it's probably the best they can do, but I think I'd take my family and go live under a tree somewhere before I'd let my children be raised in one little room with all those unmarried people, and some of them in nothing but old ragged undershirts and slips, too. Where do you suppose they all sleep? Damn this chicken; you'd think with the dues we pay they could buy themselves an occasional cow or something. And wouldn't you sell your soul for an honest whiskey sour?"

Ruth said nothing, but bent her enigmatic smile on Fancy Cobb, who misread a high-minded rebuke into the smile and flushed crossly. In fact, Ruth couldn't have cared less about the plight of the people in the Hoovervilles. The Foxes of Fox's Earth were comfortable, if not wrapped for the time in luxury. Even in that hardest of years, Paul earned a bit more than $4,000 at his law practice. Only airline pilots made more.

But on the outlying farms, cotton was bringing a miserable five cents a pound, and it was rough, drought-dried and weevil-infested cotton to boot. The silky, spindrift stuff grown at the turn of the century had commanded far more on cotton-market Saturdays. The farmers caught jackrabbits and called them Hoover hogs, and their women boiled them into watery, tough-thewed stews to sustain the children, who labored in the powdery hot fields "from cain't see to cain't see." The poor resulting crops were hauled into Sparta in broken-down automobiles, powered now by barrel-stave-ribbed mules.

It was rock-bottom time in America. Herbert Hoover had said, on the morning of the banks' collapse, "We are at the end of our string. There is nothing more we can do." He was at the end of his, at any rate. That day was his last as President; Franklin Delano Roosevelt would sleep that evening in the White House. This fact would make a great difference to the beleaguered country, and to Hebe Fox an enormous difference, and to Paul Fox the final difference. For it was under the aegis of F.D.R.'s newly conceived Civilian Conservation Corps that a handsome, whistling, finger-snapping young German-Irishman named Johnny Geiger came to Sparta to oversee the implementation of a federal flood-control project for the timorous Oconee River and stayed to capture the trembling heart and hand of Hebe Pearl Fox, and, in the capturing, to plant in the brain of Paul Fox the swift-swelling red flower that killed him.

Hebe at eighteen was much as she had been at five, and at twelve, and at fifteen: small, finely boned, fey, airy of voice and of mind, awkward, arresting, and, above all, unlike every other girl within ten years of her age in Sparta.

In her childhood, the flyaway nimbus of gilt hair that she had from Ruth and the huge, round, white-ringed gray eyes that came from Alicia's New England ancestry, together with her delicate Fox features and the wide, tremulous mouth of Cater Yancey, had made her an odd-looking child, appealing in a startling, wild way, but not quite human. It was as if Hebe's darting, restless, airborne little body was topped by the head of a pretty animal, like a lesser Egyptian goddess.

Sometime around her sixteenth birthday, the strangely assorted features of her childhood slid together as if under a spell, and she became a dead ringer for another ethereal child-woman named Lillian Gish, and as beautiful a girl as her mother had been, though in a far different and less commanding way. Hebe would never rivet eyes and stop breaths, as Ruth did even into old age, and she would have been appalled and frightened had she done so. As there was something splendid and lambent and finished about Ruth Yancey Fox from childhood on, so there was something vulnerable and unfinished about Hebe all her life.

Hebe was not a popular girl. She had always known this; it was a fact of her being, like her gray eyes and small stature, and as such did not bother her terribly. Hebe had lived since earliest childhood inside the flickering, light-struck shallows of her own mind, and nothing in the outside world could compete with that magical territory. Tutored at home, she did not learn, early or ever, the pragmatic rituals of give-and-take, arbitration, reward and retaliation with which children arm themselves for their uneasy truce with the world. She lived only with a few adults, and those adults were loving, stern, doting, and fiercely protective, as the case happened to be, but they were never permissive or accepting or, above all, objective. Going into her eighteenth year, Hebe was innocent of day-to-day experience, strictured of outlook and aspiration, ignorant of the world and its powers and pleasures and pain, and as helpless to cope with more than a broken fingernail or a stranger for dinner as she had been at ten. Because Ruth told her so almost every day of her life, she thought herself unable to choose her own clothes, drive a car, go to Atlanta on the train alone, keep a checkbook, give a party, prepare a meal, contemplate more schooling than the rudimentary amount she had absorbed from her tutor, consider any sort of career, interest a suitor, or aspire to a brilliant marriage. Indeed, Hebe envisioned no marriage at all.

This last did not bother her any more than her deficiencies in the other areas. Hebe thought that she would probably live in warmth and safety in her ruffled bower of a room upstairs at Fox's Earth forever. Marriage seemed at once exotically remote and tiresomely banal; it was clearly not for her. Hadn't her adored daddy told her over and over, "What does my pretty puss need with a date? Why does she want to spend her time with some silly old boy when she's her daddy's best girl and always will be? I'm not going to let her go; she's going to stay in her pretty house and be her daddy's girl for ever and ever."

Didn't Ruth, whenever Hebe evinced the smallest interest or curiosity about this scion of Old Sparta, or that one, lift a delicate gold eyebrow and laugh her fluting little laugh, and murmur, "Oh, Hebe, really. First it was that filthy stray kitten and now Wade Forrest. You *are* the most indiscriminate goose." Or later, "Darling, there are many, many girls who never marry and are content and happy as can be. There's certainly nothing shameful about choosing to remain single, but I have always thought it was shameful indeed to marry beneath you just for the sake of marriage. You are much too sensitive and special a girl to waste yourself on one of these dull, common Sparta boys. You are a Fox of Fox's Earth, Hebe. This fine old house is your birthright. You must cherish it and care for it always."

At eighteen, Hebe had never once thought that her mother and father and Rip would one day die and leave her alone.

Hebe had had a childhood that was cloistered and proscribed in the extreme, but, having nothing with which to compare it, she was not discontented, and in any case she had not been completely cut off from the normal young life of the town. She did the things a daughter of Fox's Earth would be expected to do; Ruth wanted least of all to attract undue attention to her daughter, and people were sure to talk if they suspected Ruth of isolating Hebe completely from the life of the town. So Hebe went dutifully

151

off to dancing school; she went to Sunday school and church with Ruth and Paul; she was taken to Atlanta once a week for art lessons at the children's museum and her regular pediatrician's and dentist's appointments, and for frequent shopping expeditions under Ruth's expert guidance. By the time she reached her teens, she was invited as often as courtesy and the Fox name dictated to parties and tea dances at the hotel and to evening dances at the country club, and her exquisite wardrobe and strange beauty initially drew flocks of young Sparta scions and well-born university men to her, all with a uniform desire to protect her even while they copped a furtive feel.

But one by one they dropped her. Hebe had no small talk and no flirtatious banter; she never mastered the breezy slang of the late twenties and early thirties, and despite her chic, expensive clothes, there was about her some Alicelike fragility that was the antithesis of the irreverent flapper. There clung to her, too, the sharp, sour, invisible effluvia of fear to which the young men could put no name, but at which they shied like nervous mules passing a charnel house. The word soon spread in Sparta that Hebe Fox, for all her beauty, did not have It, or SA; would not neck or pet; was, in short, a flat tire. Hebe withdrew in bewilderment but no real unhappiness back into the fortress of Fox's Earth, surer than ever that her lot lay there. She dived as gratefully and deeply into her movie fan magazines and endless radio dramas as her father had into his classical studies. Romance and passion flamed through her days and nights, but they were at a safe remove, far away and someone else's, transmitted to Hebe by the immaculate conduits of pulp and celluloid and crystal, not by her own red blood. The latter still ran cool and unhurried in her virginal blue veins.

Until the Sunday evening at church, in July of that bitter, blasted year of 1933, when she lifted her eyes from her Book of Common Prayer and looked full into the warm, sherry-brown eyes of a strange young man who had slipped into a seat on the pew beside her, still brushing a salting of dust from his coat. Hebe Fox looked at John Geiger, late of Johnstown, Pennsylvania, by way of Washington, D.C., and the sonorous evensong hummed away and died in her ears to be replaced by a resonant pounding that shook her head upon her slender neck and thundered in her ears, and something warm and wet and ex-

152

ultant uncurled in the pit of her stomach like a fern. He smiled, a slight, polite, and intensely personal smile that made Hebe think, suddenly, that he knew just how her silk chemise pulled taut over her breasts, and her ecru-laced panties slid tenderly between her legs, and she shifted in her seat with the warm prodding of the thought. Hebe had never before felt anything remotely like that insinuating warmth, those tickling, sly fingers of sensation, and she slid away from the stranger on the rosewood seat, closer to her mother.

Ruth glanced at her daughter and then at the young man, and in the flicker of a tawny eyelash saw in the young stranger and in her daughter's wide, unfocused eyes and flared nostrils the end and the beginning that must now come to Fox's Earth. She studied the young man . . . handsome enough, in a sharp, indefinably not-southern way; sober clothes, a bit on the cheap side; an easy smile and extraordinary reddish-brown eyes, which seemed to promise all manner of sweet things while still he fumbled with a prayer book; a facile, much-used smile and a slide of soft, rain-colored hair over a white, widow's-peaked forehead: common. Biddable, easily manipulated. Swift of appetite and short of patience. And above all, greedy. Ruth could see the greed flickering in the translucent eyes as he looked at Hebe. It was more than desire, though that was there, too, desire for Hebe in the clear, sea-blue silk-knit dress that Ruth had selected. But the greed rode over the desire like a new-hoisted ensign over a conquered flag, and Ruth knew that someone had told him that Hebe was, in fact, Hebe Fox of Fox's Earth, and that his picking of the Fox pew was no accident. So he would be the one, then. Yes. He would do nicely, this covetous and shallow-varnished young stranger. He would get lovely infant women on the shrinking flesh of Hebe.

"We got us one, Mama," Ruth whispered under the mannerly thunder of the hymn. And when the hymn was over, and the last response had been murmured, she turned to the dawdling stranger, who was edging as slowly as he dared into the aisle while Hebe dropped her handbag twice in confusion, and said, "I'm Ruth Fox, and this is my daughter, Hebe. We're so glad you joined us at church tonight. Is this just a visit, or will you be staying in Sparta for a while?"

Over supper later . . . for "it seemed the friendly thing

153

to do, darling; the young man obviously knows no one," Ruth told a fretful Paul . . . Johnny Geiger chatted vivaciously with Ruth, wrapped Hebe in the slow, caressing silk of his beautiful animal's eyes, was deferential and boyish with Paul, and looked around the great paneled dining room and the silver-freighted table with a bravado carelessness that did not mask the brilliant, avian assessing in his eyes. To Paul he looked like a young hawk, a lesser one . . . a sparrow hawk, perhaps, shabby with molt and bristling with defensiveness, just brought from the field of a farmer and jessed and verveled in the house of a lord.

He had come down from Washington only three days before, he told them, where he had gone from the house of his widowed mother back in Johnstown to get a job with Franklin Roosevelt's new government. He had not gone on to college after high school as he had thought he might, because times were so hard and his father had recently died and left his semi-invalid mother with little but the small house they had lived in and Johnny and his younger sister Deirdre for dubious helpmates.

"I went to see our congressman; he was a friend of my father's from the parish and the old days in the local. The UMW," Johnny said to Paul, happily unaware that he had introduced, in one sentence, the two largest, most incarnadine flags that could be waved before the eyes of an aristocratic southerner—the Catholic Church and the unions. "He sent me down to Washington to see some people he knew in the War Department, and as luck would have it, the corps was just getting started, and this dam project . . . without the 'n'; excuse me, fair ladies . . . needed a superintendent, and so here I am. And happy to be in the land of cotton, especially tonight, in the company of the two fairest blossoms in all of Dixie." He smiled vividly at Ruth and then at Hebe, who stared back, her soft, formless child's mouth slightly agape. Ruth wanted to shake her.

"How fortunate for us that the Oconee needs a dam," Ruth said, bending on him the full candlepower of her smile. "Will you be with us long, then?"

He smiled wryly, manfully. "As long as it takes to pay off the mortgage on the house and get DeeDee through secretarial school. Mama's strength was broken nursing Dad, and she can't work. The bank was almost ready to foreclose before I got my first check, but I sent it home in time . . . ate peanut butter for a solid month, but it was worth it.

A guy's mom is just about his greatest treasure, I always say. Until he gets himself a wife, anyway. No, I'm more than glad to have this job, even if it means putting off law school for a year or two. The law will always be there, wouldn't you say so, sir?"

He looked for agreement to Paul, who applied himself with ferocity to Sunday night's banana pudding, and only nodded. Ruth smiled sweetly and exulted in her heart; he was not only a sycophant and a liar and an opportunist, he was a fool. This was better than she could have expected.

Hebe still stared, eyes misted now with emotion. The romance of it! This handsome stranger, gallantly sacrificing his own career in the law to save the little home of his widowed invalid mother and send his sister to school, this beautiful boy, with his too-pale face and his thin, long body, undoubtedly undernourished, and his warm eyes that wanted, incredibly, her . . . for there was no mistaking that. He looked at her with a naked yearning that had nothing in it of the caution and well-bred contempt she saw in the eyes of the boys in Sparta. She burned from her fingertips to her small feet with the need to give to him; all of herself, anything that would replace that terrible yearning with surfeit and contentment.

"You'll like Sparta," she said in a breathless rush, her voice a small sighing in the still air. "There's a nice picture show and a real pretty pool out at the country club. I can show you around. We could go swimming tomorrow, maybe."

She stopped in confusion and terror. Was she being too forward? She darted a look at her mother, but Ruth only smiled at her indulgently, and Johnny Geiger did too. Paul glowered from the end of the table, but no one paid him the slightest attention.

"Tomorrow's a working day for me, I'm afraid," Johnny Geiger said. "But maybe a rain check until next weekend?"

"Oh, yes," Hebe breathed. "Next weekend."

He gave her a brilliant smile, its slowness masking the alacrity in his heart. So soon, so soon, this lovely, brainless child-belle, and this great Technicolored dream of a house, both landing lightly in his lap even before he'd fully unpacked his Gladstone in the upstairs bedroom he had let on the other side of town. He marveled at the wonder of it.

155

For in the matter of the South, if in nothing else he had said that evening, Johnny Geiger spoke the truth. His world had always been one of soot-grimed snows and dirty alleys and pool halls and pawnshops; the tubercular union-official father had in reality been a drunken miner, and the frail, invalid mother struggling to keep her small house and her decent little family together had been a fat, feckless Irish girl given to whiskey and easy tears and lamentations for her lost youth and prospects. His sister Deirdre was older than he, not younger; she had married a local beat patrolman and moved out of the stinking little house before she was sixteeen, and was now a carping, red-knuckled matron with five children under the age of ten. Compared to that bleak landscape, Sparta seemed a veritable paradise.

When, three days ago, he alighted from the train on the platform in Sparta, his reddened eyes had seen great oaks arching over cobblestone streets, and cool white columns shimmering, Atlantislike, amid the green, and pretty women and girls moving languidly in and out of the shops. He heard soft drawls and the rich laughter and music-suffused speech of the Negroes, and he smelled roses and sun-warmed dust and thick, honeyed air free of smoke and cinders, and he thought he had died and gone to heaven. Even the cool, polite reserve with which his too effusive requests for directions were met charmed him. These were not people to toss themselves easily away to any passing stranger. They knew their own worth, and when they at last awarded their friendship and approbation, those would be things for a man to treasure. That he would have them in time he was certain with the assurance of the young predator who has known only small and vulnerable prey.

Under the sun of his vivid, whimsical charm, his slatternly landlady was only too happy to supply the names and habitats of the three or four wealthiest and most prominent unmarried young women in Sparta. The following Sunday evening he dressed carefully in his good suit and slipped soberly and for the first time in his life into the sanctity of a church that was at once socially rarefied and Protestant and spied there the girl who could only be Miss Hebe Fox of Fox's Earth. That the rest was like shooting fish in a barrel because of Ruth Yancey Fox's grand design and not his own singular charm did not occur

156

to him, and it never did for the eight years, eight months, and eleven days that he lived in Sparta.

Hebe discovered sex on the third evening that Johnny Geiger called on her at Fox's Earth, and from that time on she was like a starved woman let loose in a food store; she could not get enough of him. He had called the evening after the first Sunday night, and had sat in the drawing room and conversed decorously and gaily with Ruth, while Hebe stared and breathed moistly in and out, and Paul glowered prissily. Ruth had withdrawn gracefully and early, taking Paul with her almost by force, and Johnny had been left alone with Hebe. He had quickly and skillfully drawn her out with compliments and exaggeratedly courtly manners he fancied her southern beaux employed, and she had soon lost her initial god-struck awe, and prattled eagerly to him of the romances of the stars in her movie magazines and the impossibly ethereal and pure *affaires d'amour* that poured into her room from her radio. His quick, low cunning did not fail him; this would be the tack, then. He quoted the florid verse of Robert Service, and he sang to her the cloying popular songs of the day, holding her small hands and looking into her swimming gray eyes, and he spun a wonderful, intricate web of future plans, which included service to mankind in some obscure and unnamed way, as soon as his obligations to his poor old mother were discharged. He hinted at tragic loves lost to him, and dreams that had died brutally, and a heart that would never truly heal, and he carefully did not touch her. On the second evening he took her to see Greta Garbo in *Anna Christie,* and leaned over her solicitously when she wept copiously in the darkened theater, so that his breath grazed her cheek, and tucked his own handkerchief into her hand. But still he did not move to touch her.

And then, on the third evening, after returning from a moonlight drive to which Ruth had given her indulgent sanction and which had caused Paul to retreat into his study in a perfect fury of impotent wrath, he settled her and then himself onto the glider that stood in the shadows of the wisteria bower on the side veranda, saying, "I just can't let you go in yet; let's sit out here and listen to the crickets for a while," and he put his arm around her and pulled her to him and kissed her. Hebe gave a little, low,

157

anguished animal moan, and lunged backward on the glider, pulling him after her, and when he raised himself up again, it was to glide himself, dazed and drained, out of the tightest, most explosively demanding and abandoned flesh he had ever penetrated in his twenty-two years.

Gasping, he moved a hand down to button himself up; he stared into her face, wildly groping for the whispered words that would stem the inevitable flood of tears and guilt-stricken recriminations, for she had most indisputably been a virgin. Visions of an enraged Paul brandishing his small, outraged fists and perhaps a silver-stocked pistol danced crazily in front of his eyes; Ruth's shocked and avenging face swam before him; and the spangled prospects of Fox's Earth withdrew with the speed of a meteor, leaving a sucking desolation in his heart. But when he focused his eyes on Hebe's face, a white blur beneath him in the dapple of moonlight, he saw not shock and horror and tears, but the swollen suffusion of contentment about her blinded eyes, and the beginning of a new surge of desire in her slackened mouth. He could scarcely get her to button up her blouse and pull up her panties and creep into the house; she clung to him, and ground herself against him, and moaned and laughed and wept. Finally she went, looking back at him and smiling through a sheen of pleasurable tears, and he smiled winsomely after her, and tottered on marrowless legs to his hired car and drove away, to lie for hours in his spavined bed, aching and stunned with surprised joy at the way his wildest dreams were materializing, and jittering with anxiety lest he allow her to push them to blatant indiscretion and topple the towering fantasy. Careful, he must be careful now . . . more careful than he had ever been in his clever young life. He knew that Paul did not like him and never would, and at the very least would have had him run out of town if he could have seen them on the veranda that evening. He could not even imagine what Ruth would do if she knew.

But Ruth did know. Even if she had not, by tiptoeing out onto the side balcony that overhung the bower while Paul snored fitfully in his bedroom, been able to hear the bucketing of the glider, she would have known. She had known by the sudden surge of heat from Hebe's arm as it pressed her own that first Sunday night in the church, known by the wide gray eyes as they sought Johnny Geiger across the dinner table, known by the arcana of her own blood. It had always been there in the cool flesh of her daughter, she thought, this savage thing that she had sought not quite successfully to blast and wither that long-ago day in the back garden of Fox's Earth. At best she had been able only to hold it at bay; it had been pure luck that it was Johnny Geiger, and not some invincible and omnipresent young male of the town or the South who called it from its sleep. Something very akin to fear snaked through Ruth. Luck and chance had no place at Fox's Earth. She had not foreseen this; she had been somehow lax, somehow inadequate. Nothing must be left to luck. Paul must not see, must not know. If he had heard, had seen, even she could not have stopped him from banishing Johnny Geiger forever.

The next night, after dinner, when a distinctly edgy Johnny and a desire-slackened Hebe had murmured their excuses and wandered out toward the veranda, Ruth took an astonished Paul Fox upstairs and into her own bed for the first time in many years, and there he stayed, puffing and panting and transported, for the next two weeks, while downstairs, or across town in a sagging boardinghouse bed, or in the back seat of the car out by the river, his daughter also bounced and thrashed and cried aloud in the transports of a passion stronger even than the thongs of distrust and terror that had bound her since earliest childhood.

When he came to himself again, after almost fourteen days of dragging stupefied and exhausted through the daylight hours and sinking wildly and abandonedly into his wife's inexhaustible flesh at night, Paul Fox looked about and found that his daughter had turned into a wanton. She gave off heat as a small, pearly furnace might; she was heavy of wrist and eyelid and neck and restless of step; her pretty clothes and spindrift hair were always ever so slightly askew, as if they had just been jerked and patted back into place after the hands of that really most unsuitable young man had been at them. The boy was underfoot every day and night; the flood-control project languished unrealized in a pile of manuals and missives from Washington on his desk back in his rented room, and he and Hebe were off together every waking hour.

"He isn't our sort; he's not on Hebe's level at all," Paul

fretted to Ruth over dinner one evening. Hebe and Johnny had driven into Atlanta for a chaste dinner at Hart's.

"Oh, Paul, really," Ruth fluted sweetly. "It's nothing in the world but a little summer romance. Just little picnics, and movies at night, and maybe a little drive out by the river to watch the moon. How could you deny your daughter that? Every girl is entitled to one perfect little summer romance. It won't last past Labor Day, you'll see."

"But, Ruth, what do we really know about him? No college education, no social contacts, no prospects . . . They have nothing in common. What could they possibly have in common?"

"Nothing, of course, dearest," Ruth reassured him, knowing exactly what they had in common. "Which is why this little . . . infatuation . . . hasn't a prayer of lasting. She'll realize that, soon now, I think, and it will all just . . . fade away. I'm truly not a bit worried. And meanwhile, he's a pleasant boy, and I think you'd have to admit that if you'd be fair. Sweet-tempered and polite and harmless as can be."

"Well, I don't share your sentiments, my dear, generous as they are. I don't think any good is going to come of this, and I intend to tell him when they come in that I don't want him to call on Hebe anymore. I should have done it long ago."

"Paul, dearest . . ." she began, but then she saw that he was rigid with one of his rare attacks of adamancy, and that she might as well attempt to sway a lead equestrian statue as to persuade him to come to bed and forget about telling Johnny Geiger not to darken his door again. She went to bed alone in her great tester bed for the first time in two weeks, and tossed there in barely bridled fury, trying and rejecting this course of action and that one. Stubborn mule! He must not, must *not*, be allowed to spoil this. It was too perfect, a gift of benevolent fate. It would never happen so easily again. She yearned for her mother, and rose on one elbow repeatedly to peer into the close, hot darkness beside the open French windows, but Pearl was not there. She lay awake late into the night, waiting for the faint thud of Johnny's car door slamming in the quiet street beside the old hollowed carriage block, but it did not come. Near dawn, though, she started up from a sweating, dream-haunted half-sleep to hear the fading nasal whisper of Pearl Steed Yancey. Eased, she slept fully.

When she woke again, it was to full dawn light and a terrible cackling gargle and a great, resounding thud, and a wild, endless shriek which was Hebe's, but Hebe's as a tiny child . . . in a garden somewhere? . . . and a confusion from below of running feet and bumping furniture and slamming doors, and someone calling her over and over: "Miss Ruth! Miss Ruth! Come quick, Miss Ruth!"

They had driven, not to Atlanta, but up into the mountains of North Georgia, to a justice of the peace in Fannin County, and had slept the night in a tourist camp beside a cold-running, mossy river, in a rotting, damp-slicked wooden cabin named the Punkin Vine Inn, and had come home to Fox's Earth as Mr. and Mrs. Johnny Geiger, there to encounter at the front door Paul Fox, who had not remained alive long enough to forbid Johnny Geiger his house, much less welcome him as a new son of it.

15

AT THE AGE of forty-two Rip was a great beauty, not only, as the whites of Sparta might have said reluctantly, "for a Negro," but in any right. The promise of the odalisque's magnificence that had dwelt in the thin child's high cheekbones and hawklike nose and tilted eyes had come into the full flower of its maturity, and there was a sheen of ripeness and health on her black skin. Rip was slender to the point of emaciation, but her long, fine bones and narrow skull and attenuated hands and feet were so shapely and strongly formed that they constituted a true elegance, and needed only the sheath of the skin to wrap them tautly.

"She's as skinny as a milkweed stalk," Ruth would say to this acquaintance or that who commented on Rip's stylized, Oceanic beauty. "I'm sure everybody thinks I starve her to death. And arrogant; do you know, she absolutely will *not* wear a uniform? I'd fire her tomorrow, but Hebe is still just insanely devoted to her, after all these years, and she *is* good with the children. But pretty I just don't see."

The fact was that Rip, in the cheap cotton dresses that Ruth ordered for her from the Sears, Roebuck catalog in lieu of the spurned uniforms, made anyone who stood beside her seem thick-boned and overdressed, even diminutive, immaculate Ruth Fox.

Everyone in her small world knew Rip to be long celibate and seemingly indifferent to the prospect of a man in her life and her bed. And yet she was so fundamentally and unalterably female that it was almost palpable on the air, a cloud around her. Not a few men had been intrigued and inflamed by this dichotomy in the two decades and more since Jester Tully stormed out of her life. But Rip, complete and fulfilled by the three children under the roof of Fox's Earth and the small black boy under the roof of the little slave cabin where she lived now, wanted nothing and no one to intrude upon her duties as guardian and sentinel. Paul Fox II and her grandson Jacob Lee would be her men until the end of their lives.

Her grandson had come to her two years before—when Paul Fox II was not yet a year old—a long, painfully thin, huge-eyed child of four with Rip's own elegant bones and the blank, smooth face of a melon. Nothing seemed written on his face, which was the lustrous melted caramel that his mother's had been as an infant. He did not cry and he did not laugh; it was days before Rip realized that he could speak. It was as if he had no past at all; Rip herself had had that timeless, untouched air when she was young, but in the case of the boy this seeming lack of a personal history sprang from the brief life so harsh and bereft of warmth and surety that the child had simply buried the reality of it away. For all his life, Jacob Lee's first four years remained a cipher to Rip, unimaginable. He never spoke of them, and his mother did not remain in Sparta long enough to do so, if indeed she could recall them.

She had come home in the spring, on a night when the mimosa's breath struck the warm air around Fox's Earth to heartbreaking urgency and the first of the peepers cried in the dark garden just outside the kitchen windows. Rip was upstairs in the small cubicle that was still her only home; she had not left it when Hebe married Johnny Geiger and moved with him into the big room that had been her father's. Rip might have been expected to leave

162

the small room now that her charge was grown and married and the nursery long empty, but no one questioned her right to it. Hebe spent as much time with Rip in the kitchen and schoolroom as she ever had, and Ruth Fox found all manner of tasks for Rip's deft hands. It was as if they were all waiting . . .

"I guess you's in hog heaven these days, sittin' up there arockin' like white fo'kses, without no chirrun to nuss," an overworked and failing Pinky had sniped at her once, her illness adding fuel to the fire that age had lit under her temper.

"They be chirrun soon," Rip had said tranquilly, and stayed to help with the fancy tea sandwiches Carrie was struggling over.

"Bet you that li'l ol' snip of a gal cain't git her no chile," Pinky snorted. "Too po' an' too spooky; she too rattle-headed to know where they comes from, ne'mine how to carry one."

Rip only smiled her rare, splendid smile, starred now with a gleaming gold tooth that did not in the least mar its impact but only lent it an exotic richness. She knew where the flush of languor that Hebe wore during that time came from. She had worn it herself, joyfully, like a rich red ensign, in the full, hot young days of Jester Tully. And besides, the jaunty, escalating gallop of the creaking bed-springs in the night would have told her, even if artless Hebe had not run in on the first morning after she and Johnny had slept at Fox's Earth to hug her and blurt, "Rip, there's just nothing in this world as wonderful as doing it! I could do it and never stop! Did you ever do it, Rip?"

"They be chirrun soon," she had repeated to Pinky, and that had been the end of it. She had stayed in her little room.

So it was to this room that Rusky came pattering on that April night, almost twenty-five years to the day after Rip entered it for the first time, came pattering and knocking and calling softly, "Rip! Rip! They somebody here wantin' to see you!"

The woman who sat swaying and muttering in the kitchen chair was so starkly alien to the shining, orderly kitchen of Fox's Earth that she might have been from another planet. She wove back and forth in the chair, cobralike; her eyes were closed as in some transport of mystic ecstasy, and she smiled and hummed as she swayed. Her face was yellow, as yellow as lye soap, and swollen, but beneath the spongy mask of edema the pure, clean bones of the highlands of Africa could be faintly seen. She reeked powerfully of raw, cheap whiskey and wore an astonishing slit-skirted dress of viscera-red satin, which rode up her knotted thighs to expose soiled lace underpants. At first Rip did not know who she was, and stared at her silently. And then, with a leap of recognition that sprang straight from the blood and womb, she did know. Her heart constricted so painfully that the breath stopped in her throat, and then lurched in her breast with a wildness that rocked her backward, but she said nothing. Rusky, hovering avidly in the doorway, saw her long, smooth eyelids slide slowly down over her eyes, and then lift again. Rip looked at Rusky and made a small sign with her hand: Go. Rusky went.

"LeeAnne."

Rip's voice cracked harshly around the name that had not passed her lips in more than a quarter of a century.

Her daughter stopped rocking and opened her eyes.

"Hey, Mama," she said, and laughed long and joyfully and insanely. She closed her eyes and began to rock again, and hum the dreadful, tuneless little song.

Rip sat down on the chair across the table. Her tireless legs, spring-steel pistons for forty years, were water.

"Open yo' eyes an' look at me, LeeAnne," she said in the same thin, rusty voice. "You ain't so drunk you can't look at yo' mama, is you?"

The eyes opened, and Rip saw that more than liquor glittered in them. Madness. Madness and sickness. Sorrow swept her, a fierce, debilitating sorrow she had not felt since this gaunt, crazed, drunken woman went away from her a chuckling golden infant.

"What happen to you, baby?" she said, choking on the words. "Where you been all this time so bad that you ackin' like this? Befo' God, baby, I thought you was dead, I thought I never see you again no mo' in this worl' . . ."

"Been right there all the time, Mama," the woman caroled. "Right there all the time. Right there in 'Lanna, an' N'Awleens, an' Memphis, an' . . . someplace else, I forgits. Then I thinks, I b'lieve I'll go see my mama, whut give me away when I was a young'un 'cause I ain't got no daddy . . ."

"No!"

It was a shriek of enormity and outrage, and it tore itself from Rip's throat like vomit.

"I ain't never give you away! He took you away, took you away from me in the night like a thief and run with you when you wasn't even big enough to walk, and all them years, Lord God, all them long, hard years I thought you was dead . . . Did that no-count nigger tell you I give you away? *He* was yo' daddy; he took you 'cause I wouldn't marry him, but I always knowed who yo' daddy was. I thought, I hoped, at least he take good care of you 'cause you his chile, but just look at you. . . . "

The woman stopped swaying and stared at her, and for a moment the madness and drunkenness lifted, and incomprehension and pain looked clearly back at Rip.

"I ain't never had no daddy. I ain't remember nobody takin' care of me, much lessen no daddy. There was a man used to stay with me some at night when I was real little, for a spell, an' he the one tell me I got a mama in Sparta what don't want me, but he ain't my daddy. He say he ain't. An' he go off 'fore long. After that, I always tooken care of myself."

Slow red rage mingled with the great, heavy sorrow in Rip's chest. She shut it out.

"Well, it don't matter none now, 'cause ain't none of it true. I yo' mama an' I ain't never give you away, an' I gon' take care of you now. LeeAnne, baby, if you'd knowed all the nights I laid awake hurtin' in my heart over you an' wonderin' where you was, an' if you alive . . . but you's here now. I git you some coffee to git rid of that whiskey, an' somethin' to eat, an' then I go talk to Miss Ruth. She fin' you a place to sleep till I can git us a place to stay. . . . "

The woman began to laugh again, and jerked to her feet and took several steps toward Rip. Her gait was stiff and stumbling; it was not the fluid, boneless lurch of drunkenness but an uncontrolled stagger on legs that were petrified into stilts. Rip saw then the paralyzed arm hanging loose at her side, and the scars and craters of sores that pitted her yellow arms and legs, and the great, thick tongue that lolled from her mouth with the laugh. The mustardy yellowness too . . . Rip had seen it before, on deathbeds in Suches. The last terrible stages of syphilis with severe liver involvement, though Rip could put no name to it. But she knew it meant that her daughter had probably been a whore since early childhood, and would soon and without question be dead.

"I ain't come all the way from 'Lanna to live in no white bitch's house," her daughter shouted gleefully, waving her arms. "I ain't need you to take care of me, ol' woman. I got me better than you'll ever have in this white cunt's house. I jus' come to bring you a li'l present . . . li'l gift from yo' daughter what you ain't want. Jus' a li'l ol' present . . ."

She laughed hugely, then stopped and looked around the kitchen.

"You got some whiskey, Mama? Got a li'l drink fo' you' baby girl?"

Rip tried to speak, but she could not force the words past her parched throat. She tried again, and produced a frail whisper.

"How you git here?"

Her daughter flung a scabbed yellow arm toward the back door, and nearly went over with the motion.

"Come in a big ol' new car a block long. Come with my man, what takes care of me good as my mama. Better, even! He gits me white men to fuck; I ain't fool aroun' with no sorry niggers what ain't got no money. Got me a fine room in a *ho*tel an' clothes like a movie star an' all the whiskey I can drink. He got me this here dress; you like it, Mama? An' these lace pants . . ."

She jerked her sleazy satin skirt high, and Rip saw clearly the scars and the sores that still yawned redly. Bile flooded her throat but she swallowed against it.

"Baby . . ."

"I ain't yo' baby!"

The woman shrieked it, close to Rip's face, and the sick sweetness of liquor and decayed teeth and something else gusted into her nose. Rip's lips drew away from her teeth in a silent snarl. Death was in there, in the corrupted flesh of the baby she had borne and lost and found again too late. Her old enemy breathed its cave breath on Rip and froze her silent.

"But I brung you one."

Before Rip could collect herself from the chill breath of death, her daughter had whirled and lurched from the kitchen and stumbled out the back door into the perfumed night. Rip followed, and peered out the door into the darkness to the gravel drive that led to the old stables, where

Mr. Paul's Chrysler and Miss Ruth's smart little coupe rested now. The little apartment over the stable-garage where the new chauffeur lived was dark, but Rip knew that Robert was leaning close to the window looking down at the car that stood in the moonlit driveway, its motor chuffing huge puffs of exhaust out into the damp night air.

It was a great, gleaming yellow car, and it was iced baroquely with sworls and bars, and cartouches of chrome that glittered in the pale light from the high-riding moon. A fox tail hung limply from its aerial, and four shining-black new tires gave back the moonlight defiantly. There was nothing like this in Sparta; the car's throbbing purr as it idled in the rear drive of Fox's Earth spoke of extravagance and excess and expensive gasoline bleeding away into the night. The man who sat at the wheel wore yellow, too: a yellow suit, with a fat yellow-and-dark-striped tie exploding under the blackness that was his face, and a thin flicker of gold from his watch chain and on two fingers of the hands that rested on the steering wheel. Rip could not see his face in the shadow, but then he turned his head and she caught the gleam of white that was his teeth, and the blind flash of light that might have been from the rims of spectacles or from the pits that were his eyes. The hair lifted at the base of Rip's skull, and her lips drew back once more from her teeth.

Rip's daughter appeared and fell against the back door of the car, and fumbled at it, and the man reached back and opened it, and Rip heard his deep laugh, and a cracked, skidding answering screech from her daughter. She turned away, sickly, and leaned against the kitchen table with both hands, her head hanging slackly. The oilcloth felt cool and hard under her palms, good.

A slam of the back door and a great, sighing breath of honeysuckle-smelling air, and the woman was in the kitchen again. Rip raised her head and looked at her. At first she did not see the child, shrunk away behind the woman, but then her daughter reached back and jerked him out into the light by one thin arm, and Rip saw him plainly then.

At first she thought he was a toy, or some sort of monstrous dwarf or midget that her daughter had produced to further punish her, and she could only goggle in incomprehension. He was so small and wizened that it seemed impossible he could stand, much less walk; it was as if a human infant had been wrapped in the loose, badly tanned skin of some yellow animal . . . perhaps a hyena . . . and dangled from adult hands like a puppet, so that it had the appearance of standing and walking. He did not even look like a monkey; his skin did not fit him well enough for that. His eyes were huge and black with terror and at the same time as flat as thin-washed river stones with unsurprise. His arms and legs looked like river reeds, or charred kindling. The skin was so slack that Rip could have picked it up and wrapped it neatly about his limbs and pinned up the excess. His head was huge, and long and narrow like her own. The stretched skin of his face was surprisingly lovely, smooth and lightly sheened and a pale golden color that she had never seen before except on the body of Jester Tully, long ago. Except that it had a nose and mouth and the great flat eyes, it might have been a balloon or a hammered disk of gold. Perfect nothingness looked back at Rip.

Rip's daughter threw back her head and roared with laughter; she balanced herself on the table and howled with glee, and slapped her thigh.

"How you like yo' present, Mama?" she squalled. "He all yourn to keep fo' youself, lessn you ain't want him neither. If you ain't, thass all right, 'cause I jus' th'ow him out 'side the road in the ditch on my way back to 'Lanna. I ain't want him neither."

Rip's hands reached out for the child of their own volition, and touched the razor-sharp ridges of thin bone beneath the shapeless, filthy pullover garment the child wore. It had a reek of old excrement and a child's thin sweat and stale dirt, and she could feel that he wore nothing under it. He did not pull away from her, but he went as rigid as stone. She relaxed her grip, which had bitten cruelly into his shoulders.

"He yo' baby?"

Her voice seemed to her own ears to come from a long way away.

"Naw! He yo' gran'baby!" shrieked her daughter. "I ain't got no baby!"

"What his name?"

"Ain't got no name!" The woman roared with the hilarity of it. Madness was as tangible in the room as the sweet, light wind that came in at the windows.

"That his daddy out there in the car?"

"Shit no! That ain't his daddy! He the one say I got

168

to come down here an' give him to you, else he gon' take care of him for me. I 'spec he wring his neck like a li'l ol' chicken. I don't know who his daddy is . . . was. Could be lots of fo'kses. Could be white fo'kses, all I know. He ain't got no mo' daddy than I got."

"LeeAnne. Stay here with him. Stay here with yo' mama. Don't go back with that man. I take good care of both of you. I git you well an' strong . . . you goes back an' you is as good as dead. You hear me? You a dead woman . . ."

"Naw, ol' woman! What I want with a li'l ol' yaller bastard an' a ol' skinny black woman what cleans up white fo'kses' shit all day long for a place to stay an' somepin' to eat? I got me ever'thing I wants in this worl' back in 'Lanna; I makes money fo' my man, an' he takes care of me . . ."

Silent tears were running down Rip's cheeks. "If you goes back you ain't no daughter of mine . . ."

"Shit," said the woman gaily, "I knowed that all along."

When Rip raised her face from her hands, the kitchen door was slamming and her daughter was gone out into the night. The purring of the car's engine rose to a growl and then settled into a mellow throb, and the man in yellow nosed it around in the driveway and headed it out toward the road to Atlanta. The last Rip saw of her daughter was the twin orbs of its taillights, blinking redly through the moon-silvered night like dying stars in a dead, cold cosmos.

She took the silent child in her arms and carried him up to the little room. He did not whisper but hung still in her arms, so light that she might have carried a soiled bundle of feathers. She pulled the grimy garment off him in the dimness and winced at the chicken's ribs and the gray carapaces of keloids on his meager trunk. He smelt gamily and powerfully. She would bathe him in the morning, and feed him; tonight he needed sleep most of all. She laid him in her narrow bed and pulled the spotless covers over him.

"Can you say somethin' fo' yo' granny, baby?" she whispered, her hand light on his forehead. She did not want to frighten him by cuddling him in her arms too soon. Time enough for that . . .

"Can you say good night to yo' granny?"

He looked at her flatly and said nothing.

She sighed and went into the bathroom that had connected Hebe's nursery with her little room. She would sponge away the worst of the encrusted grime tonight, and tomorrow she would clean him thoroughly and find something from Hebe's old chest to dress him in before she went to Miss Ruth and asked for shelter for him. Maybe the little house that had stood empty for so long behind the hedge of the back garden. The house where she and Jester once had thought to live . . .

When she returned to her room with a warm, damp washcloth he was gone from the bed, and her eyes went frantically around the room until she saw him lying on the bare boards of the floor in the corner, naked as a tiny plucked chicken, his knees drawn up to his stomach. When she approached him he sat up and held his arms up to her. She thought he wanted to be taken up, and was bending to do so when she noticed that his hands were held oddly: closed into fists and tightly together, palms in. Solemnly he held them there, looking into her face, waiting, palms and wrists pressed together.

"What you want me to do, baby?" she whispered, perplexed. And then she saw, in the light from the bathroom, the circle of scar on each wrist that manacles had made.

She held him all night and rocked him in the little rocking chair in which she had lulled favored little Hebe to sleep so many nights, so long ago, and all through the night her tears fell from her chin down onto the downy, napped head of her grandson. But none of them were for her daughter, and none ever were again.

16

THEY WERE AT WAR, and on a stormy day in March 1942, when Rip sat in the kitchen of Fox's Earth looking down in sorrow and pity at the face of Hebe's last child, a new daughter, they had just had the news on the radio that General MacArthur had left Corregidor. It was a day of grief and ironies; earlier that afternoon Hebe had found the note from Johnny Geiger, laid on the bedside table beside her little plastic radio and anchored with his heavy gold wedding ring, that said he was leaving her and the children and not coming back.

"I know I am a hound but the sad truth is I was never cut out to be a husband and father," Johnny wrote in his childish, parochial hand. "You are a good wife and a fine woman and do not think this is your fault for it is all mine. You can have the Wedding Ring to sell and you can divorce me if you want to for I will not come back. There won't be any problem with the Church as you are not Catholic. Goodbye Heebie. I will always remember you. I will not worry about any of you for I know your mother will take good care of you."

"I shall return," Douglas MacArthur had written from Australia. Johnny Geiger wrote no such message from the bathroom of Fox's Earth, where he retreated to pen his note to his wife. He simply waited until she went into the nursery for her morning visit with small Yancey and Paul and infant Nell, left the note in their bedroom, and went whistling out to Paul Fox's Chrysler, which he had appropriated, and drove away as if he were leaving on his daily round of job hunting.

He did not stop until he had reached Memphis. He spent the night in a crowded railroad hotel; it was shabby and smoke-grimed and sadly beneath him, but he was satisfied to hoard the cache of new bills in his pocket for as long as possible. They, and the proceeds from the Chrysler, would set him up in a business of his own when he reached war-booming California. Never again, he swore to himself over the hotel's glutinous meat loaf and gravy, would he work for another man. The Chrysler and a brand-new C card in his name were a part of the bargain he had made with Ruth Fox, as well as the bills; God only knew how she had obtained the C card, but apparently it had not caused her undue inconvenience, for her smile as she handed him the envelope containing the card and money and the car's papers had been silky and dazzling. Johnny knew his mother-in-law to be a woman of considerable resources.

Rip sighed in the kitchen and pulled Nell closer to her. It had taken her an hour to quiet the baby's screams and almost another hour of rocking to restore the huge, slate-blue eyes to their lucent roundness. She was a good baby

171

as well as a beautiful one; since her birth the previous December she had regularly slept through the nights, and cried only when she was wet or hungry, and broke into winning, trilling gurgles and coos and wreathing grins whenever anyone bent over her crib. When she was left alone, she slept peacefully or lay and burbled quietly to herself and waved her hands and feet; it took little to please Nell. It was as if from the moment of her birth, which had been endless and agonizing compared to the births of Yancey and Paul, she had been motivated solely by the desire to please.

Rip loved both the older children of Hebe and Johnny Geiger, but to Nell she felt from the beginning a tie that was almost physical, as if the birth cord had connected the baby with her own body instead of Hebe Geiger's. Not even to small, sweet-tempered, thriving Jacob Lee, whom she loved with a fierce and protective passion, did she feel such a powerful, mystic tie.

The baby stirred and waved her tiny fists, and Rip saw that the angry purplish red on the side of her face and head was fading. There would be a bruise, though. Witch hazel would be good for that. Her long hand went to the baby's crown and gently sought out the soft spot buried under the drift of silky, silver-brown hair. Like clean baby mouse fur it was; her father's hair. The spot was all right, not touched by the incarnadine smear. Rip's heart was still thumping uncomfortably with the aftermath of the baby's fall. She had not watched as carefully as she should; she had been lax in her primary purpose. Johnny Geiger's disappearance should not, after all, have been a total surprise to her. True, she had not heard the words that he and Miss Ruth had exchanged in the little parlor the previous night, but she had seen the money change hands. Rip had long been a watcher in the nights. She should have been able to figure it out, should have known when he did not return for lunch, and Hebe began to fret . . .

But she had not, and so she had not been present when Hebe, with Nell cradled in the crook of one arm, went into her bedroom and found on the bedside table the note and the ring that weighted it down. And when she had read the note and screamed the terrible scream that galvanized the household, and had fecklessly dropped the baby to the rug and run shrieking down the hall to her mother, there had been no one there to pick the stunned and mewling infant up from the floor and rock her and bathe her small head. Rip had rushed in from the nursery to find Hebe howling incoherently in Ruth's arms, and Ruth rocking her back and forth crooning, "Hush, now. Hush, now. Everything is going to be all right. Mama's here. Mama's not going to leave you, not ever again. Mama will take care of you."

Hebe had gone off into one of her convulsions then, a mild one, but strong enough to leave her limp and dazed and vague, and to cause her to soil herself. And so it was only after Dr. Hopkins had been called and Rip had sponged Hebe off and was bundling her soiled under-clothes into a ball for the laundry that Hebe whispered, "The baby. Oh, Rip, the baby. I don't know what I did with her . . ."

And Rip had dashed into Hebe and Johnny's bedroom to find Nell on the floor, only then just recovering enough breath for the piping shrieks of pain and fear and outrage that had lasted through and beyond the doctor's visit. He had examined her carefully and pronounced her all right before seeing to Hebe, but had told Rip that she must be taken away from the confusion and kept very still and quiet, and watched through the night for signs of concus-sion. Rip had rocked and crooned and rocked and crooned until the screaming subsided into whimpering, and then into hiccuping, and then into drowsy silence, and after that had brought her down to the warm haven of the kitchen to heat a bottle for her. She had been taking bottles regu-larly, supplemented with Hebe's thin milk whenever Hebe felt she could nurse her, but Rip knew that after today Hebe's milk would be bitter gall to the baby and would soon dry up.

She knew, too, that by bedtime all of Old Sparta would be shaking their heads and speaking of the abandonment of poor Hebe Fox by that strange Yankee (and Nazi, like as not) she had married, the one that had killed dear Paul Fox as surely as if he had pointed a gun at him and pulled the trigger. All their sympathy would be for wispy little Hebe Fox (no one in Old Sparta had ever called her Geiger), who never did have gumption enough to spit in a privy, and her three poor little children. One did not think of Ruth Fox in terms of sympathy.

"Here, Rip," said Carrie, who had replaced old Pinky in the kitchen of the Foxes some time before, on this day of departures. "Give that baby some of this here custard on yo' finger an' see do she like it. I cool some in a bottle for her if she do. Well, like I says to Red while ago, it ain't like he one of us. He ain't never belong here in this house."

And he had not. If Johnny Geiger had lived in the South longer than the three weeks he had dwelled in Sparta before marrying Hebe, he would have seen that he might sleep and eat and beget his children at Fox's Earth but he would never truly live there. Ruth Fox knew this, of course; Paul Fox had known it for perhaps the forty or fifty seconds left to him after finding that this sycophantic Irishman was his son-in-law; Rip knew it, with sorrow and fear deep in her bones for Hebe; the other servants knew it instinctively and snubbed him unbearably out of the sight of Ruth and Hebe. But Hebe never knew it at all, and Johnny Geiger, when he wondered why his place at the dining table of Fox's Earth did not earn him the fellowship and good will of the born sons of the other great white houses and the smiles of their pretty wives, could only conclude, miserably and fuzzily, that they all blamed him for Paul's death. This was true, but it was not the reason he was never accepted in Sparta.

It had not originally been in Johnny's mind to live at Fox's Earth from the beginning of their marriage. Even he could not have aspired to that soaring pinnacle of perfection. He had thought to rent a neat little house on one of the tree-graced old streets near the university, where most of the faculty lived, until such time as Paul Fox should relent and welcome his daughter and son-in-law back forever under the flat ancestral roof . . . perhaps after the children had begun to arrive.

But Paul Fox's death had changed his plans. For once in her life Ruth Fox seemed to lose her awesome composure and went crashing down to sorrow and despair. She had cried and sobbed so that a grim-faced Dr. Hopkins had had to give her a powerful sedative by injection before he could raise her up off the supine body of the obviously deceased Paul and certify him dead.

Hebe was all but destroyed with grief. Johnny, who wanted only to turn tail and flee from the house of the man who had died staring and pointing and gobbling wordlessly at him, found himself forced to stay and tend to a brand-new wife who had turned into a stranger, one who screamed witlessly and uncontrollably and then slid into an eerie sort of fit in which she jerked and ground her tongue and wet herself and finally lapsed into unconsciousness. Rip and the doctor took her upstairs along with the stumbling, lolling doll that was Ruth, and it was Johnny who sat silently and guiltily in the foyer of Fox's Earth beside the sheeted figure of Paul Fox and waited for the hearse from Cromartie's to come and take him away.

After that terrible dawn, there was never any question that they would live at Fox's Earth. Ruth was inconsolable; no one could comfort her but Hebe, and she would have no one in her darkened bedroom but Rip and this ineffectual daughter to whom she had always been bulwark and fortress. That Hebe herself was sodden and prostrate and no use to her at all did not seem to matter. For the rest of that first day she clutched at Hebe's weeping form and sobbed over and over, "Don't leave Mama, baby! Promise Mama that you won't leave her!"

When Hebe at last remembered that she was married and had a husband lurking uncomfortably somewhere outside in the upstairs corridors and byways, and rose to go to him, Ruth gave a great cry and hissed, "You made me a widow, you and your fornicating and your running off in the night like rabbits to get at each other sooner! You can at least stay with me now!" And Hebe collapsed again in guilt and despair and sorrow, and stayed at her mother's side. Johnny Geiger slept that second night of his marriage in a small bedroom he found down a hall in the back of the house, as far away from that room of sobbing women and recriminations and the staring eyes of servants as he could get. He never knew that it was the room Alicia Fox had died in. Indeed, in all his eight years at Fox's Earth he never heard the name of Alicia Fox mentioned.

They buried her son, Horatio Paul Fox, in the graceful white marble Fox mausoleum in the old Confederate cemetery beside her and his father, Claudius, and it seemed to Johnny Geiger that all of Sparta was at the cemetery, and all of Sparta was in decorous tears, and all of Sparta fixed him with cold, remote and accusing eyes. These were precisely the people he had thought to move among, trading jocularities and back slaps with the men and pretty gallantries and occasional discreet pats lower down with the women, and he shifted miserably under their stares. It did not seem an auspicious beginning.

Afterward Johnny had gone back to Fox's Earth with

his wife and mother-in-law, and Rip had appeared at the door and borne Hebe off to the upstairs region of the house. Johnny was left alone to bob crazily like a castaway cork in the wake of Ruth Fox as she moved graciously about in the sea of mourners who had come back from the cemetery to nibble at the platters of ham and turkey and chicken, and the cakes and casseroles and molded salads that adorned the Hepplewhite dining table. It was an astonishing display of food for the depths of the Depression, and it had, Johnny knew, been arriving in a steady stream since Paul died two days before. He had answered the doorbell himself on several occasions, when Robert was off on an errand in the big Chrysler, and some of the people who stood there with covered platters or baskets looked as if the offerings they held had been the last in the chicken coop or larder. Johnny thought it strange and foolish for the clearly indigent to bring their humble provender to this house of staggering plenty, but he noticed that Ruth nodded at each new offering without turning a gilt hair, and so he held his silence. There was much, he concluded, that he did not understand about these attractive southerners.

An inkling of the depth of his incomprehension came when, casting about for something to say to a deaf, purple-haired old lady with whom he was marooned in a corner of the dining room, he attempted to make a joke about Paul Fox. Johnny had concluded, upon seeing the crowd and the food, that this ritual was, after all, only a slightly more elegant version of the Irish wakes which had regularly made the days and frequently the nights clamorous back in Johnstown and, grateful that he knew the drill, bellowed a little anecdote about Paul Fox's great girth into the dried-persimmon ear of the old lady. The resulting slow, freezing stare was unique in his experience, and his humiliation was complete when the old lady shouted in the clarion tones of the long-deaf to a middle-aged woman standing behind her, "Who is that tacky boy? That's not Hebe Fox's husband, is it? I can't believe Ruth Fox would give that common trash house room . . but then they ran off, didn't they? Well, he's probably been in her bloomers and they had to get married. A Yankee can't keep it buttoned up, you know."

The younger woman, obviously her daughter, tried in an agony of embarrassment to shush her mother, but the entire assemblage had heard the old harridan, and her words followed Johnny Geiger as he fled in full rout up the curving stairs to their bedroom, where Hebe still whimpered in the dark arms of Rip. There was not a soul present who did not agree with the old lady; he could read it in their eyes even though they would have died before saying so in his hearing, or in that of Hebe or Ruth. Johnny Geiger crept away to the little room where he had spent the first night at Fox's Earth and locked himself in with only the unfelt, ineffectual shade of Alicia Fox for company, and he did not come out until hunger forced him forth to forage at midnight in the darkened kitchen for leftover funeral meats. He did not sleep well that night, and in truth he would never sleep really well under the roof of Fox's Earth.

Ruth Fox seemed to bloom in her widowhood into a new dimension of beauty and fulfillment. It was not that she obviously reveled in that state (though alone in her room after the funeral she had laughed in silent exultation and paced the room like a triumphant tigress, whirling as if an ermine cape swirled about her ankles, holding her white arms out as if to embrace a lover). Rip, passing Ruth's door with a tray for Hebe, had heard her cry, "Oh, Mama, it was worth it! You told me truly; it was!" There was a small, charged silence, and then Ruth said, with all Rip would ever hear of love and tenderness in her voice, "Good-bye, Mama." On the other side of the closed door, Rip shivered as if in some visitant wind that passed by, and down the stairs, and out of the house. But she never again heard the voice of Ruth Fox lifted to the mother who was not there, never until another twilight exactly forty-three years later, and then upon that same stair.

No, the new radiance of fullness and beauty was more an ontological phenomenon, as if all the rhythms and tides of Ruth's life had moved inexorably and by intricate design toward this moment and this state, and had culminated in the perfection that was Ruth Yancey Fox as a widow of forty-three years. And, indeed, they had.

After an entirely suitable period of mourning for Paul, there began a time at Fox's Earth that Hebe always thought of later as the Good Time. Ruth was going out again. She went out far more as widow than she ever had as wife, though she never again in her lifetime left the great pillared portico of Fox's Earth on the arm of any man who

177

was not her kin. Gradually, as the period of mourning receded further and further into the town's collective memory, she began to become overtly active in civic and charitable affairs, and eventually sat on as many boards—indeed, some of the same ones—as Paul Fox had. Those with whom she served came to depend on her near-mystic financial intuitions and her utter and surprising lack of cluttering feminine sentiment, and they soon came to admire these qualities even more than her ripe and dizzying beauty and silvery voice and slow, sensual smile. "If you want it done, give it to Ruth Fox" became a watchword in Sparta, and Ruth's influence moved out from the affairs of Fox's Earth to embrace those of the entire town.

During these days she was more loving and attentive to Hebe than she had been even in her childhood, lavishing hours of time and motherly attention on the girl and gradually loosening the determined grasp of Johnny Geiger. She planned small treats . . . little drives together in the Chrysler, shopping trips with lunches or stops for ice-cream sodas or afternoon movies . . . and brought home from Atlanta drifts of ruffled, girlish dresses and fragile silk underwear. She redecorated Paul Fox's bedroom for the young couple, making of it a virtual bower of frills and swags and ribbons and flounces, so that Hebe in it was a fragrant baby in a perfect nursery once more.

But Johnny Geiger could not get his breath in that room. He caught his feet and hands in cobwebby flounces, and was afraid to put his feet up on the silken surfaces of things, and could not sit comfortably on the frail, spidery chairs and love seats, and had no room in the bulging closet to hang even his meager wardrobe . . . for Ruth's largesse did not extend to her son-in-law.

"A man doesn't want his mother-in-law picking out his clothes or giving him money, for heaven's sake," she would cry when Hebe, opening yet another Rich's box, would protest that Johnny had no gift. And she would smile extravagantly at Johnny, and he would grin back, his mouth hurting with the effort. The point of honor which she so blithely assumed for him escaped him entirely; he thought it niggardly and malicious of her to neglect him while heaping his wife with exquisite clothes, and ground his white teeth in his answering smiles. But he dared say nothing to her. It was his own intermittently jobless state that prohibited the purchase of suitable clothes.

But Hebe noticed none of his resentment. Within a year she was more the helpless, cosseted daughter of Ruth Fox than she had ever been as a child. In that golden time Hebe had everything in the world she had ever wanted . . . the undivided attention of the beautiful and adored mother, heaps and billows of lovely clothes, days full of treats, her ubiquitous movie magazines and radio romances . . . and the hot, delirious nights tumbling with her handsome young husband in the organdy-canopied tester bed. But for Johnny Geiger, drowning in ruffles and suffocating in the musk of women, the bedding of Hebe was the only spontaneous and unalloyed pleasure in his life, and even that was beginning to pall by the time she became pregnant with Yancey, for Hebe was genuinely and exhaustingly insatiable.

But in the beginning, and even up until the birth of his second child, Paul, he was hopeful that the perfectly carved, gemlike life he had envisioned for himself might still materialize, even though considerably modified. Ruth had gone out of her way to be helpful to him and make him feel welcome. She had never once, by so much as a gesture or an eye-blink, made him feel responsible for the death of her husband. Only the silent eyes of the servants and the town blamed him, and as his first days at Fox's Earth became a year, those eyes seemed to accept him, as even the steeliest eventually will.

But they did not warm to him, nor brighten at his approach. No matter how hard he tried, Johnny Geiger could not seem to make glad the heart of Sparta. He did not know why. It was not, he didn't think, the southerner's traditional and truculent dislike of the federal government and its representatives, for Ruth took care of that stigma not a week after he had married Hebe.

"Johnny, honey," she said to him one morning at breakfast, resting her pointed chin in her hands and leaning toward him entrancingly in the sunlight of the little breakfast room, "Are you really and truly devoted to that old job of yours? I mean, is your heart just set on it?"

Johnny, who had not given the neglected Oconee flood plain a thought since he had become a married man and moved into Fox's Earth, came back to workaday reality with an uncomfortable thud. He had not even been back to his mournful rented room to collect his mail; he could just imagine the tone of the letters and telegrams that

179

would be piled up there now. He leaned forward across the table toward his mother-in-law, switching on his winsome smile and crinkling his sherry eyes.

"Not so's you'd notice it," he said gaily. "What did you have in mind, Mom?"

Ruth's teeth ground at the "Mom," and the easy familiarity scalded through her veins like boiling water, but she smiled even more vividly at him, and put her shining head to one side.

"Well, I was just thinking. I could help you, if you aren't too proud and silly to accept a little help from your mother-in-law. Chiles Davenport was telling me at the bank board meeting just the other day that he needs somebody to help out in his office since that ungrateful boy of his up and went into the Baptist seminary. It wouldn't be much right now, with practically nobody buying or selling land, but it would be a steady little income and a nice office, and of course the Davenports have been in Sparta almost as long as the Foxes, and Chiles was one of my dear Paul's closest boyhood friends. He would be glad to have my son-in-law in his firm. The prospects could be quite good if you're patient and willing to work hard, and the social contacts would be . . . awfully nice . . . for you and Hebe."

Johnny's heart leapt up. If he could not penetrate their ranks by charming or marrying his way in, he would work his way into the inner circle. Gradually the business camaraderie would expand to include real masculine friendships; Johnny would hunt and fish and golf with the men of Church Street (though never in his pale, city-pavemented life had he held a gaming gun or a rod and reel or a golf club), and would drink with them in the men's locker room and grill of the country club, and would greet them at the great front doors of Fox's Earth with a highball in his hand and perhaps a velvet smoking jacket as they came to the dinners and cocktail parties that he and Hebe would give. Ruth, of course, would remain the grande dame of the house, but as the only man in residence he would soon come to be accepted as the man of the house, and whenever they thought of Fox's Earth, they would think of it as "Johnny Geiger's place" . . .

As sweet and heavy as opium the images clouded and swarmed in his brain, and he stared at Ruth, unaware that his eyes were a trifle glazed and his lips slightly and moistly parted. She thought he looked like a boated shad.

"Well, what do you think of my little idea?" Ruth asked finally between clenched teeth, and he focused on the present again.

"I'm truly and humbly grateful, Mom," he said earnestly and seriously. "I'll work hard and be a credit to you and Hebe, and I won't forget your generosity. I'll call Mr. Davenport . . . Chiles . . . right after breakfast."

"I took the liberty of doing that for you," she said, looking up at him obliquely through her lashes. "He's expecting you at eleven. Johnny dear, do forgive me if I seem a meddlesome old woman and an interfering mother-in-law. It's just that I want the best for you, and Hebe, too, of course, and it seems silly not to use the poor little influence I have when it might make things a little smoother for my handsome son-in-law."

"I could never feel that way, Mom," he said fervently, and rose from the table and came around and aimed a swift and egregious kiss at her cheek. She flinched, and Johnny, surprised, planted the kiss on her neck. The flesh was cold and the cords in her neck stood out like bas-relief. He looked at her, disturbed; had he been too familiar? But she smiled gaily up at him and said, "Run along now, and get all dressed up for your new career, and do go by the telegraph office and tell those silly folks in Washington you've got bigger fish to fry. The idea of *you* in khaki!"

So he went off up the stairs whistling jauntily, and when Hebe drifted by on her drowsy way down to breakfast, still in her rumpled nightgown, and said, "Where are you going in such a hurry, you handsome thing?" he replied, with a lilt in his voice, "Off to catch this town by the tail and show it who's boss!"

Johnny did not catch Sparta by the tail. To the contrary, Sparta soon had Johnny Geiger by the tail and its well-shod foot firmly if gently upon his neck, and it became gradually obvious who was boss. Johnny was duly and with much florid and flat-eyed rhetoric welcomed into the realty firm of Chiles Davenport (who was, unbeknownst to anyone but Ruth and her lawyer, struggling to make regular payments on a note which she held), and presently a discreet and properly engraved announcement went out to all of Sparta that mattered in such things, heralding the inclusion of Johnny Geiger into the old firm. Johnny fingered the raised lettering on the card with something approaching rapture; who in Sparta could refuse him their homes when it would be he who bought and sold them?

But a year went by, and he made no sales to speak of. The fact was that he was naturally and abysmally inept at his job, never perceiving the complex, bone-deep and earth-old web of emotion these volatile southerners wove about their lands and their homes. They would no more put their properties into the sly white hands of an urban northerner than they would hand over the care of their children to some sallow, sharp-faced poor white woman.

Johnny's daughter Yancey was born in 1935, a long, elegant infant with Ruth Fox's blue eyes and a headful of gilt hair and a finished, rather imperious small face, and from the very first breath of her life she demanded . . . and commanded . . . the attention of almost everyone in the household. Her cries were strong and clear and piercing and constant; she was not ill or puny, simply unwilling to be left unattended. Ruth had been inordinately pleased by the birth of her first grandchild, and had taken her from the nurse's arms and held her at arm's length when she was first brought to the fuddled Hebe in the hospital, studying the small, red, indignant face and listening to the insistent cry.

"A big, strong girl," she said to Hebe, who did not miss but did not understand either the odd note in her mother's voice, which was triumph. Rip, who had come with Ruth to the hospital to see her new charge, looked assessingly at Ruth Fox as she held the baby aloft, but said nothing.

"She'll be named Yancey, after my family," Ruth said, handing the child matter-of-factly to Rip and turning to Hebe.

"Oh, no," Hebe said drowsily. "I'm going to call her Greta. For Greta Garbo. Because it was after seeing *Anna Christie* that I knew I wanted to marry Johnny. Greta Geiger. Don't you think that's pretty?"

"I think it sounds like an immigrant hairdresser," Ruth said icily, and Hebe was silent. There *was* a rather harsh, Teutonic ring to it . . .

"But Johnny and I decided . . ." she ventured weakly.

"Johnny is a reasonable man who wants the best for his new daughter," Ruth said, smiling radiantly at him. "He knows that in the South, in certain circles, it is always proper for children to be given the names of their families.

Especially when the names are as old and respected as Yancey and Fox."

Johnny, seeing the wisdom of this, agreed eagerly with Ruth and abandoned the exotic "Greta" in an instant. He did not know . . . and never would . . . that his daughter bore the name of a mad drunkard, for Cater Yancey had suffered a sea change with the passage of time, and even Hebe knew her grandfather only to be a minister come to Sparta from farther north in Georgia. She envisioned him, on the rare occasions she thought of him, as a white-haired, silver-tongued old gentleman in the pulpit of some dim, time-smelling old church similar to the one in which she had grown up. Rip alone in the household knew for what and whom the first grandchild of Ruth Fox was named, and the name crashed in her ears with a long resonance. It rang like an omen: YANCEY. Once again Rip must try to guard well.

She took over the child's care when Hebe came home from the hospital, and again there was a baby in the old nursery, and Rip's days and nights at Fox's Earth were round and full. Hebe gratefully abandoned the care of her daughter to Rip, and took her husband back into her bed with alacrity, and her days spun on unbroken much as they had before Yancey was born. She tried to nurse the child, but the sharp, beaklike ridges of the voracious little gums hurt her breasts and the enforced stillness bored her, and after Johnny had stormed from their bedroom twice because she had flinched her sore breasts away from his hands, she abandoned the nursing to a wet nurse Rip found in Suches. Small Yancey became the true child of Rip, as Hebe had before her, and Johnny, especially, often had to stop and think, when he heard the faint, peremptory cries from the nursery, what baby there was at Fox's Earth. He was never to feel like a father; the most profound and honest emotion Johnny Geiger ever felt for his children was the mercurial fondness of some self-absorbed older brother, and that came later.

But he was glad of the baby, for he felt that now, as a married man with a child, he would automatically increase in stature in the world of downtown Sparta; he would be seen anew, washed in his new luster of responsible fatherhood. He went back to his work after Yancey's birth with renewed vigor and hope. But though they congratulated him heartily, and slapped him on the back, and made properly goatish remarks about his prowess as a husband, and two or three of them even asked him to have after-work drinks in the men's grill at the club, nothing really came of it, and he was soon back where he had been when he first joined the firm, moving unimportant papers around on the polished surface of his desk and chasing about on dusty back roads on the poorer fringes of Depression-sapped Sparta, following up non-existent leads on drought-blighted and about-to-be-foreclosed properties.

Piece by piece, shard by shard, the dream disintegrated. He came to realize, finally and bitterly, that he was not one of them and would never be; the North and the harsh, abrasive "Geiger" lay around his neck like an albatross. A son was born on December 16, 1939, at two o'clock in the morning, after a wild, skidding ride back from Atlanta, where Hebe had cajoled Johnny Geiger, against his better judgment, into taking her for the premiere of *Gone With the Wind*. She had been beside herself with joy, had pressed herself recklessly into the crowd around the spotlit, bunting-draped Loew's Grand Theater, and the crowd, recoiling from her vast pregnancy, had made way for her. Johnny had fought his way behind her, in mortal terror that she would deliver on the spot, and so it was that they stood at the very coveted curb itself when the stars who had shone on the screen and in Hebe's head so long and vividly walked in the shining flesh directly in front of her. Ecstasy flooded her as her fingertips brushed those of sleepy-eyed Leslie Howard, but pure rapture buckled her knees when Clark Gable, seeing her lovely, blinded face gaping at him above her jutting belly, reached over and picked up her hand and kissed it.

The shock of that kiss, Hebe maintained forever after, broke her water, and it was so soon after their wild drive back to the hospital in Sparta that Ruth Fox later said it was "common as gully dirt" that the boy child was born.

"He's got to be Rhett," Hebe mooed mindlessly, when they told her that she had a fine son. "He absolutely *has* to be Rhett Geiger. It was an omen, as plain as day. An omen."

And, "nonsense," Ruth snapped again. "What kind of a common movie-star name is Rhett Geiger? He's going to be Paul Fox Geiger, just like we planned. What on earth would people say if your firstborn son wasn't named after his maternal grandfather? Unless..." and she looked at

184

Johnny benevolently . . . "you'd rather he be called after *your* poor father, darling?"

Johnny shook his head wordlessly. His father's name had been Padraic; he had stubbornly kept to the old spelling. Even Johnny knew that Paddy Geiger could never enter the same doors that Paul Fox Geiger could. What was more, he knew that Ruth knew that he knew. Some of the exultation of the night and the birth of his son bled out of him, and he heard the familiar faraway sound of great doors shutting once more, firmly and finally.

This time they did not open again. The world went to war, and while the United States again held coyly back, there was little doubt in the minds of most people that it was only a matter of time until American boys once again tossed and bucketed across the gray Atlantic to fight alongside the young Britons against the revived and ravening Hun. It was not a good time to be a German in America; it was not a good time even to have had, however far back, a German perched on the limb of one's family tree. Johnny Geiger was as Irish as Paddy's pig, as they said in the streets of Johnstown when he was growing up, but his good Austrian great-grandfather had left him his stolid, proper burgher's name as well as his strange, sunlit sherry eyes, and in provincial and truculent Sparta, that name soon became his final nemesis. The harshness of the syllables that to drawl-soothed southern ears had once sounded only citified and northern now became alien and ominous, a blunt and brutish club that hammered at their tender, touchy, war-sharpened sensibilities.

"What kind of name is Geiger?" Johnny overheard one venerable octogenarian blurt at a Kiwanis meeting one day, after he had passed the group in which the old bastard sat.

"Sounds like some kind of Nazi name to me. God only knows what he's up to out there on those country roads all day, by himself. God only knows who he's meetin' and talkin' to."

The old man was joshed and shushed and jeered hastily, but Johnny heard the level of the men's voices settle swiftly into a low and earnest drone, and his back burned with the smoking pits their eyes left upon it.

He did not go back to the Kiwanis Club, or to the Rotary or the Chamber of Commerce meetings, either. And he began to plead extra work when Ruth or Hebe suggested an outing to the country club. Ruth had heard the talk, and kept her own counsel. It would need only a nudge from her now. She could afford to bide her time.

His third and last child was born on a soft gray December Sunday, after almost twenty hours of brutal, grinding labor that left Hebe faded and confused for weeks after. Johnny had spent the day putting up a swing for six-year-old Yancey in the back garden; he had been banished from the hospital by Ruth, who had said that Hebe did not want him to see her like she was. This suited Johnny perfectly well. Hospitals frightened and intimidated him with their frowning hushes and acrid odor of mortality.

He had found recently that he enjoyed his oldest daughter more than he could have imagined. She was more a distinct and delineated miniature person than a child, and had a polished and complete perfection about her that drew and held the eye as surely as her splendid grandmother did. She was a pretty sight that morning in her plaid skirt and saddle shoes and argyll socks that matched his own; Rip had dressed her like her father on this day of scurrying and strangeness and the absence of her mother and grandmother, thinking that it would amuse and distract her. And it had; she had gone to play with her father in the back garden just as if her mother had not been taken away in screaming agony a scant five hours before, and would not be coming home with another usurping bundle in her arms. Yancey doted fiercely on two-year-old Paul, with an intensity that was, at times, almost alarming, but she did not want a sister.

"I'm your only little girl," she said to her father, as he straddled the low limb from which he was hanging the rope swing, his gleaming brown-and-white saddle shoes swinging in time to the tune he was whistling.

"That you are," he said cheerfully, thinking how pretty she was going to be when she grew up. Not like him, though; she was Fox down to her delicate bones. The boy, too. Johnny found that this no longer bothered him in the least.

"What if Mama gets another girl, though?"

"Well, she'll just have to be Mama's girl, because I've already got one, and you're it," he said.

"Always?"

"Always."

Not an hour after the call came from the hospital to tell

him that Eleanor Steed Geiger had come wearily into the world via Caesarean section, he switched on the radio in the little parlor to hear that the Japanese had bombed Pearl Harbor in Hawaii, and the United States of America was at last at war.

In March of the following year, Johnny found that flat feet were going to keep him out of that last man's refuge, World War II, and when he came gray-faced and dead-eyed into the foyer of Fox's Earth from his physical, Ruth knew that her moment had come at last. After dinner that evening, with Hebe tucked up into her organdy bed and the older children asleep in the nursery and the new baby staring bluely at Rip as she rocked her in the kitchen, and the other servants gone home, Ruth smoothed her skirt down her slim hips and wet her lips and climbed the stairs to the little room where Johnny Geiger was sleeping once again, until Hebe recovered enough strength to take him back into her bed. He had come to care very little when this would be; Johnny Geiger cared very little about anything anymore. Ruth found him lying on his back on the narrow iron bed, arms crossed beneath his head, staring at the ceiling. Horace Heidt and his Alemite Brigadiers brayed from the bedside radio, but Johnny did not appear to be listening. His sherry eyes were as fixed and opaque as those of a cooling squirrel.

"Johnny, sweetie," said Ruth Yancey Fox softly, "could you come down to the little parlor for a minute? There's something I'd like to talk to you about."

In the kitchen of Fox's Earth the next day, in the dancing stipple of rain light from the walls and ceiling, Rip looked down at the baby in her arms. Where the red had seeped out of Nell's cheek it was as white and pure and sweetly polished as it had been when she came home from the hospital. Because of the Caesarean section, Nell had been a lovely baby from the very beginning.

Rip began to rock with the baby from her waist, back and forth, back and forth. She hummed under her breath, a tuneless chant. The baby looked up at her roundly and gravely. It was very still and quiet in the kitchen. Ruth and Hebe, mother and daughter now and nothing else, were huddled together upstairs in this great house of women, and Carrie had gone to take the boiled custard to Yancey and Paul, being minded by Rusky in the nursery. There was no one in the great, echoing downstairs of Fox's Earth but Rip and small Nell Fox. Nell Geiger, Rip amended to herself.

Aloud she said to the baby, "Po' little child what ain't got no daddy. Po' little baby. Rip help you. Rip be here. God gon' help me help all these here chirruns without no daddy, 'cause ain't nobody else in this house gon' do it."

Part Three

❧ ❧

NELL

17

UNDER THE steep wooden steps that led from the back porch down to the rear veranda of Fox's Earth was a small space enclosed by a cage of green-painted lattice strips, a close, damp, mold-smelling cave that housed the electric and water meters. The meterman could reach the meters through a little square door cut into the lattice strips for the purpose, of a size that would admit a man's hands and arms, or a medium-sized dog, had a dog been able to reach that high from the veranda. Nell Geiger had found when she was four or five that by standing on a cinder block she could just barely reach the door and wriggle, snakelike, through it, and drop down into the earth-floored lattice cage, where she could regard the comings and goings of the rear world of Fox's Earth through the black and brilliantly golden diamonds of lattice light, in a small and somehow magical house that was, in all the vast richness of space in the big house where she lived, uniquely her own place.

No one else came to the cage; the adults could not have fit into it; her tall, imperious sister Yancey was too vividly self-absorbed to care about it had she known of its existence; and her brother Paul, gentle and remote and abstracted into his world of books and boy's comings and goings with Rip's grandson Jacob Lee, had somehow never discovered it. The cage was a sort of gift that only a solitary dreaming child might receive, a child who had need of shadows and nooks and secrets, and Nell spent a great deal of her childhood staring out at her altered world through the magical scrim of the harlequin lattices. The altered perspective was rich and strange, and the closeness of the cage around her was like arms that held her in perfect love and safety. Like a mouse admiring from the security of its hiding place the larger world of great fabulous cats, Nell never loved and admired the god-inhabited world of Fox's Earth so much as when she viewed it from her secret lair beneath the back stairs. Then, curled into the nest of filthy old quilts that she had shoved through the little door when she first discovered the cage, munching apples or tea cakes from Carrie's oven, it seemed to her that she was one of them, the beautiful, powerful, golden people of Fox's Earth; that she rested in her own den only momentarily and out of choice before moving indolently back out among them to take up the heroic communal life they shared; that when she appeared among them again she would be as tall and lithe and radiant to look upon as they, and they would know her as their own and equal, and would greet her as such.

But always, when she crawled from the cage and stood blinking in the oddly flat and unpatterned sunlight of the back veranda once again, she was only small Nell Geiger after all, slight of form and voice, strengthless and powerless, forced to tip her silky, silver-brown head far back and lift her great topaz eyes far up to the tall pillars of light that were Gamma and Yancey, the shining totem of bronze that was Rip, the slender, wavering foxfire that was Mama. Even to Paul who shone in her eyes like the sun and whom she loved totally, she had to lift her head, to look up. Out of the cage, the great winds of God seemed once again to blow unchecked around her, and she became only inconsequential Nell, the baby, the youngest and the last of the Foxes of Fox's Earth.

So the cage was to Nell refuge and comfort for many of her earliest years on earth, and this was well, for despite Rip's best efforts, Nell Steed Geiger often had need of comfort.

On a bright, diamond-hard January afternoon in 1951 nine-year-old Nell huddled in the quilt nest in the cage and squinted at the diamonded veranda through tears, her hands pressed tightly over her ears to shut out the chorus of voices that called for her over and over: "Nell! Nell! Come out here this minute, young lady, or you'll wish you had! Nell! Where are you, Nell?"

There were three voices in the chorus now: Gamma's, Mama's, and Rip's. This morning there had been only one, Rip's, and it had not threatened or thrummed with distress and exasperation but had sought her softly, bearing the same heavy freight of grief that she felt in her own chest, but without the anger and outrage. Even for Rip, whom she loved as she loved Paul, Nell had not come out of her hiding place, for the enormity of the morning was too large to be borne outside the arms of the cage, and for a long time it was Rip's voice alone that ranged through Fox's Earth seeking the smallest Fox.

For a long time the others had not known she was missing. They had thought she was still asleep in her room upstairs next to Rip's in the merciless bright dawn when they bore Yancey away to the train station, and it was hours before they returned home again. Gamma was driving the Chrysler herself . . . odd in itself, on this strange and terrible day . . . and she parked it on the oval just beyond the back veranda, so that Nell saw and heard Mama when they came in, heard Mama's familiar but still terrifying sobs and cries, heard Gamma's soothing sing-song in reply, heard Rip's indistinct murmur and caught her own name, heard Gamma's answering snap of annoyance and alarm, heard Mama's keening howl: "Oh, dear God, am I to lose my baby now, too?"

She saw them, too, saw them pause and look around the bare brilliant back yard, then hasten up the back steps and into the house, where, dimly, the long litany of her own name began: "Nell, Nell! Where are you, Nell?" It was four o'clock now, and the golden diamonds of the lattice light were dulling into lead, and Nell could no longer feel her feet or her fingers or the tears on her face. She had been in the cage since seven o'clock that morning.

The departure of Yancey from Fox's Earth had been a sickening, breathtaking blow to Nell, but, huddling numbly in the quilts now, she thought to herself that it was not exactly a surprise. It had happened before, the previous spring, when it had been Paul who was taken in the pearled, mimosa-heavy dawn and half led, half dragged to the Chrysler, his cries of outrage and ineffectual fury quickly stilled as the solid, upholstered doors of the back seat closed upon him. That time, Nell was not awake and did not see Paul go; she woke only later, after Gamma and Robert were back from the train station, to find that Paul was gone and his room was as stark and neat and desiccated as if no boy had ever lived there, and that her sister Yancey was in a state of screaming hysterics in her room upstairs. Nell had fled that day, too, to the cage under the steps. She was there when Jacob Lee stumbled down the back steps over her head, snuffling heavily and mumbling under his breath in anguish, and loped through the shrubbery at the back of the garden toward the little house where he had lived with Rip before he moved into the boys' haven of the garage apartment to study with Paul. Nell saw with alarm and astonishment that he was crying; great, milky tears left opaque snail's tracks on his polished cheeks, and his face was twisted grotesquely.

Jacob Lee was four years older than Paul and a scant half-year older than Yancey, but he was as large as a man, and he cried as a man would cry, roughly and reluctantly, and with a rusty, unused sound that shocked ears used to the easy tears of childhood. Nell had never thought of him as any particular age; he was larger than she by far, of course, but then so was Paul . . . so was everybody. He had a bright, clear child's face and a child's soft, untroubled eyes, and his smile was quick and sweet. He laughed and sang and capered around Paul with an uninhibited animal glee and energy that was a perfect foil for Paul's fragility and gentle gravity. Their friendship ran deep, and was as simple and spontaneous as earth and air.

Paul had been, from his birth, a frail child. By the time he was ten he had largely outgrown the asthma that had kept him confined to the house so much of the time, but the compensating passion for books and solitude that sustained him during the time of his illness never flickered or waned, and the biddability and sweetness of temper that sprang from constant association with soft-voiced, indulgent women were never to leave him, either. Yancey, four years older, adored her grave, quiet, small brother as she never did Nell, but her quick, imperious ways and boisterous vitality were curbed and shushed around him, lest he begin the terrible, choking coughing, and so for the first few years of his life she treated him gingerly, waiting for the time that he would be wholeheartedly hers, and Paul burrowed into his beloved books undisturbed by anyone at Fox's Earth. And when at last he shrugged off the constricting swaddles of illness and asthma and stood blinking in the sunlight, starved for adventure and mischief and his very childhood, the first figure his newly cleared blue eyes lit upon was the brimming, grinning golden person of Jacob Lee.

From that moment, their friendship absorbed and delighted both boys. That Jacob Lee was on the brink of adolescence altered none of the egalitarian quality of the relationship. Indeed, it nurtured it. Paul's naturally assumed superiority, born of whiteness and mental acuity and privilege, was offset by Jacob Lee's size and age and athletic prowess and intimate acquaintance with the woods and creeks and byroads of Sparta, and, in the manner of black and white children of a certain South, they were together at every waking instant that was not occupied by Paul's schooling and Jacob Lee's intermittent and enforced tenure at the small black public school in Suches. When they were not away on their mysterious business in the woods or the kudzu jungle . . . in the wettest of weather, for instance, or a black February ice storm . . . they would hole up in Paul's room, and Paul would tell to a wondering Jacob Lee the stories in his books of myths and adventures, adding his own creative embellishments, or would instruct the older boy in the arcana of erector sets, stamp or butterfly collecting, his ant farm, or the Lionel train and the black tracks that laced his room like a spider's web.

Rip smiled her infrequent, gold-flickering smile to see them together in the sunlight or on the rug before the grate fireplace in Paul's room, and Hebe laughed to hear their whoops of raucous laughter, and Nell tagged after them determinedly and futilely, yearning to share the bright, perfect world that their synergism created and wrapped them with. Paul would not be unkind to her, but was discouragingly remote in his small sister's presence unless he was alone with her, and Jacob Lee was, like virtually all the black male children of the South, uneasy and circumspect with the white female children of the big houses, so he avoided her when possible. So Nell was never permitted inside the golden circle, but it never occurred to her to resent Jacob Lee. Instead, he became one of the tall gods who walked the world of Fox's Earth, and she included him in her private devotions.

Only Yancey resented Jacob Lee's presence in the house and Paul's life. In his later childhood, from about age seven on, Paul had seemed to truly see Yancey for the first time, and bent the full force of his grave, intense personality upon her, and she responded to the pull of this intensity as if she had been waiting all her restless young life for something capable of totally absorbing and engaging her. It was as if, somehow, she became focused only in Paul's eyes. They became inseparable in a way that Paul and Jacob Lee would never be, in a way that Nell and Paul would never be, worship her older brother though she might, and share from the marrow out his love for books and reading though she did. There sprang up between these two tall, slim, golden children of Hebe Fox Geiger an almost twinlike bond; it was not unusual for one to catch the unspoken thoughts of the other and finish them, and often Yancey would know, suddenly and surely, that Paul, closeted away upstairs with C. S. Forester or Richard Halliburton, had thought of something he wanted to tell her, and would rise to go and see what it was. Likewise, he knew, not infrequently, when Yancey was feeling unwell, or had flown into a temper away from home.

"Paul wants me," Yancey would mumble over her shoulder to Hebe and Ruth when they asked her where she was going, as she lifted and cocked her pale head and scrambled to her feet from the rug before the fire in the little parlor where they habitually sat in the evenings after dinner. And Hebe and Ruth would exchange looks over Nell's head but say nothing.

"Yancey's really going to be in for it now," Paul would say, not raising his eyes from his grandfather's limp leather Bulfinch that he was perusing at his Great-grandmother Alicia's escritoire, and Nell would see the same look arrow between Hebe and Gamma. And when Yancey returned from her after-school cheerleading practice, they would see that she was flushed and incandescent with temper, and would learn that she had flared up impertinently at the squad's faculty adviser and been suspended from next Friday night's game.

"How do they do that, Rip?" Nell asked once, envying Paul and Yancey both this unspoken communion that could leap miles and penetrate walls and the unfailing, if silent, attention it earned them from Mama and Gamma.

"Do it with they inside ears," Rip said, going on with her ironing. It was clearly a familiar phenomenon to Rip, and Nell was intrigued.

"Have you got inside ears, Rip?"

"Reckon I do. Know I got inside eyes. How you reckon I knows when you doin' somethin' you ain't s'pose to?"

Nell studied her respectfully. Rip did seem to know a great deal about her that she seemed to have no way of knowing, far more than Mama or Gamma.

"Are you a conjure woman, Rip?"

"Where on earth you hear that trash, Nell? Carrie, I bet. I gon' bus' her head for her. Ain't no such thing as no conjure woman."

"Well, how do you know when I'm bad, then? And how do Paul and Yancey know that stuff? If it's not conjure, why can't I do it?"

"You can, mos' likely."

"No, I can't; I've tried and tried. All I can do is make Bucky turn around and look at me sometimes."

" 'Spec that fat ol' pony smell the col' biscuit you got in yo' pocket, Nell. Hearin' an' seein' inside is for fo'kses and fo'kses, not fo'kses and animals."

"Well, then, but . . ."

"You ain't done it yet, Nell, 'cause you ain't foun' the person that goes on the other end of you. Everybody got one person in all the world what's the other ha'f of they inside eyes an' ears. Paul an' Yancey, they goes on the other end of each other, an' so they can talk and lissen to each other ne' mine where they are. When you finds the person what belongs on you' other end, you can talk to 'em jus' like Paul an' Yancey."

Nell was enchanted. "When will that be?"

"I don't know. Some fo'kses fin's they other end right at first an' has 'em all they life. Some fo'kses don't never fin' 'em. It jus' luck."

"Oh, Rip!" Nell was smitten with the awful possibility; her heart hurt her with this newly discovered potential for loss.

"What if I never find my other end?"

Rip looked at her and smiled her slow smile.

"You find 'em, Nell. Not in this house, I don't 'spec, but you find 'em."

"Where, then? When?" Nell wriggled in an agony of impatience.

"I don't know. Won't nobody ever know but you and t'other."

"Has Mama found her other end? Does Gamma have one?"

Rip wrinkled her brow indulgently.

"Yo' mama got no mo' business with no other end than a June bug. She don' need nobody to finish her up; she got ever'thing she want right here in this house. It ain't never come in her head that she need nobody or nothin' else but whut she got right here."

"Wasn't Daddy her other end?"

"No'm. Yo' Gamma come closer to bein' the other end of yo' mama than anybody, but even she ain't it. It ain't always who you loves most what's yo' other end, Nell; it's who you need to finish you up so you whole. Yo' mama, she as whole as a flitterby or a li'l ol' moth buttin' 'round a light. She as finished as she ever gon' be."

"What about Gamma? I don't guess Gamma ever needed finishing up, did she?" Nell could not imagine her grandmother in need of communion with anyone, corporeal or not; she was as magisterially and unarguably complete to Nell as a mountain, or an egg.

Rip's face closed.

"Oh, Miss Ruth, she got another end, all right. She just ain't need 'em for a long time. But they still there."

"What about you, Rip? Did you ever have an other end? Have you now?"

"Oh, I had me one, yeah, I sho' Lord did. And now I got you, ain't I?"

And Nell, knowing that she was someone else's other end even if there was not under this great flat roof anyone who belonged on the other end of her, was satisfied, and content to wait for the magical words out of the air that would someday ring in her own inside ear, and did not envy Paul and Yancey their magical community of spirit.

But Yancey, feeling Paul lost to her as he was drawn deeper and deeper into the wash of his involvement with Jacob Lee, hissed and whipped and struck about her as a mortally injured snake might, and hated wary and bewildered Jacob Lee, and vented her jealous misery upon Paul when he was present and upon Nell when he was not, as was more and more often the case.

"It looks tacky and it brings disgrace to everybody in this house," she said to Paul in the flat, cold drawl that so perfectly mimicked Gamma's at times. "You spending all your time with that big old trashy, imbecile nigger. You aren't any better than a nigger yourself, and I'm not going to the picture show with you anymore. I don't associate with niggers."

"Suit yourself," Paul said to her equably, leaving Yancey to sulk and slam doors and nurse her hurt in her room like an animal in its lair. Once Nell went into her room to keep her company and to watch her brush out the flying cornsilk hair, but Yancey whirled on her with such white-faced, blue-sparking fury and called her such unbidden and terrible names that she flew downstairs to Rip sobbing, and never went unasked into Yancey's room again.

But even as she stumbled down the stairs, a tiny, placating crystal voice in Nell's head said to her, "You can't really blame her. She's lost her other end."

At five or six, Nell's one identifiable talent was a clear and touching gift for rationalization.

One other at Fox's Earth watched the bond between Paul and Jacob Lee cement itself with less than pleasure. Often, when she worked at the heavy leather ledger in her room in the mornings while Hebe still slept or drowsed beside her radio, Ruth Fox would pause and lay the ledger aside, and walk out onto the floating balcony beyond the French doors and lean her arms on the white railing, looking out over the gardens of Fox's Earth and watching the two boys at their play. If she thought, on those mornings, of another woman in drifting white like her own who leaned, long ago, on this same balcony to look down upon children, her face gave no hint of it. Her blue eyes would go dark and narrow against the sun, and she would think with annoyance that it really was not at all seemly, young Paul Fox playing mumbletypeg on the front walk of Fox's Earth with the hulking nigger grandson of a servant, for all the world to see, and that she really should speak to both Paul and Rip about it.

But then she would think that the friendship was no different, really, from the ones between half a dozen young white sons of the old houses on Church Street and Negro boys from Suches, and that no other household took any notice at all of them, and besides, something deep within Ruth Fox was reluctant to tax Rip with any situation in which the deck was not loaded in her own favor. And so she was, for a time, content to let the alliance rock along, for she sensed no threat to herself or Fox's Earth from the relationship or either boy in it.

Until the day in 1949 when she suffered a sudden and agonizing gallstone attack, the first illness outside her one pregnancy that she had had at Fox's Earth since the pneumonia she contracted the day Pearl Steed Yancey vanished. On the day of the gallstones, with the breathless, sweating pain finally diagnosed and eased by Dr. Hopkins, Ruth determined to go at the first opportunity to the office of Stuart Hill, the son of old Thaddeus Hill under whom her husband Paul had read the law, and make the will that, somehow, she had never gotten around to.

And so the long time of sweetness at Fox's Earth ended.

18

WHEN HE had told her the terms of her husband's will, Stuart Hill thought the indomitable and porcelain-beautiful Ruth Yancey Fox was going to faint and fall to the floor of his office before his very eyes, and he rang in agitation for his elderly secretary, who floundered in with a carafe of water. Between them they managed to splash most of it over Ruth's smart shantung suit, and the secretary was on the point of calling Dr. Hopkins when Ruth recovered herself and waved them away.

"But, Miss Ruth," soft, fussy, pear-shaped Stuart Hill protested, still chafing mindlessly at her white wrists, "you haven't been well; you said yourself that you'd seen the doctor for an attack of gallstones not two days ago . . ."

"I'm quite all right now, thank you, Stuart," Ruth said. "You needn't fuss over me. I was foolish enough to walk this afternoon, instead of having Robert drive me, and it is colder than I thought outside. Now. You were saying about my husband's will . . ."

"Yes, well, I thought you knew. At your . . . er, passing . . . Fox's Earth goes to the oldest male child of Miss Hebe or to the university if there are no children . . . which, of course, there are; little Paul, a fine boy, and Miss Yancey and little Miss Nell. But Paul, Senior, could not know that when he made this will; we drew it up before Miss Hebe was . . . ah, even considering matrimony. It isn't uncommon, Miss Ruth; so many of our old houses go to the oldest male in the line, you know. Your husband undoubtedly wished it so for your own protection; he didn't want you to have to worry about the disposition of the house."

"But you said, back when he died, that the house was mine . . . that I was to stay on, no matter what, and not to bother my head about it . . . I asked you, and that's what you said . . ."

"Well of course, and it is. It's yours until your death, no questions asked. You have no worries on that score, Miss Ruth. And then, of course, it stays in the family; it's not as though Fox's Earth would pass into hands that did not deserve it. And we don't care about the roofs over our heads after we're . . . ummm . . . . gathered, do we? So long as they stay in the family. But I did think you knew about it . . ."

"No. Paul did not tell me."

Ruth said no more, but her head roared with betrayal. How could he? To sit there, so fat and fawning and foolish, so stupidly, dotingly fond and fatuous, while she did all the real work of Fox's Earth, and all the time, this monstrous . . . trick . . . this *ruse,* this *treachery,* had lain in his heart like a cancerous spider . . . Red rage howled in her heart, but she sat still and quiet in the wing chair across the desk from Stuart Hill, her translucent eyelids shuttering her eyes. She did not trust herself to speak or look at him; a pragmatic voice far back in her mind told her that it was one of the most important things that she would ever be charged to do, the masking of her surprise and betrayal and fury from this pursy little lawyer. No man must ever find her vulnerable.

And presently she was able to look up and say, "And if, God forbid, anything should happen to little Paul?"

"Then it goes to the next of Miss Hebe's children who will stay and live in it and maintain it. That would be Miss Yancey, or, if she did not choose to live there, to Miss Nell. If neither girl wanted it, it would then pass to the university."

"But not to Hebe? My daughter?"

"Well . . ." he hesitated uncomfortably. "I'm sure your husband was certain that any child of Miss Hebe's would naturally maintain her there for the length of her life. We did talk about that, I remember, or at least I was in the office when Mr. Fox and my father were talking about it. Mr. Fox . . . your husband . . . felt that Miss Hebe was perhaps too . . . fragile and vulnerable, you know . . . too

201

unworldly . . . to have the burden of a huge old house like Fox's Earth put on her shoulders. You know how Mr. Fox doted on Miss Hebe, Miss Ruth. And, of course, he didn't know at the time whom she would marry. In this way he insured that Fox's Earth would always be there for Miss Hebe, just as it will be for you, without the onus of worrying about its ultimate disposition. It might have been possible that Miss Hebe's husband would not be as . . . careful of Fox's Earth as he might be . . ." and the poor man went scarlet with embarrassment as he thought of Johnny Geiger.

". . . and so he took this way of protecting both her and the house," he finished up lamely. "I'm sure a smart, competent lady like yourself can see what he was thinking."

"Oh, yes," Ruth said, feeling finally the great irreducible distance between the Yanceys of the mill village and the Foxes of Fox's Earth yawning under her feet, "I can see what he was thinking."

After that she dictated to Stuart Hill the now-inconsequential terms of her own meaningless will and left to walk home to Church Street over the crazily canted brick streets where, nearly half a century earlier, her bare feet had contorted themselves in impotent shame and fury, coated with the dust of the mill village, the feet of an outsider, an intruder.

As they were again, these forty-five years later.

When Ruth reached Fox's Earth, she was aware from the varnished tips of her small, bejeweled fingers to the polished crown of her head that she walked into the house of a stranger, and that the pale, bookish boy child who had hardly even intruded upon her day-to-day consciousness was now truly the enemy.

Ruth found that her path was clear. The plan was all there, whole and of a piece, when she woke the morning after her visit to Stuart Hill. She lay awhile in the vast tester bed that had been Alicia's, studying the intricate and lovely pattern of it on the underside of the rose-sprigged chintz canopy while she mulled over the scheme. It was a good plan, so tight and smooth that it was clearly a Meant thing. Ruth knew that it would work.

"I've been thinking," she said pleasantly to the assembled Foxes at the breakfast table. Even Hebe, who usually did not venture downstairs before noon, was there, at Ruth's request; Rip was there, too, still and watchful, summoned from the kitchen by Ruth. She would meet new danger this morning, she knew; meet it in the young sun of the breakfast bay.

"I've been thinking for a long time that we really should do something about Paul . . ." Eyes flew from her face to Paul's; his was grave and remote, only his blue eyes going darker with apprehension. Gamma let the pause spin out, and looked around the breakfast table at them, one by one. And then she smiled, a bright, dimpling smile that seemed to light the crystal-blue aura she sometimes wore about her like a match touched to a gas jet. The entire family of Foxes smiled back at her in relief; it was Gamma's rare playful smile, and it always meant that something pleasant was in the offing.

But Rip saw a rictus, and breathed deeply and secretly within herself.

"And I think what we should do is turn the old yard-man's rooms over the garage into a dormitory for Paul and Jacob Lee, and hire us the best tutor money can buy, and get some real schooling into both of them. I've been watching Paul for quite a while now, and it's obvious that he's such a sight smarter than those children at that dinky school in town that I'm afraid it's actually harming him. And I've been watching Jacob Lee, too; of course he hasn't had Paul's advantages, but I think he has a real gift for creative expression . . . Now, he does, Rip; don't be modest. You know his drawings are fit to be in a story-book. We could get a tutor who was good in art as well as smart in Greek and Latin and all those highbrow things Paul is interested in, and he could take Paul in the mornings while Jacob Lee does his chores, and then he could work with Jacob Lee on his drawing in the afternoons, and they could still have the evenings free for their rambunctiousness, whatever it is. I have a lot of respect for tutoring; Paul's own dear granddaddy was tutored in this house, and his great-grandaddy, too, and they were both fine, cultivated men. Well . . ." for they were silent . . . "what do you think? Do you like my little idea, or am I barking up the wrong tree?"

"I . . . gee, Gamma, I don't know . . ." Paul could not think clearly; his eyes were dazzled by the light that came from her, and the leap from unwitting sinner awaiting unimaginable punishment to favored son of the great house was too much for him to manage in so short a time. He

203

blinked at Ruth. No one else spoke; they all stared stupidly at her.

"I thought you'd be pleased, Paul," she said in the dying little voice that meant that one of them had hurt her to the heart. "I thought you'd like spending all the time you wanted on those big old books of yours, and I truly did think you'd enjoy living up there over the garage, especially if Jacob Lee could be there with you. We could fix it up real nice; bunk beds, maybe, and a radio, and room for your train and your ant farm. You could even get that guinea pig you've wanted so long, maybe; there'd be room for the creature out there. I thought it might be like a tree house . . ."

He looked at her cautiously. What was the catch? It was so nearly perfect a boy's dream that Paul could not believe he would not be asked to trade some essential piece of himself for it, something of infinite value. But he could not think of anything he had that she might want.

"Could we put a hammock up in there?" he asked presently.

She smiled. "You can put up fifty hammocks if you want to. It's all yours, yours and Jacob Lee's. The only condition is that you keep it halfway tidy, so your poor tutor can get to his books and blackboard. Beauty or Salome will clean it once a week, but you all are on your honor the rest of the time."

"There would be, like, lights out, though, wouldn't there? You know, like we couldn't talk or play the radio after nine o'clock, or something?"

"Well, I would hope you had sense enough to go to bed at a reasonable hour, but who in the world would there be to hear you if you whooped and hollered like two wild men from Borneo all night? I figure any boy old enough to live off by himself like that is old enough to get himself to bed on time. It would be strictly on your head. Do you think you could handle that?"

A smile of pure joy spread across Paul's narrow face and illumined it; it was really going to happen, then. It wasn't a trap to catch him out in some grievous sin of omission or commission. There weren't any strings.

"Oh, boy, Gamma, sure! Sure I could handle that! Jacob Lee, he could too! We'll study so hard, you'll be so proud of us . . . can I go tell Jacob Lee? I'll come right back, but I want to go tell him . . ."

"Go tell him, then. But come right on back here. We have some practical arranging to do."

With a dazzling grin and a shy, spasmodic little jerk toward her that might have been the beginning of a hug, he was gone from the room and the remaining Foxes looked from his bobbing, weaving figure back to Gamma, still in fascinated silence.

"Well, has the cat got all your tongues?" she said, smiling, but with a tug of impatience in her voice. "Don't you think it's a stroke of genius? Growing boys need room to ramble around in, and it will get them out from underfoot. You can barely hear yourself think around here as it is. And there'll be fewer distractions from their studies. Hebe? What do you think?"

"Well, Mama, he's still just a little boy . . . you don't think he might be too young to be all the way out there where we couldn't hear him if he got sick, or scared, or something?"

"Nonsense, Jacob Lee could run in and get Rip if he needed her. I think it might be the making of him, Hebe. Sometimes I think Paul is dangerously close to turning into . . . a sissy, shall we say. He needs more men in his life. All the more reason for a tutor. But, of course, the main one is the need to develop that fine mind. To my way of thinking, it's either a tutor or a good private school in the East somewhere, and you always get in such a state when you think about him going away from home . . ."

"Well, if you think he's old enough, I think it's just a wonderful idea, Mama," Hebe said hastily. Relief at having the perplexing problem of Paul's further education lifted from her helpless hands lightened her voice until she gurgled with joy. "I never would have thought of it, but you're so clever . . . and so *good,* Mama, to let Jacob Lee live out there with him and study. Think of the advantages! You're just the best thing . . ."

"You didn't ask Rip if Jacob Lee could do it," Nell piped punctiliously from her youth chair. She had listened to the proceedings with rapt attention; they seemed to her so fabulous as to be lifted from the whole cloth of a fairy tale; not something that her brother Paul and the tall Jacob Lee whom she worshiped silently would actually be doing at a specific time in the future. It was her innate sense of order and fitness that made her want all the strings tied and the i's dotted. If Rip's permission were not secured and her own elbow kissed three times, the wonderful thing would not come true.

Ruth, misunderstanding, frowned at her smaller grand-daughter. "It's hardly your place to remind me of my manners, Nell," she began, and Nell's eyes filled with topaz tears.

"It be fine with me, Nell," Miss Rip spoke from her place beside the door into the kitchen. "Miss Ruth doin' a mighty generous thing, seem lak to me."

Her voice was rough, as though the words were frozen in rust in her throat, and she must cough them out by force. Ruth Fox looked at her narrowly. Rip looked back; she nodded but did not smile.

"Won't you miss him, Rip?" Nell said.

"Oh, I be lookin' out for him, don't you worry none. I keep up with him, whether he down to my house or out there. I gon' keep an eye on both of 'em wherever they is."

She spoke to Nell, but her eyes did not leave Ruth's face. Ruth looked back steadily. Something leaped between the two pairs of eyes and left a sort of silent buzzing in the air. Nell squirmed under it uncomfortably.

"I think it's the tackiest thing I ever heard of," Yancey said suddenly and clearly into the buzzing, and they turned to look at her. Her face was white to the point of blue-ness, and her eyes had widened until a thin ring of white encircled them. She looked bleached and terrible; ugly; an albino; a skeleton.

"Yancey . . ." Hebe began.

"I think it's just . . . obscene! Paul, *Paul,* that skinny, pracky little ole baby, living out there in the help's house with that big, dumb, horrible, grinning, idiot nigger like he was his nurse or his keeper or something! Like he was white trash, and couldn't afford a separate house to live in! How *can* you, Mama? What on earth will everybody think of us? The best thing they'll think is that we're common nigger lovers; the worst . . ."

"Yancey! That is quite enough out of you!" Gamma's voice was a frozen lash. "I will not have such language under my roof. If there is common behavior in this house, it is yours. You will go to your room *right now,* and you will remain there until I tell you you may leave it, but first you will apologize to Rip. If I were she I would never forgive you."

Yancey went even whiter, and her long fingers flew to her mouth. She turned a miserable face to Rip.

"Oh, Rip!" she whispered. "Oh, I'm so sorry! I didn't mean . . . I wasn't thinking . . ."

She sobbed, a great, hiccuping sob, and scrambled up from her chair, and bolted from the breakfast room and up the stairs. They heard the crying begin in earnest, and rise to heartbroken howls before the solid thud of the carved old door to her room cut them off. They sat in silence. Nell's face burned with Yancey's shame and misery, and pain for Rip stung her throat and nose. She was terribly afraid she was going to cry herself, and struggled desperately against the tears.

"Please, please," whimpered Hebe. "Don't be mad at her, Rip. She loves you just as much as the rest of us, and she didn't mean a word of that awful stuff about Jacob Lee. You know how she's been lately; I don't know what gets into her . . ."

"I ain't mad," Rip said tranquilly. "Yancey jus' upset 'cause she think she losin' Paul. She see 'em goin' off together to live by theyselves out there, an' she scared things ain't never gon' be like they was. She 'fraid somethin' gon' happen . . ."

"It was inexcusable," Gamma said crisply. "This time she's gone too far. I promise you, she will be punished."

"No'm. I sho' don't want her punished 'count of me or Jacob Lee. I understands Yancey; ain't I done raise her from the time she born? I knows what she really sayin'."

There was another pause while the two women looked at each other once more, and then Gamma dropped her eyes and pushed back her chair and rose from the table, and Rip turned and went back into the kitchen. And the day hummed on.

It took only a scant seven months, after all. The old gardener's quarters were renovated and snug by the first of December, and the two boys moved in on Christmas Eve of 1949. The whole household turned out to help with the moving; Beauty and Salome had the last of the fresh saw-dust swept out early that morning, and made up the sturdy, raw-smelling new bunk beds with sheets and quilts and new plaid bedspreads, as tight as drums. Robert, swollen like a bantam rooster with the indignity of the task, made several muttering trips with Paul's clothes and

207

books and records, and hung thick, serviceable curtains under Gamma's direction. Paul followed, carrying the ant farm, and Jacob Lee, skittish, brought up the rear with the Lionel train. He did not seem to realize that he would be staying with Paul when the other servants left to go back to the big house; he grunted and sweated and worked silently and earnestly, and looked to Rip for further directions when he finished each task.

Nell and Hebe danced about the airy, low-ceilinged rooms, exclaiming over the neat built-in storage drawers and closets, the twin worktables under the window of the big room that would be used as a schoolroom, the corkboard walls already filling with snakeskins and birds' nests and posters and Paul's other treasures. They jostled each other on the braided rug and got in everybody's way, and Nell admired this kingdom of boyhood with a whole, full heart untainted by envy. Rip dusted books and put them away silently; even Carrie came creaking and puffing up the outside stairs with a tin full of tea cakes. Jacob Lee, having nothing to hang on the corkboard or stow in the cedar closet that was his except two spare pairs of overalls, some shirts, and an extra pair of shoes, disappeared for a longish space of time, and returned, just as they had begun to miss him, bearing a perfect, freshly cut small pine tree. Its fragrance was a blessing, a benediction in the room, and they all smiled involuntarily.

"Got us a Christmus tree," he drawled softly, grinning around at them. "Foun' him in Miz Calhoun's cow pasture over to Suches."

And they all applauded the Christmas tree, and Jacob Lee grinned even wider, and shuffled his feet in pleasure. It was the perfect gesture; Jacob Lee had a delicate gift for fitting the right gesture to the moment; it brought much small pleasure to Fox's Earth that no one had ever stopped to analyze.

Only Yancey was not there. She stayed in her room all that Christmas Eve, and did not go near the new retreat, and in all the months that Paul and Jacob lived there above the garage, she never entered it.

Soon after the first of the year, the young man from the university whom Ruth had engaged to tutor the boys came for his first session with them, and they settled into the new routine as though they had been born to it. The family saw less and less of Paul, and soon they saw him only at meals. Jacob Lee continued to eat with Rip in her little house behind the box hedge. Both boys were very happy.

"What on earth do they *do* out there, do you think?" Hebe said one evening after dinner. Her light voice was wistful; she might have been envying the boys in their magical, no-girls-allowed fastness.

"They rassle," Nell said importantly. She had taken to creeping out to the garage lair in the early mornings, ostensibly to waken them, and Paul had relented and let his small sister stay while he and Jacob Lee took turns in the spartan bathroom dressing to come in for breakfast. He would not permit her presence at any other time, but something in her small, pointed white face and yearning caramel eyes spoke to the remembered loneliness and alienation in his own heart, and he decreed that early morning could be Nell's time in the retreat.

"But just till we're ready to go to breakfast, Bean," he said. "No girls allowed after that. You'd just get in the way."

And Nell accepted the condition with alacrity, both because he had made it and because it was infinitely superior to nothing.

"Wrestle?" Gamma said, pausing over her coffee cup to look at Nell. "What do you mean, wrestle?"

"You know, rassle. Everytime I go out there they're rolling around on the floor in just their underpants with their arms around each other. Oh . . ." for she caught the queer, stilled look on Gamma's face . . . "they're not really fighting. They're just playing, you know, playing rassling. They don't hurt each other. They're laughing and hugging all the time they're doing it."

"That . . . is . . . dis*gust*ing!" Yancey cried, and whirled away from the table and out of the room.

"Oh, dear, I do hope they'll be careful," Hebe sighed. "Jacob Lee is so much older and bigger than Paul. Mama, I wish you'd speak to them."

Gamma did not answer her; she said nothing. Finally she resumed drinking her coffee, but her eyes were far away.

Rip also said nothing. She watched Gamma, and then she went out of the dining room and into the kitchen.

It was the next morning that Gamma came dragging the two boys into the house with flaming eyes and a frightening face. Nell understood nothing except that Paul and Jacob Lee had done something too terrible even to speak of, something so utterly, unimaginably awful that it resulted in Jacob Lee's exile from the house and Paul's inexorable dispatch to a military boarding school in Virginia. He did not go right away; after the scalding interval of shouting and tears upstairs in Gamma's room with Mama and Rip, Paul went into his old room and closed the door and did not come out again. Rip took trays to him, and left them on the floor outside his door, and Beauty or Salome, eyes darting with trouble, would collect them later and take them back to the kitchen. Clean clothes went up and down via Rip, but she did not try to enter Paul's room, or attempt to coax him out of it. Nell knew this to be true because she had haunted the landing outside Paul's room ever since he disappeared into it, occasionally calling out in pain and bafflement to him on the other side.

"Hey, Paul. The Palace has got Johnny Mack Brown."

Silence.

"I made a hopscotch on the front walk. Want to play with me?"

Silence.

"Hey, Paul, if you'll come out you can have my aggies and taws. Not the old ones; the new ones that I got for my birthday."

Silence.

"Hey, Paul, you want me to bring you up some tea cakes? Carrie just made some."

"Go on off, Nell. You're bothering me. I don't want you in here."

"Well . . ." The grand gesture, defeat and appeasement at once: "Then I'll go get Yancey for you, okay? Okay, Paul?"

"I don't want her either! I don't want any of you. Go on and leave me alone, Nell; you're a pest."

After this exchange, Rip found Nell in tears once more and hustled her downstairs to the kitchen for a plate of tea cakes and a glass of milk.

"I don't know what's the matter with everybody," Nell wailed in blinded misery. "I don't know why Mama cries all the time, or Gamma goes around looking like she's about to die. I don't know why Paul won't come out of his room, and I don't know what happened to Jacob Lee, and nobody will tell me. Yancey won't even speak to me."

"Nell, there is some things that you jus' ain't s'posed to

210

know, an' this is one of 'em. All you needs to know is that ever'body be all right terreckly, an' things will work out. You jus' leave Paul an' Yancey an' yo' Gamma an' Mama alone for a spell, an' then you see. It all be done blowed over. Jacob Lee, he workin' out in the town an' makin' lots of money, he likin' it jus' fine. He ain't never cut out to be no artist; things is better this way. You don't worry none about Jacob Lee. Paul, he jus' poutin'. He come out when he git hungry."

And so, for a small space of days, Nell was soothed, even though she still understood nothing about that dreadful morning. She thought that it had something to do with fighting, because, just before Gamma's door had swung shut on them all, she had heard Paul's voice spiral up in a howl of outrage and incomprehension, so high that it cracked:

"We were just wrestling! Gamma, we were just *wrestling!*" And there was a note in that last high, desperate sound that she knew, surely and certainly, to be terror. But what was there in being nabbed for fighting that would so terrify Paul? Nell did not know, and in the murky depths of the not knowing swam monsters and terrors. But still, Rip had said it would be all right; Rip had said that Paul would come out . . .

But when he did, it was in the dawn before she was even awake, before Yancey was awake, and it was not to pad downstairs to the dim, May-cool kitchen but to be herded in fury and fear and incomprehension into the back seat of the Chrysler with Gamma and thence to be driven by Robert to the train station, where he was given into the care of the conductor and borne off up the clicking rails toward the pedigreed prison of the boys' school in Virginia, where a straight-backed, hard-angled, gray-as-rain Commandant waited to meet him.

And in that morning, when Nell awakened, there was Paul's room as sterile and barren as if a slim, remote, blue-eyed boy had never lived there, and there was Mama sobbing and moaning and sometimes crying out as if red-hot coals were being applied to her feet behind her closed door, and there was Gamma stalking about the great house with such a look of tragedy and strangeness about her that Nell would as soon have questioned a ghost, and there was Rip gone still and quiet and far away back into herself, and there was Yancey in a fit of screaming rage in her room, shrieking terrible things to Gamma through her locked door in a mad, piping voice, and it was not all right after all. It was worse than it had ever been, unimaginably bad, and something in Nell went cold and still and small and dead under the weight of the awfulness and mystery in the house. She spent a great deal of time in the pile of sour quilts in the cage, and she asked no questions and listened at no doors.

It seemed to Nell very important, during this time, to be still and quiet and attract no attention, for in this house you never knew what would bring calamity and horror and irrevocability down on your head. Anything was now possible, for Rip had said that it would be all right, and it wasn't.

Once, passing Mama's room, Nell had heard Gamma's voice crooning in a singsong over the monotonous mewling that had been emanating from Mama's room for the past two days. She paused and listened, poised for flight. She heard Gamma say:

"It's the only thing for him, puddin'. Strong, vigorous men and strict discipline, the stronger and stricter the better, and for as long as they'll keep him. No women, no women at all. He's had too much of us women, and you see what it's made of him. It may not be too late yet. Of course, if his father had stayed around . . . but it's all going to be for nothing if you give in to those phone calls and all that crying and let him come home. He must *not* come home again while Jacob Lee is around, at any rate, and I simply can't ask Rip to send him away. Poor, sick creature, where would he go? No, Paul is safe as he can be right where he is, and you must *not* let him talk you into telling him he can come home. Hush, now. Hasn't your mama always known best?"

And Nell went stiffly and in pain on down the stairs of Fox's Earth, knowing that Paul would not come home again soon, and knowing on some level that he would not ever truly come home again. And young Paul Fox, the small boy who had mattered so little and who now mattered so terribly and so much to the chatelaine of Fox's Earth, remained in bondage in his barren man's fastness and set his narrow Fox feet on the road toward that very thing with which his birthright had been betrayed and stolen. And between Ruth Fox and the great white bulk of the house for which her soul panted, there loomed only time.

19

YANCEY CHANGED after that; the changes, though nascent before Paul went away, seemed accelerated by his absence, so that by the summer of 1950, only weeks after his departure, Yancey was a different person altogether. No one seemed to like the changes especially, but everyone noticed them.

In the second half of her fifteenth year, the prickling, lumpy, disparate clay that was Yancey was transmuted, seemingly in the space of a single spring night, into a woman and a beautiful one. It was not a beauty that Nell or Hebe or Ruth or even Yancey's small society particularly admired, for instead of being petite, delicate, ladylike, wholesome, or cute, Yancey crawled from her tangled bed one morning and assembled her long limbs and sharp bones into something as exotic and seductive to the eye as a peacock or a griffin or a unicorn. She was as tall then as she would ever be, and her head was small and rectangular, and her neck was only saved from exaggerated, giraffelike length by the suddenly tamed mass of her moon-pale hair, which never darkened and no longer flew about her head like a frantic nimbus but swung, bell-like and luxuriant, at her slender shoulders. Her chin and cheekbones flowered and stretched themselves against the taut, golden-white Fox skin in proportion to the patrician pirate's nose she had had since childhood, and after her other features had grown up to her face, the acetylene-blue eyes did not seem so mad and fevered. Her mouth remained the one softness about Yancey: it was like a delicate, bruised rose in her face, infinitely vulnerable and somehow palpably sexual. When Yancey licked her lips, as she did often, it was said in her junior-high-school circle that half the boys in the school ran for the gym to take cold showers. It was Hebe's mouth, and Nell had it, too, and would see it again in the face of her own daugh-

213

ter, Abigail, but it was somehow, in all the hawklike golden fierceness of Yancey's countenance, the decisive element, the catalyst that resulted in startling beauty.

But because it was that . . . a startling beauty, and not the pert, scrubbed, ingenuous cuteness prescribed in the early fifties by M-G-M and *Seventeen* magazine . . . it had the effect of disquieting those who came in contact with it, and brought little joy to those around Yancey. Ruth Fox would draw her delicate brows together in silent disapproval as Yancey strode through a room, her long, polished legs scissoring in shorts rolled so high that they showed the tiny, tender crease of her buttocks.

"Go and put some clothes on if you're going to parade around the yard, Yancey," she would say. "You look just like a naked heathen savage in those shorts. I declare, it's just trashy."

"Everybody else wears them this short, Gamma," Yancey flung back carelessly, not stopping or looking over her shoulder.

"Well, you don't look like everybody else," Ruth said, unwittingly fingering the source of her dissatisfaction. "You're always going to have to be careful about how you dress, or you'll end up with everybody thinking you're a tramp. If they don't already."

"Mama, do you think Yancey is going to be a peculiar-looking woman?" Hebe would murmur worriedly to Ruth, watching Yancey scrambling into a car full of teenagers that had careened to a stop beside the hollowed carriage block at the curb of Fox's Earth. She would be wearing not a calf-brushing sea of starched and crinolined skirt and a high-necked, sleeveless blouse, like the other girls in the automobile, but blue jeans washed to milk-whiteness and shrunk so that they forced denim fingers into every hollow below Yancey's slender waist, and a severe, crisply ironed oxford-cloth shirt with a button-down collar. She looked elegant, spare, expensive . . . and odd.

"Yancey may be a beauty, but it will never bring her happiness," Ruth would say, paying grudging tribute to the powerful, shining thing she saw in her granddaughter, but hating it. That it was her own strange blue-edged aura —and that of mad Cater Yancey before her—that she saluted and feared in her granddaughter never seemed to occur to her. Hebe would sigh.

Rip seemed to like this incandescent new Yancey, however.

"You looks mighty pretty, Yancey," she would say as Yancey slouched into the kitchen on her way to dancing class, dressed in the odd, dark, linear linen upon which she had insisted for her best summer church-and-party dress. "Where them high heels you bought in Atlanta last week?"

"I can't wear them to this stupid old dancing class," Yancey spat impatiently. "I'm already taller than everybody else; those dumb little boys would be leaving teeth prints on my collarbone. God, I *hate* being so tall and skinny! Nobody decent is ever going to ask me for a date, I know they're not."

"Yes, they is. You wait and see. Now go git them shoes and put 'em on and hol' up yo' head an' go on to that dancin' class. You be the bes'-lookin' gal there. Ain't nobody be able to take they eyes off you."

And Yancey, quiescent for once, would go and put on the new high heels and weave off upon them to her dancing class, a slender new reed quivering with the furled promise of great distinction.

"You know what?" Nell said once, looking after Yancey and then at Rip. "Yancey looks just like you. If she was colored instead of white and had her head wrapped up in a rag, she'd look *just* like you, Rip. I bet that's why you think she's so pretty."

Rip smiled at her. "That a mighty fine compliment, Nell."

"Really?"

"Sho is."

"Well," Nell said doubtfully, "maybe she's not so funny-looking after all. But I know Gamma thinks she looks like a horse. I heard her say so."

"Yo' Gamma know she got to keep tight aholt of the reins on that hoss, else she got her a handful," Rip said.

"What do you mean, Rip?"

"Don't mean nothin'. Go on now, Nell. I got to finish this here ironin' befo' yo' mama and Gamma wakes up from they naps."

Aside from Rip, Yancey alone seemed to relish her sudden metamorphosis. But she did not use it as any other young girl newly sprung to beauty might: she did not flirt, pose, posture, preen herself at mirrors, practice gestures

215

and try on personas, closet herself in her room for hours with creams and lotions and the potently scented arcana of the new Rexall drugstore. Yancey went from egg to eagle in the blink of an eye, without interim fledgling training, and this surefootedness with her new splendor was as unsettling to the Fox household as the splendor itself.

Her pain and rage at Paul's exile provided the thrust for this quantum leap from childhood into perverse maturity, a leap that soared above and past all the tentativeness and shyness of adolescence, although Nell did not realize this until much later. All she saw in that strange, troubling spring of 1950 was a splendid, feral stranger who dwelled in her sister's room and set about scrambling the household into total turmoil with a fierce singleness of purpose that bordered on a religious passion. Though she did not go out from Fox's Earth until early the next year, Yancey Geiger went away from Nell . . . from all of them . . . on the same morning as her brother, Paul, and, like him, she did not ever truly come home again. In that terrible hot spring, Nell's acquaintance with abandonment . . . and her fear of it . . . became as living and pulsing and sophisticated as another organ in her body, and as permanent.

They were living in a stew of decaying sexuality, although no one at Fox's Earth recognized it as such. Nell would, one day, be able to put a name to the *pot au feu* in which they simmered, that year of the leaving of Paul and Yancey, but at the time she knew only that there were strong forces loose in Fox's Earth, and that those forces were not vigorous and fresh, but sly and sucking and corrupted. Nell thought of the forces in the aggregate, and called them "it"; "it" had fingered and mouthed at Paul and Jacob Lee and spat them out into the world beyond Fox's Earth, leaving them forever stained with its saliva. "It" had swept Rip up into an unimagined early ecstasy and then fled, leaving her silent and husked dry. "It" had caught Mama up into a wild abandonment of young animal excess and taught her great, shameless, bawdy joy, and then sneaked off into the West with Johnny Geiger, never to return, and had so desolated her that all her womanly humors thinned and dried to accommodate the chaste old child she became. Nell did not know this, but she lived daily with the results. "It" had been twisted in

Gamma so mightily and early that it could only burrow deep within her, there to roil ceaselessly with such a powerful intensity that it seemed to blaze about her like a fire about a fat chunk of pine light'ard at times. Nell did not know this either, but "it" was the force that shaped all their lives, and she sensed its presence even if she could not name it. It rode over Fox's Earth like a fathomless, thick, drowning sea, and no one in the house was untouched by it.

Yancey was nearly destroyed.

From the moment she became aware of her new beauty and the power it dealt her, she saw clearly its potential as a weapon, and she set out to become the bane of Ruth Yancey Fox's existence, as well as the talk of Sparta. Restraint and deference and all the pretty, mannerly graces that Ruth had so labored to instill into her granddaughters seemed flash-burnt out of her along with her swift, boyish childhood. The frightening new Yancey snarled and spat; she lounged indolently or strode carelessly whenever the spirit moved her, rolling her hips; she dressed as she pleased and flaunted her young body in front of whomever she wished; she scratched when and where she itched, literally and figuratively. Her grades took a dizzying slide and she laughed when Gamma taxed her with it; she got into numerous scrapes at school, along with her hard-edged new set, and shrugged when Hebe wept at the summons from the high-school principal to come and talk over Yancey's latest transgression. Her pretty, expensive clothes, brought back from Atlanta or ordered from New York by Gamma, piled up in soiled drifts on the floor of her room and she shrank her blue jeans still further and rolled her shorts higher and unbuttoned still another button on the oxford-cloth shirts, so that her unfettered young breasts winked plummily in and out of view when she walked. She began to smoke, showily and with some style, and she did not care who at Fox's Earth knew it.

She began to go out at night with a group unknown to them, taller and older than her contemporaries on Church Street, a shadow band of faceless, taciturn shapes that stayed massed in darkened, souped-up cars throbbing at the curb, honking raucously for Yancey to come out. Nell saw them from her window only briefly and in the nights, beneath the streetlight or in the lurid flare of a match held in cupped hands. The boys had dark wings of oil-sheened hair slicked back into duck tails, and tee shirts with the sleeves rolled high on the shoulder, or sports shirts with the sleeves cut out altogether. They wore leather jackets and blue jeans that cupped their genitals like codpieces, and they spoke only in monosyllables. The girls wore nylon sweaters so tight over their high-hiked, extruded breasts that the concentric stitching of their Peter Pan brassieres showed through, and their slick gabardine skirts cupped under their jiggling buttocks and slipped into the clefts between them. Their frizzed hair fell forward over their sharp faces to hide their flat, mascara-spiked eyes and brush their heavily lipsticked mouths, and their voices were nasal and tired. Catching sight of Yancey as she emerged from the dark bulk of the veranda and ran lightly down the front walk to one of the waiting cars, her hair pulled austerely into a pony tail so that her narrow, elegant skull stood out in bas-relief in the opalescent streetlight, her tall, loose body as attenuated and stylized as a fashion sketch; hearing her cool voice as it rose in greeting over the nasal flatnesses and thick slurrings, Nell would flinch unconsciously. These were not Yancey's people; she was as alien from them as she was from her own family. Where was the place for Yancey, then? Nell took the matter to Rip.

"What does she want to run around with those trashy old mill kids for?"

"How you know they mill chirrun?"

"They look like it. They're ignorant and common-looking. They're po' whites."

Rip regarded her equably. Of the three adult women inside the walls of Fox's Earth, she alone had not scolded Yancey, or wept over her, or threatened or cajoled her to mend her ways.

"Who tell you about po' whites?"

"Well . . . Gamma did. Or at least I heard her telling Yancey last night that those kids she went out with were po' white trash. She said it was a disgrace; that everybody in town was talking about her. She said Yancey was bringing disgrace on Fox's Earth."

"Well, I 'spec yo' Gamma know po' white trash when she see it."

Something in Rip's voice jerked Nell's head up from her absorbed picking at the ragged cuticle of her thumb, but the mahogany face was mild and agreeable, and she dropped her eyes back.

"Well, but what does she want to go around with 'em for, Rip? They're stupid. Most of them drop out of school when they're sixteen; I bet you none of those kids she went off with last night goes to the high school. They don't ever *do* anything but drive up and down Main Street in those cars and holler at each other and beat on the sides of 'em, or play their stupid old radios. They don't even go get barbecue or milk shakes. They just go out to the Blue Lantern or the Wagon Wheel and drink liquor and dance all scrunched up together, if they go anywhere. I don't see why she wants to do that stuff."

"How you know they drinkin' liquor? How you know they goes out there to them jukin' places? Yancey tell you she went out there?" Rip's voice was suddenly stronger.

"Naw," Nell said. "Yancey doesn't even talk to me anymore. I saw some matches from both those places in her purse, though. And I can smell the liquor on her all the way from the landing when she comes in. I wait up for her sometimes."

Rip was silent, her black eyes far away. Nell was out of sorts and impatient. Yancey had been the focus of Rip's eyes all too often recently. Nell wanted them to see only her once again.

"Rip? Why *do* you think she's so crazy about them all of a sudden? She wasn't ever before. She used to call 'em lintheads, and laugh at 'em."

"I don't 'spec she crazy about 'em. Nell. She jus' want yo' mama and Gamma to think she is. Yancey know they ain't her kind of fo'kses; she know takin' up with 'em be the one thing that rile yo' Gamma up worse'n anything. She jus' tryin' to rile up yo' Gamma."

"What for? Because she sent Paul off? Yancey's been funny like this ever since Paul went off. Does she think it was Gamma that made him go?"

Rip's face closed in upon itself; the remoteness that was all that remained of her when she went away inside herself hung about her. Nell's heart chilled, but then Rip spoke, and the distance receded.

"Yancey jus' actin' hossy. She tryin' to show yo' Gamma she ain't the onliest boss around here. Some fo'kses jus' cain't stand to knuckle to nobody; Yancey be like that, I 'spec. She stubborn and she strong-minded. She goin' through a little spell of actin' bad; some gals does when they gits to be her age. She act better when she git to feelin' more comfortable in her skin."

Nell went away feeling somewhat better about the rebellious, scornful stranger who lived in her sister's room, but the autumn wore on, and deepened into the dry, iron-hard cold of winter, and still Yancey laid her outrageous siege to Fox's Earth. She was dropped from the cheerleading squad for smoking and swearing and missing practice, and thereafter spent the nights of the ball games in one of the powerful, throbbing cars behind the stadium, emerging to blink in the lights of the half-time band show with her mouth a soft pulp in an angry scarlet smear of lipstick and beard burn, often with her skirt slipped around so that its zipper rode crazily down the front of her. She smoked on the school grounds and in the drugstore now, as well as in her room at home, and her breath often smelled of the sly-sweet cheap bourbon they drank. Nell knew that she kept a pint of it in her school purse, but she did not know if Rip or Mama or Gamma knew. She thought not. She did not think the whiskey would be borne.

The entire high school was buzzing about Yancey that winter; her teachers could do little with her and soon stopped trying, and the beleaguered principal stopped sending notes and letters to Hebe and Ruth to come in and discuss "the little problem we have with Yancey." As angry as she was at Yancey . . . and at home she bubbled with rage at her . . . Ruth Fox would brook no criticism, implicit or overt, from outsiders. The principal was reminded . . . and sweetly told to remind his teachers . . . that the school board had hired him in the first place because they had faith in his ability to run his school without creeping continually to outsiders for assistance; they would be disappointed indeed to find that this was not so. Since Ruth was a long-time member of the school board, and in line for its presidency, the summonses soon stopped.

The town talked, too, Nell knew in the way a child always knows such things. The club, the Episcopal Church, the merchants and service people, the board rooms and coffee shops of Sparta, and, in a smaller way, the faculty homes and lounges over on the hill . . . all buzzed and clattered with the abrupt debauch of Yancey Fox Geiger. But most of those who whispered and watched through that fall and winter did so mechanically and without malice, with only the automatic relish of the gregarious, easily diverted southerner. There was in the watching and the whispering none of the ugly savor and glee that might normally have been there at the wounding and weakening of one of the great families in the huge old white houses; spite was too pale and familiar an emotion to be easily applied to the Foxes of Fox's Earth. It had been so ever since Ruth Yancey Fox had taken the reins from her husband Paul. She had always been careful to maintain a sort of Olympian distance from even the natural peers of the Foxes, and as a result the gossip of Sparta was without sufficient teeth to hurt her or Fox's Earth. Ruth knew this, and paid the talk no heed. Her energies were needed elsewhere.

For the real threat came from inside the walls of Fox's Earth. Yancey, the little Fox, was eating at her grandmother's vitals with deadly relish, and even as she kept her head high and her porcelain face still and calm, Ruth Fox gnashed inside herself with pain and rage and something that was not quite fear but was not far from it. Yancey would not be stopped or silenced, and, worse than that, there was in her blue eyes something that looked at her grandmother and probed her to the depths of her being.

Not since her own mother, Pearl, had stopped coming into her room to stand in the shadows, there and not there, had anyone looked at Ruth Fox and known her wholly and in her heart. She would have been surprised had anyone told her that Rip often came close, but she would not have been alarmed. Rip would not, she knew, move against her, not until the last Fox girl child was gone from Fox's Earth, and Ruth did not intend that that should happen in Rip's lifetime. Now someone besides Pearl and Rip had looked at her with eyes that saw, and that someone was her older granddaughter, the princess she had once thought to prepare all this vast kingdom for, and instead of the approbation she had had from Pearl, she saw in the fierce blue eyes of Yancey hatred and harm and something that was not full understanding . . . yet . . . but that reached inexorably toward it.

"But now listen good, Ruth," a remembered voice seemed to say out of a time long dead and past, a flat voice full of bitterness and rusted love. "A woman's different. A woman can know your mind like no man ever can. You be careful around a woman, especially a woman like that."

Ruth listened to the voice and knew the time of Yancey's reckoning was coming, the time would be soon . . . Ruth knew this as she had known all the other things she had needed to know. She had only to wait. In her torment, Yancey would strike finally at herself like a scorpion. And then the comprehension in those light-spilling eyes so like her own would be rendered impotent, and Ruth, after meeting and vanquishing the sudden looming threat of young Paul only a few months earlier, could, at last and truly, rest.

Yancey undid herself at Christmastime.

With the house awash in preparations for Ruth's annual party, her outrages reached new excesses. She came down to dinner two evenings in a row smelling of bourbon and more than a little silly, but Gamma was having her dinner on a tray upstairs with her lists and telephone, an indulgence she permitted herself only at the time of the party, and did not witness Yancey's condition. The others looked at her in dread, but said nothing, and Rip shepherded her angrily up to her room after each appearance and thrust her, spitting and howling, into a tub of cold water. It was one of the few times Nell had ever seen Rip angry with Yancey.

Three days before the party, Yancey went out to the omnipresent jalopy that waited at the curb in a silent, hissing sleet storm and she did not come home at all that night.

Finally, all pretense of normality was abandoned. The women gathered in the little parlor downstairs to wait for Yancey, Rip and Gamma silent and stone-faced, Hebe snuffling monotonously and fidgeting with the fluttering ribbons and ruffles of her chiffon dressing gown. At two o'clock, Nell scuffed downstairs in her bathrobe and bunny slippers and sat down on the hearth rug, glaring defiantly at them as though daring them to oust her. Gamma looked through her with blue-black, blinded eyes and said nothing. Hebe began a fretful protest and Nell screwed up her face to sass back. Rip murmured and touched Hebe's shoulder; she quieted back into her sniffling and Nell settled herself to stay.

At three o'clock, Gamma rose silently and cast a glance through the heavy curtains at the sleet, which ticked down inexorably outside on the veranda. She belted her heavy blue slipper-satin robe closer about her slender waist and went out into the hall and called Chief Gerald Minnich of the Sparta City Police. They listened in silence as her light voice began its silver fluting into the telephone.

"Gerald? This is Ruth Fox. I'm sorry to waken you at this hour, but my granddaughter Yancey left here with a . . . young man whom none of us know . . . at half-past seven, and she is not at home yet. The storm is really getting quite severe, and we are naturally very concerned about her. This . . . person . . . she is with is accustomed, I understand, to hanging around those . . . ah, places . . . out on the old highway, and I have heard that he is frequently intoxicated. I would appreciate it very much if you would go and see if Yancey is by any chance there with him, and if she is, bring her home at once. If she is not, I will appreciate your searching the roads 'round about until you have found her. There may have been an accident. I will wish to press charges against the young man . . . for contributing to the delinquency of a minor, or whatever charge applies; I'm sure you can find one that will . . . so please detain him. I will wait to hear from you."

There was a pause.

"Oh, no, Gerald, tomorrow morning won't do at all, not at all. My granddaughter is not 'lots of girls,' and her previous behavior is hardly any concern of yours, is it?"

Another pause; Nell, who had crept across the room to stand in the archway into the hall, digging at one slipper with the toe of the other, saw Gamma's face go white and her eyes light and leap like a jack-o'-lantern when the candle inside is lighted. Nell stared in fear.

"I remind you, Gerald," she said, "as I shall remind my fellow members of the city council when we meet next week, that my granddaughter is only fifteen years old. She is a minor in the eyes of the law, and, as such, she is not responsible for her own conduct. If she comes to harm, I shall have no trouble remembering that you were reluctant to leave your bed and go out on an unpleasant night to look for her. It's not the sort of thing a parent would forget. I shall see that none of them do." Another, shorter pause.

"Thank you, Gerald," she said, and hung up the telephone. Nell fled back upstairs to her room.

Yancey came home in a Sparta City Police car at six forty-five that morning, driven by Chief Minnich himself. She sat huddled in the back seat wrapped in her scarlet winter coat, and in her lap was a tight ball of her underclothes. The nineteen-year-old hot-rodder she had gone out with the previous evening, a meatily handsome, acne-pitted mechanic at the RoyCo Transmission Shop in town named T. C. Coggins, had been left blustering and swearing in one of the seldom-used cells in the makeshift city jail behind the Ford place, waiting for one of the tribe of great taciturn brothers at home to come and spring him.

Gerald Minnich had found them in the end cabin of the Red Rose Motel off the ice-slicked highway between Sparta and Titusville at six that morning, and had hustled them into the squad car so quickly that Yancey had not had time to dress completely. She had been asleep in the sour, sprung bed when Minnich and the white-eyed manager had burst into the icy cabin. Coggins, beside her, was passed out. Both had been naked.

Perhaps the most frightening thing about all of it, to Nell, was that Gamma did nothing. Nell had heard the slam of the patrol-car door in the dawn and scrambled to her window, scratching a round hole in the rime through which to peer down upon Yancey's teetering progress along the front walk. Seeing the bare white legs and soiled feet jammed into black suede pumps, seeing the ball of underclothes and the unsteady gait and the mountainous blue bulk of Chief Minnich looming up behind her sister, Nell felt her heart skid sickly, and she skinned out of bed and down to the landing where she could see and hear without much danger of being spied and sent back to her room. She watched and listened as the Chief's flat drawl, burying itself away from their shock and shame in official police terminology, laid it all out in the tired gray light of the foyer. She heard her mother's shriek of pain and grief, saw her bury her flaming face in her hands and scuttle into Rip's arms. She saw Rip put her mother gently aside and go to Yancey, who stood weaving in the center of the domino marble floor, her hair tangled and matted, her face white, her eyes blazing, her mouth, looking chewed and bruised and swollen, stretched in a ghastly smile. Nell could smell the sickly sweet whiskey gusting up the stairs.

But Gamma did nothing. She only stood and regarded Yancey with what looked to be great interest.

Nell watched as the Chief turned and went out the door, watched as they all turned to face Yancey, and then Gamma. Gamma still did nothing. They were all silent, and then Yancey spoke.

Rather, she shouted. She teetered up to the small, erect figure of her grandmother, and she bent into Ruth's face, and she shouted; she screamed.

"How do you like your little granddaughter now, Gamma? You like my outfit? You want to smell my new perfume? It's called Oh-dee-*screw*, Gamma, and you ought to try some. I sure am going to try some more; I'm going to use it every chance I get. And you know what, Gamma? I'm not ever going to be afraid of you anymore. Because I know all about you, you horrible old woman! I KNOW WHAT YOU ARE!"

Nell covered her ears against the uproar; she could not believe what she was hearing. Gamma would move now; now Gamma would act, must act; something terrible, something final was going to happen now, right now.

And there was movement; Rip, from the shadows under the curve of the stairs, moved out like a dark fury, faster than Nell had ever seen her move, and grasped Yancey roughly by her shoulders, and whirled her around and pushed her hard toward the stairs. Yancey stumbled ahead of her; her coat flew open and Nell could see that Yancey's crumpled skirt was unzipped, and her angora sweater rode so high up her young torso that one white breast showed, bobbling in the dirty light of dawn. Rip squalled at Yancey as she pushed her along, her low voice gone off into a strident cat's squall that Nell had never heard:

"*Git* on up them stairs, git on up there right this minute an' don' open yo' mouth! Just shut yo' mouth an' git upstairs *now!* Actin' like trash, comin' in here like some trashy ho' offen the street . . . *git* on up there!" In the dancing stipple of ice-light from the veranda, Nell saw that Rip's face was contorted into unrecognizability with anger, and that overlaid upon the anger was a stark and helpless terror. From her vantage point, Nell whimpered; Yancey, her own face white and raw-burnt and utterly blank, stumbled past her on the stairs and lumbered up and out of sight, with Rip behind her. Nell knew that neither saw her.

Downstairs, Hebe hugged the newel post and sobbed and sobbed.

And still, Gamma did nothing.

There were three days left until the party, and after the terrible scene in the dawn foyer of Fox's Earth had ended and they had all gone back into their rooms, the house settled back into a caricature of normalcy that was, to Nell, more frightening than the aftermath she had expected. Her misery was so intense that it embarrassed her. She felt shame at her own pain, as though she had earned it by some unspeakable inadequacy or deed, and must wear it about her neck like a rotting albatross until her atonement was sufficient. She shrank aside when she passed anyone on the stairs, and smiled gummily, and fawned like a beaten cur, and hated herself for the fawning; the great golden lions of Fox's Earth did not fawn. They would despise her even more. But she could not seem to stop the craven shrinking. And it did not seem to matter anyway; they did not notice her. By the evening of the party, bathed and dressed in a new dress of topaz velvet that did astonishing things to her eyes and rain-colored hair, she had stopped much of the hurting and most of the fawning, and felt better.

Banished to the upstairs so that she would not be underfoot during the last-minute preparations, Nell crept down the corridor to Yancey's room and, to her surprise, found the door open for the first time in three days. She put her head around the door; nothing happened and Yancey did not shriek at her or hurl anything, so she edged into the room. All Yancey's lamps were lit, and she sat at her dressing table, her back to Nell, her long legs buried in the starched dotted swiss of the vanity skirt. She was brushing her hair; it licked about her head like snapping fire. Nell always loved to watch Yancey do her hair. She ventured farther into the room. Yancey wore only panties and a blue satin garter belt and a strapless bra; the long line of her back, with the velvety knobs of her vertebrae nudging against the pearly skin, was beautiful to Nell. She must be going out; she would miss the party, and that would set Gamma off for sure, but on the other hand, the bra was an auspicious sign. It had been a long time since Yancey had worn one. On balance, Nell was heartened, and made bold to speak to Yancey. The open door behind her would facilitate a quick escape if Yancey should erupt again.

"Whatchou doin'?"

"What does it look like I'm doing? I'm brushing my hair. Oh . . . for God's sake, Nell, don't stand there gawking. Come on in if you're coming."

Nell sat down on Yancey's bed and looked about her. A sea-green taffeta dress hung from the mantelpiece on a padded satin hanger. Nell had not seen it; it was one of Yancey's severe and beautifully tailored shirtwaists, but it was softened with a delicate ruching of tiny ruffles down the deep V of the neckline. In it Yancey's long neck and small head would look tender and elegant, like a snow-drop rising from its foliage. What was happening here? Where were the blue jeans and the oxford-cloth shirts?

"Are you going out?"

"No . . . I'm fixing to go to bed. That's my new night-gown." The hairbrush flew; silk fire crackled and leapt. Nell could not think of anything to say that did not sound as stupid as what she had just said. She was silent.

"I'm sorry, Bean."

"Huh?" Nell raised her head; was Yancey talking to her?

"I said I'm sorry. Oh, look . . ." Yancey's face in the mirror looked at her in an odd mixture of impatience and despair, and then she swiveled on her vanity bench and rose and crossed the room in her slender high heels and sat down beside Nell on her bed. Incredibly, she put her gleaming naked arm around Nell's shoulders and gave them a small squeeze. Nell was transfixed in sudden embarrassment, and ducked her scarlet face into her new dress's inevitable lace collar.

"I've been absolutely rotten to you lately, haven't I, baby?" Yancey said. "To everybody else, too, but they don't count. Well . . . Rip does, but Rip understands . . . but I'm sorry about you. It's just that I . . . oh, I guess I miss Paul a lot, but you do, too, don't you? And things just seem so shitty awful . . . and it's all Gamma, Bean. You're too young to see it, but I've just begun to see . . . it's all Gamma . . ."

"What's all Gamma?" Nell mumbled in dread, digging in her nose with her forefinger. She felt that something terrible and inevitable was about to be imparted to her, something she should have known always, something she could never unknow. Yancey gently removed the finger.

"I don't know . . . but I *do* know, somehow . . . I mean I almost know. It's like real soon I *will* know . . ."

"Know *what?*" Nell wailed.

"Know about Gamma. Know what . . . I need to know. What there *is* to know. Whatever that is. At least, if I don't screw up and make her so mad that she yanks me out of here like she did Paul. I've really been dumb; I've been playing right into her hands, with all this smoking and drinking garbage, and all . . . the other stuff . . . I've just been *asking* for her to kick me out. God, I really thought I'd done it the other night. But I guess she's washed her hands of me. Thank God. It only occurred to me yesterday that I wouldn't ever know all there is if I got her so mad she ran me off. It just made me want to throw up, to think how close I came. So I'm mending my ways; the worm has turned. As of tonight, I'm starting to be the most perfect Miss Priss Yancey Geiger of Fox's Earth you ever saw. Everyone will be amazed. Gamma will cream her jeans in joy."

"What's cream her jeans?" Nell lifted her head and stared at Yancey in fascination. The mental image of Gamma clad in milk-smeared blue jeans was ludicrous to the point of absurdity.

"Oh," said Yancey, beginning to laugh, "you'll soon know, Bean. I promise you, you will all too soon know!"

And her gay, throaty laugh was so unexpected and delighting that Nell did not nag her for further illumination, but laughed with her sister in a caroling moment of closeness that she would remember the rest of her life.

A sudden thought struck Nell.

"You're not going out; you're coming to the party!"

"Right you are. I'm coming to the party and grin like a possum in the middle of a cow plop; till the bitter end shall I bob and grin and coo and carry on. No one will know me."

"I'm real glad," Nell said simply, a great anthem of thankfulness swelling her heart. Yancey caught the joy and hugged her again.

"I really am sorry for the way I've treated you, Bean. It'll be better from now on, I promise. With Paul gone, we Fox girls have got to stick together, don't we? Say you aren't mad with me?"

"Oh, naw. I'm not mad. I didn't care, anyway."

"Well, then. Stand up and let me look at you. Wow, Bean, what's *happened* to you all of a sudden? You look *beautiful*. That color, and your eyes and hair . . . and you're getting tall, too. You're going to be a knockout; did you know that? Come over here and look at yourself. Don't you think you look grown up and pretty?"

"Gamma says I look like a Beatrix Potter mouse," Nell said almost inaudibly, but new joy rang in her ears. A knockout. Grown-up. Tall. Yancey had a magic she could bestow at will: for a moment small Nell Geiger was tall, prowling, golden Nell Fox, padding proud and invincible down the great curving stairs of Fox's Earth into the adoring stew of her party below. Nell went fiercely scarlet and crept back into her lace collar, and Gamma came into the room.

The two sisters froze in front of the mirror, their faces still with danger, and looked at Ruth Fox, who looked back at them in cool amusement. She was dressed in black satin with an enormous portrait collar that framed her marble shoulders and set off the creamy triple strands of her pearls . . . the "Fox Pearls" as she always referred to them. Her hair was piled in a shining coil on her small head, and her eyes swallowed the room in their intensity. The light that seemed to shine from somewhere behind her slim bones was as bright this evening as Nell had ever seen it; the very air around her quivered and trembled with showered light. Her pupils were so large that her eyes were black. She looked beautiful and somehow terrible, but her voice was mild and light and chiming, and her smile was serene. She was carrying a small tole tray covered with a white linen napkin.

"Hello, chickies," she fluted, as if the last words she had spoken to her older granddaughter had not been terrible, tearing, searing things, as if, indeed, the anguished descent of Yancey into her tawdry alienation had never occurred at all.

"Hey, Gamma," Nell mumbled. Yancey said nothing, but she smiled tentatively, and Gamma gave them both her brilliant smile that spurted blue light at them.

"I have a little favor to ask somebody," she said. "Yancey, I think, since I heard Rip say she still had to give Nell's sash a lick and a promise. Honey, would you just slip on your coat and run out to Rip's house and take this tray to Jacob Lee? You don't even have to dress; just slip your coat on over your undies. I think *your* dress could stand a little lick of Rip's iron, by the way; I'll tell her while you're gone. It's a mighty pretty dress, isn't it? You're going to look real sweet in it tonight."

"Jacob Lee?" Yancey said stupidly. She did not move to take the tray.

"Jacob Lee," Ruth said, smiling even more brilliantly. "You know what a sweet tooth he has, and it seems a shame for him to have to wait till Rip can get there after the party with some goodies for him. Besides, I know he's missing his supper. She's been busy in the kitchen all day. Would you be a lamb for me and run these out there?"

"I . . . well, gee, Gamma," Yancey said, staring at her grandmother. Nell knew how she felt. Hardly anyone in the house had seen Jacob Lee since Paul's departure, and no one had mentioned his name, Gamma least of all. That she should be so concerned for him now, on this of all nights, was somehow nearly incredible. On the other hand, it was an incredible night.

"Please, honey?" Gamma said, even more incredibly.

"Well, sure," Yancey said, and took the tray. Her blue eyes narrowed with puzzlement; Nell thought, looking at them as they stood facing each other, that in profile like this Yancey and Gamma might have been struck by the same mint. It was an unsettling thought.

"Thank you, puddin'," Gamma said, and was gone from the room in a crackling slither of black satin and a drift of Joy and a spatter of staccato heel taps.

"Well . . . gee," Nell said, for want of anything else to say. Something seemed required of her in the face of Yancey's nearly palpable silence.

"Gee, indeed," murmured Yancey, still looking at the door through which Gamma had vanished. "Now what, I wonder . . ."

"She's actin' real funny, don't you think?" Nell said chummily, wanting to preserve the warm-wrapping air of Yancey-and-Nell that had pervaded the room before Gamma had come in. But Yancey was gone away from her again.

"When isn't she?" Yancey said briskly. "Oh, well. Scoot, now, Nell. Go get your sash ironed and take my dress with you, will you? The neckline *is* wrinkled. Christ, of all times . . . where's my coat? Oh . . . there."

She skinned into her red coat and belted it tightly. She might have been fully dressed beneath it, instead of nearly and pearlily naked.

Still, Nell lingered. The night had turned large and strange.

Yancey grabbed up the tray and hustled Nell out of the room ahead of her.

"Go *on,* Nell! I don't want you rooting around in my room when I'm not here. I'll be back in a minute, tell Rip."

"Okay. Uh . . . Yancey?"

"*What,* Nell?"

"Tell Jacob Lee I said hey."

"I will."

She went down the stairs in a glissando of heel taps, her loose hair flying behind her like a cloud of fire, the tray balanced lightly in her long hands. Nell, dawdling along the stair railing and swinging idly on the landing newel post, heard her shout something to Rip as she passed through the kitchen, and then the back door slammed and she was gone.

Five minutes after she left, Ruth Fox slipped on her own coat, a melting new Autumn Haze mink, picked up another, smaller covered tray, and went out through the kitchen door behind Yancey.

"I forgot to put Jacob Lee's fruitcake on his tray," she said to Rip as she pattered through the kitchen on her tiny heels. "And that's the part he likes most. I'll be back in two shakes of a sheep's tail, Rip."

Nell, standing impatiently at the ironing board as Rip steamed her trailing velvet sash, looked around sharply as the smell of damp cloth became the curling stench of smoking silk velvet, and saw that Rip's face was blasted to black basalt with something that looked to be a stunning terror. It was so intense and naked a look, focused on the door that Ruth had just closed behind her, that Nell swung back to stare at the door in sour, heart-stopped terror: what unimaginable horror stood just outside in this December night? But there was nothing there. For a long, long, velvet-smoking, heart-hammering moment, there was nothing there at all, and then there was.

Gamma was there, standing motionless in the open doorway, her face whipped and white and truly dreadful, a woman who has seen ghosts, the devil, unseeable evil.

231

The wind whipped behind her. Sick and unable to breathe, Nell waited for whatever it was to loom up behind Gamma on the porch, but there was only the empty back yard, moon-silvered and whispering with the wind, and, through the cold lace of the box hedge, the warm lights of Rip's cabin. Yancey was nowhere in sight.

Still holding her small covered tray, Gamma walked slowly into the kitchen. She walked through the kitchen and into the dining room, and only then did she speak. She did not turn her head, but her voice drifted back to them with exaggerated clarity:

"Rip, I want to see you in my room immediately. On your way up, stop and tell Miss Hebe that I wish to see her there, too. Right now. Nell, go to your room and stay there until you're told you may come out."

"Gamma . . ."

"Go."

"Rip!" Nell was frantic; her voice whistled out of control in her throat, and she could not breathe around the sick bucketing of her heart inside her rib cage.

"Rip, what's the matter? What's wrong? Where's Yancey? Rip . . ."

"Go to your room, Nell," Rip said in a voice that Nell had never heard before, and Nell said no more, but turned and flew up the stairs to her room.

20

YANCEY WENT away on the second of January, 1951. This time Nell was not surprised. The same signs that had foretold the going away of Paul were as vivid in the bright air as sheep's entrails laid out, or the spilt dregs of sacramental wine. This time there was an additional portent, one that shrieked in the air of the holiday season like a huge night bird: the leaving of Jacob Lee. For he was gone the next day after the party that, insanely, went on as though Gamma had not come staring in from the black night with the face of a woman who has looked on death; as if a humming Yancey had not come drifting in from Rip's cabin and been snatched up the stairs, stunned and furious, by Gamma and summarily locked into her room; as if Rip and Gamma had not emerged from this latest hissing, sobbing meeting in Gamma's room with old, dead faces over which, later, they pinned party smiles that were as ghastly false as the smiles of corpses; as if Mama had not collapsed and not come down to the party at all.

Jacob Lee was gone, and all that Rip would tell Nell . . . all that she ever told her . . . was that Jacob Lee had been sent to the home of a great-aunt in Detroit who had fallen and broken her hip, and had need of his strong back and willing heart. And Nell did not question Rip, for her energies and her small passions had all simply shut down, had curled up within her like the new fronds of ferns against the cold of winter, and her sole concern was the navigation of each day in that great, hurting house so that no one noticed her or singled her out in any way. Nell could afford no further engagement of any essential part of herself with the world.

It was not difficult in those few terrible days after the party, to be an invisible girl at Fox's Earth. As after Paul's leaving, Mama kept to her room, and the wailing and keening that emanated from it seemed to Nell, when she passed in the hall upstairs, to be a tired and perfunctory outcry, as though she were not yet up to form after her virtuoso performance at the time of Paul's departure. This was Nell's first cynical thought, and she was not aware of having it, but it struck against the wholeness and integrity of her childhood and left there a tiny pit of scar tissue.

Gamma was not abroad in the house to notice her, either. She spent most of her time, when she was not closeted with Mama, in her own room, and she spoke little to Rip and not at all to Nell, who in any case stayed in her own room or in the cage under the back steps as much as possible. No one went into Yancey's room that Nell saw; she would hear the door open and close sometimes, in the nights or the early mornings, so she knew that Yancey was not still locked in, but she did not see Yancey again after watching, transfixed, as her sister was hustled, squalling in genuine confusion and outrage, up the stairs by Gamma the night of the party. Once, on that same night, after the party had ended and Rip had gone silently back to her own cabin, and Gamma had gone upstairs in her black satin and white grimness, Nell had heard shouting from Yancey's room, heard her sister's voice cracking with fury and frustration: "But *why?* Why? I don't understand why you're doing this!"

And later that same evening, from Mama's room, she heard Gamma's voice, pure and true: "Hebe, darling puddin', I wish I *had* been mistaken, but it was just as I passed the window, not five feet away, and the room was as bright as daylight. No, I know what I saw. And you and I both know what we must do. We've left it too long as it is; I tried to tell you, but you wouldn't listen."

But though she heard them, she saw almost no one, and though Rip was there in the kitchen as she always was, she was gone so far away inside herself this time that not even a glimmer, not a flutter of her Rip-ness flickered in her obsidian eyes or lit her vacant face. She did not sing or hum, as she usually did, or call out after Nell in passing in her rich voice; her steps were slow and measured, and her eyes did not seem to see the tasks that her hands did, and Nell knew that there was nothing in this Rip for her. She did not mind, somehow. All that mattered now was to seek the solace of the cage and to wait.

She was in the cage so often, wrapped dreaming and silent in the cold quilts, or in her room buried deep in a book, that she saw and heard none of the preparations that surrounded Yancey's leaving. Trunks came down from the attic and were carried into Yancey's room without her noticing; and clothes were washed and ironed and carried upstairs by Beauty and Salome; and, she supposed later, there were phone calls back and forth to the expensive boarding school in Virginia . . . near Paul? Afterward, Nell wondered about this, but incuriously. If Yancey was near Paul, she would see him somehow. If she was not, she would keep close to him in other ways. They would be together in some sense; they always had been. This knowledge was a small, sere comfort.

But all this washed over Nell's curly mouse head unnoticed, for she had drowned in something deeper and older.

But still, on the morning that they took Yancey away in the Chrysler to the Sparta train station, the morning that they thought her still asleep and oblivious in her bed,

Nell woke and stirred and heard the muffled commotion down the hall and on the stair, and knew instantly that Yancey Geiger was going out from Fox's Earth and, like her brother, would not be truly coming back; and when the Chrysler had turned the corner she got out of bed and dressed herself in her blue jeans and one of Paul's old striped jerseys, over which she pulled Yancey's discarded cheerleader's sweater with the grand blue S, and over it all she buttoned her own hated burgundy wool winter coat with the velvet collar, and then she stole down the back stairs and went into the cage. And there she stayed until the sun was low and bloody, and the January cold had chapped her tear-scoured cheeks and nose raw, and her hands and feet had long since gone numb. There she stayed, through all their calling and scolding, and it was not until the house had been silent for over an hour that she crawled stiffly out of the lattice cage and stood alone in the darkening back yard, feeling, not the leonine afterglow of grandeur that often lingered about her after her times there, but only a whistling emptiness and the strange and radiant beginnings of the flu.

Rip found her first, still standing at the foot of the steps, shivering and wavering and pinched blue with cold and loss. Rip merely looked at her, and then she knelt and put her arms around Nell, and pulled Nell into her thin-corded neck where, incredibly, Nell felt the scalding warmth of tears. And the tears seemed to melt the great ice chunk that filled most of the interior of Nell Geiger on this January day, so that by the time Mama and Gamma came pounding down the back steps, fussing and chirring and demanding to know where she had been, Nell was crying outright and furiously, and was able to pull herself away from the healing arms of Rip and look her grandmother in the eye, and aim a thin stream of ineffectual spittle at her. The spittle fell far short of Ruth Fox's high-heeled slippers, but the effect was enormous: she paled, and gasped, and stared at her granddaughter as though she brandished a smoking pistol.

"I'm not going to tell you where I was," shrieked small Nell Geiger. "I won't ever tell you where I was! I hate you and I wish I never had to see your awful old face again!"

Ruth did not blink or drop her eyes. Nell felt her bones soften and curl; the stiffening fury ran from her legs and spine like used water, and the back-yard wind howled around her smallness and aloneness until she had the eerie sensation of feeling herself disappear.

"That can be arranged, Nell," Gamma said softly. "And it will be arranged if you ever say that again."

Nell never did.

She was alone then, in the house of the Fox women. She remained curled into herself until a sort of healing was complete, and by the time she could allow the tender, red new tissue of herself to creep out of her shell, the currents of grief and loss that ran free in Fox's Earth had lessened. They had not stopped, but they had slowed. Nell knew that she could live with the small, rhythmic rockings. It was the great storm tides she feared.

In those years, only Rip truly lived in the fervent, arid little heart of Nell Steed Geiger. But she was an older, slower, more silent Rip now, since Jacob Lee had gone away to Detroit and it became apparent that Paul and Yancey would not return to Fox's Earth. For though there were fleeting visits between quarters and after summer camps, it was two remote, formal, neutral-eyed strangers who came to sleep briefly in their old rooms; beautiful, narrow-boned strangers who spoke politely about nothing of consequence and returned to their schools as soon as decency permitted. But still, there was Rip. The gold-flickering smile was seen seldom now, and Rip did not sing at her ironing board anymore. But her fine, corded arms were still there to encircle Nell when she wept with loss after Paul and Yancey had come home and gone away again, or when Gamma's bridle chafed too heavily on her, or some citizen of her small world transgressed against her. Rip, always. Rip, there. In Nell Geiger's mind, when she thought, abstractly, "Fox's Earth," she saw first the blue-golden flare of Gamma and then the bronze warmth of Rip.

Nell was not, for all her early isolation, an acutely lonely child. Her world soon became the raucous, comfortingly banal world of public schools, first grammar school and then the consolidated high school that served Sparta and its surrounding rural school district. Nell had friends; she was popular and strikingly pretty, though not so flamboyantly beautiful that she alienated her contemporaries, as Yancey had. Unlike Yancey, Nell was, and

236

remained, almost totally without vanity. This was less a tribute to some pure innate ore in Nell than the result of the smashing ambiguities and losses with which she had lived early, but it was an attractive trait, nonetheless, and gave Nell the child and later Nell the woman a real and touching vulnerability that drew the solicitude of others to her, whether or not she wished it. Usually she did not, for she found early on that solicitude quickly became dominance, or at least the attempt at it, and nothing in Nell's life had armed her to resist dominance. So she shied away from this easy and unasked solicitude, but still it rained down over her silken head in an unceasing shower from the day she entered school, and so she had friends even though she was a shy child.

Ruth, as serene and gracious as if she had not only lately cast her two oldest grandchildren forth from Fox's Earth, ran her woman's world and soothed and petted her aging daughter and tended her remaining grandchild like a flower. She saw to it that Nell was carefully schooled in piano and drawing and watercolor, sent to dancing school, taken once a week to Atlanta to the preteen classes in fashion and deportment offered by the largest department store. Ruth picked her clothes, chic, feminine miniatures of her own. Hebe, emerging blinking and slumbrous from her bower for dinner or a matinee with her mother, would look contentedly at her slender daughter in one of that season's exquisite dresses and, perhaps remembering Yancey's fiercely sexual armor of faded denim, would smile and murmur that Nell looked pretty and nice, like a real lady. And though Nell yearned for pedal pushers and back-buckled Bermuda shorts, she warmed in the frail sun of her mother's approval and did not change out of the pretty clothes Ruth picked.

But Nell's real love, her real gift . . . a rich, glinting, entirely spontaneous facility for words and an odd, haunting perception with which to illumine them . . . Ruth Fox subtly discouraged. That way lay power for Nell; that way lay escape. That way must be barred. But Ruth knew that that way must not be dynamited, only eroded. So she walked softly and moved slowly. There was time . . .

And so Nell's first small, stumbling, inventive essays and poems were dismissed with a vague smile or a faint frown.

"You draw so beautifully, honey," Ruth would say. "I

hate to see you wasting your real gift fiddling around with something that can't ever take you anywhere."

And Nell, knowing already the gnawings of self-doubt and anger and the guilt that anger engendered, began to know them now in a new and mature way. And she rebelled, even though the rebellions were small.

She drifted effortlessly through high school. Ruth and Hebe agreed that she might attend the county high, instead of going away or having a tutor, because "it's really quite good now, with the new principal, and we can't do without our baby." And the writing, unsuspected and unapproved by Gamma, persisted.

Nell quietly dropped her elective art courses for more journalism and English literature. She ran, without mentioning it at home, for editor of the school paper, and won the position. She began to spend afternoons with her journalism adviser, a young New Hampshire woman so far undaunted by the fetid weight of the South, who saw Nell's gift and was pleased to nurture it with hours of talk and career planning. Under her direction, Nell began to prepare for application at Columbia University's School of Journalism.

"My brother goes there," Nell said. "He's going to be a journalist, too—a real one, I mean. He's terribly talented."

"Well, so much the better, then," her adviser said. "Does he like it?"

Nell hesitated.

"I don't know," she said finally. She didn't. All she knew of Paul's world now was that he was a freshman at Columbia and shared an apartment in New York with Yancey, who had gone there like an arrow after graduation from Wellesley and was rising in the advertising agency in which she had found a job. Nell knew that Yancey loved "housekeeping for my helpless baby brother," as she put it in a rare letter home, but she did not know how Paul felt about the arrangement, for he did not write or call and had not been home since he left the Virginia military school. News of him came via Yancey.

"Columbia is the place for you, too," the young adviser said. "With your grades and your other activities, you shouldn't have any trouble at all. It will be the best thing in the world for you, to be out in the real world for a while."

"This is real," Nell said, puzzled.

"This is about as real as Rudolf Friml," her adviser snorted, and Nell smiled.

Under the guidance of the young teacher, she entered a national essay contest, and won it. Happiness turned to throat-aching joy. Nell ran all the way home to tell them. Surely now, surely this . . .

And, as she had always been, she was punished. Ruth became desperately ill in the night with heart palpitations; the night was an explosion of calls and soft-running footsteps and the frantic summoning of Dr. Hopkins and Hebe's banshee wails and Rip's low shushing. Ruth was in bed for two weeks in silence and stillness, in lieu of hospitalization; she flatly refused the tests ordered by a frowning, puzzled Dr. Hopkins. Hebe was utterly unable to cope; there was no question of Nell's going to Washington to accept her prize. It was mailed to her, and came weeks afterward.

This was perhaps the most dramatic punishment, but it was not the first or the last. But always before they had been subtle punishments, so that she was seldom aware of them . . . only of the dull, ever-present anger and helpless frustration that she felt, and the guilt . . . always the guilt.

"They've given me everything in the world," Nell would think, because she had been told this so often. "How can I be so angry at them all the time? What kind of selfish monster am I, to disappoint them this way?"

The punishments were clever and effective and were carefully concealed from Nell. After a quiet visit to the young curriculum adviser from Ruth Yancey Fox, Nell found herself steered away from the elective journalism and English courses. Ruth had inherited her husband's position on the county board of education at his death; she was now president. The young adviser was supporting an emphysematous mother and two small brothers in a blighted, desperately poor New Hampshire farm village; she had no stronghold from which to fight. The year of Nell's editorship of the school newspaper, Ruth was by turns delicately scornful and deeply sorrowful that she was neglecting her art courses. Hebe, sullenly resentful of the attention-getting commotion that her last child was causing and shrinking from conflict, sided with her mother.

Nell did not enjoy the year, and did not make a good editor. Her self-doubt deepened.

"Maybe they're right, and I am just not a writer," she thought bleakly. "No matter what Miss Henderson thinks."

In any case, it proved to be an academic point, for the young faculty adviser did not receive her tenure, and did not return to school for Nell's senior year. The young woman never knew why, but she had her suspicions. Only Ruth Fox knew for certain.

And Rip.

During that time it was Rip alone who offered encouragement.

"Read me somethin' you wrote, Nell," she would say in the kitchen in the afternoons, and she would cut Nell a slice of freshly baked gingerbread and settle herself to listen.

"Soun' mighty fine," she would say, nodding, her eyes closed, when Nell had finished. "You makes them words soun' like music. Bet you gon' be a famous writer one of these days."

"It's just a hobby," sullen, guilty, grateful Nell would murmur, loving her. "I'm really a lot better at other things."

"Soun' mighty fine to me. Make me wisht I could read an' write. You do what yo' insides tells you, not what yo' head say."

"Or what *they* say" hung in the air, but it was never spoken, and the afternoon recitals were never mentioned, by tacit agreement between the black woman and the girl.

But after all, she was only silent, loving, illiterate Rip, and Nell paid her little heed.

Nell was popular with boys, but had no steady: "Really, Nell, don't you think he's just a bit . . . well, you know, honey, his folks were mill people until just recently. Just wait till you get to college. So many really fine young men to meet, and you *are* a special girl. What's your hurry?"

And so Nell, in the last bright autumn of her senior year in high school, let her writing slide and dutifully applied herself to her English and art classes, and went to football games and pep rallies and sock hops and slumber parties and a few dress-up dates in Atlanta, always in a crowd of her brushed and burnished peers, always home by her curfew, always and essentially unengaged by any life that could not have come straight from the pages of *Seventeen*. Gamma's and her mother's approbation were warm on her shoulders like the sun.

But always, in the back of her mind, like a diamond hidden in a cave, Columbia and New York shimmered.

"Can I? Can I, really?" Nell would think. "Can I really leave them and go there and learn to be a journalist?"

And, faintly, faintly, would come the faraway answer: "I can try."

21

AT CHRISTMAS that year, Paul and Yancey came home for the first time in four years, and Nell saw that something had come upon them there in the East, something that changed them so that they would not ever truly be familiar to her again. There had been changes before, of course; on their few fleeting visits home from their Virginia schools Nell would see clearly the metamorphoses wrought by passing time and their changed worlds, and there was always upon them the formal remoteness with which they armed themselves against Gamma.

But where before there had always been the almost tangible forces of their twinlike bond and their delighted absorption in each other, now they seemed poles apart, alike only in their long-boned, fair-haired physical beauty. Nell marveled at the beauty of them even as she wondered at the alienation; she had forgotten how alike and how compelling they had always been. But this Christmas Yancey was hollow-eyed and nervous and caustic, prowling about the house and chain-smoking and snapping abruptly at Paul, and he was at once aloof and humming with an undischarged energy. He met Yancey's gibes with a sort of secret, banked excitement that lit his cheeks and eyes.

On the morning they would leave to go back to New York, they sat late at the breakfast table, Yancey heavy-eyed and pale after a late party the night before, looping her hair behind her ears with a thin, impatient hand, Paul abstracted over his coffee, jumping whenever the phone rang. Hebe chattered ingenuously at them as if they had been older and more sophisticated contemporaries from a far more exotic world. She never tired of hearing the details of Yancey's job and Paul's studies and their lives in Manhattan. Gamma sat silently, smiling and studying them both.

"Christ, I feel awful," Yancey said, sizzling out her cigarette in her coffee cup. "I forgot what eggnog could do to you. I'm too used to martinis."

"You were very late last night, weren't you?" Gamma said companionably. "I heard you come in around five. Goodness, you sophisticated New Yorkers. Did you have a good time with Sykes Claiborne? I guess you haven't seen him in . . . oh, at least seven or eight years."

"I wasn't with Sykes Claiborne," Yancey said, stretching enormously. "Sykes Claiborne is a horrible bore. Sykes Claiborne has a beer gut. Sykes Claiborne is a *Jaycee*, for God's sake. I dumped old Sykes Claiborne right on his fat behind and spent the evening out at the Wagon Wheel with old T. C. Coggins. You remember T.C., don't you, Gamma? Who works in the transmission place? The last time I saw old T.C. he was in the back of a *po*lice car in front of the Red Rose Motel, on his way to jail with Gerald Minnich. And you know, he hasn't changed a bit."

Nell stared at Yancey; was she crazy, goading Gamma like that? Really, she was in the most horrible mood. Hebe looked around the table, as if waiting for someone to tell her how to react. Paul drank his coffee steadily and calmly. Gamma's face showed nothing at all. She smiled at Yancey.

"Well, whoever, I'm glad you had a good time," she said. "It's always nice to see old friends again, isn't it? How about you, Paul? Did you have a good time with Molly Longshore? Such a pretty girl, and such a fine family. You were sweet to humor your old granny and take her to the party. Now, tell me the truth, wasn't there at least a little teensy spark? I thought when I met Molly that you two would be just perfect for each other. I know Yancey is too busy with her exciting career to think of it right now, but your mama and I do hope for wedding bells before we're too old to hear them without hearing aids. Maybe you'll be the first. You certainly can't live in that tiny little apartment with your sister forever."

There was a silence, and then Yancey exploded into laughter. Paul's face was mild and still, his eyes shuttered.

"Excuse me," he said. "I want to catch Jean before he gets away; the rent's due and he always forgets."

He rose, a long streak of narrow grace, and left the room. Still Yancey laughed. It was not a merry sound.

"I hate to tell you, Gamma," she sputtered finally, "but you'll be waiting a long time to hear Paul's wedding bells. Send not to know for whom the bell tolls, Gamma. It do not toll for Paul."

"Well, you two are just beyond me," Gamma said indulgently. "Who on earth is Jean?"

"Ah, Jean," Yancey drawled. "Jean François Leclerc de Valery, or some such. Jean is Paul's new roommate. Jean is Professor of Sub-remedial French or something equally esoteric at Columbia. Jean is twelve years older than Paul and very French and very, *very* pretty and very, very, *very* crazy. In fact, I would venture to say that Jean is downright demented. *Un homme dangereux, c'est Jean.*"

"When did Paul move in with . . . Jean?" Gamma said mildly. "I thought he was all settled and cozy with you. You've been together so long, and it seemed to work out so well for both of you, sharing the rent and all . . ."

"Yes, well, he's been all settled and cozy with Jean since September, and it's working out even better for him because Jean is footing all the bills," Yancey said sweetly.

"Why, that's nice of him," Hebe chimed.

"Oh, yes, Mama, it sure is," said Yancey. "He does lots of nice things for Paul. Takes real good care of him, does Jean. Guards him like the crown jewels. Why, once, when I'd gotten Paul a date with a girl I work with and they were doubling with me and my date, darling Jean tracked us to the restaurant and made an absolutely glorious scene. Said Paul should be home studying. Hollered and cried and carried on."

"My goodness, how embarrassing," Hebe said. "What did Paul do?"

"Go up and left with him," Yancey said. "We took his date home. It made quite an impression on her. If you want to know what I think, I think Jean is really dangerous."

"Oh, dear," Hebe said, her delicate brows drawing to-

243

gether and her luminous gray eyes filling. "Mama, maybe you should speak to him. If this professor is really dangerous . . ."

"Oh, nonsense, Hebe," Ruth said. "The French are emotional; it's just their way. Paul is a grown man now. The last thing he wants is for his mama and his grandmama to interfere with his life."

"Well, then, Yancey, maybe you can keep an eye on him. He always listened to you."

"Forget it," Yancey said. She looked white and in pain, ill. "Jean won't let him near me. Thinks I'm a bad influence. He doesn't even give Paul my telephone messages."

"Well, what can it hurt, after all?" Gamma rose to leave the table. "I for one am not displeased to have an experienced older man interested in Paul's welfare. New York is a mighty big and dangerous place. Come on, Hebe. Get your bath now. Fancy Cobb's do starts at eleven, and it's almost ten."

Her face as she left the breakfast room was rapt, as if she kept a splendid secret. Formless apprehension swept Nell. She wanted to pursue the matter with Yancey, but her sister rose and stalked away, and Nell was left alone in the quiet sunlight. Rip. She would go out into the kitchen and talk it all over with Rip. . . .

Paul put his head into the room.

"Bean? Could you come into Granddaddy's study a minute? There're a couple of things I've been meaning to talk to you about."

She followed him into the dim-shuttered room, and he swung the heavy paneled door shut and sank down into his grandfather's old leather chair. He held out his arms to Nell, and she ran across the carpet and perched on the chair's arm, and he put his arm around her and drew her head down to his shoulder. He rested his chin on the crown of her head, as he used to do in his rare moments of overt affection when they were children.

"I've missed you an awful lot these past few years," he said. "You've gotten so grown up and so pretty. I'm sorry I haven't been here to watch you grow up, look out for you a little."

"I don't need looking out for," Nell said, loving the clean smell of him and the good, remembered strength of

244

his arm around her. "Gamma has given me everything in the world I need, and more. And there's Rip."

"There's always been Rip, hasn't there? Tell me, Bean. What are you going to do about college? Go to art school somewhere?"

"I . . . haven't decided. Gamma and Mama want me to go here, to the university. The art school's awfully good . . ."

"What do *you* want?"

"Well . . . I *have* been thinking about Columbia—for journalism."

"I was just going to suggest the same thing," he said, holding her off and looking at her. His face was serious and intent. "You're really a good writer. This art stuff is a waste of time. Besides, you need to get away from here, and Columbia would be perfect for what I've been thinking about. It's a grand idea, and I want you to apply the minute school starts back."

"But I don't really have much hope of getting there," Nell said. "Gamma and Mama are truly set on the university, and I don't have any money of my own. And then, Columbia may not take me."

"They'll take you," Paul said. "You're better than me, and they took me, didn't they? And I have some money. That's the other thing I wanted to talk to you about."

"What?" She hardly dared breathe.

"I'd like to pay your tuition at Columbia. I have enough money now that I'm sharing with Jean. I'll have even more when I start working next summer. And I'd like to get you a little efficiency right in the same building. They're not much to look at, but they're clean and safe, and I'd be there to look after you, and Yancey isn't far away. In fact, I've already talked to the super about one on the same floor with me. It'll be available in September, and I can swing it with no trouble. I want to go back and put a deposit on it, if you'll agree."

"What would . . . Jean . . . say? I mean, he doesn't like Yancey bothering you all the time . . ." Nell did not look at him.

"Jean will think it's a terrific idea. He's a nice guy, Bean. You'll like him. I gather Yancey had a few things to say about him while I left the room, right? Don't pay any attention to that. Yancey's always been a trifle possessive. Now, what do you say?"

245

"Oh, Paul. Oh, Paul!" Possibility rang in the room like struck bronze. "Oh, if I really could . . . I did so want to do it, but I had no idea how I was going to. I promise I won't get in your hair . . ."

"I always want you in my hair, Nell. Remember that, no matter what happens. Now. I'll be in touch after the first about how we'll do this, and meantime, you just fill out that application and sit tight. And don't, for God's sake, say anything to Gamma or Mama about it until it's set. The closer to September the better, in fact. You're over eighteen, aren't you?"

"The seventh of this month."

"Good. No problem, then."

"I'll die if Gamma won't let me."

"Gamma can't stop you. She may make things pretty hot for you, but she can't stop you unless you let her. Remember that, Bean. You badly need to get out of here."

"Oh, I *love* you!" Nell hugged him fiercely, feeling the strong, straight, unfamiliar man's bones of his back and shoulders. He hugged her back. His smile as he opened the door of the paneled study was whole and free, a boy's smile. Even through the grateful tears that thickened her throat, Nell laughed aloud to see it.

In the arched niche under the curving stair that housed the telephone, just outside Horatio Paul Fox's study, Ruth Fox smiled, too, but there was no one to see it, not even Rip, and in any case, it was not a smile at which to laugh.

On the seventh of January, late in the evening, a telephone call came from a doctor at Bellevue Hospital in New York. Paul Fox Geiger had been shot, presumably by the man with whom he shared an apartment, who had then turned the gun on himself. The building superintendent had heard the shots and, getting no response to his knocks and calls, used his pass key to open the door of the apartment. Both men were dead on arrival at Bellevue.

For the first time in her life, Nell found herself unable to cry. From the moment Gamma put down the telephone and came into the little parlor where they were watching Ed Sullivan, her face blanched and wild, a perfect, airless orb of impenetrable numbness descended of its own volition over her, and there it stayed. Within it, Nell found that she could function as well as she needed to; it was

246

she who fetched the brandy from the sideboard when her mother gave a sharp yelp and fainted, she who summoned Dr. Hopkins and his ubiquitous needle, she who walked steadily out through the box hedges to Rip's little cabin to fetch her and tell her that Paul was dead.

After her mother's first predictable storm of weeping and shrieking, she did not cry again either, but grew vaguer and mistier and more shadowed, often forgetting that death had robbed her once more, not recalling who had died when she did remember. The exotic older man-child who had visited her and charmed and awed her was no more, but what had that to do with any son of hers? Afterward, Nell saw that the real deterioration of Hebe Fox Geiger began then.

Nor did Gamma cry. After a night shut away in her room, shades and curtains drawn, Ruth Fox rose in the bright January dawn of the next day and dressed in one of her exquisite Norell frocks and lit into the details of tidying up after the decidedly messy exit of her grandson from the world. First she called old Angus Cromartie at the funeral home and arranged for him to see to the details of sending for Paul's body, cremating it, and selecting a suitable urn. Under the circumstances, she said to Rip, who stood in the hall watching her telephone, it was unthinkable that there should be a funeral. Rip, who alone of the Fox women had wept for Paul, started to protest, but seeing Nell's blank white face and huge, staring eyes, fell silent. Rip thought that for all her vigilance she had not been able to protect Paul, but she could at least guard the other two Fox children to whom she was pledged.

"I 'spec that best," she said to Ruth, who was preparing to dial the editor of the Sparta weekly newspaper and silence any mention of the tragedy. "What you gon' tell Miss Yancey?"

From the swift look of blankness on her grandmother's grave white face, Nell knew she had forgotten about Yancey.

"Oh, my God," Ruth Fox said. "Of course, someone has to tell Yancey. Oh, poor child. It will kill her."

She was saved from the unpleasant duty of calling her granddaughter, at any rate, for the telephone shrilled under her hand and when she lifted the receiver it was to hear from a colleague of Yancey's at the advertising agency that her boss, concerned at her unaccustomed absence and getting a constant busy signal to his repeated calls to her apartment, had gone there, routed out Yancey's super, and found her sitting on the edge of her bed in her nightclothes with the telephone in her hand, as still and cold and white as if it were she who was dead and not her brother. Later they learned from the doctor at Bellevue that he had found Yancey's name and address in Paul's leather address book along with Ruth Fox's, and had called Yancey immediately after telephoning the Sparta number. So far as they would ever know, her sleepy "hello" to his call was the last word she spoke aloud for almost four months. Yancey slipped as naturally and, perhaps, gratefully into catatonia as a frozen traveler into a hot bath, and so of all the women in his young life, only a thin black woman with the fine head and shoulders of a pagan idol shed tears for Paul Fox Geiger at the hour of his death.

Quickly and quietly, Ruth Fox arranged with Yancey's boss to get her granddaughter into the care of his own psychiatrist and into an unobtrusively elegant and ruinously expensive small private clinic in the East Eighties, and that evening Stuart Hill from her husband's law office flew north to "see about this little tailspin Yancey has gotten herself into," taking Rip with him. "Because," Ruth told Nell, "I thought maybe they could bring chickie home with them, you know, and Rip could always handle Yancey when nobody else could." Rip, who had never traveled fifteen miles out of Suches in her life, made the trip with the same impassive calm and grace with which she would have embarked to the grocer's or the moon, and forever after, all she would say about New York was that it "ain't all that diff'unt from Sparta."

Yancey's kind and halfway infatuated boss had made his small East Side apartment available to the exasperated Stuart Hill and Rip, and met them at LaGuardia and chauffeured them to and from the clinic. They spent a day and one night in the city, Rip sleeping on the brocade sofa, Stuart Hill talking with doctors and making arrangements, and both looking at Yancey, who did not look back, or at anything else except the square of dirty-water-gray sky outside her wire-meshed window. While they were gone, a silken young man from Cromartie's called at Fox's Earth with the discreetly wrapped urn containing all that was mortal of Paul Fox Geiger, and Nell, serene and safe within her bubble, answered the bell and took the package into her room and unwrapped it and placed the urn on her mantelpiece. It did not look very different from the silver trophy she had won in the national essay contest. The next day, Stuart Hill and Rip came home again without Yancey.

"She is not well enough to come home, Nell darling," Gamma said that evening to Nell. "Very frankly, I do not know if she will ever be well again. I don't mean to be brutal, but we must face facts. You are old enough now for me to speak openly to you. We need you to help us bear it all."

They were in the little parlor, where Gamma had taken her for the purpose of a "serious talk," and Nell sat not on the couch or the hearth rug, her accustomed places, but in her mother's wing chair that was the twin of Gamma's own, on the other side of the fireplace. She was thinking nothing at all except that Gamma looked uncommonly well, with bright eyes and cheeks as pink as though she had just come in from vigorous, healthful exercise in the fresh cold outside.

"We have known all along that Yancey is not . . . terribly stable, haven't we, darling?" Gamma said, reaching over to take Nell's long, cold hands in her small ones. Hers were soft and warm. "And I've never felt that her fanatical attachment to poor darling Paul was in the least healthy, if you know what I mean." Nell didn't.

"You are our good, whole, healthy girl, Nell, and I know you will be strong for mine and your poor mama's sake. We must all be strong now."

Nell looked at her grandmother but said nothing, and presently Gamma patted her hand again and rose and went up to Hebe.

Gamma *was* strong. On her fragile shoulders she bore them all, fragmented, bewildered Hebe, zombie Nell, silent, grieving Rip. From early morning until late at night, Nell would see and hear her going about the echoing house, stilling the sorrowing litany that rose from Carrie and Robert and Beauty and Salome in the kitchen, ordering food . . . for, incredibly, they continued to sit down to meals in the vast dining room . . . crooning and singing to her daughter up in the crazy bower of a girl's room.

"I can't let down," she would say to people who phoned.

"If I did I think we'd all just give up and drown in misery."

There were many callers. Whether they knew all the lurid details of Paul's death and Yancey's incarceration Nell was not sure, but she doubted it. She was aware that the editor of the newspaper owed her grandmother a formidable sum of money, and that she had long since ceased to press him for payment. More than once she had heard Ruth say that she considered the uncollected debt a good investment, and it must have been, for no mention of Paul Geiger appeared in the paper at all, and none made its way across the sixty impenetrable miles of brown kudzu and "Jesus Saves" signs to the Atlanta media. Sparta could have no way of knowing very much.

But Nell knew that they talked, furiously, endlessly. It was as inevitable as children's chatter at a circus. The talk did not touch her. She could not imagine Paul dead, could not see his narrow, carved face and fair hair sheeted with blood, anymore than she could see volatile Yancey silent and in a place of wire and bars. And since she could not physically imprint the images on retina and brain, she was in some way unmarked by them. Neither was she touched by the image of her brother in the arms of the faceless Jean, for brain and retina rejected that picture, too, and this last, betraying love of Paul's stayed outside the globe of glass in which she walked.

Yancey did get well. One morning in April her physician at the private clinic called with jubilation in his dry voice to report that Yancey had that morning wakened as naturally as if she were in her own narrow apartment bed, sat up and stretched, frowned at the attendant who had come with a pan of water to bathe her, and said, "What time is it? I've got a meeting at ten I can't miss," and from then on her return to work and her Manhattan life were only a matter of time.

"It's as if she had stayed shut away somewhere until she could heal, and then just opened a door and came out and got on with it," the young doctor said. He seemed amazed by this, but Nell, who had taken the call, understood it perfectly.

If the Yancey who came out of the clinic was not the same quick, ardent young woman who went into it, she was, nevertheless, whole, and took up the flung-down ends of her life with an energy and singlemindedness that was astonishing in one so young and so recently seriously ill. She remembered fully Paul and the details of his death, but she did not speak of them again, and she refused the outpatient therapy recommended by the clinic, and moved back to her old apartment on the day she was discharged, rejecting all offers from Gamma and her friends at the agency to come and stay with them awhile. She plunged into her job with a passion bordering on monomania, working long hours on nights and weekends, bringing work home with her, volunteering for more. Everyone at the agency agreed that it was probably therapeutic for her, and gave her all the extra work she could handle. Within a year she was given a few small accounts of her own, and within two she was a full-fledged account supervisor, and soon the name Yancey Geiger became synonymous on Madison Avenue with a certain rakish, daring, bold-stroked style, a brittle panache. Before she was out of her twenties, Yancey was something of an industry legend, clearly destined for a top executive niche, if not *the* top one.

To Nell, at home in Sparta, she was a legend made more fabulous by a scrim of distance, for from the time Yancey left that last Christmas, she did not come home again. There were phone calls back and forth, and infrequent letters, but essentially Yancey had cut away the long roots of the South that bound so many refugees from that red land, and walked alone in her adopted life. But never again, from the time she left the small, barred clinic room on the Upper East Side, did she sleep alone.

In late April of her senior year, an envelope came for Nell from Columbia University. She folded it carefully over upon itself once, and then twice, and threw it into the kitchen garbage pail unopened. For the rest of her life, she never knew whether or not she had been accepted.

22

NELL ENTERED the local university in September. She majored in art, as Gamma wished; she flinched away from the very thought of journalism, of writing. In a way she was almost grateful that any such ambition had been scourged out of her and the decision wrested from her hands. Columbia and New York were unimaginable to her now. The East was a cold and distant star. There was no way home from there; not for Paul or Yancey. Not for her.

Ruth and Hebe were pleased.

"You were born to this house and this town and this life," Gamma said approvingly when Nell announced her enrollment. "You bring your own special grace to it. You understand it like Yancey never would have. Of course you'll stay here and go to school. This is your home; this is where you belong."

"This is where you belong," her mother parroted sweetly, and smiled mistily at Nell.

And to the youngest Fox, so long a stranger in a cage under the back steps amid a world of great golden beings, the word "belong" was sweet. Nell went off to her first classes in a mantle of contentment that was as warm as it was mindless.

Insofar as it could be after the numbing pain of her senior year in high school, college was pleasant for Nell. Realizing that they dared not cage her, that to do so would be to risk waking her and driving her from Fox's Earth, Ruth consented to her moving into her sorority house on campus, and Nell became something of a belle. There were men, then, cool, attractive fraternity men blissfully unencumbered with serious thoughts or the brains to house them: the "right" men.

Reveling in the social approval and the soft, pleased smiles from Ruth and Hebe that these young men's attendance earned her, but shying violently from the inevitable fumblings and gropings in the backs of their cars, Nell determinedly played the field. She dropped the ones who became serious. She drifted from alliance to alliance. She accepted no jeweled pin, though several were offered. She earned the reputation for being an elusive and desirable tease; the allegation did her no harm at all. It served to increase her popularity, in fact, and carried its own license to dodge the petting sessions. Nell cultivated the image; it was, in truth, a godsend. Commitment to any man now meant only one thing to her: pain and loss.

Nell's grades were good. She was busy. Campus and sorority activities absorbed her free time; she was engaged by none of the sluggish, colossal stirrings of the civil rights movement that was being born, slowly and in fire and portent, in Alabama and Mississippi. She was, she thought, enjoying college very much.

But it was different from high school; now they could not keep her from her required college English, even though she was an art major, and in these classes her anesthetized mind and heart began, slowly and tentatively, to sing to her once more. She began to take extra English and journalism electives again, this time telling no one. She worked hard on her themes; she reveled in her literature courses; she wrote often, late at night, in her journal.

She did not try out for the college literary magazine or the student newspaper. She simply wrote. She jangled with guilt at this betrayal of Gamma; she throbbed with fresh pain at the evocation of Paul that the writing brought her.

But she wrote.

Nell met Phillips Jay in September 1961, at the start of her senior year. She walked into the contemporary-style fiction class she had been saving as a special treat for herself in some quarter when there was time to savor it, and thought for one sick, dizzying moment that Paul stood at the blackboard, covering it with a list of required books for the course. Then he turned to the class and she saw that it was not Paul, of course, but a slim, blond stranger with Paul's narrow head and long-boned, negligent grace. He wore a tweed jacket with leather elbow patches and desert boots, and Nell thought he must be about twenty-eight or -nine. Through ringing ears, she strained to hear the words that his mouth was shaping.

"I'm sorry to tell you that Dr. Oakes had a bad fall at

253

his mountain cabin last week and broke his hip, and will not be taking contemporary fiction this quarter," said the blond young man, and Nell heard the long, flattened, oddly close-mouthed drawl of New England and prep schools and Harvard in his voice, which was surprisingly deep for his height and slightness.

"So you're stuck with me, which is probably your bad luck but my extreme good fortune, since I haven't got God's bit of tenure and have been in the fair Southland exactly three days and came here from a fine old rock-ribbed New England academy for young ladies so small and exclusive that its four alumnae can't remember its name to write it on endowment checks. But for the little acorn that felled the mighty Oakes, I would undoubtedly be dispensing Longfellow and Robert Service to the varsity football team, and you would have missed the cultural millennium. I am Phillips Jay from Boston by way of Harvard, and it's too late to do anything about any of that, so let's try to make the best of it, shall we?"

The class tittered uncertainly; with his blond hair and faint, lingering summer tan and unsuitable but becoming tweed over blue oxford cloth, he was an attractive man, and the added fillips of Boston and Harvard lent him an air of exotica and cultivation. On the other hand, there was an ominous northern sharpness about him. The class, which had anticipated coasting through the treacherous shoals of twentieth-century fiction on the familiar, sonorous balm of old Dr. Oakes's drawl, shifted in its collective seat.

Would those murky, razor-spined waters now be further booby-trapped by the elliptical, condescending wit and notorious tongue of a Yankee? More than one student decided when Phillips opened his mouth to drop the course and seek another, safer elective, but none of these students were women. The women students, almost entirely unconsciously, looked at Phillips under their lashes and patted their softly waved flips and cast their lot with contemporary fiction. Only Nell Steed Geiger did not sit up straighter, and wet her lips, and lean a little forward in her seat. But then, Nell would not have done so if Cary Grant had walked into Pressley Hall and told them he was taking contemporary fiction. Receding shock and anger at him for not being Paul pounded in her veins. What she felt consciously was sharp disappointment and a flush of anger at Dr. Oakes and his flaccid old ankles. She had looked forward to his class for three years, and this glib, fox-faced easterner was not going to charm her out of that cheat easily. She frowned, slightly and unconsciously, and Phillips Jay caught the frown, alone in a sea of penciled eyebrows arched over widening eyes. He thought nothing in particular about the small frown, but he noticed Nell.

Two weeks into the class, he caught up with her as she was leaving the classroom and asked her if she had time for a cup of coffee at Guido's across the street, and when he had settled her in a booth there and brought back two cups of swarthy coffee and a handful of elderly glazed doughnuts, he looked long at her in what Nell took to be displeasure, for his golden brows were drawn together over the sharp, webbed blue eyes, and the clever, wide mouth was a straight line.

Nell thought with a sinking heart that he was probably going to suggest that she drop his class and seek one less challenging, for he was as sharp-tongued and critical with his students as they had feared initially, and his sarcasm had made more than one tender, smitten woman student cry. He had not spoken sharply to Nell, in class or out; indeed, he had not spoken to her at all, but the three papers she had turned in to him had come back with two C's and a B-minus, and she could not seem to please him no matter how late into the nights she wrote. It was a new experience for Nell so far as her college English went, and the old self-doubts that had been born in her high-school years came flooding back over her. She had buried his resemblance to Paul so deeply in her subconscious that she would have been honestly surprised now if anyone had remarked upon it, but it bulked there nevertheless, immovable and solid, and sent eddies of discomfort and unsureness boiling into her awareness whenever she was in his presence. Nell was more than a little intimidated by Phillips Jay.

"I pulled your file from Admissions this morning and read it," he said. "I see that you've been majoring in art for the past three years. What the hell are you doing? Don't you know you're a natural writer, and a first-class one at that? Why have you wasted all this time? Oh, Jesus, don't cry. I didn't mean to yell . . . here, have a doughnut. Please, Miss Geiger. I always thought I knew something about women, but you southern ladies are going to do me in. Please?"

And Nell, who had been startled into tears of pure relief and childish joy and a great vindication, found herself laughing at the plaintive, unfeigned dismay in his voice, and looked up at him, and fell in love with him through the melding clouds of steam from their two coffee cups.

Phillips Jay was a newcomer to Sparta in more than one sense of the word. He was one of a new breed of young college professors who appeared in the South in the decade or so after World War II, a second wave of visionary carpetbaggers borne into Dixie on a swelling tide of opportunity and challenge. He and his counterparts were a curious phenomenon, in a way: idealists in a time when America's honor lay tattered on beaches in the Gilberts and Solomons or charred in the crematoriums of Europe or flash-burned into the incandescent rubble of Hiroshima; crusaders in a land where the only popular quests were for cheap housing and two cars in every carport and a Hula-Hoop for every toddler.

But idealists and crusaders they were, undoubtedly, as only the cloistered and prepped and ivied young princes of the East can be, and they saw in the overflowing, G.I.-billed colleges and universities of the South a sort of last frontier for classical education. Phillips Jay was at once one of the best the East had to send to this rare new Jerusalem below the Mason-Dixon line, and one of the worst. By birth and breeding he was so faultlessly begotten, schooled, summered, clubbed, and advantaged as to be almost laughable; later in the decade, he and his type would be the butts of much scornful abuse in the new egalitarian movement that threatened his very species, and they would seek to redeem themselves by streaming south to march with stoic blacks in burning little towns whose names were unpronounceable, whose speech was indecipherable, and whose white inhabitants loved them not and set upon their fair, lofty heads with clubs and dogs and fire hoses. And redeem themselves they would, for there was in Phillips Jay and his ilk no lack of decency or honor or courage; only, perhaps, of sense and sinew.

Unlike many of his kind, Phillips did not plan to put in his conscience time in the stricken South and then drift north and east again, there to slide comfortably into the English and humanities departments of the hoary universities that had spawned them, or into great family mercantile empires. Phillips had cast his lot with the South even before he set out for Sparta and the university, and he departed the ancestral roof amid great bitterness and acrimony on the part of his father, who roared of betrayal, irresponsibility, softheadedness, bleeding hearts, knee jerks, and niggers. It was the first time Phillips had ever heard the word on his father's lips, and it lent his southern quest the glow of nobility and the iron of commitment, so that he arrived at the southern university fully determined to make his stand and his career and his life there, and the family fortune be damned. Theirs was a bitter and basic estrangement that never healed, but only grew wider and deeper.

Much later, when the intractable South had begun closing in upon him and the cool groves of his own eastern academe began to seem sweet once again, he looked homeward and found the family door closed to him and his prodigal's portion given to his brother Charles, and the classrooms and board rooms in which he might have sat he found long filled. He raged inwardly then, cursing the bright, trashy bitch that was the South and cursing himself that he had not foreseen this exigency in that charmed landscape to which he came, bringing his pure and gemlike flame, in September of 1961. But it was a moot point, for again, like most of his sterling kind, Phillips did not at first see the South plain, and by the time he did, it was far too late for him ever to be truly of it. Like another easterner long before him . . . the father of the girl he would meet and marry . . . he never truly reconciled himself to that alienation.

But all this was still before Phillips Jay when he met Nell Geiger, and he was, by and large, charmed with the fauna and flora of the world he had come to save. The welcome he received from the courtly, soft-voiced academics of Sparta had been warm and flattering, and he found them surprisingly and reassuringly cultivated and charming. There would, after all, be good companions among them, good talk. The university itself was mellow and beautiful, a graceful neoclassical city crowning its wooded hills, seeming to float in purity and gold in the slanted, mythic light of September. The town itself, or what he had seen of it, was equally beautiful, and wrapped with the same reassuring patina of graceful age, and the rooms that had been found for him in a great, cool, white-columned house on a tree-vaulted street near the university were large and high-ceilinged and furnished with massive old pieces that were kept glassy and redolent of lemon polish by the petulant, muttering old black woman who apparently came with the house. Phillips had not liked the idea of the poor old black woman having to turn out his two rooms and bath, and had offered to do them himself, but the decayed gentlewoman from whom he rented had seemed so honestly scandalized that he did not persist.

"Clothilde would simply have a *fit* if she caught you doing for yourself; I swear she'd leave me that very minute, and then where would I be?" Mrs. Bondurant had fluttered at him with the hyperbole he found so bewildering and yet so charming in these women of the South. "Besides, she *owns* this house. I do exactly what she tells me."

For a moment, Phillips thought, "My God, does this house really belong to that old Negro woman? I wonder if Mrs. Bondurant rents, or what?" and then he realized that he had been cast ashore on the shoals of southern rhetoric once again, and he produced a belated smile. "Well, far be it from me to get such a charming lady in hot water with *her* landlady," he said archly, with a playfulness that was alien to his mouth, and hated himself for it, but the sally earned him another smile and a toss of Mrs. Bondurant's floridly hennaed head.

"How you do run on, Mr. Jay," she said, and he thought wildly that she was parodying herself, so exactly a caricature of a bad comic's routine were the words. But she wasn't. "When you're through putting your things away, you come on down to the veranda and we'll have a Co'Cola. Or a little nip of something stronger, if you'd like. I take a little bourbon along about this time of day myself, every now and then."

The old black woman, who had been hovering about the room frankly itemizing the contents of his suitcases, gave a great snort and rolled her eyes showily to heaven and stumped out of the room, muttering; Phillips was fascinated to see that she wore an honest-to-God kerchief on her head, and mentally began setting her into the letter he would write that evening to his college roommate, who was teaching, entirely by choice, in a small liberal arts college in Arkansas. He looked at Mrs. Bondurant to

258

see how she would react to this monstrous effrontery; his own mother, calm-voiced and patrician-tempered in the extreme, would have fired the old woman on the spot.

"Bossy old thing," Mrs. Bondurant said, dimpling up at him. "Raised me and now she thinks she owns me. Still thinks I'm too young for spirits. What I do put up with!"

And she pattered away down the stairs in her high-heeled sandals, leaving Phillips to feel as if he had just dropped in from a distant star.

"All the women are flirts, even the old ones, and they let their servants take the most God-awful liberties with them," he wrote in his head to the roommate, who, like him, had hopes of bringing light and air to the blacks of the South as well as literature to the whites of it. "It may be trivial and flippant, but by God, it *is* attractive."

And so the one woman who did not flirt with him, the owner of the one pair of eyebrows in his contemporary-fiction class that drew together ever so faintly over large lynx eyes, became the woman that he noticed above all other women. Before the class was over that first day he had ascertained from his student roll that her name was Nell Geiger; when she handed in her first paper on Sinclair Lewis he had seen, with a not unmixed pleasure, that she was a writer of real talent and substance, though with lamentably little discipline and polish. At first he thought her merely lazy; surely such a writer was an English major and had had at least three years of university training. He saw little excuse for such sloppiness of syntax and form, such haziness and formlessness of concepts, sensitive and original though they might be. And so he graded her harshly.

But he watched her, too; she seemed perplexed and upset with her grades, and she took copious notes in class, and listened attentively, straining forward to hear, and she stared at him with the great lynx's eyes as though she wished to possess, not his body and his bright head, as the other girls in the class did, but what was inside his head. He was puzzled by her, and when, at the receipt of her last poorly graded paper, he saw the sheen of sudden tears in her eyes, he went after class to the registrar's office and pulled her file, and found that she was a first-quarter senior in advertising design, and had had little English at all, though she had taken what electives she could manage. He saw, too, that though she lived on campus in her sorority house, she was a town student. Over lunch in the faculty dining room that day he asked the elderly professor who took the Shakespearean overview class, a native of Sparta, if he knew a town student named Nell Geiger.

"Oh, yes," said the old man. "Nell Fox. Well, Geiger, really, I suppose. Indeed I do, I've known her people since her own mother was born. Interesting family. Mainstays of the town and all that. Been there in that old hulk of a house since...oh, well before the Civil War, I suppose. Some real tragedy there, too. Her father ran off and left them when Nell was just a baby, and her brother was shot to death—accidentally of course—four or five years ago, in New York. And her older sister was in a clinic of some kind up there for months afterward. She and her mother live in the house with the grandmother, or Nell did till she started college, and Miss Hebe still does. Miss Ruth Fox. Now *there's* a woman for you. Pretty as a picture to this day—lots of folks think her child and grandchildren aren't a patch on her—and holds just about every honor and office this town has to give, and runs that big old white elephant to boot. You'll undoubtedly meet her if you stay in Sparta any length of time. She's one of our natural resources, is Miss Ruth Fox. Why do you ask, by the way? As if I couldn't guess. Nell's a pretty girl, isn't she?"

"Yes," said Phillips Jay absently, a rich and uniquely southern collage of images forming in his mind: white columns, dainty women in lawn and dimity and sunshades, white-aproned, silent-footed black servants, tears and death and madness. It was the stuff of Gothic tragedy. The romantic in Phillips Jay cocked an ear, even as the cultivated sophisticate penned yet another letter to the roommate: "Guess who I've got in my class? Little Nell, right out of *Gone With the Wind* by way of Tennessee Williams. Lives in a house with a name, and what a name: Fox's Earth."

"But the reason I wanted to know," he said to the old man, "she's a born writer. Just a natural. But she's an art major, of all things. It's an awful waste. I wondered if art ran in the family or something."

"Not so far as I know, and I'd know," said the elderly professor. "I'd have said books did, though. The library there is full of them, some of them really fine. It's a fine

260

house, in fact, really one of the best of the Greek Revivals in the South. You should try to get in and see it sometime."

"I plan to," Phillips Jay said. And when, on the day that he bought her coffee and shocked her into tears and saw, with alarm and exhilaration, the dawning love in the eyes that met his through a cloud of dank coffee steam . . . and when he felt a thoroughly dismaying answering tug of feeling for her somewhere behind his ribs . . . he realized that it was not only a girl named Nell Geiger with whom he was falling in love, but a house called Fox's Earth.

From that morning on they were together whenever they could manage. The university had a very strict policy about professors seeing students socially; a serious liaison would ordinarily have been deemed unthinkable, and Phillips would have been warned in no uncertain terms by the head of his department to break off the alliance immediately. Nell, too, would have been spoken to by any number of guardian females under the university's aegis. But somehow, even to the raptor-eyed dean of women, the case of that nice, new young Mr. Jay in the English Department and sweet little Nell Fox was different. For one thing, the Fox name was still a potent totem on University Hill, and rumor had long had it . . . erroneously . . . that under the terms of her husband's will, Ruth Fox planned to leave the bulk of her vast estate, including the great white house, to the university at her death, and the school was in undeniable need of a proper president's residence. Then, too, Nell herself was held by all to be a young woman of uncommon maturity and breeding; one never saw her mooning about the campus clinging to the hand or arm of some pampered fraternity boy, or sidling into her sorority house at curfew flushed with beard burn and smeared lipstick and lust. And as for young Jay, well, his background was, of course, beyond reproach, as were his grades and credentials, and there hovered about his slim person a delectable aura comprised of some of New England's bluest blood and greenest money.

And on the face of it, their relationship was largely that of mentor to pupil. For Phillips worked her hard, and she responded gladly. For hours each day, after class, in the empty classroom in Pressley Hall, in a corner of the Student Union Lounge or a booth at Guido's, he drilled her as, long ago, his eastern compatriot Alicia Fox had drilled her grandmother Ruth, though in other things.

"Read E. B. White for clarity and eloquence, Nell. You're getting entirely too ruffly here."

"But he's just a magazine writer, Phillips."

"And Proust was just a list maker. Read him in this week's *New Yorker* and think how he'd handle this passage here. And then do it over and bring it back to me tomorrow."

"Read John Marquand for style. And while you're at it, get some O'Hara and see what he does with dialogue. He lets it carry the entire characterization. I'm not saying you should emulate him, but you should know that there's another way to make dialogue work for you."

"Dr. Oakes always says that popular fiction trivializes both the writer and the reader," Nell said mulishly, simply because she so seldom contradicted him, and felt that this must look to him as though she had no gumption.

"And so God put an acorn under Dr. Oakes's great flat foot and dumped him on his ass for the pompous old fool that he is," Phillips said. "Don't be a snob as a matter of policy, Nell. It's stupid and childish, and it's the worst sort of provincialism. You are not a provincial girl."

They were not lovers. Nell would have fled for her life had Phillips pushed her beyond the gentle embraces and not-so-gentle kisses that left them both racked and breathless, and he knew this, and did not push her. She had told him, whispering under the weight of the pain, about Paul's death . . . about Jean, about Yancey's breakdown, all of it, and he saw the scars of that terrible winter on her heart and spirit far more clearly than she did. But a time came, not far into the slow bronze of October, when they both knew that they would be lovers by now if circumstances were different; if she had been unknown in the town and he had had more private quarters, for example, or if the fear of commitment that underlay her hesitancy had not lain so deep. Both knew, too, that some future together would soon have to be taken up and discussed, but for the moment they were content to let themselves go with the dreaming tide of that enchanted autumn, to drift, to be. Nell worked and learned and wrote and laughed and was in love, totally and conventionally. Phillips was exhilarated and absorbed with her, stirred to fierce desire by her, and on the whole, rather exalted by her. More

262

than his love, Nell was rapidly becoming his creation, and a Pygmalionlike pride of authorship underlay all his feelings for her. Throughout that fall, Nell did not propose that he come home with her to Fox's Earth to meet her family, and he did not mention it. "Time enough when she is more sure of herself and of me," he would think. "Let her find her own time for it."

But in truth, the thought had not even occurred to Nell.

It did, finally, at Christmas of her senior year, and then it occurred first not to Nell but to Ruth Fox. As sometimes happened since she had moved into her sorority house during her freshman year, two or three weekends slipped by without Nell's leaving the campus to spend an evening or weekend with her mother and grandmother at Fox's Earth, and it had been at least that long since she had seen Ruth when, on the morning of the last day of exams before Christmas break, Nell looked up from the booth at Guido's where she and Phillips were having coffee and saw her grandmother looking at her from the doorway, smiling. For a moment, Nell merely stared blankly. The sight of Ruth Yancey Fox in Guido's was as unimaginable to her as Guido himself, hair exploding exuberantly from his melon head, in the drawing room at Fox's Earth.

Something in her stillness stopped Phillips's conversation; he was reading aloud to her from the letter he had written his former roommate about William Faulkner's *The Mansion*. Irony was the order of the day in this correspondence; both wrote, Nell thought mutinously, as though they intended to be Significantly Biographied one day, and their letters to each other hailed as profound and poignant communion between two sensitive young academicians alone in a land of savages.

At any rate, he stopped reading and lifted his head and looked at her. "What is it?"

"It's my grandmother," Nell said mildly, her heart racing unaccountably. "Gamma. Right up there in the door. How strange. I hope there's nothing wrong at home . . ."

Phillips skewed around on the booth seat and stared in the direction of Guido's front door. And thus it was that he had his first glimpse of Ruth Yancey Fox, wrapped in her lambent self-light and a lustrous richness of dark mink, looking, within the scabbed, green-painted, sweating walls of Guido's, like a Fabergé creation set carelessly down in a boiler room. Her smile dazzled like a darting flock of scalpels; all the exam-weary student heads had lifted and turned toward her, and a silence fell like the silence of a flock of sparrows at the approach of the golden hawk. Portent flew up Phillips's arms and legs like novocaine; she will mean much to me, boomed through his head.

"God, how beautiful she is," he whispered totally involuntarily, and then turned guiltily to Nell to assure her that her grandmother's beauty was no match for her own, which was not true. But Nell did not notice.

"Yes, isn't she?" Nell said absently and without rancor; she had said it herself many times in perfect truth. "Something *must* be wrong, Phillips, she never would come into Guido's otherwise. I didn't even think she knew where it was. Hey, Gamma, over here . . ." and she lifted her hand tentatively, and waved.

But nothing was wrong. Ruth walked the length of the room to the booth where they sat, seemingly oblivious to the silence and the stares, and slipped onto the leatherette seat beside Nell. She smelt deliciously of Joy and cold fur, and she smiled winsomely at her granddaughter and then at Phillips.

"I had a few minutes to kill before Sally Fickling's open house, and I was right around the corner at the bank board meeting, and I thought to myself, 'Well, puddin' has been neglecting her mama and grandmama lately, so why not go see if she might just be at this famous Guido's I've heard so much about?' And here you are, and I'll bet *this* is the famous handsome Yankee English teacher I've also heard so much about, isn't it?"

She dimpled up at Phillips, who gaped at her for a moment, like a goldfish drowning in air beside its broken bowl, feeling once again subtly outmaneuvered by the Janus-faced charm of a southern woman yet unsure that it was anything but what it seemed: simple charm. Phillips hated feeling unsure. He opened his mouth to reply, was mortified when no words emerged and Ruth's dimples deepened, and tried again.

"How do you do, Mrs. Fox? You can't be anybody but Nell's fabulous grandmother; nobody talks about anything else but you. I think I'd have known you anywhere. I'm Phillips Jay, Nell's English teacher and her good friend.

And may I say I can certainly see where she gets her good looks?"

"You may indeed, Mr. Jay. Aren't you sweet to say it, too? I'm Nell's Gamma; do call me Ruth, though. I'm safe in thinking we really should be on a first-name basis, aren't I?"

Nell cut her eyes at Ruth apprehensively; there was something too creamily arch in her voice. Nell had heard that musical tremolo before. Like the happy, sunlit gurgle of running water, it masked rocks and deep places. But Phillips smiled; his shoulders relaxed in ease.

"I'm very happy to meet you. And, yes, I do think we should be on a first-name basis. I've been wondering when Nell was going to get around to asking me home to meet her folks. I'd begun to think I was going to have to ask myself to dinner."

Ruth giggled, a small, shining sound. Nell stared; this was getting stranger and stranger. She felt like Alice; everything was canted and awry and ever so slightly and cheerfully insane. Gamma did not giggle. Gamma did not come into Guido's and sit down in a booth with her granddaughter and flirt with a man Nell had not thought she knew existed. Gamma did not come to anyone, people went to Gamma. But here she was, giggling in Guido's, looking conspiratorially up beneath her extraordinary lashes at Phillips, who was acting a perfect fool.

"Well, I thought so too," Gamma fluted, "and, knowing my granddaughter, I knew it might be *years* before she got around to bringing her young man home . . . oh, yes, Nell, I know he's your young man; I have my little spies. And a handsome one he is, too . . . and so I thought, well, shoot, I'll just go and surprise her and grab him and bring him home myself. Nell is *such* a shrinking violet sometimes. But we love her."

Nell colored to the roots of her hair. The months with Phillips, the days and weeks of healing and sureness and joy, fell away, and she was the smallest Fox in that house of great, leonine demigods again, impotent and yearning in the dappled cage under the back steps. "I was going to ask him home to meet you all next quarter, Gamma," she said. "He's going home to Boston for the holidays day after tomorrow, so there wouldn't have been any point to it until then."

She kept her voice level and uninflected, so they would know that she considered their jarring jollity unseemly.

"Oh, really? What a shame. I was thinking a little family dinner party this coming Saturday . . . that's Christmas Eve, you know. But of course, I should have thought: you'd want to be with your own family, Mr. . . . Jay."

"Phillips, please. And . . ." He seemed to swell, and gave Ruth a smug, goggling look that deepened Nell's fury. "I'd love to come. I can see my own family any time. Besides, who knows? Maybe I'll be with my own family, in a way."

It was such an astoundingly coy thing to say that Nell forgot her anger and stared frankly at him, openmouthed. She had seen Gamma reduce young men . . . old men, too . . . to gabbling platitudes before, but they had been the lesser game of small-town Sparta. This arch stranger was *Phillips;* this was the mind with which, along with the graceful golden body that housed it, she had fallen in love for its freshness and acuity and control.

"Maybe you will, at that," Gamma said, and, incredibly, reached over and patted his hand. Nell had never seen her touch any man but Paul, and that not since he was a small boy, years ago.

"Well, then, we're just tickled to death that you'll come, and we'll expect you about six. Nell can show you the way, or ask anybody. And now I've got to run; Sally's got me pouring again, the little nitwit, and I'm late as it is. Goodbye, Mr. Jay. 'Bye, chickie."

She kissed Nell's flaming cheek, her own cool and sweet-smelling, and patted Phillips's hand again, and was gone in a swirl of Autumn Haze and a fusillade of heel taps. Guido, holding his stomach in, held the door for her and actually bowed as she swirled through it, and there was an even deeper silence in the big room, as though many deep breaths were being taken, and then a muted buzz curled upward into the silence, and heads turned toward Nell and Phillips's booth. Nell ducked her own head until her hair swung forward to hide it, and sucked at the remaining liquid in her water glass until she made a rude, rattling noise amid the ice cubes on the bottom. She put the glass down abruptly, but she did not lift her face to Phillips.

"Nell?"

"What?"

"Well, look at me. I can't talk to you when you're hid-

266

ing behind your hair like that. What's the matter with you? You were almost rude to your grandmother.''

She did not answer.

''Nell?''

''What?''

''Will you *look* at me? You're acting like a child!''

''And you're acting like an ass.''

She flung her head up. He saw that there were white lines from her nose to her mouth, and a tiny ring of white around her great golden eyes. It might have been rage that he read in her face, but he knew somehow that it was fear. He made his voice gentle.

''What upset you so about seeing your grandmother? Did you think I was too familiar with her, all that talk about being in the family? I was just going along with her, answering her in kind, sort of. She *did* ask me to dinner, you know, and I assume she wouldn't have if she hadn't wanted me to come. It's more than you've done. I really was beginning to think you were ashamed of me . . . or your family. Only now that I've met your Gamma, I know it couldn't have been them.''

''You were *flirting* with her. It was disgusting,'' said Nell, near tears.

''Goddamn, Nell, I was *not*,'' he said. ''I was only taking the same tone she took. She comes on a little . . . flirtatiously, maybe . . . but most of you southern women do. My God, my *landlady* talks to me the same way. I don't think anything about it. I thought she was perfectly charming.''

''Of course you did. Everybody does.'' Nell knew she sounded like a mulish and truculent eight-year-old, but she could not help herself. The warm, invulnerable cocoon of Nell-and-Phillips in which she had moved in peace and security for the past quarter was receding from her at a dazzling speed, leaving her once more alone and vulnerable and cold. She curled in upon herself. ''I want Rip,'' she thought clearly and from nowhere, for the first time in two years. The thought did not surprise her.

''You really are acting like a spoiled brat,'' he said, his Boston accent sharpening to tiny clipped pellets as it did when he was seriously annoyed. ''I thought you'd be pleased that I'd stay in Sparta and come meet your folks. If you'd rather I didn't come, just tell me. There are a lot of people at home that I want to see, anyway.''

Nell's throat closed around an enormous, cold lump of desolation. She saw in her mind Phillips walking in snowy lanes, blue drifts piled against stone fences, swinging mittened hands with tall, serious-faced blond girls whose fine blue eyes and firm, sweet mouths were innocent of make-up, whose long hands and strides matched his own. They would speak of Smith and Wellesley and Harvard and Groton and childhood summers spent together in places like Maine and the Cape and Martha's Vineyard. She heard the solid-as-stone slide and click of like worlds coming together and meshing, the deep, eternal surf of communities of blood and interest washing together. She was small and whipped and still with misery. The tears ran over the edge of her bottom lids and spilled down her face and into the corners of her mouth.

"Please don't go home, Phillips," she whispered desolately. "I do want you to stay. I would have asked you myself, only I was afraid you wouldn't. I'm . . . really sorry."

He should have leaned across the table and taken her into his arms then; it would have been the right thing to do, despite the eyes on them and the silence in Guido's. It seemed such a right thing that she waited, her eyes on the swimming table, for his touch. But it did not come.

"Well, okay, then. I guess it's settled. Now, I've got to get back and post grades, if you're finished," he said remotely, and she knew that she was being punished for the diminishing of the pleasure he had felt at Ruth's fulsome words.

"If we knew each other better, we would have a real fight about this," she thought with bleak prescience, following him out of Guido's and across the campus to his office, where she had left her school satchel.

That night, in the back seat of his car on the black flood plain of the Oconee where everyone from the college went to neck and have sex, she tried for the first trembling, whimpering time in her life to have intercourse, but her bare legs and buttocks were rigid with cold and fear beneath the driving weight of him, and he was urgent and fumbling and hurt her so that she cried out in agony and lunged away from him. He finished outside her, mortified and only slightly apologetic. This simply did not happen to Phillips Jay. They drove back to her sorority house in silence, and she knew that his perfunctory words of apology to her were hollow and forced.

"Please, Phillips, it wasn't your fault, it was mine," she whispered, and was rewarded by the returning flood of warmth in his eyes. He kissed her and held her, and she thought, her face pressed into his parka shoulder, "I can always get him back if I apologize. It's really very simple."

But from somewhere deep in the pit of her, a diffuse anger began to pound.

The next day she gathered her dirty laundry and went home to Fox's Earth, where she closed the door of her old room behind her and fell into her narrow tester bed and slept for fourteen hours without stirring or dreaming.

23

RIP WAS TROUBLED. The Christmas Eve dinner party was not going well.

"Might as well of fixed possum and sweet potatoes, for all they's enjoyin' it," Carrie grumbled from the stove, where she was stirring syllabub. She was shelf-lipped and wall-eyed with resentment at having to spend her Christmas Eve cooking for the Foxes; she and Robert and Beauty and Salome were habitually given that holiday off, coming in only in the midafternoon of Christmas day to cook and serve the traditional Christmas night dinner at Fox's Earth. Carrie knew that the pale, sharp-faced Yankee stranger in Mr. Paul, Senior's, place at the vast Hepplewhite dining-room table was the reason that she and the other three servants labored late on this holy night over turkey with cornbread and oyster pan dressing, sweet-potato soufflés in orange cups, English peas and pearl onions in cream, cranberry relish, hot rolls, and the cloying, devilish syllabub to go with the slices of fruitcake that were cut from the great wheel of whiskey-reeking cake that had steeped and fermented on the back porch under a shroud of muslin since she had made it the previous October.

Carrie turned to Rip, who was sitting in the kitchen rocker by the stove, mending Nell's forlorn underclothes.

"Reckon he Miss Nell's lovin' man," she grumbled. "Cain't think of no other reason he be settin' there in old Mr. Paul's own place on Christmas Eve. He sho' ain't much, is he? Po' as a shikepost an' lookin like the hin' axle of hard times. An' don't he talk funny though? Look like that pretty little gal do better for herse'f than a po' skinny Yankee. Unhhh, *unhhh*. Another Yankee 'roun' here. Reckon do she plan on marryin' him, Rip?"

Rip did not look up from her mending. She had seen the flame that burned on Nell's face, and heard the softening of her voice as she spoke to the pale, thin boy at the table. It was a look and a sound she had waited long to see and hear in Nell's eyes and voice, but never had before. Rip knew Nell as she knew the lining of her own heart; she sighed and drew her thin shoulders together slightly at the icy little moth that walked up her straight spine.

"I reckon she do," she said.

"Unhhh, *unhhh*," Carrie clucked again, conveying sympathy and inviting confidence, and settled herself more comfortably into the old felt bedroom slippers of Mr. Paul, Senior, with the slits cut in the sides to accommodate her corns, that she wore in the kitchen. But Rip said nothing further, and, in fact, was silent for the rest of the evening, and Carrie had to be content with glimpses of the pale young man at bay before Miss Ruth's cane-syrup tongue through the swinging door. Maddeningly, she could hear nothing of what was being said, and somehow she did not like to ask Robert with Rip sitting still and straight as a sapling in the kitchen. Oh, well. She would wait until tomorrow and corner Robert then. Rip couldn't spend all her time in the kitchen like a silent basalt sentinel.

Rip could not hear the words that were being said in the dining room, either, but they were insignificant; she knew their import. This young man was important to Nell, therefore he was dangerous to Ruth Fox. She had known that something was afoot since midway in the previous week, when Miss Fancy Cobb had come by one afternoon for a cup of Carrie's Russian tea and a visit with Ruth. The women had settled themselves by the fire that Rip had laid in the grate of the fireplace in the little parlor, and she had been carrying in the heavy old Sheffield tea

270

service that had come south with Miss Alicia when she heard Miss Fancy's breathless gurgle saying, "Well, Ruth, I hear you're about to have a Yankee schoolteacher in the family," and had heard Ruth's cool, offhand reply: "Why, Fancy, whatever are you running on about now?"

"Why, Nell and the new young Yankee English teacher over at the university," Fancy Cobb gurgled happily. "Don't *tell* me she hasn't even mentioned him to you. Why, they've been virtually inseparable since school started; everybody knows about them. It's just the love affair of the year! Oh, you needn't worry about anything *funny,* Hebe . . ." for Hebe had seen the sudden ice in her mother's eyes, and whimpered in confusion . . , "he is a thoroughly nice boy, they say. Has family and money back to Adam, practically, from what Eloise Bondurant tells me. He's rooming with her. She says he's so Boston blue-blooded that he wouldn't bleed red if you cut him, says he's got beautiful manners and never gives a minute's trouble. And she says she's *definitely* never known him to have . . . you know, a girl . . . up to his room, so there's nothing to worry about on that score. I'm sure it's all very honorable your dear Nell . . . such a *good* girl, we've all said. We all think he's a real catch . . . for a Yankee, anyway. I'm really surprised that you didn't know about it, Ruth."

"Not a word," Ruth said serenely; only Rip would have known that flames roared inside her. "Which only means that he doesn't matter a doodly-squat to Nell. She never has wasted much breath on any of her young men. Frankly, there just hasn't been anyone in town who interested her, I'd know if there was. Nell doesn't keep things from me."

"Oh, I never thought for a minute that she did," purred Fancy Cobb, smiling at Ruth over the rim of Alicia's Rose Medallion teacup. "But I'll bet you a nickel you're wrong about him not meaning anything to her. *I'll* bet that you're going to have a new son-in-law this time next year, and a handsome Yankee one at that."

Miss Fancy Cobb left soon afterward, wreathed in smiles, and Miss Ruth smiled and kissed her guest's heavily rouged cheek as she left. A casual observer would have thought that the entire conversation had rolled off Miss Ruth like water off a duck's back, but Rip was no casual observer.

Later that evening Rip had been in the kitchen when

Miss Ruth came sailing in through the swinging doors from the dining room, her cheeks burning with high pink flags. She looked like a tiny figurine of some beautiful, half-mad czarina. Carrie and Robert and Rip fell silent and looked at her in apprehension, but she only smiled after all.

"Robert, do you know a place called . . . Guido's, I believe it is?" She said, "It's a coffee shop or something, it's near the university. I think I've heard that a lot of students go there."

"Yas'm," Robert said chattily, relieved that this whirling dervish of a woman had not come to castigate him. "It over there on Rutherford, right behind the bank there. Used to be Mr. Ell Cooper's grocery sto' fo' he died. Belong to an Eye-talian man what got his hair standin' up all over the place now. What you want with a place like that, Miss Ruth? You let me drive you out to the club do you want to set an' have yo' coffee in a nice place . . ."

"No, I was just wondering where it was, Robert, I don't want to go there. Mrs. Cobb mentioned that her son Wade and a lot of other students went there, and it just struck me that I'd never heard of it . . ."

And thus it was that Rip knew that her last and best-loved Foxchild had found a man and, in the finding of that man, had mobilized her grandmother's terrible daimon against her once again. The tides that had slept dormant in Fox's Earth for many years stirred sluggishly; Rip could hear them lapping at the very foundations of the house, down there in silent darkness, gathering strength, gathering force. Somewhere across town, on the nearby university campus, Nell walked with a man who threatened Ruth Yancey Fox because he had it in his power to take Nell far away, and so, once again, Rip sat down to guard.

Phillips Jay did not know what had gone awry. The evening had started smoothly; indeed, it had had about its earliest moments the aura of floridly romantic fiction that he had envisioned it would when he thought about it alone in his room. Fox's Earth itself, when he drove up the long, boxwood-fringed driveway and parked the car on the gravel turnaround and got out in the tender Christmas dusk, had taken his breath away for a moment. In three months he had become used to Sparta's sweet symmetry of column and pediment and peristyle and flat roof, but this great house, glowing in the Della Robbia blue of early evening with Christmas candles and the soft-nimbused lights of a towering cedar glimpsed through tall French windows behind the veranda, was a rhapsody of proportion and grace that stilled his jaunty, half-nervous whistling and widened his eyes, even accustomed as they were to the opulence and stateliness that furnished his world back in Massachusetts.

"Holy Mother of God," he breathed reverently, and Robert came to the front door and opened it, and the full cedar-and-spice-and-lemon-polished breath of Fox's Earth at Christmas swept out to meet him.

Ruth Fox, in floor-length burgundy velvet, with her hair swept up onto her elegant small head and diamonds twinkling like Christmas stars at her ears and throat and fingers, glided down the right side of a magnificent double staircase, her little white hands outstretched to him, her blond head tipped entrancingly to one side. Behind her, in an oddly old-fashioned long topaz velvet dress that he had never seen, came Nell, so tall and slender and radiant of face and misty of eye that she looked like a lighted taper, and Phillips's heart turned over with joy at the simple fact of her.

This is right, this is what has been meant for me, said something near his heart. This girl and this house . . . and, yes, this other woman, too. All of it, all of them, are a piece of the same thing, are a unit, an integrity. This is what has waited for me here in the South all along.

"Welcome to Fox's Earth, Mr. Jay," Ruth said.

It was just about the last pleasant thing that was said to him all evening.

Oh, they weren't overtly rude. Looking back over the evening in his bitterness as he lay in Eloise Bondurant's canopied guest bed that night, he had to admit in all fairness that he couldn't point to one single thing that any of them had said or done of which it could be said, by an unbiased outsider, "There, now, *that* was intentionally hurtful, *that* was meant to wound." But Phillips was not unbiased, and he knew with a prickling certainty that Ruth Fox, that smiling, gracious, beautiful mistress of Fox's Earth, had meant to annihilate him in the eyes of her granddaughter, and he knew that she had in no small part succeeded.

Ruth Fox had started in on him almost at once, after she had, with much ceremony, seated him at the head of

273

the table, where "my sweet Paul . . . *big* Paul, you know, my husband, always sat. You look a little like him, Phillips, in the candlelight. Like he did when he was young, anyway, before he got stout."

"Nell says I remind her of Paul, only she meant her brother, I think," Phillips said volubly, then fell silent at the enormity of his gaffe. He glanced at the three women around the great table apprehensively, but no one seemed upset. He smiled tentatively at all of them. Ruth nodded to the hovering Robert to refill his wineglass, and he drank deeply and gratefully. It was a smooth claret; perfect, he thought, with the roasted turkey and the stuffing that was not stuffing at all, but a savory sort of cornbread affair in which he detected onion, sage, celery, oysters, and some other flavors that pleased and eluded him. It was the sort of wine that his father might have chosen, and Phillips lit into it with pleasure. He realized that he was becoming quite drunk, but it was a realization accompanied only by a gleeful inner hilarity. He felt suddenly, despite the unfortunate mention of Paul, that he could do no wrong.

"Oh, does she really?" Ruth Fox said, looking at Nell. "How odd that she would think so. Except that you're towheaded, I don't think you favor a bit. You are unmistakably northern, and my poor Paul was just pure southern to the core. A sweet old Georgia cracker."

Her eyes caught the light and flashed like sapphires struck by the sun, and a small silence fell. Nell murmured into it, "I only thought so when I first knew him, Gamma." The evening began to change then.

"Well." Ruth put down her fork and leaned slightly toward Phillips Jay from the waist. "Tell me what you think of our South. We aren't really the ogres y'all think we are up there in the North, are we, now that you've gotten to know us? You don't really think this silly business with the Negroes is going to amount to anything, do you? Or did you come down here to save them all from us meanies?"

She smiled so entrancingly at him that he quite forgot that Robert was at his elbow with a platter of sliced turkey.

"I certainly haven't found any who seem to want saving," he said waggishly, and then remembered how he had so often held forth at length to Nell about the cause of civil rights, and its great and noble ramifications for the country and the world, and how he had been so gratified that she had responded to this new way of thinking with all the fresh, if naïve, ardor of a newly awakened conscience. He darted a glance at her; she was obviously remembering, too, for she was staring at him in bewilderment. So he said, hastily and pompously, "But I have certain views that I feel I can't compromise, even for such charming company as you, Mrs. Fox. Ruth. I do feel that the Negro has been done a grave injustice . . ."

And then he slowed to a halt, for the Negro of whom he might have been speaking was departing ostentatiously through the swinging door with his ramrod back bespeaking indignation and injury, and Phillips realized that he had just been guilty of an action he had always loathed in his privileged set back in Boston: speaking of the servants in the third person while they were in the room. And this servant, moreover, was a Negro . . . the very being whom he had come south, in part, to champion. And an obviously contented and well-tended and conspicuously unoppressed Negro at that.

So he said, "Though your servants certainly seem happy and well taken care of. I didn't mean to imply that you *personally* were oppressing the Negroes . . . there are Negro servants in the North, too, you know. *We* don't have any, but many of my parents' friends do. I certainly have never seen anything *wrong* with it; it's just that our servants have always happened to be white. Irish, mostly; well, you'd expect that in good old Boston, wouldn't you? Even my family's cooks. I really think Negroes make the best cooks, though, don't you? Certainly, if tonight's dinner is any example . . . ah, I was just assuming that your cook is a Negro, but maybe not . . ."

He could hear his own voice in his ears, clattering dismally; nothing like this conversational ineptitude had ever even remotely afflicted him, and he was as much at a loss to explain it as to stop it. He saw that they were all staring at him: Ruth with the sweet, playful smile that had so soothed him at Guido's the other day; Hebe with simple pleasure; Nell as astoundedly as if he had grown antlers. Her cheeks were stained red, too; embarrassment? His voice sank and died again.

"No, Carrie is a Negro," Ruth said serenely. "I'd be real uncomfortable with a white person in my kitchen, I think. Besides, like you say, it's up to us white southerners to make things better for our Negroes, and the more of them we can employ in our homes, the better, don't you think? It's easier for white people to get all the other jobs down here. If I hired white help for the house I'd be taking food out of the mouths of Negroes."

His own face flamed. "Of course," he mumbled.

"You said, 'cooks,'" she went on brightly. "Goodness, how many do you have?"

"Well, four," he said quickly, grateful for the change of subject and the chance to demonstrate that his family, too, was guilty of having servants. It was suddenly important that the Jays of Boston seem, to this beautiful woman and her family, as frail and human and possessed of faults and foibles and servants as any southern family. In fact, in the manner of one who seeks to reassure a guest who has just spilt coffee on the rug by saying, "Oh, that's nothing; last week I spilt molasses," Phillips set out to embellish the ranks of the family servants with gusto.

"There's Janie, the main cook at the Boston house, who's been with us for years. And then Deirdre helps her. And Mary Ellen is at the Cape house full time; she cooks when we're there and keeps things going when we're not. And Manuelo . . . well, he's Filipino, not Irish, obviously . . . is at the New York apartment."

"Mercy sakes, *three* houses," Ruth Fox said admiringly. "Your mother must be a truly remarkable woman. I'd just go out of my poor mind, trying to keep up with *three*. This old white elephant keeps me in a tizzy as it is."

"Oh, well, of course, she has more than enough help," he said hastily, seeking to cut the paragon mother down to manageable size in those great ingenuous eyes. "She has upstairs maids and downstairs maids, and housekeepers, and gardeners, and Selfridge to buttle, and Jeffries to drive her, and Dad has O'Keefe, to do for *him*, and Ryan, who drives him, and then there's a skeleton staff at the other two houses. It's an embarrassing lot of people to look after a small family, but the houses are pretty big, and some of our staff have been with the family since my grandfather's time, back when the business was new. You feel a certain responsibility . . ."

"You do indeed, don't you? *Noblesse oblige* and all . . ." she murmured. He shot a look at Nell. Her head was bent over her plate and her hair swung forward so that he could not see much of her face, only her forehead. It was crimson. She was mincing turkey into tiny, exact pieces with great skill and precision.

"What sort of business was your grandfather in?" Ruth Fox asked, interest and attention leaping in her eyes. Something else was there, too; what? She had very strange eyes, he realized. He answered gratefully. Surely here was the stuff of common interest. He had heard somewhere, vaguely, that Nell's family had had connections with Dixie Bag and Cotton Manufacturing Company in the dim past.

"Textiles. A cotton mill, or mills, actually. Seneca Mills, over at Framingham. Dad's still active there; my brother Charles will take up the flag one day, I suppose. It's a coincidence, isn't it? That both our families should be involved in the textile industry, I mean?"

There was another silence; in it, her strange eyes went flat and still. He stopped smiling.

"I thought someone told me that Nell's great-grandfather, or somebody . . . well, that would be your father, I guess . . . was connected with the mill here? Or was I mistaken? . . ."

"My father was a minister," she said. "I think you must have been misinformed, Mr. Jay."

In the kitchen, Rip, who had heard the exchange, actually shivered and rubbed her arms against the little cold, furred feet that pittered up them.

"Now we for it," she said under her breath. "Lord, let me be strong enough this time," she thought. "I gittin' ol'."

"But you decided to teach English, instead of going into the mill," Ruth said, and all there was in her voice was bright interest. But his reply was guarded and neutral.

"I . . . yes, I've always loved English. I don't think there's a higher calling than that of a writer; nothing seems to me to be so valuable both to the person who does it and the people who read it. It's one of the first things I noticed about Nell. She's one of the most gifted natural writers I've ever seen; I think, with work, we can make her a writer of real substance. She's been working like a little demon for me, and she's produced some things that I believe could be published right now. In time, you'll have reason to be proud of Nell . . ."

Nell, from across the table, made a sudden, odd sound, a hopeless small whimper. He looked up at her. Her hand stabbed the air helplessly before her, as though to ward off some blow; her face was hidden further beneath the silvery mouse-hair, but he could see from her forehead that it had paled. Again he stopped. What in the name of God was *wrong* in this beautiful, treacherous house?

"Well, I declare, Nell a writer," Ruth Fox said. "I always knew she was a smart girl, but I thought she would make her mark with her art. She's a real little artist, you know. I thought she'd been working hard on *that* all this time. Well, fiddle, what do grannies know, anyway?"

"Nell's art is *nothing* to her talent as a writer," he said, feeling himself on firm ground once more. "I'm afraid she's wasted a lot of time there. I wish she'd had more English, done a lot more writing, but we're taking care of that now. I'm really privileged to be working with her."

"Well, I guess another writer would be the best judge of that," Ruth said. "And I'm sure she's a lucky girl to have you. Tell me, I'm embarrassed to ask, but you'll understand it's the question of a total ignoramus and no reflection on you... what have you written? I'll have to get some of your books from the library, or better still, I'll buy them."

Phillips looked at her. Something swam in her blue eyes before she dropped them to her plate. It was, Phillips saw, triumph. Humiliation and outrage swam over him. She had found his Achilles' heel, the one pitifully vulnerable spot in all his bright, beautiful Brahmin armor. Phillips wanted more than anything in the world to write and publish novels that would change the shape of the world around him; he thought constantly of those novels; he could see them, see their tasteful, shining covers, in a row in a bookshelf near a fireplace in some amorphous future home of his, and he knew in that moment that he would write none of them.

"I... haven't actually had anything published yet," he said. "It's pretty hard to teach and write, too, though when I'm a little more settled I'll be starting... I have my first book all drafted now. It's difficult to get the kind of thing I want to write published... it's sort of specialized and esoteric, you know... academic stuff. There's only a very small, if select, market for academic writing... but, of course, well worth the effort..."

"I'm sure that's true," Ruth said sweetly. "Well, now. Let's have dessert in the little parlor, shall we, so Carrie and Robert can get on home? I believe Carrie's made syllabub. Do you have syllabub in the North, Mr. Jay?"

"Ah . . . I don't think so. No," he said.

"Oh, goody, syllabub! I could eat the whole bowlful," Hebe chortled suddenly, clapping her hands together. Phillips stared at her wildly: he saw an old child in incongruous gray chiffon.

Nell was on her feet even before Ruth's rising signaled the end of dinner. Her face was whipped and drawn, her eyes riveted to the carpet. He saw then that he could easily, so easily, lose her, and if he did, he would have only his own mutinous tongue to blame.

"I really couldn't eat another thing," he said. His ears were roaring so that he could hardly hear himself speak. "Thank you, but I believe I'd better get home. I promised my family I'd call tonight, and it'll soon be their bedtime."

"Well, if you're sure," Ruth Fox said. "It's been a lovely Christmas Eve for us, having you here. And I'm sure it's made Nell a very happy little girl. We'll be seeing you sometime tomorrow, of course?"

"Oh, of course," he murmured.

"I'll walk you to the door," Nell said.

They stood in the cold dark on the veranda, just outside the circles of light left by the porch light and the pyramid-shaped electric Christmas candles, and they quarreled. At first Nell said nothing; he saw that she could not even bring herself to speak to him but could only stand beside him, automatically rubbing her upper arms in the chill and staring at the tiles, and he thought he would simply kiss her chastely on the forehead and leave quietly and with dignity, but then the fountaining injustice of it all rose in his throat and came pumping out between his lips. Like his callow, boasting prattle at the dinner table, he could not seem to stop it.

"Well, that's some little family of southern aristocrats you have there," he spat furiously. "Your wonderful, precious Gamma is a class-A castrating bitch if I ever saw one; she led me on and set me up and made me look like a pure and simple goddamned fool in front of you; I'm sure she thinks that no Yankee schoolteacher could ever be good enough for her precious little Nell, and she was determined to make you see that, wasn't she? And your mother is as crazy as a bedbug; she's right out of Tennessee Williams."

"She is not!" Nell cried furiously, but of course sometimes she was, and she had known this for some time.

Grief and shame for her mother swept over her; tears coursed down her cheeks and she licked them away like a child. The small action infuriated Phillips even further. He took her shoulders in his hands and shook her.

"Yes, she is. They're a . . . a collection of freaks . . . southern Gothic freaks is what they are, your Gamma and your mama and no doubt your crazy sister and your dear departed fag brother, too. The whole frigging South is a freak bed; I don't know why I ever thought it wouldn't be. Stop that damned crying, Nell, you're acting like a baby, like that old infant of a mother of yours. That's exactly what your dear Gamma wants you to be, do you realize that? A baby, just like your mama. So you'll be tied to her apron strings all your life, just like you are now. Like your mama is. So you'll stay in that famous, rotting old pile of bricks and keep the flame, like a good little Fox baby girl . . ."

"They're not freaks! Damn you, Phillips, you sounded like a jackass tonight; why did you let her make you carry on like such a fool? And I am *not* a baby! I am *not* tied to Gamma's apron strings: I do what I want to, I am *me*, Nell, my own person . . ."

"Marry me, then."

"I . . . what?"

"I said, 'Marry me.' God, Nell, you look like you'd seen a ghost. You know perfectly well we were going to get married eventually, don't you? Oh, Christ, of course you do, don't cry. Well, then, if you're your own person, marry me tonight. Just go in there and get your coat and walk back out and get in this car and we'll drive up to North Georgia and get married."

"Phillips . . . I can't do that! Tomorrow is Christmas!"

"Well, so what? Come on, Nell. If you mean what you've said about loving me . . . if you mean it when you say you're your own person . . . do it. Tell me this: do you love me?"

"Well . . . Yes, I guess so. Yes. But, Phillips . . ."

"Do you want to marry me?"

"I . . . think I do, yes. Of course, sure I do. But . . ."

"Will you come with me tonight and marry me?"

"Phillips, no. I can't just do that. It would kill Mama, you don't know about Mama's wedding, but . . ."

"Then I was right, and you are a baby, just like your mama, and you'll never be free of your Gamma's apron strings as long as you live. Good night, Nell. Have yourself a merry little Christmas, as the song goes."

He turned and went down the walk to his car, which Robert had brought around for him and left idling to warm up, and got into it and drove away. Nell watched him out of sight. Then she went back into the house and straight up the stairs to her room, where she cried until precisely the blue hour of the Christmas dawn when she used to get up as a little girl and creep into the lighted splendor of the living room, to see what Santa Claus had brought her.

Over breakfast, Nell faced her grandmother. Ruth was smooth-faced and rested in a pale-rose satin kimono. There was no one else in the room except Rip, who looked on silently as she poured coffee. She knew from Nell's ghastly face and swollen eyes that Ruth Fox had drawn first blood, and her veins burned with impotent fury, but she thought perhaps that penance had been done and Nell's long night of tears would be tribute enough for Ruth. In any case, she was powerless to do anything but watch while Nell still lived under this flat roof. Ruth's long-ago threat of expulsion, of banishment, was still potent today.

"I thought you liked him," Nell said without preamble to her grandmother. "You came all the way over to Guido's the other day and practically danced on the table in front of him, you practically begged him to come last night. Why did you egg him on like that? You know you made him look like a fool. You know he's not like that."

"I know nothing of what he's like. But I do know it is not possible to make a fool of someone who is not a fool, Nell," Gamma said, looking with artful compassion at her granddaughter. "I'm afraid your young Yankee friend showed his true colors last night, that's all. Better you see him as he really is now instead of later. I'm sorry, baby."

Hebe came into the room rumpled and pink with sleep. Her hair stood up like duck down on her head.

"Merry Christmas, Mama, Nell," she said, putting a finger into the strawberry preserve pot and popping it into her mouth. "Honey, I was telling Mama last night, I like your young man. He's very like your father. Don't you truly think so, Mama? Very . . . eastern. I've always liked that."

Nell said nothing. She looked at her mother.

"Very like him indeed, Hebe," Ruth Fox said sweetly to her daughter. Her face wore a look of madonnalike suffering. "And you of all people should know the upshot of that. I would spare Nell and all of us the pain of another John Geiger, but she is a grown woman and will make her own decision. I hope there is enough strength and heart in us to bear it."

Hebe's face clouded and her small mouth pursed and trembled. She looked from Nell to her mother and back. Nell still stared at her grandmother. She saw, as in a nightmare or what she had heard of drowning, not just Ruth now, but a melting montage of Ruths, of Gamma; Gamma from now back until her earliest memory of Gamma; Gamma always and infinite.

"Why," thought Nell mildly, "Phillips was right. She is trying to make me into Mother. She means to keep me here, here in this house, always. To be another of the Fox women of Fox's Earth all my life. It's what everything has been about, always. It's the sum of everything she has ever said or done to me."

Later that morning, while Phillips Jay still slept fretfully in the prissily garlanded guest bed of the Widow Bondurant, Nell dressed and drove to the Bondurant house and told the old black woman who answered the door to please tell Mr. Jay that Miss Geiger was waiting for him in the downstairs drawing room. The old woman was cross and reluctant, but since her mistress was at Christmas morning services at the Sparta First Methodist Church, and since she had known little Nell Fox since her birth, she went stumping up the stairs and pounded, muttering, on Phillips's door until he answered.

"Does the offer still hold?" Nell said to him when he appeared in the drawing room, his hair standing up in still-damp spikes on his head.

They were married that afternoon in the same scabrous little marriage mill in North Georgia where, twenty-eight years before, Hebe Fox had fled to marry Johnny Geiger, but the irony of this was lost until later on Nell Geiger Jay, who came home to find her grandmother familiarly grim-faced and silent once again and her mother plunged deliciously into the same hysteria with which she had greeted the lethal consequences of her own marriage. Rip, her face drawn down to bladelike bone, met the newlyweds on the veranda of Fox's Earth with a packed suitcase and a long, trembling, silent hug for Nell and a formal handshake for Phillips.

"Better you goes an' fin's you a place to live an' gits settled in 'fore you sees yo' mama an' Gamma, Miss Nell," she said. "Yo' mama carryin' on considerable, but I be able to calm her down do she know they ain't nothin' she can do 'bout it. I git yo' Gamma settled down terreckly, too. Ain't no sense in stirrin' up nobody jus' now. You light someplace an' let me know where you is, an' I'll tell you when's a good time to come see 'em."

Nell's heart smote her. "Oh, Rip . . . is Mama sick? Has she had a real spell? Or Gamma? I'd better just run in for a minute . . ."

"Miss Nell, you a married woman now. You go on home with yo' husban'. He look after you, jus' as good as I does. I aims to look after yo' mama now. An' yo' Gamma . . . well, she ain't never need no lookin' after, do she?"

"Oh, Rip! What on earth would I ever do without you?"

"You ain't gon' have to, Miss Nell. Not for a spell yet."

She turned to Phillips Jay, who stood diffidently behind Nell.

"You look after Miss Nell, Mr. Phillips. She gon' need strong arms now."

"I'll take very good care of her, Rip," he said. "We'll have this business settled and forgotten in no time."

Rip looked after them as they walked back to his car in the driveway, still iced with the dust of North Georgia.

And so Phillips and Nell Geiger Jay spent the evening with a wildly elated Miss Eloise Bondurant in her parlor, and retired for their wedding night to the newly made-up guest bedroom, where Nell found that sex did not, after all, hurt so badly as that first dry and furtive attempt out by the Oconee had led her to believe, and where they both fell asleep and slept like tired children until noon of December 26, 1961. By then Miss Eloise Bondurant had been on the phone to everybody who was anybody in Sparta, and was also able to report that a neat little bungalow in the brand-new subdivision that had become the unofficial faculty housing project on the west side of the campus was available for sublet, furnished, from a fussy bachelor professor of economics who had gone on sabbatical to Geneva. Nell spent almost a week in the house, her first married home, before Ruth Fox had the heart palpitations that put her to bed, white and spent, and sent Hebe sobbing to the telephone for her daughter to come home, despite Rip's glowering protests. "Because she keeps calling for you, Nell, and crying, and what if something happened to Mama and you didn't come . . ."

And Nell, who had spent all her hastily marshaled strength of will on her one overt act of defiance of Ruth Fox, flew home to Fox's Earth in agony of remorse, and stayed there for three weeks nursing her grandmother and soothing her mother while her new husband fumed alone in his honeymoon cottage. And Ruth Fox, who had at first been so enraged with herself for overplaying her hand that for once the palpitations were quite real, came quickly to realize that Nell's guilt and her subsequent miserable, ceaseless propitiations were stronger bonds to Fox's Earth than any she herself could have forged, and she smiled in misty forgiveness of her errant granddaughter and asked, in a weak, bled-out voice, if she might have another cup of tea.

And so began the marriage of Nell Geiger and Phillips Jay.

24

IT SEEMED to Nell that after that her grandmother was never truly well again. Nor was she truly ill; it was just that, for the first time in her life, there seemed to be an abating, an ebbing, of the blue vitality that had seemed to lick almost visibly through Ruth Fox's veins. She did not age; there was not about her any sign of degeneration that Nell could see. And she did not fade. The blue eyes still snapped and sparked in her face; the air around her still seemed to burn with a candle's flame at times. Rather, she just seemed to slip into a lower gear, as if some perpetual internal motor was slowing, imperceptibly but inevitably, leaving her to languish later and later on the piled pillows of her bed with her leather ledger and her correspondence, or to have her luncheons more and more often on trays in her room or in the little parlor, with Hebe hovering in anxious attendance, or to curtail her civic and social and altruistic engagements until she hardly went out at all anymore.

More and more often, in that first year of Nell's marriage, a call would come from Fox's Earth, and it would be Hebe, whimpering breathlessly into the telephone. "Honey? Do you think you could run by for a minute on your way home from the grocery store? Mama has the painters and plasterers coming for the dining room and she just can't get up to deal with them, and I wasn't ever any good with workmen, you know."

"Mama," Nell would say in exasperation, "all you have to do is ask Gamma what she wants you to tell them and just go down there and *tell* them. You don't have to stay with them while they work. Rip or Robert can look after things while they're there. Just tell them what Gamma says. You don't need me to do that."

"But what if I get it wrong?"

"Then ask her again. Mama, for heaven's *sake,* it's blocks out of my way, and I've got a term paper due day after tomorrow." Nell was finishing her degree before settling down to keep house or write full time; Phillips had urged her to do so, though she felt little interest in it anymore. It seemed part of another Nell, in a life that no longer interested her. But she persevered for his sake, and found studying easier in the little house alone. It disturbed her, though, to leave her studies for Ruth and Hebe's endless errands, and she found herself angry and then riddled with guilt at the anger whenever she did so, and it became harder and harder to get back to work afterward.

"Mama asked me to ask you," Hebe would whimper, and Nell could hear the tears bubbling up from her mother's inexhaustible well, and would snap in irritated defeat, "Oh, all right. I'll be there about four. But I am *not* going to stay for supper, Mama, so don't start on me again about that."

"I won't, sugar. I sure won't. Oh, and, Nell, since you're coming anyway, would you just run by the drugstore and see if the new *Photoplay* has come in? Mama didn't go this morning, and Robert almost snapped my head off when I asked him to drive me. I declare, he's getting to be the meanest old thing . . ."

The sound of the receiver's slam would reverberate in

Nell's head for long minutes after she had hung up, and often she would put her work away, knowing that it was useless to try to concentrate on it until much later.

Sometimes it was Rip who called: "Miss Nell? I hates to bother you, but Miss Ruth ain' go to the bank this mo'nin' an' they ain't no money to pay Beauty and Salome, an' they done wait a week fo' they pay as it is."

"Oh, Rip, really, *can't* Mama go just this once? I'm so far behind . . ."

"She done run up to her room acryin', an' I cain't git her down right now, Miss Nell. It my fault . . . she say she cain't go without Miss Ruth, an' I tell her she a useless ol' baby, an' by the time I gits her to hush up now the bank done be closed. I sho' am sorry. I ain't like to bother you. I go myself, but you know they ain't gon' cash no check for me . . ."

Nell knew that they would not, even though everyone at the Sparta First National Bank and Trust, from the president down to the newest teller, knew Rip as one of the Fox household. She knew also that the regret in Rip's voice was genuine. Rip *did* hate to bother her; indeed, at times Nell thought that Rip did not want her to come to Fox's Earth and sought to speed her on her way as quickly as possible when she did come by on an errand of mercy for old Ruth.

"Are you trying to get rid of me by any chance, Rip?" Nell said once, after Ruth and Hebe had pressed her to stay for afternoon tea and Rip had said, quickly and firmly, that there was no more of the seed cake left and Carrie had spilt the last of the tea into the sink that morning.

"No'm. You know I don't never see enough of you, Miss Nell. Jus' seem lak to me yo' place over there in yo' own house now. Spend too much time fussin' roun' over here doin' things what we could do for ourse'fs, seem lak to me. Seem lak we leanin' on you too hard; seem lak we gittin' spoilt, lettin' you do aroun' for us all the time."

"Well, I am *not* spoiled, either," Hebe began indignantly, and Rip said, "You been spoiled ever since you was a little bitty girl, Miss Hebe," and Ruth Fox said, "That will be enough, Rip. I'm sure Nell won't stay if she hasn't the time to do so. I just thought a cup of tea with my granddaughter would be pleasant, seeing as how she and her husband never even come to dinner."

She looked directly into Rip's eyes, her own narrowed,

and Rip returned the look levelly and serenely for the space of a minute before she said, "Yes'm," and turned and went into the kitchen. Nell, smarting under the remark about dinner, made her escape as soon as possible. It was true; Phillips would not, that first year, put foot into Fox's Earth under any pretext, and forbade Nell to ask her grandmother into his home, and Nell knew that Ruth kept a careful tally of the invitations not issued. She wondered if Rip suffered any sort of retribution at her grandmother's hands on the occasions when she openly defied her as she had that day. It seemed unlikely that Ruth Fox would let one of her servants get away with such behavior unscathed, even Rip. On the other hand, Nell could imagine no one assailing Rip's immense dignity with attempts at discipline or reprimands. It struck her again that the relationship between her grandmother and Rip was both unknown to her and, perhaps, unknowable. Gamma and Rip: they simply *were*.

Nevertheless, things at Fox's Earth were not as they always had been, and it made Nell vaguely uneasy when she thought about it. There was some shift in the balance of things, minute but somehow of great moment, some delicate but portentous realignment, as though a tiny fissure had opened in the crust of the earth and set all things upon it into a slight but irrevocable new relationship. Was it because Gamma was slightly less well now than she had been, slightly slower, a bit indisposed for the first time in anyone's memory? Was the motive power that ran the great house flagging ever so slightly?

"What's really the matter with Gamma, Rip?" Nell asked once. "Is she sicker than we think? Dr. Hopkins just brushed me off when I called him; he said she just needed a little rest and would be herself in no time. Said she was basically sound as a dollar. But she's been like this ever since I . . . since we got married. I thought maybe the doctor was so used to brushing Mama off that he just automatically treated me the same way."

"You listen to him. Ain' nothin' the matter with Miss Ruth. You think I ain't gon' tell you if somethin' be the matter with her? I knows when she sick an' she well, an' she ain't had a sick day since them gallstones when you was jus' a little thing."

"But she really was so weak when . . . after her heart. She looked awful. She couldn't even raise her head, Rip.

And she hasn't really been right since. I don't know, something's changed . . . I can't put my finger on it . . . something isn't like it used to be. She *is* getting on, you know, even if nobody ever thinks about that. If I'm going to have to take over and fill in for her here, I need to know about it . . ."

"Miss Nell, ain't no need in this worl' fo' you to try to take care of yo' mama and yo' Gamma an' this ol' house when you got a house an' a husban' of yo' own. You listen to me, Miss Nell. Ain' nobody sick an' ain't nobody need you over here yet. Someday, maybe, but not yet. You comes over here way too much as it is; you jus' go on about yo' business next time yo' mama call an' leave everything to me. Ain't nothin' here I can't take care of, but they plenty here can tie you down an' mess you up, do you let it. Leave it to me, Miss Nell. I knows the ways of this house an' ever'body in it, better'n you ever will."

"Oh, Rip," Nell murmured in guilty gratitude, hugging her. "We dump too much on you. All of us do. We always did."

"Miss Nell, that's what I here for. It's what I come here for. It's all I knows how to do, look after the Foxes."

"Well, I hope to God we're worth it. Sometimes I don't think the whole kit and caboodle of us are worth a hair of your head."

"Oh, yessum," said Rip, smoothing Nell's pale-brown crop of curls off her forehead. "You worth it, all right."

And so Nell went less and less often to Fox's Earth, taking comfort in the fact that Rip was always there. By the time she and Phillips celebrated their first anniversary, Nell was going to Fox's Earth perhaps only once or twice a week, and Ruth Yancey Fox became less and less an oppressive presence in her marriage.

Nell was happy. She loved her husband; the moment of fierce, flooding doubt and embarrassment for him she had felt at the dinner table on that terrible Christmas Eve had dissipated without a trace, leaving no residue of bitterness or memory. Away from the corrosive presence of Ruth Fox, Phillips Jay became himself in Nell's eyes once more, the strong, quick-witted exotic young eastern prince who had, incredibly, wanted her above all the women he might have had in all his favored, unimaginable life; who had, even more incredibly, given her back her writing; who had, most incredibly of all, married her.

And he made love to her with a frequency and ardor that left her weak-legged and drowsy and indolent, most nights and in the daytime, too, hurrying home at noon to take her to bed or push her down on the deep-piled carpet of the prim little sitting room, flinging her skirts over her head or hastily dragging down her slacks to her ankles, entering her quickly and deeply, smothering her protestations with his open mouth, driving himself hard and long in her until he came with a cry and a great flailing of arms and legs. At first this overwhelmed and frightened Nell; she would struggle against him, would turn her head away, flinch her hips up and away from the great ramming length of him. But with repetition she learned to open herself to the times in the bed and on the carpet, learned to arch her back and thrust her hips up to him so that he went deeper still, learned to move with him and under him until a sly warmth came creeping, then flooding, then exploding and shuddering deep in her pelvis, like great hiccups, and soon she was crying aloud as he was, and even sliding up behind him to rub her breast and thighs against him while he stood looking into the refrigerator or shaved before the bathroom mirror. He would take her then on the kitchen table, or in the glossy green bathtub of the economics professor, who would, Nell thought with glee, undoubtedly go into cardiac arrest if he could see what they were doing in his spotless kitchen and sanitary bathroom.

Nell did not know how it was with the other young faculty couples who were their acquaintances, but she thought that their sex lives could not possibly be so rich and innovative and satisfying as hers and Phillips, and she smiled indulgently and a little distantly when the conversation at parties on hot, postage-stamp patios became suffused with innuendo, as it invariably did. She thought them all sniggering children, and deprived children at that. Men friends, seeing the full smile and soft, sated eyes, felt a palpably sexual attraction to Nell, but her natural remoteness effectively stopped the usual high-flown, boozy passes before they were made, and the young professors-to-be contented themselves with saying to each other, "Something there, all right, if you push the right button." And "I'd like to have a whack at the Snow Queen there; I bet she'd melt your fillings once you turned her on." Their wives, themselves awesomely M.A.'d and Ph.D.'d, intense, older than Nell by five to ten years, wearing Marimekkos and tortoise-rimmed glasses and no makeup at all, saw the attraction that that strange young Nell Jay, with her cool little smiles and her white-columns background and her great cat's eyes, had for their men, but did not understand it or Nell, and Nell, feeling shy and insecure in the face of all their casually competent talk of babies in backpacks and advanced degrees in sociology and ab psych and natural childbirth and Modern Language Association meetings, retreated even further into the beautiful shell of her childhood, and so she did not make friends among them. But she did not miss the friendships then, early on; she had Phillips and her toy house and her writing and the deep, tumbled bed that waited for them when they left the back-yard patios, and she wanted little else.

Indeed, the only fly in the satiny ointment of their early marriage was Phillips's continuing animosity toward Ruth Yancey Fox. The bad feeling did not, as Nell had thought it would, abate naturally with the passage of time. She could understand his reluctance to open himself too soon to her grandmother after the humiliation and betrayal he had suffered on the evening of his first and only visit; she did not blame him for that. Her own indignation at Ruth's treatment of him rose like bile in her throat whenever she thought of the evening. And, of course, their elopement had taken a bitter toll from Gamma. Nell could understand easily that Phillips would not feel comfortable in the face of Ruth's tacit disapproval and would wish to avoid her. On the other hand, the breach would never be healed if Nell continued to go alone to Fox's Earth; he must make the step himself. She could not imagine that her grandmother would not ultimately be won by Phillips's charm and substance; it was only the sour residue of that first meeting and the elopement that hung in the air like a stench from a stagnant pool. It could so easily be dissipated by some small gesture from him. But he would not make it, and he would not go to Fox's Earth with her, and he would not discuss his reasons for refusing.

"When she invites me herself, then we'll see," he would say, and that was all he would say, and Nell knew that, failing some small initial gesture from him, this would not happen. On the few occasions that she found it necessary to speak to him of her grandmother and Fox's Earth, she thought there was something in his voice and manner that smacked of respect and . . . incredibly, faintly . . . fear.

But this she felt to be impossible; Phillips's self-possession was complete and shining, and she thought that he feared nothing in his world, and so she put the impression down to the vagaries of her own hypersensitive antennae, which had always reverberated like a stuck tympan when it came to her grandmother.

Why the continuing estrangement should bother her so she could not have said. True, Nell was utterly a creature of a South in which family and the ties and webs of blood and birth were all. But it was not she who was alienated from the great white house of her people. Did she not, herself, chafe with conflicting emotions each time she felt herself pulled back to Fox's Earth by the bonds with which her mother and grandmother held her? Had she not a hundred times wished herself free of the two women of that house, only to shrink away from the wish in hasty guilt, thinking, "How could I? They are my people; they gave me everything. They have done all for me."

But the cleft between her two great allegiances did bother her; it underlay and undermined every step she took, so that she was conscious of straddling the crack between her worlds at every turn. Nell moved through her days mostly in joy and contentment and sunlight, but the great bulk of Fox's Earth stalked her like a monstrous fish in the dark beneath the sunlit surface of the sea.

Nell finished her studies and graduated with her class at the end of their first spring of marriage. She took a *cum laude* in her art program; it had, they both agreed, been too late for her to change her major—it would have accomplished nothing. Phillips contended that under his tutelage she had come far enough to go on with her fiction on her own. The art degree was nice, an added fillip; they hung it over the fireplace in the professor's toy house along with Phillips's own lofty diplomas and degrees from the venerable East, and it had a fine, cultivated look to it, there among the certifications of his excellence. It was, also, the indirect instrument of their first serious fight.

"It really gives us a touch of class, doesn't it?" Nell said, wriggling to fit herself into the hollow of his arm and hip while they stood admiring their wall full of self-authentication. "The perfect marriage of art and literature. I know, Phillips; let's start a salon. You can sit before the fire and be brilliant and profound while Evelyn Carras and those other post-Bennington earth mothers kneel at your feet and adore you, and I can paint bold, cryptic abstracts over by the window and smile enigmatically at everybody from time to time, and we'll be the absolute toast of the campus. Everybody will clamor for invitations to our little evenings, but we'll be very selective, and only have who we want. Don't you love it?"

"Our own Bloomsbury." He smiled indulgently at her. "What a romantic you are, Nell. There aren't two people in all of Sparta, including my own department, who would know and care what a salon was, much less come to one. Mencken was right."

"About what? I thought you loved the South, anyway. You said last fall that it was the only region left in the country with any vitality, with anything at all to challenge a good teacher."

"What Mencken said was that it was the Sahara of the Bozart," he said. "And the fact that you, my charming and culturally deprived wife, have never heard that only bears me out. It's one of the most famous quotations to come out of the twenties. *And* if I said otherwise last fall, it was because I thought for sure I'd be a full professor by March, when Courtenay left for Sweet Briar, or wherever the hell it was he went."

Nell's elation fell away. She looked up at him. His blue eyes were hidden by his sweep of golden lashes, but the faint lines of discontent that had crept into his face, bracketing his mouth and furrowing his forehead, seemed deeper. When had they begun, what secret acid was etching at them when she was looking the other way? Anxiety fluttered in her stomach.

"Phillips, you've only been here nine months," she said. "It sometimes takes *years* to make the jump from associate to full. You said so yourself."

"Yeah, well, I was talking about the run-of-the-mill English associate. Not to put too fine a point on it, Nell, I'm the best they've got and they know it. There isn't anybody in this southern-fried playpen who can touch me on the contemporaries, and more than one of them have told me so. Dr. Crandall himself told me so when—ah, shit."

He had gotten angrier and angrier, and Nell could have bitten her tongue for starting the conversation in the first place.

"Do you want to go back East, then? We can always do that. I know you think it would be hard for me to leave

292

Mama and Gamma and the South, but it wouldn't, Phillips; truly it wouldn't. I'd do it in a minute. You could teach in any school in the East you wanted to; you could have your choice. You know you could."

"No." He shrugged impatiently and she moved out of the circle of his arm. "I came here to do some good and try to help get some changes made, and I'm not going to give up on that. I told you, I'm finished with the East."

"Is it because of . . . you know, that fuss you've had with your father? You could reconcile that in a minute, Phillips; all you'd have to do is pick up the phone. I wish you would. It would open up so many other doors for you in your career; it would give you all sorts of options for later that you've cut yourself off from, and besides, I've got to meet your parents sometime. I can't go through my life not knowing my in-laws."

"I am not going to go crawling back to my father and ask for his blessing and his stupid money," he said tightly. "If he wants to see me and meet my wife, he can pick up the telephone himself. Mother would already have done it if he'd let her, so that tells me how it stands up there as of now. If you want a crack at my famous inheritance, Nell, *you* go crawling to the old bastard and lick his boots. That's what he'll think, anyway . . . that you married me because you thought I was going to be rich as Croesus one day. I don't want his fucking money. I don't need it. My family is going to live just fine on what I make."

"That's not fair," Nell said, tears stinging in her nose. "You know I didn't marry you for your money. You *know* I knew you'd renounced your family's money long before I met you. If your father thinks that of me when he's never even met me, then I don't ever want to meet him. That was an awful thing to say, Phillips, and I don't think I dserved that."

"Ah, shit," he said again, and banged out of the house and went to his office. Nell waited miserably for him to call or come home and apologize, but he did not. She sat on the little chintz love seat in the living room and wept, and by the time he did come home, she had cried herself out and fallen into a heavy doze on the love seat, and when she awoke he was in the kitchen making them drinks and humming along with *The Moldau*. He was cheerful and expansive and suggested that they drive into Atlanta and have themselves a really good French dinner, and she was so relieved by his high spirits that she rushed to shower and dress and the fight was mentioned no more. It was a pattern that was to be repeated many times in the course of their marriage, until Nell finally abandoned all discussion of his family and the progress of his career.

She spent that summer keeping house. He settled himself to work on the novel he had put aside three years ago, realizing then, as he said, that he was not ready to write it. Now he thought he might be, and with a whole summer ahead and no plans to go to the seashore or mountains or travel in Europe . . . for an assistant professor's pay in a southern university was far from spectacular . . . he holed up in his office and stayed there for hours each day.

And Nell, alone, puttered in her miniature rental house and was endlessly charmed with the novelty of it. It was her own; she dismissed the pristine apparition of the absent economics professor as easily as she might shoo away a troublesome fly, and did not spare a thought for the day when he was bound to return and they would have to seek other housing. She devised her own small household routine and did not vary from it all summer; it gave her a satisfying, womb-deep feeling of continuity and strength and permanence to wake each morning and go so carefully and with such relish through each step of her formal little ritual. There was a hypnotic, earth-old rhythm to it; each step was like a small amulet. Do it perfectly and you would have good fortune. Step on a crack and you'd break your mother's back.

But inevitably, the charm of her proscribed little routine began to fade, and by the time the summer ended and Phillips put away the thin stack of paper he had amassed in the hot little office, she was bored and restless.

"I'm wasting my time, really," she said to him. "I should be doing more than this. What should I do? Go back and start my master's?"

"No," he said. "It's time for you to start writing in earnest now. Do me some short stories, Nell. Get yourself some of those women's magazines and see what they're publishing and do me a couple. You're better than three-fourths of those people they publish right now."

"Oh, I couldn't, Phillips! Could I? Shall I?"

"You won't know till you try, will you?"

And so Nell bought herself a ream of typewriter bond at the drugstore and brought out the old portable manual typewriter that had seen her through high school and college, and set herself up a work place on a card table in the bay window of the little dining room, and began to write. She was in an odd, nervous, vibrating stasis that autumn. These first halting sorties into fiction were different from anything she had ever attempted before.

"It's like everything I try to do is some kind of preliminary," she would tell Phillips in the evening. "I get so impatient; I want so to get on with it, but I don't know what I'm in such a hurry to do. Lord knows, it's hard enough to get one little short story the way I want it. It's not like I had delusions of being a Great American Writer."

"God, I hope not," he said. "The things you're doing now are charming and inventive, Nell, even if they're still clumsy. But spare me any Great American Authors."

On April Fool's Day, 1963, Nell got up to put on the breakfast coffee, threw up into the toilet, and knew immediately and without question that she was pregnant. The first thing she thought after she flushed the toilet was, "I'm going to send that new short story to *Redbook* before I tell anybody. That way, if they take it, it won't be like it was a reward for getting pregnant or something, it will be because it's a good story. I'm going to do it today, too."

"Did I hear you throwing up?" Phillips said, his head appearing around the bathroom door.

"No," Nell said. "The toilet made a funny noise when I flushed it, though. That must have been what you heard."

And from then on until she heard from *Redbook,* she got up half an hour earlier to allow for the morning's one clockwork siege of vomiting, which she veiled with the roar of the shower, and she said nothing to anyone about the baby.

The letter came seven weeks later, when Nell was beginning to worry about the fact that her waist was definitely, if faintly, growing broader and tauter of skin, and her heavy Fox breasts were engorging with blue veins. She knew she could not hide the fact of the pregnancy from Phillips much longer, but it had become a matter of stubborn importance to her that she hear from the magazine one way or another before she told him.

The letter said that they liked the story very much indeed, and would like to publish it in their special July fiction issue, and that she was due heartiest congratulations, and would she send a photograph of herself and a short biographical sketch to them as soon as possible? They would, they said, pay her $250.

Nell sat on the love seat in her too-tight slacks the rest of the afternoon, holding the letter in her hands, feeling as though she were totally encased in a plastic bubble, with all feeling waiting outside the sphere for the time when she would lift it.

"I sold a story to *Redbook*," she said to Phillips when he came in that afternoon. "And I'm three months pregnant."

And the bubble burst, and Nell began to cry.

They wrote his parents but never received any response to their letter. Phillips was bitter about this, but Nell did not mind. The second trimester of her pregnancy brought with it a stupendous feeling of well-being, a glow of health and contentment so profound that she seemed to hum and shimmer with it. She moved as through a lake of serenity: calmly, with infinite relish. She wished to do nothing but read silly, inconsequential novels and lie dreaming for hours on the love seat or on the patio chaise in the hot, fragrant spring, and to sleep. She slept for endless hours, deep, dreamless, drifts of sleep that took her suddenly and submerged her totally and cast her up on the shores of wakefulness hours later, refreshed and yet ready again for sleep in only a few hours.

She did not seem to want to make love, and Phillips did not push her on this, for he thought often that she had become someone he did not know, a self-contained and benevolent stranger, not at all the adoring, anxious, bed-besotted Nell that he had married. He felt, obscurely, that this woman in his house was as round and complete as an egg, and in no way needed the intrusion of his seed. He quite forgot that it was his seed that had transformed Nell into this shining carrier, and while he was glad about the child, and solicitous of Nell, he was also unaccustomedly wary and tentative around her. He never admitted to himself that part of Nell's new and imposing stature in his eyes was that of a soon-to-be-published author, and would have denied it if anyone had pointed it out to him. The fact of her publication became entwined in his mind with the fact of her pregnancy, giving her burgeoning procreativity a double dimension of height and breadth in his mind. Nell blooming in both body and mind was awesome.

296

When she mentioned, later into the pregnancy, that she did not feel like writing somehow, he rushed to assure her that she must rest and do exactly as she felt like doing. Writing would always be there. Writing would wait.

Nell went to Fox's Earth in early June to tell them about the baby. She had not been going so much in the past few weeks; the warm lassitude that wrapped her had kept her dreaming on her own patio or in the dank cool of the air-conditioned bedroom. She told them in the wisteria bower on the veranda, where they sat in the sun-dappled coolness and rocked in the old white wicker chairs that had been there ever since Nell could remember. Mama, predictably, burst into a flood of tears and upset her glass of lemonade into her lap. Gamma, ringing for Beauty or Salome to come with damp cloths and a fresh pitcher, looked at Nell silently for a long moment over the head of her daughter and then smiled. It was a strange smile; lovely, as all Gamma's smiles were, but oddly triumphant, as though Gamma herself had caused the pregnancy-to-be, and was pleased.

"Well, well," she said, in her light voice. "So I'm going to see at least one great-grandchild before I die, after all. I should have known you wouldn't let us down, sugar. Our dear baby Nell a little mama herself. And a new little girl for Fox's Earth . . . isn't that lovely, Hebe?"

She patted her sniveling daughter automatically, continuing to hold Nell in the intensity of her eyes.

"*Or* a little boy, Gamma," Nell said, vaguely annoyed. "Just as likely a little boy, and not for Fox's Earth, either. For Phillips and me. For *our* house."

"Of course, or a little boy," her grandmother said, dropping her lashes. "I imagine Phillips wants a little boy, doesn't he? Do hush now, Hebe. Here's Rip with some fresh lemonade. For crying out loud, you'd think it was you who was fixing to have a baby, you goose."

Rip looked down at Nell. Her rare, slow smile broke the ebony planes of her face.

"Well, Miss Nell," she said.

"How about that, Rip? A new baby. And *my* baby to boot; just imagine, *me* with a baby. I won't know which end of it to pick up first. You'll have to help me. Are you surprised?"

"No'm," Rip said. "I ain't surprised. You done had that look about you for a long time."

"Oh, come on, Rip! I haven't really started to show."

"No'm, but I knows. You ain't lookin' at us much these days; you lookin' inside, like. I knows what you sees in there."

"Will you help me take care of him? I can't imagine a Fox baby . . . *listen* to me; I mean a Jay baby . . . without you to help raise him."

"Yes'm, I be there. I was meant to look after Fox babies, look like. I watch over her for you."

"Her?" Nell said in exasperation. "What *is* it with you and Gamma?"

"Seem like to me I sees a little girl sittin' on yo' shoulder whenever I looks at you, Miss Nell. But the light funny in this ol' bower. Cain't go by what you sees."

"I hope not." Nell shivered in the gold-dappled gloom. "That's spooky. You're a witch, Rip. I don't want to know yet."

"Well, then, it's settled, Nell," Ruth said gaily. "We'll have to celebrate. A special supper, and champagne, and a no-holds-barred dessert. What's that thing you told me Phillips carried on over so when you went to Rémond's last time? Cream . . ."

"*Crème brûlée*," Nell said automatically, holding her breath. Did her grandmother mean to invite Phillips to dinner, then? Oh, if she only would! And if only he would put his stiff-necked New England pride aside for once, and accept with grace . . . "I think I could be completely happy, then," Nell thought. "Gamma *is* a trial, and so is Mama, in another way, but they're all the family I've got, and all Phillips has, too, really, if he'd only stop to think about it. I don't want my baby to grow up in a divided family."

"*Crème brûlée*, that's right," Ruth Fox said. "Well, it all sounds too grand for us, but if you'll stop by the kitchen and tell Carrie how to make it on your way out, we'll give it a try. Could you come Friday night? Or I tell you what, I'll call Phillips at his office. That would probably be better, wouldn't it?"

"That would be grand," breathed Nell. "That would be just wonderful, Gamma."

Nell never knew what her grandmother said on the phone to Phillips, but she knew how persuasive she could be when she set her mind to it, especially when it was a male she wished to captivate. So she was not entirely surprised when Phillips said, casually, "Your grandmother called and asked us to dinner . . . in honor of the baby, I suppose. I said we'd go. Is eight all right?"

"Eight is all right," Nell said, hugging him. "Oh, Phillips, eight is just fine!"

It was a pleasant dinner. It was more than that; it was comfortable and somehow inevitable. It seemed to Nell that they had dined with her mother and grandmother at the great Hepplewhite table each week since they married; there was about the evening a strong sense of continuity rather than a sense of beginnings. Gamma wore a water-color blue and lavender Pucci that Nell had never seen, that turned her eyes to pansies and set her smooth cheeks to glowing as with fever. She laughed and tossed her head so that the pearl-drop earrings in her tiny pink ears swung in the chandelier's light, and she leaned toward Phillips, whom she had seated in Paul, Senior's, chair at the head of the table as on that other night . . . but with such a difference, now . . . and she trilled and fluted and exclaimed with interest whenever he spoke, and he gradually capitulated, first smiling at her foolishness and then laughing aloud. He did not babble nervously, or posture and boast and embroider, as he had on that other, terrible night. He answered Ruth Fox's charming excesses with gravely ironic courtesies of his own, and flashed Nell little "She's-just-too-much" smiles, so that Nell knew he was pleased, and she felt ready to burst with pride and gratitude at his behavior. "See? See what you've missed all this time? This is my husband, this is how he really is," her smile said to her grandmother, and Ruth smiled back at her.

Hebe, in a flower-sprigged, floor-length sun dress incongruously tied in the back with a trailing sash, bubbled merrily at each sally and quip, and looked from one of them to another like an enchanted child at a circus, and even Robert and Beauty and Salome, and Carrie in her kitchen, in the midst of producing a perfect, glass-sheeted *crème brûlée*, grinned with delight and good feeling. Miss Nell and her Yankee husband were back home and a new baby was coming, and Miss Ruth was smiling and laughing as she had not done since Miss Nell was a little girl, and it seemed that a new sun shone on Fox's Earth. Only Rip, in the rocking chair by the stove that had become her own chair, did not smile and chatter. She rocked steadily, back and forth, back and forth, her slim black fingers busy with the mending of Hebe's interchangeable and endless ruffles, her calm black eyes fixed levelly and without expression on the swinging door into the dining room.

"What you lookin' at, Rip?" Carrie asked her in the middle of the evening, for Rip had not moved from her rocker, and had not taken her eyes off the door.

"Ain't lookin' at nothin'," Rip said, but she did not move her eyes.

"Well, sho' look to me like you fixin' to bore holes in that do' with them eyes," Carrie said.

"Jus' tryin' to see what comin'," Rip said. "Jus' tryin' to hear if Miss Nell be all right."

"Sho' she all right, you sees how all right she is, don't you?"

"I ain't mean tonight," Rip said impatiently. "I mean, do she be all right down the road. That's what I tryin' to hear, 'roun' the soun' of yo' mouth flappin'."

Carrie was silent. She looked at Rip out of the corner of her eyes. Sometimes Rip walked and talked with things that Carrie did not see and did not want to, and at those times it was best to be quiet and still and ask no questions. Carrie knew that she would not have liked the answers.

After that, they went regularly to Fox's Earth. Nell was fussed over, tempted with little treats from Carrie's kitchen, showered with frivolous small things that Ruth had picked up in town or ordered from Atlanta or New York. She was tucked onto sofas and chaise longues and covered, protesting, with afghans and throws even in the heat of summer, and great plans for the baby were spun in the air around her head, until finally she had to call a firm halt to them. For she could tell from his sudden silences that these plans displeased Phillips, and she feared a lapse of their new relationship with Ruth back into the old, hurtful one. Already a sort of attrition had eaten away the fine edge of that first night's good feeling; Phillips and her grandmother had slipped into a kind of guarded, neutral politeness that neither degenerated nor ripened into anything warmer. It was as if they had settled something between them, and if the solution was not entirely to the liking of either of them, it was certainly livable. Nell sorrowed briefly for the one fine night of camaraderie they had had, but the new and continuing relationship was so far preferable to the old estrangement that she soon came to count herself fortunate, and rested in her deep new pool of content.

Only once did the new *politesse* threaten to erupt into enmity, and then it was avoided largely through the grace of Ruth Yancey Fox, who simply and with amiable dignity dropped the subject.

It happened when Ruth said, early on, "Tell me what Dr. Hopkins says about the baby. A new Fox baby: he must be thrilled to death."

"I'm not going to Dr. Hopkins," Nell said unwillingly. She had been dreading this moment. "I'm going to a man in Atlanta. He's real good, Gamma; he's young, and he has some pretty innovative ideas about having babies. He thinks he can fix it so Phillips can be right in the delivery room with me. All the faculty wives go to him."

"Well, aren't you modern," Gamma said, and there was something in her voice that made Nell look at her. She saw that Phillips was looking at her grandmother too, with his chin raised and his nostrils flared as though he anticipated, not without some pleasure, a fight.

"To have Phillips right there when the baby comes, I mean," Ruth went on. "You young people are so brave. Not to care that it's so messy and all. But, honey, I had so hoped that my first . . . and probably only, the way I'm going . . . great-grandbaby would be born right here in Sparta. And that you would come here from the hospital for a week or two, so we could look after you and Rip could tend to the baby like she has all the Fox babies. Sort of carry on the tradition, you know? Wouldn't you just think about that?"

Nell was silent. All of a sudden it sounded wonderful: the calm and silence of the great white house, where all sounds and smells and resonances were as familiar to her as the textures of her own skin. The protective arch of her own narrow bed's canopy over her in the linen-scented darkness, the peaty, warm smell of morning coffee coiling up the stairs from the kitchen, the heart-swelling smell of drying cedar and pine . . . for the baby would come, if the smart young Atlanta doctor was correct, just after Christmas. And Rip . . . the measured sound of Rip's slender feet on the stairs, the gentle, long hands, the rich, crooning voice that sounded always in Nell's ears the way woodsmoke smelled.

"I don't know, Gamma . . ." she began.

301

"No," Phillips Jay said. "Nell is going to Atlanta, and that's final. She's too far along to change doctors now, and I want her where she can get the best care and equipment possible. And when she comes home with the baby, they're coming to our house. I'll see that she has a nurse if she needs one."

Nell looked at him nervously, and then at her grandmother. His words had been downright belligerent and rude; it was not at all like Phillips. But Ruth Fox only smiled graciously at her grandson-in-law.

"Well, of course, Phillips," she said. "Your own house. How exciting! I knew it was about time for you to give up that darling little rental house, but I didn't know you'd picked out one of your own. Tell me about it. Is there a nursery? Well, of course, you'd have a nursery. And a room for the nurse. Oh, Nell, honey, I *hope* it's one of those pretty brick Colonials you liked so much out on the river. We talked about them one day when Fancy Cobb was here; Fancy and Tom bought one of the first ones for Sissy and her husband when they married, remember? It was the day you brought those dresses of your mama's back from Atlanta for us . . ."

"I remember," Nell said, not looking at her.

"It's one of the faculty duplexes," Phillips said loudly. "It's behind the intramural athletic field, and it's just temporary, until we can find something we really like. It's not fancy, but it has two bedrooms, and it will be just fine while the baby is small. I didn't think it was smart to buy right now, until we're really sure what we want."

Ruth was quiet. Nell looked with interest at her foot, and then at the pattern in the little oriental. She dreaded the move; she had loved the immaculate little toy house, and the faculty duplex was bleak and charmless in the extreme. It was, in fact, almost shabby. Nell thought yearningly of the graceful, azalea-planted new brick Colonials out by the river, with their pierced-brick patio walls to catch the river breezes, and their acre and a half of level lawns, and their three and four spacious bedrooms and walk-in closets and high ceilings. More than anything else, Nell found that she needed space around her. It came, undoubtedly, from growing up in the vast reaches of Fox's Earth, and it was just as undoubtedly a pampered and shameful need. Nevertheless, there it was. To be cramped made her feel angry and desperate, like a trapped

animal. She would be able to touch both sweating con-
crete-block walls of the duplex's tiny bathroom when she
sat on the toilet, and the closet door in the bedroom would
not open fully when a double bed was in place in the
room. She was suddenly vastly annoyed with Phillips. Why
must he be so stiff-necked about accepting financial help
from Gamma? Not to mention his own parents. It was
not as though he couldn't patch things up with his father
with a single telephone call. Just a small apology . . . But
she knew he would die first.

Ruth Fox still did not speak, but "can't provide" hung
as palpably in the room as if the words had been spelled
out in neon tubing.

"Well, a new baby only needs about three square feet
of space, anyway," she said finally, gaily, and rang for
Rip to bring ice cream and sour-cream pound cake. Phillips was sullen and quiet on the way home, but at least
he did not launch into a railing tirade against Ruth Fox,
as he might once have done, and Nell had the sense of
having stepped back from an abyss.

But still, she knew that he was not happy, not truly
happy, and because her own well-being was so nearly
complete, she felt a guilty anguish at this. She did not
know precisely why he seemed to simmer gently and per-
petually in a stew of his own discontent lately, only that
he did, and she did not ask him, fearing that to have it
articulated would somehow be to deepen it. And he did
not discuss it with her, for in truth he did not know exactly why himself.

There were several reasons, on the face of it. He was
still not a full professor and could not anticipate being
one in the foreseeable future. He still had not published
and knew, somewhere at the very bottom of his heart,
that he would not . . . at least not the novels with which
he yearned to leave his stamp on the world of letters.
Money was tight, especially with the new baby coming,
and there was no immediate prospect of any more coming in. Phillips was not used to this. Moreover, he was
tiring rapidly of the company of the young assistant and
associate professors of English and history and psychology
and the other liberal arts with whom he spent his time; he
found them pretentious and boring, and the invitations
from the great white houses that were the counterparts of

the ones in which he had lived and visited so casually at home in New England did not come.

Nell could have told him they would not; she had known when they eloped that she had effectively cast off many of the moorings that had held her secure in her world before she met him. Nell did not care, but Phillips came to. Moreover, he had not succeeded either in converting any of the whites he had come South to convert or in saving any of the Negroes he had thought to save, and now the moment was passing and the great movement was giving way to the peevish tantrums of the terrifying young in their costumes and amulets, and Phillips suspected that should he seek to join them, they would jeer at him. He was right.

And he could—or would—not go home again.

And so as the days passed toward Christmas and the birth of his child, and Nell grew greater and more clifflike and incandescent with each passing day, he clung to the thought of the child, and the glorious moment in the immaculate delivery room far away in Atlanta, that bravest of new world, where his son . . . his! his own! . . . would come howling out into his very hands, to reshape his sagging world and reaffirm his stagnating life.

But he was cheated of even that brief moment of participatory glory, for on Christmas Eve as they sat with tray suppers of oyster stew in the little parlor at Fox's Earth, Nell's water broke and she went so immediately and efficiently into deep labor that there was hardly time even to get her upstairs and into bed, and instead of the innovative young doctor in Atlanta, it was Rip and Ruth Yancey Fox who brought his child, who was not a son at all, but a raging small daughter with the unmistakable gold of the Foxes on her narrow head, into the world, with a puffing Dr. Hopkins arriving from his own hearthside only afterward, to deliver the afterbirth and pronounce both Fox mother and Fox daughter in excellent health.

And so Phillips Jay passed into the third year of his marriage in the house of his enemy, alone in the fine old paneled study where Claudius and Paul Fox had paced in turn on the birth nights of their children so many years before; waiting, as they had waited before him, for a new voice to affirm him not only man but father.

And in the quiet Christmas morning air of Fox's Earth, still another Fox woman child cried aloud.

304

25

BUT ABIGAIL FOX JAY was not, after all, destined to be a child of Fox's Earth, and this fact was evident from the moment of her birth. She was born screaming, and she howled lustily for the first three weeks of her life . . . which were, after all, spent at Fox's Earth as old Ruth Fox had wished, and not in the mean little faculty house of her father.

The birth had been easy for Nell, and almost indecently quick, but because there had been no chance to do an episiotomy and Abby was a large child for her not quite nine months, Nell was badly torn, and was grateful to rest in her tester bed at Fox's Earth, taking heat-lamp treatment and antibiotics, for the prescribed three weeks following the birth. She lay drowsing in the dim, quiet room, reading or listening to her radio and eating the special meals concocted to tempt her by Carrie and brought up by a tiptoeing Beauty or Salome. In this high-ceilinged, flower-sprigged room of her childhood, in this house where she had never been mistress or even equal, but only small Nell, the littlest of the Foxes, it was harder than it might have been otherwise for Nell to accept the reality of her motherhood; sometimes she lay listening to the faraway, angry hornet's wail of the baby from the old nursery and wondered, "Whose baby can that be? How funny, to hear a baby at Fox's Earth." And once or twice, waking in the early morning and hearing the cries, in that suspended state between sleep and wakefulness, Nell would feel sharp resentment at whatever usurping infant cried in the nursery that was, by rights, her own, as the baby of Fox's Earth.

And then she would remember that it was her own child who cried in this house of her ancestors, and that presently she would have to take it home and begin to care for it, and would have the care of it forever after, and a shameful, helpless fear would roll over her.

"Oh, God," she would whisper, turning her head in the cool darkness, burrowing deeply into the lavender-scented pillows that had been put fresh on her bed only the night before. "Oh, God. What am I going to do with that baby? I don't even know how to be a grown-up yet. I don't even know how to be a real writer. What ever made me think I could be a mother?" And she might cry a bit, a few helpless, hopeless tears.

But she always fell asleep again before she could cry very long. And when she woke again, there would be a steaming, laden breakfast tray, and a fresh nightgown and new ruffled bed jacket, and there would be Gamma with the morning paper and new magazines and small plans for the day, and there would be Phillips, looking clean-scrubbed and handsome, if sullen, stopping by to kiss her and see his daughter before his first class of the morning, and there would be Mama, hovering and chattering like a girl friend or a sister, and, finally, there would be her baby, bathed and powdered and dressed in lace and ruffles, instead of the sensible Carter's shirts and diapers Nell had bought, waiting in Rip's eternal black arms to be put, howling and kicking, into Nell's timid ones.

And in this way Nell learned to handle her daughter, at a comfortable remove, with an army of doting family and servants in attendance, ready to take the baby away and minister capably to her needs if she should so much as whimper in the inept and uncertain arms of her mother. It was, by and large, a happy, almost magical time for Nell.

But it was not a solid foundation for motherhood, and on some deep and basic level Nell knew that it was not, and fretted even as she basked in the hiatus she had miraculously been given. It was as if Abby was a dangerous and unpredictable wild thing that waited on the fringes of Nell's consciousness for the day when she would finally be alone with her mother, and must then be dealt with on her own savage terms.

And Abby was a wild thing. Even Rip, who loved her best and had the constant care of her away in the old nursery on the third floor, had to admit that this newest Fox was another matter entirely from all the other blond, fine-featured babies who had wriggled and thrived in the big old room. Even when she slept, Abby did not rest in sweet-faced peace, but stirred and kicked and waved her tiny fists in general protest, knotted her silvery-blond traces of eyebrows together, snapped her gums open and shut like a furious turtle. The bubbles of spittle that she blew seemed not the classic effluence of babyhood but boiling effluvia of the bile that kept her shrieking and kicking from dawn until dusk.

"What on earth is the *matter* with her, Rip?" Nell would say, near tears. "Is it me? Look at her; she looks like she's just going to explode! I honestly think she hates me. Oh, dear God, what if she's . . . mentally wrong, or abnormal, or something?"

"She jus' mad," Rip said. "Ain' nothin' wrong with her mind."

"But she's been crying for almost three weeks now. She's been crying ever since she was born. The only time she doesn't cry is when I'm nursing her, and then she bites me. Phillips is getting so he won't even come by here after work; he blames me. I know he does; he blames me for not having the baby in Atlanta at the hospital and being back home by now. But, Rip, Dr. Hopkins *said* not to get out of bed yet . . . listen, Rip. You have to tell me. Nobody else will tell me, but you've never lied to me, and you've got to tell me now. Have you heard him . . . Dr. Hopkins, I mean . . . have you heard him tell Gamma or Phillips that there's something the matter with the baby? He tells me he can't find a thing, and that some babies just naturally cry a lot, but, Rip, no baby cries this much. There must be something they're not telling me . . ."

"No'm," Rip said truthfully, for she had worried about the same thing, and had listened and watched until she had satisfied herself about the matter. "He say the same thing to Miss Ruth and Mr. Phillips, not two days ago. He say there ain't nothin' wrong with the baby that he can see, an' that he's seen lots of babies in his time. He say they can take her into 'Lanta to a special doctor, do they want to; he say he give 'em the name of one, but he say they ain't gon' fin' nothin' wrong. He say she jus' a crier, an' she git tired of it pretty soon, an' then she stop. He tellin' the truth, Miss Nell. I could have tol' 'em that."

"Then what's the matter with her? *Why is she still crying?*"

"She cryin'," Rip said, "because she don't like it here.

307

She stop soon as you gits her home. You wait an' see don't she, Miss Nell."

"That's absurd," Nell said. "A three-week-old baby doesn't know where she is."

"This'un do," Rip said equably. And, eerily, she was right. Because from the day they carried Abby out from the veranda of Fox's Earth into the world for the first time, wrapped in the featherweight lacy white wool blanket that had been Alicia Fox's, she stopped crying, and the first night she spent in the dismal little linoleum-floored cubicle that served her as a nursery in the faculty duplex, she slept around the clock and woke bubbling and gurgling quietly in her crib, looking like a Gerber baby. And from then on, though she always had a swift and imperious temper and was quick to howl her outrage and frustration, she never cried again in that terrible, monotonous, marathon manner in which she had shrieked away the first three weeks of her life at Fox's Earth.

"I don't blame her," Phillips said, watching while Abby nursed peacefully at Nell's aching, blue-veined breast on their first night home. "I'd like to scream that place down myself sometimes. Poor kid. Look at her. I never even knew she had white skin till now. I thought she was going to be that boiled-owl red all her life."

"She's going to look just like you . . . and like Paul," Nell said, so grateful for her child's new tranquility that for the first time she did not feel the ache of old grief at the thought of her brother, but only a deep, sweet fondness. "She's going to be a great beauty. She's really got Yancey's temperament, though."

They had heard so little from Yancey during their marriage that Nell sometimes forgot about her sister for months on end. And though Phillips had met her once, when he and Nell spent a weekend in New York, he had not liked her, for she was coolly mocking to him, so they did not visit again. But ever since Abby's birth, Yancey had, surprisingly, kept in touch. She would call once a week, in the evenings, and she seemed so eager for news of the baby, so uncharacteristically and genuinely interested in Abby, that Nell was deeply touched and grateful. She had told Yancey, when she phoned her to tell her about the baby's birth, that although everyone said she was a carbon copy of Paul as a child, she was temperamentally so like Yancey as to be laughable.

308

"It's like having your baby around all the time, instead of mine," Nell had said, and Yancey had laughed her now-clipped New York laugh and said, "God help her. Gamma will put her in a gunny sack and throw her in the river."

Put after that she had begun her once-a-week calls, and she kept them up throughout Abby's childhood and into her adolescence, even when she and Nell no longer talked except to argue futilely over the responsibility for the two women in the great white house. She begged so often for photos of Abby that Nell habitually had prints made whenever they took snapshots of the child, and sent them to Yancey. Nell would live to see the day when she would regret with all her heart ever having made that first phone call to her sister to tell her of her niece's birth. But for now she was as abjectly, mindlessly grateful for her older sister's attention as she had ever been as a child, when Yancey had cast some small, careless token of benevolence her way.

"It never did take much," she told a man who was not Phillips once, much later. "Just a little tiny bit of Yancey always did buy her an awful lot of me."

"Pity," the man said. "You're worth forty of Yancey."

Nell's short story had appeared in *Redbook* the summer before Abby's birth, a sharp, finely wrought little character study of an introspective child on her thirteenth birthday in a small southern town in the first year of World War II, and it surprised all who knew Nell with its bite and perceptivity. Nell called it, banally enough, "Rite of Passage," and it brought her three thick manila envelopes full of fan letters which the magazine passed on to her, and earned her considerable favorable comment in the cramped, hot faculty apartments and duplexes in which they visited, and by the members of the old guard, who had known her as a child. The older faculty wives, who had drawn themselves into a protective circle against her youth and sensuality and breeding and essential otherness, opened their ranks slightly; if they did not admit her into their choruses of degree requirements and creative crafts endeavors, neither did they ignore any longer her shyly proffered comments and tentative smiles. Nell was more than a child bride in the ranks of women now; she was a writer, albeit a writer of what they privately comforted each other by calling "slick women's stuff."

But the story was better than that, and their husbands,

many of whom taught one level or another of literature, knew that it was, and they looked at her with new respect and interest even as their lewd speculations as to what Nell Jay was like in bed escalated. Phillips knew that it was better than the average magazine fiction of the day, too, and he was proud of Nell and generous with his praise, for it was, after all, still women's magazine fiction, and it did not threaten him. Even Nell was finally able to see that it was a good piece of work, and this knowledge led her to do other stories, a few at first while Abby was still a baby and slept most of the time, more later on, when Rip came to them at noon every day and stayed through the afternoon to care for the baby, and Nell was free.

In these early years, while Abby was still a curious and vivid-faced baby whose volatile temper and bright, nervous quickness were soothed and charmed by the serene presence of Rip, and while the long-awaited promotion to full professor kept Phillips, for the moment, secure and eased in his skin, Nell was as happy as she could imagine being. The little duplex was still too small, but Nell's clever eye for color and texture and the extravagant largesse of Ruth Fox had made it charming and almost luxurious with pillows and plants and small accessory pieces and bibelots. And with Rip to rock the baby to sleep or take her out on campus for walks in her almost indecently costly English carriage, and later to the playground with other faculty children, Nell could retreat to her typewriter, settle a pile of Vivaldi and Handel and Palestrina carefully onto Phillips's pampered Fisher turntable, and let the deep water of her fiction settle over her for three or four hours at a time. When Abby finished her nap or her outing and was bathed and fresh for the evening, and Rip hugged her and handed her to Nell and let herself out the squeaking little fake Dutch door of the duplex, Nell would have a satisfactory pile of fresh pages squared and paperweighted on the card table, and could start their supper in the detumescent glow of a good day of writing and a right and ordered world. Almost everything she wrote, moreover, sold to one respectable women's magazine or another; by the time Abby was a kindergartner, Nell realized that hers was a familiar name in the world of "women's fiction," and in the main she was content and grateful with

310

this status. It was so much more than she had ever dreamed of having.

It was not a perfect time. But Nell, having learned in her childhood to aspire only to the maintenance of a livable status quo, found the sweet, uneventful days as pleasing and satisfying as a Technicolor movie. They charmed her; she never tired of them. Even the increasing fragility and dependence of her mother and grandmother, even the escalation of the fretful, nattering telephone calls and the fussy, stale, old-woman crises and talcumy pets that emanated from Fox's Earth had lost much of their power to annoy and smite her. Nell felt as removed and insulated from the fluttering fingers of Hebe and Ruth as she had in her pregnancy, but with a new and heady sense of peace and power and competence. Her mother's excitement when one of Nell's stories appeared in the new issue of one of her magazines touched Nell as little as her grandmother's elaborate and chilly silences about her writing.

But there were other fruits of her writing that were bitter on her tongue. The most notable among them was Phillips's attitude about the money it brought. Generous with his praise of her writing ("It's a valid form, even if it's not world-shaking. You do it better than anybody I know"), he was adamant and irrational about the rewards it engendered. They fought about it more than once.

"I won't sit on it," he said loudly of a beautiful little Regency love seat Nell bought when enough of the small magazine checks had mounted up in the separate account he had opened for her at the Sparta Bank and Trust. "And I will not allow Abby to sit on it, and I will have none of our friends into this house until you take it back. I don't care what you do with your money, Nell, as long as I do not have to hear of it, or see evidence of it. I've told you this before. Give it to the Peace Corps or the SCLC, for all I care. Start a home for unwed cats. Better still, endow the Nell Geiger Jay Chair of Trivial Literature here at good old Kudzu U. But I will not have one penny of your money going over our heads, or onto our backs, or into our mouths. I am not even going to discuss it any further with you. You knew my feelings, and you chose to directly flout them. I want that thing out of here tomorrow."

"Phillips, that's not fair," Nell shouted, caution for once swept away on a flood of injustice. "I live here too, Abby lives here too. It's a horrible little dump of a place, and you know it is, and yet you'd let your daughter continue to live in a . . . a rathole where she'll be ashamed to ask her friends when she's old enough to care about those things, you'd do that rather than let your own wife help make it better. I'm half of us, Phillips; I'm on the team. I count, too. With my money, we already have enough for a down payment on a halfway decent house; in another year we could afford one of the river houses. If you're too damned stiff-necked to let your own in-laws help you with a loan . . . a loan, for God's sake, Phillips, not a gift . . . or to make up this stupid, ridiculous thing with your father, who's never even met his daughter-in-law or seen his granddaughter, you could at least consider what the other half of this family wants to do. You aren't the whole show!"

His face went white, and the cords in his neck leapt out into the pulsing bas-relief she had come to dread, and she knew before he even spoke again that she would call the shop in Atlanta the next day and have them come for the love seat. The weight of his anger was too much for the smallest Fox, who crouched forever, in Nell's head, in the harlequin-dappled lattice cage beneath the back steps of Fox's Earth.

And because she did not oppose him during those years, the money mounted up in the account. And though sometimes she burned with resentment for the nothing that the money was doing for them, still, they did not often fight about it. And that was the main thing, the not fighting. It kept the years of Abby's childhood and Nell's short stories good years, calm years.

And after all, things did get better, for not long after Phillips received his full professorship, his nearly forgotten Uncle Corydon Jay died in Tucson ("he was my drinking uncle, the black sheep. I didn't think he even remembered that I existed") and left Phillips fifty thousand dollars, and at last they had the four-bedroom brick Colonial with the pierced old-brick wall to catch the river breezes, and a level yard full of azaleas and dogwood, and were able to spend the summer in England, where Phillips gathered material on the Bloomsbury Group for his oddly conceived book on Vita Sackville-West as the mother of the moderns, and where Nell and seven-year-old Abby learned to eat huge cream teas and did cathedrals and stately homes.

Phillips's book was finished the following year, and was published with due academic acclaim by an impeccable little university press, and he was wined and dined in the department, and took to having five o'clock sherries with old Dr. Crandall, the head of the English Department, in his study at least twice a week. He grew rounder and full of face, and his fair hair dulled to proper and becoming pewter at the temples, though he was only in his middle thirties, and he began smoking a pipe, which he left to smolder and stink in a litter of scorched dottle in overflowing ashtrays as he began work on yet another book, this time tracing the influence of what he termed the popular mass-market press on the development of the fiction writers of the twenties.

"I have a theory," he told Nell and an assembled crowd of dinner guests at his newly acquired antique gate-legged dining table in the river house, over moussaka, "that that most American of all mediums, the popular magazine . . . Nell's forte . . ." and he raised his wineglass to her . . . "not only gave the enduring writers of the day—Fitzgerald, Hemingway, Lewis, et al.—a leg up, it actually shaped the way they wrote; the magazines dictated the eventual *oeuvre* of each one. Who knows what body of work Fitzgerald might have produced if he hadn't, for better or worse, spent a lot of his creative vitality on 'Bernice Bobs Her Hair' and that sort of thing? It may turn out that Nell's nice, innocuous, slick little lady magazines are in reality very efficient, apple-cheeked small assassins of genius." And he smiled hugely at her, and the other people at the table . . . older, sleeker people now than at those early spaghetti and jug-wine suppers that had been Nell's introduction into Phillips's world . . . smiled, too, indulgently.

"Well, if that's what you think before you've even started your research, Phillips," Nell said, stung, "you probably won't have any trouble fitting a theory around it."

He hastily changed the subject, but Nell again had the sense . . . one she had increasingly and inexplicably, in these days of greater affluence and a lessening of stress over Phillips's career at the university . . . of stepping back from a great crevasse in the nick of time.

But for the most part the days and months and years of roundness and goodness continued unabated. They summered sometimes on Sea Island, where Gamma took a house for them, though she herself rarely came down, hating the sun and the competitive opulence and expensively tended flesh of the wealthy women from all over the country who flocked there like wattled, hard-beaked birds of prey. They went once more to Europe, this time to Italy, just for a vacation, where small, white-blond Abby grew accustomed and then inured to the fervent cluckings and cries of *"Bella, bella, bella,"* and where, Nell came to think later, the child first fell under the spell of the music that so consumed and transmuted her for the rest of her life, when they took her to see a brooding, red-and-black production of *Nabucco* in the gardens of the Pitti Palace in Florence.

After that, in the winters, while Nell worked at her stories and Phillips wove his clever, ironic spells in his classrooms and Rip rocked in a new chair in the relentlessly charming copper-and-ruffled kitchen of the river house, waiting to go and collect her small charge, Abby studied piano with a fine young instructor in the university's Music Department. This was a real tribute to the astonishing talent that had lain locked in her starfish baby fingers, for Abby was the youngest student in the class by ten years, and was something of a legend on the campus at the end of her first autumn of instruction. And at Christmas of that year, Phillips bought an exquisite little upright piano for the pine-paneled den, and for hours on end, after her class was over at three o'clock and Rip had gone home to Fox's Earth, the den became Abby's own preserve, just as the seldom-used guest room was by day the preserve of Nell and her typewriter.

"Kallen said Friday she was just about at the end of what he could do for her," Phillips said one evening as they sat listening to Abby practice etudes. "He thinks we ought to see about enrolling her in a good performing arts school where she can just submerge herself in her music and see what happens. He thinks she might be one of the few who really have a crack at it, I mean in an international way. The big time. He knows several schools that he says would take her in a minute. None of them are around here, but the New York High School of Performing Arts and of course Juilliard and Eastman come to mind. Not now, maybe, but before too long. She ought to get in while she's still young and flexible. I know it sounds like a long way away, but if it were New York, Yancey could look after her. You know Yancey's mentioned it before, and Abby lights up like a Christmas tree when she does. She ain't much, Nell, but she *is* family, and she wouldn't let anything happen to Abby."

"No," said Nell.

It was not a new battle. Ever since Abby's first faltering swipes at a piano had so rapidly been transformed into grace and order and fire, Yancey had been caught up in the notion of a musical career for her. She called often to hear of Abby's progress, and she wrote the child encouraging notes on cards on which she had drawn swift, clever cartoons of a tiny Abby at a Steinway concert grand in a vast auditorium that she labeled "Lincoln Center," and she subscribed to *Musical America* in Abby's name, even though it would be years before the child could comprehend the articles. She sent Christmas and birthday gifts of expensive classical piano albums and biographies of Liszt and Chopin and Schumann-Heink, and checks for extra lessons, and it was a rare phone call to Abby that did not end with some mention of "when you come to New York to live with your old Aunt Yancey and study at Juilliard." So that even before Abby could comprehend the parameters of her own gift, or understood what Juilliard was, she was teasing and pouting to go and live with Yancey, and flaming into her quick, bright tempers when they told her it was out of the question.

While Abby was still a small child, Phillips had objected to the invitations as strenuously and impatiently as Nell did, though for entirely different reasons. To Phillips it was simply out of the question for an eight- or nine-year-old child to be entrusted to a hard-driving career-oriented stranger, aunt though she might be, in a merciless city and an even more mercilessly competitive *métier* a thousand miles away. But when she was nearing her thirteenth birthday, and it was no longer possible for him to ignore the mounting evidence of Abby's extraordinary talent, the plan began to look more feasible. Phillips might be resigned to the less than tender mercies of the Deep South for himself, but he had no wish to limit his child to what he considered laughably second-rate creative resources. He would sadly miss Abby, who was more and more the strong-minded volatile child of her father as she approached adolescence than the precocious small companion to her mother she had been as a tot, but he would risk much to see her soaring free.

But Nell's objections ran much deeper, and she knew that the day would never come when she would capitulate and send her child away from them to boarding school, no matter how much the child herself might wish it. Nell had watched too many leave-takings from beneath the flat roof of Fox's Earth; those who left her did not return. Abby would not follow Paul and Yancey into the murderous, polite fiction of boarding school "for her own good," and that was that. Her very heart withered within her at the idea. Fierce anger at Phillips for even considering the possibility, pure rage at Yancey for attempting so treacherously and persistently to seduce her child away from her, licked at Nell like St. John's fire whenever the subject was mentioned. Soon she stopped producing careful, level-voiced, adult-sounding reasons for Abby and Phillips and simply snapped, or screamed, as the intensity of the occasion seemed to warrant, "No. NO! I won't talk about it any more, so you're wasting your breath. NO!"

And sensing some dangerous, razor-honed edge in Nell that they had never before perceived, Phillips and Abby would leave her alone. But more and more often Abby would return to the subject, and lately Phillips was becoming exasperated and belligerent at Nell's refusals to discuss it.

"You're irrational about this, Nell, you know that, don't you?" he would say. "You're sounding like a crazy woman. You look like the madwoman of Chaillot; your eyes light up like your Gamma's when you scream like that. You can't hold Abby back forever; her kind of talent is going to come out, no matter what you do. Far better if you gave in gracefully and helped us make some workable arrangements for schooling than to keep on being a blind fool about it. You're going to drive her away from you faster than Yancey could ever lure her, if that's what you think she's trying to do. Don't you remember how it feels to be held back from something that's simply second nature to you? Don't you see some parallel to the way you're carrying on over her music and the way your famous Gamma sat on you about your writing?"

"Oh, it's not the same thing at *all*, it's not," Nell cried, stricken to her heart; but a new fear was born in her, a fear of losing her daughter forever through her own neurotic fears, and so her adamant objections shrank to, "We'll talk about it again when you're sixteen," and with this Abby and Phillips and Yancey had to be content. At least the wind had tempered a bit. In time, perhaps . . .

And time passed, and time melted away, and as in most moderately happy . . . or at least, not measurably unhappy . . . families, everything happened, and nothing did. Abby grew in stature and beauty and talent and temper. Phillips reached inexorably toward the chairmanship of his department. At Fox's Earth, Hebe and Ruth fussed, fluttered, frittered and dreamed away their days, and were cared for exquisitely and faithfully by Robert and Carrie and Beauty and Salome and Rip. They reached fretful fingers out more and more often to Nell, bound her closer and closer with tiny, sighing, silken threads. Hebe faded into a shadow childhood; Gamma slipped into a fragile Dresden stasis; Rip endured into magnificence. Nell's vulnerable mouse-child sensuality ripened into real beauty, though so slowly that her mirror never gave it back to her; only strangers truly saw it. No one was seriously ill; no one died. The hills and valleys of the wheeling southern days absorbed them all more than the larger topography of the years.

And in the house by the river, one aching April day in 1973, Nell put away her short stories and rolled a sheet of clean bond into her typewriter, and on it she typed,

THE BLOOD REMEMBERS

A NOVEL BY
NELL GEIGER JAY

317

26

NELL WORKED on her novel for two years, writing in the mornings for an hour or so after Abby had gone to school. The hours of writing gave an authenticity, a validity to her days; she never omitted them, no matter how hectic the rest of the day became.

She told no one she was writing a book. At first this was because she dared not think of it as a book at all, lest the fragile concept flee her mind and leave her alone once again with her short stories for *McCall's* and the *Ladies' Home Journal*. She did not know how one went about writing a book, and since she knew no published authors except Phillips and a few other author-academics in the department, and their work was esoteric in the extreme, and she feared their gentle patronization or, worse, their oversolicitousness, she did not ask them. Moreover, she planned the novel . . . if it ever turned into such . . . to be a surprise for Abby and Phillips.

It was easy to conceal the fact of the book. Ruth and Hebe were accustomed to receiving no answer to their pettish phone calls during Nell's writing hours, and had long taken a special gleeful malice in saving up their implorings and grievances and spewing them over Nell at the precise end of the time; they assumed that she was working on her usual short stories, and did not ask how her work was going. They had never asked. Even Phillips, absorbed in the delicately vicious politics surrounding the imminent retirement of old Dr. Crandall, gradually stopped asking, "How's the writing going, love?" and only once remarked that it had been a long time since she'd had a new story to read to him over their predinner martini.

"I just haven't felt much like short stories lately," Nell told him. "And now that I'm driving Abby into Atlanta twice a week for her lessons with Upshaw, there's just no more time. Gamma and Mama are getting worse and worse about calling, too. Do you mind awfully if I stop for a while, Phillips?"

"No, of course not." He patted her absently, already absorbed in the stack of departmental business he had brought home with him. "Time enough to pick it back up when this thing with the department chairmanship is finally settled and Abby's lit one place or another. Relax and just be a mother and a wife for a while. Or is Gloria Steinem allowing that these days?"

"It's allowed, I think."

For a long time, Nell was content to savor these secret hours during which the satisfying small pile of white pages grew taller and taller. Then, after almost a year, she sat back one day and read the pages through in one sitting, and realized that what she had done had turned from a pile of typed pages into what would unquestionably be a novel one day, and a good one. She could not turn back now, or pretend that she was simply experimenting with forms and styles. *The Blood Remembers* had, sometime in the quiet year past, transmogrified itself into a living, breathing, shouting, demanding book, and she was going to have to be accountable for it. A great wind of terror and joy and wonder shook Nell, so that she could not stand up from her chair for a space of time, and when she did, her legs and arms were heavy and weak, and her breath came in shallow gasps. She went into the bedroom and lay down across the twin bed that was her own, and cried from gratitude and humility.

But she still told no one, except Rip. Somehow, that same afternoon, she found that she could not go on with the comfortingly banal ritual of everyday that had sustained her for so long until she had driven over to Fox's Earth and told Rip about her book. She pulled her car into the back drive and went up the back stairs through the porch and into the kitchen, very quietly. She knew that her mother and grandmother would be napping in their rooms at this hour; she did not want to see them now. She wanted only to tell Rip about the book and then go home and go on with her life, and that was what she did.

Rip looked up from the rocker beside the stove. It was very quiet and still in the kitchen; Carrie would not be back until five, and Robert was polishing the Chrysler out in the turnaround. Beauty and Salome had not yet come from their homes in Suches. Rip was alone. Her dark eyes took in Nell's burning cheeks and amber-lit eyes with affection and welcome, but without surprise.

"Miss Nell," she said.

"Rip," Nell said, "I just came over here to tell you that I've been writing a book for the last year . . . a novel . . . and that I just today realized that it's a very good book, and I think it will probably be published when I'm finished with it. It's a surprise for everybody, so please don't tell a soul, but I wanted you to know about it."

"Well, I'm real proud of you, Miss Nell. Wondered when you was gon' write yo' book. Wondered if you ain't be up to just that, these here las' few months."

"Oh, Rip . . . I can't ever surprise you! How did you know?"

Rip's eyes rested quietly but with intensity on Nell's face. "I don' 'spec you ever surprise me none. But that don't mean I ain't so proud of you I be about to bus'. I knowed because you be lookin' inside you'se'f at somepin' that be growin' in there, like you done when you carryin' Miss Abby, and I knows it ain't no baby, so I thinks it got to be a book."

"You old witch, Rip . . . how did you know it wasn't a baby?"

"Miss Nell, I think you done had yo' babies. I think Miss Abby all you an' Mr. Phillips gon' make between you. I ain't see no more babies for you. But I sees that you gon' make things by you'se'f, an' I says to myse'f, she gon' make books, an' that as good as babies fo' some fo'kses. It be better for you, I 'spec."

"Yes. Well, I needed to tell you, Rip. I felt real happy about it, all of a sudden, and I knew you would be, too."

"Course I is. And so proud, Miss Nell. Proud fit to die. But now listen, Miss Nell . . . everybody ain't gon' be proud. You know yo' Gamma gon' git riled up. You remember that, an' you be ready for it."

"Oh . . . Gamma. Of course she'll turn white and noble about the whole thing, and carry on about how I'm wasting my time and neglecting my family and my art. But, Rip, it's such an *innocent*, silly little book. There's nothing in it that anybody could really get upset about. Don't you worry about Gamma."

"It ain't just yo' Gamma I's worried about," said Rip.

"Well, good grief . . . who else *cares?* It's not like I was writing an exposé or something. It won't even affect any-body much except me and Phillips and Abby."

"Yes'm. I knows that."

"You don't mean Abby and Phillips? Lord, Rip, Abby's so absorbed in herself and her music that she doesn't even know I'm in the world, except as a chauffeur to drive her to her music lessons, and Phillips has *always* encouraged me to write."

"I 'spec you right, Miss Nell. I jus' wants you to be on yo' guard a little bit. That way, don't nothin' nobody say or does hurt you none. You never did have much extra skin when it come to what fo'kses was gon' do or say. Always did expect they was gon' treat you as nice as you treated them, an' always gittin' hurt."

"Well, I'm not a six-year-old anymore. I'll be careful; I'll buckle on my armor the very day the book comes out, and not a single arrow will touch me. Thanks for worry-ing about me. I've got to go now. Abby will be home any minute, and I haven't even started supper. 'Bye, Rip."

" 'Bye, Miss Nell."

She thought back over the conversation driving back to the house by the river.

"I'm awfully sure of myself all of a sudden," she thought. "Talking as though it was just a matter of time before it was published. I don't even know where to send it when it's done, if it ever is. I may have to eat those fine words."

But she knew that the book would be published.

Nell worked on it for another year, and when it was done, she went to an old family friend of the Foxes in the History Department who had published an exquisitely boring but nationally respected trilogy on the Civil War in Georgia with a mainstream publisher and obtained from him the name of his editor at the big New York publish-ing house. The elderly professor sent the manuscript off for her, with a note to his editor, and a letter came back al-most immediately saying that the editor did not work with fiction but was turning the manuscript over to the house's executive editor, who did. Nell, the editor said, would hear; please give them a few weeks to get the book through channels.

Nell sat back to wait.

Three weeks later a telegram came from the publishing house saying they wished to publish *The Blood Remem-*

bers and would be in touch with her shortly to discuss terms. When Phillips came home that evening, Nell and the telegram and a chilled bottle of Taittinger were waiting for him on the patio, and for fully five minutes after Nell silently handed him the telegram, hugging herself and pacing to and fro, he stared at it, saying nothing. Then he laid it on the white wrought-iron table beside him, and looked at her. She had taken a long time bathing and dressing, and had dabbed on her Christmas Calèche and an unaccustomed touch of bronze eye shadow, and a new coppery Halston caftan she had bought in Atlanta, and looked, she knew, with the fever of excitement in her eyes and cheeks, as well as she would ever look. She stared back at him, her soft child's mouth trembling with a little smile of joy that would not stay tucked inside. She felt the ridiculous, happy tears start in her eyes, and blinked them back impatiently. She waited. Somehow, all her life seemed caught and focused and prismed on this moment, like a rainbowed universe shimmering in a raindrop.

"Well, aren't you the little sneak," he said.

After that, everything changed.

During the next seven months, before *The Blood Remembers* was published, Phillips would not read the manuscript of her book.

"You obviously meant it to be a surprise," he said, "and I'd rather it be a total one. I'll read the first copy off the press, and then we'll celebrate."

So she put the manuscript away in her desk drawer.

They did not speak of the book for weeks on end, and sometimes even Nell, burrowing determinedly back into the soporific routine of her ordered, mindless days of errands and meetings and duties, forgot that she was to have a first novel published in the spring. Her mother and grandmother did not remember it either, or seemed not to, though she had told them briefly the day after the telegram had come, for neither one alluded to it. Even Abby did not know, and the rest of Sparta had no idea, and, in truth, would not have cared if they had known.

For most of those weeks, Nell was content to let the matter lie, but sometimes, at odd moments, a wave of bleakness, of deadness would wash over her, and in those moments she would think, "Is this all there is, then? All those hours and all those words . . . for this?"

Phillips became chairman of the English Department in January, and for two or three months they rode high on the glow of his well-being, and she was able to bury the deadness under real joy at his pleasure. He was expansive once again at dinner, almost vivacious, and full of talk and the academic gossip that was permitted him now the department was, in effect, his. He took fewer classes, and then almost none, keeping only the contemporary-fiction class that he had wrested from the desiccated hands of old Dr. Oakes those many years ago and incorporated into his own legend. Nell was sometimes aware that Phillips talked in quotations, as if he was consciously weaving a mythic cloak with which to wrap himself. Once she would have found this amusing, even endearing. Now, she admitted to herself, reluctantly, it made her weary.

Gradually that winter Nell slid into a sort of dreaming suspension; she closed in upon herself, her world pared itself down to such minimal engagement with outside stimuli that she went virtually nowhere socially beyond the obligatory departmental functions with Phillips. She ran her errands, drove Abby to and from Atlanta, and listened to her daughter's escalating pleas to go and live with Yancey in New York with detachment; she cooked their meals, smiled and nodded at Phillips over dinner, retreated into a detective novel as soon as she could afterward . . . was often in her bed reading by eight in the evenings . . . and slept. Incredibly, if anyone had asked her, Nell would have said that, yes, she was quite happy. Quite content.

In April, *The Blood Remembers* was published, and the content shattered.

It was a small novel, swift and spare, sharply limning the world of a small southern town in the thirties and forties. It was gentle in tone, but stingingly perceived, and its characters leapt and flamed with Nell's characteristically odd and inventive insights. It did not sell well, and it might have dropped without a ripple into the bottomless pond that swallowed so many first novels but for two facts: it received, quixotically, a spate of splendid reviews in the literary and academic press and, to some small extent, the popular press, and it had for its central figures a family of poor, uneducated blacks living in a niggertown much like Suches, who managed to emerge as intelligent, sympathetic, vital, and, most of all, quirkily individual people.

The first fact was enough to seal Nell's doom with

Phillips. The second cooked her goose very effectively at Fox's Earth and in most of the other great white houses in Sparta.

Nell did not clip her reviews. She refused all invitations to speak at book clubs and libraries around Georgia, would not agree to the small author tour of three southern states that her publishers urged upon her, and refused to drive into Atlanta and appear on the three housewife-oriented talk shows offered by the local television stations. She did not sign her books in department stores, and she temporarily stopped going to campus and departmental functions where people she and Phillips knew came up and took her by her arm, looked at her as if she had surprised them by taking to roping Brahma bulls in rodeos, and congratulated her on her book. But she could not stem the tide of letters that poured in by way of her publishers, nor the phone calls that came at all hours from well-wishers and the occasional hate-whisperer who threatened to burn a cross on their lawn, and she watched as Phillips grew redder and redder of face and whiter and whiter of lip, until finally he stormed downtown one Saturday morning and engaged a post-office box for her, and had their telephone unlisted.

"It's going to cripple my effectiveness in the department severely, having an unlisted number," he snapped at her on his return. "You might have thought of that when you first put pen to paper, my dear."

He stopped calling her "love," but he frequently called her "my dear." Their friends thought it had a quaint, courtly ring to it, and invariably smiled when he addressed her thus. Nell flinched. She knew that she would not soon be forgiven for the good reviews. The teacher would punish the pupil who had had the effrontery to outstrip him in front of his entire world.

He stopped work on his own book. He said nothing about it, but the stilled typewriter and the unchanging pile of pages in their neat typewriter-bond box sat so accusingly on the desk in his study that they might as well have been painted red and shouted aloud, "Nell did it. Nell murdered me," whenever she walked into the room. When she asked, as she did once . . . but only once . . . how the book was going, he said, "It isn't going at all, Nell, as you can plainly see. One author in this family is more than enough, don't you think?" and he gave her a smile of such exquisitely twisted pain that she did not ask again.

She stopped work on her own sporadic writing and did not resume it. She could not seem to make her fingers work at the simplest tasks, and her thoughts were scattered and thick, as though they struck against damp, spongy clay. Much of the time she felt stupid and fragmented and stunned with lethargy.

Inside Fox's Earth, the book seemed to accomplish what all the doctors and nostrums and anxious, meticulous ministrations by Nell and Rip could not: Ruth Yancey Fox flamed into roaring, voracious life once more. She was furious; her anger and energy seemed to know no bounds. Where for so long she had lain abed propped on her pillows, tinkling her peevish little bell and fussing weakly and fretfully for Nell to come and set this petty wrong or that aright, dozing away her afternoons and spending entire days in her trailing Pucci house robes, now she rose and scourged through the kitchen and pantry . . . indeed, the entire downstairs . . . like a small, fierce wind, setting the servants to grumbling and rolling their eyes and the benign dust of careless years to boiling. She turned her long-neglected household inside out and on its ear; she inspected and railed and chastised so terribly and constantly that Beauty and Salome, who bore the brunt of her anger, quit in a huff on the same day and went to work in the black beauty parlor in Suches, and shortly after that Carrie gave her notice, too. She was, she said, too old to be talked to like po' white trash, and she intended to go and live with her daughter in Macon and be cooked for, for a change.

Robert lasted three weeks after that, and then simply vanished one day, leaving the keys to the current Chrysler lying ostentatiously in the middle of the silver card tray that he had long kept gleaming on the gate-legged table in the great marble-floored foyer. They heard later that Robert was driving for a limousine service in Atlanta, and was considered very elegant.

Then Rip was alone with all of Fox's Earth and two old women to care for, and Nell's guilt soared to a new intensity, for there was no doubt at all that it was her book that had relighted the terrible fire in the heart of Ruth Yancey Fox. Old Ruth had spoken to her of it only once, but it had been a truly dreadful session, with her grandmother so blue and white and burning that Nell was sure she was going to die of her anger, and with Nell stilled and shrunken into one of the wing chairs in the little parlor, a head taller and fifty-two years younger than her grandmother, but as diminished by her molten presence as she had been when she was a small, desolate child alone in the vast battleground that was Fox's Earth.

Gamma's words had been very quiet, but they had burnt and frozen and bloodied Nell; she would never forget them. Nell had used them all; Nell had exploited them, her own family, all she ever had or ever would have of kin, of blood; Nell had mocked and betrayed and abandoned them; Nell had brought shame on the Fox name. Nell was not fit to call herself a Fox anymore. Nell had heaped offal on the heads of all her dead, and Nell had probably killed her mother . . . all with the treacherous, trashy writing that she, Ruth, had always known in her heart would bring ruin upon them. *"The Blood Remembers,* my foot," Gamma had hissed. " 'The Blood Betrays' is more like it."

After that they did not speak of the book again, though Hebe was silent and bewildered and even more vague than usual in Nell's presence, and Gamma's controlled fury simmered on unabated. Nell could see it through the windows of her eyes whenever she went to Fox's Earth, and she went often, for without Robert and Beauty and Salome and Carrie, there were far more household mishaps and incidents to be seen to, and many more errands to be run in the car. Nell burned with anger at the new impositions, for she knew, rationally, that it was not her fault that her grandmother had driven her servants away in her rage, like a blindly snapping dog. But the new freshet of guilt that followed predictably in the wake of that anger . . . for this trouble had, after all, been engendered by her book, hadn't it? . . . overpowered the rationality, and she assumed the heavier burdens of the two old women without complaining.

She broached the subject of old Ruth to Rip one day.

"I'm sorry about all this," she said by way of preamble, indicating the pile of ironing that was stacked up beside Rip's ironing board in the white kitchen of Fox's Earth. It was only late May, but already the heat was piling palpably into the corners of the room. Nell's face was pearled and pale with it, and perspiration ran down inside her open shirt collar to her waist, but Rip's straight back and slender waist were unsplotched by dampness, and her fine, high-planed face was untracked with moisture. She hummed as she ironed, slowly, methodically, atonally.

"Sorry 'bout what?" Rip said, looking up at her to smile. The gold tooth flashed.

"Sorry you've got all this extra work to do. All the ironing, and the cooking, and God knows how much cleaning . . . Gamma's going to have to get you some more help. If only I hadn't made her so mad . . ."

"I ain't got more'n I can do, Miss Nell. We shuts off lots of this big ol' house, an' I sends out the hand wash, an' they don't eat 'nuff between 'em to feed a bird. We ain't need nobody else, an' to tell you the truth, I ain't lookin' to train nobody new. This house knows my ways; we has all we needs here. It ain't yo' fault; don't you go thinkin' that. I don't care what yo' Gamma tell you. It don't be yo' fault do she have one hissy after another'n. You ain't come over here an' make her swell up like a turkey gobbler . . ."

"Well, but it was my book; you know it was."

"I know that jus' what she wants you to think it was. An' I know that what you do think. But that ain't the way of it, Miss Nell. She usin' you lak she always done; she usin' that book of yourn to git holt of you better. An' she got you right roun' the neck, too, ain't she? Ain't you come over here five times a day to pet and fuss and drive her somewhere, or go fetch somethin' for her or Miss Hebe? What she need with a chauffeur or maid when she got you?"

"Well, you may be right, but I can't help that, Rip. I can't just not come, and that's that. She sure can't drive herself."

"Yessum, she can," Rip said, looking at her again. The smile was gone. "She can drive an' she *do* drive. She take that car out twice last week when you was in Atlanta with Miss Abby, an' off she go like she twenty-five again. She think I ain't see her, but I do. But I 'spec you right about one thing. You cain't not come when they calls you. It jus' ain't yo' nature, Miss Nell, an' I ain't go' try to change you none. You come on and do what you got to. But don't you go thinkin' you done harmed her none with yo' book, because you ain't. She gittin' round better now than she have in ten years, and I hears Dr. Hopkins tellin' her that whatever it is lit a fire under her, he's grateful for it. He say she ain't look so good since she a young married lady. And she do, too; jus' look at her."

And it was true. Ruth Yancey Fox was as beautiful

again as she had been in the middle years of her life: erect, vivid, seeming to snap and shimmer in the very air. It was as if some sort of protective scrim had been peeled away from her, and she could be seen again in the old full radiance that threatened to dazzle the naked eye. Even in repose she seemed to smolder and thrill; Nell often had the fancy that if she put her hand to Gamma's flesh, she would feel something like the deep, powerful purring of a big cat.

To Rip she said, "Well, I won't worry so much about her, then. But I'll come every day to see what I can do to help you, anyway. If she won't hire anybody else, at least you and I can keep things straight. But, Rip . . . please watch them for me. Watch her, especially. She *is* in her eighties, after all."

"Oh, I watches her, Miss Nell. I watches her real good. I be moved back in my old room upstairs, did you know that? I stays close to her all the time. Don't you worry none about that. I growed up watchin' yo' Gamma, that what I was meant for. To watch after you Fox chirrun and yo' Gamma. An' I 'spec I does it right well."

"You do it better than anybody in the world, and we don't deserve you," Nell said, kissing her on the cheek. "I wish there was some way we could ever really repay you, but that's not possible."

"Well . . ." Rip hesitated.

"Name it, Rip. Anything in the world."

"Well, Miss Nell, I sho' would like to have one of yo' books with somethin' you wrote to me inside it. You know, like you wrote with a ink pen, for yo' mama."

"Oh, Rip . . ." Tears started in Nell's eyes. She had not thought of it, for she knew Rip could not read, and now her insensitivity choked in her throat. "Of course. I'll bring it tomorrow when I come. I'll write the best and prettiest thing I know on the flyleaf, just for you. What would you most like me to say?"

"Well . . . I recollect that Mr. Claudius give Henry . . . Henry what drove the car before Robert came . . . a Bible once, and he wrote in it, 'Well done, good and faithful servant.' That do me just fine, Miss Nell."

"Oh, Rip," Nell whispered, and the tears did spill over her lower lashes, and onto her cheeks. She went to Rip and buried her face in the corded hollow of the long neck, as she had done so often when she was a child. "Oh, Rip. I think I can do better than that."

Often in that long, anxious spring, Phillips was too tired for lovemaking, and when he did come into her bed, it was in silence and with a perfunctory haste that bordered on indifference. Straining and laboring up to meet his driving thrusts, their limbs slick with sweat, Nell would feel, over and over again, the climax that had begun to build in her loins drain out of her and escape, and a violent impatience would shake her, almost a fury at his hard, intrusive, silent thrusting. She would grit her teeth and pump with renewed effort, to hasten him to his climax and end the hot charade that forced the breath from her lungs and pinned her to the sticky sheets. Once, when he seemed to be taking an eternity to come, she had thrashed her head aside from his wet, searching mouth and hissed, totally involuntarily, "Oh, for God's sake, Phillips, get *on* with it!" And had felt him stiffen, and still, and then go limp. Silently he got up off her and back into his own twin bed, and turned over so that his back was to her, and he did not move for the remainder of the night. Nell was appalled and remorseful, but somehow she could not bring herself to speak, or go to him. She, too, lay in silence until, finally, she slept. In the morning when she awoke, he was gone, and there was a note under the coffeepot in the kitchen that said he had an early meeting and would get some breakfast on campus. They did not speak of it when he returned that evening, and he did not come into her bed again.

The glass bell that had sheltered and sustained her after Paul's death descended around Nell once more, so that instead of feeling anguish or grief, she could only watch with astonishment as the decay of her marriage touched and seared Phillips and Abby and turned them into people she no longer knew, caustic, unloving people who would have had immense power to hurt her had it not been for the impenetrable shell. She and Phillips continued their daily routines, continued to see their friends, but the occasions were strained. He would aim small snipes at her: "I don't know; that's strictly the department of our minor regional novelist here," and "Don't ask me, ask the author." The end of their public life together came when, at the last faculty cocktail party of the spring, a new associate professor who was in charge of the program for the MLA meeting in Atlanta the following autumn blundered enthusiastically up to them as they stood in a group and asked her to read from her work at the keynote meeting; Nell muttered a hasty refusal, but the damage was done. Phillips accepted no more invitations for them as a couple, though he often attended official department functions alone. She did not mind; in any case, the invitations soon slowed to a trickle, and the coming of the summer hiatus was a reprieve to them both.

Conversation at home diminished to the point of occasional tepid carping: "Have you really looked at this house lately? You could carve a frieze in the dust." "Good God, Nell, is this the third day with this stew, or the fourth?" "I don't know if you've noticed it, but I'm sure everybody at her school has . . . Abby looks like a rag-picker's child."

And Abby, feeding like a wounded, feral young thing on the discord in the house and her mother's vulnerability, changed from the self-involved but essentially ardent and guileless child she had always been into an open foe, a terrifying changeling, the enemy. She who had said little about her mother's book, except to note matter-of-factly that all the kids in school were talking about her, now came home each day with a new and more fantastically wrought tale of the lurid mistreatment she received at the hands of her classmates because of her mother's writing. She became flagrantly rebellious and disagreeable to Nell, ridiculing her openly and often and flying into towering rages at Nell's continuing refusal to let her go to New York and live with Yancey. Sometimes, in the hot nights of that summer, when she could not sleep, Nell would hear Abby sobbing in her room, sobbing the lost and out-of-control sobs of a terrified and utterly helpless child. Remembering her own tears in the night, when she was a child at Fox's Earth, Nell would think, "I *must* get up from here and go to her. She must not cry alone in the night like that. It's inhuman that I would let her."

But the glass dome would not let her rise, and the endless languor swept her, and she would slump heavily into sleep before she could rise.

And the next day she would wake numbed and fragmented once more. The pain of the self-estrangement hovered off beyond the dome of the bell jar with the host of other pains that waited to be dealt with, but somehow they did not get in.

She spoke of her feelings once late that summer to

330

Phillips, as they lay on chaises beside the pool at the country club. Later she remembered that it was the last time they attempted to talk about anything important. She would not have spoken then, she knew, but she was tired and hungry and half drunk, and her tongue had seemed infused with a strange, roistering life of its own. It was a cool night, foreshadowing autumn; the brilliant green water was warmer than the air, and they wore sweaters. They watched as Abby and a group of silverfish teenagers dived and preened and jeered. It was their turn to chaperon the bimonthly club Teen Swim, otherwise, Nell knew, they would not be lying there side by side on chaises, drinking daiquiris. Already Phillips was fidgeting irritably on the plastic webbing of his chaise.

He listened to her without comment, for so long that she thought that he simply was not going to speak, but presently he said, without looking at her, "I find something essentially ludicrous about a middle-aged woman lying beside a country-club pool drinking rum and wailing that she's hollow and empty and doesn't know who she is and can't pull herself together. On a scale of pain priorities from one to ten, Nell, I'd give you about a point three."

Hurt and fury flickered along Nell's veins briefly, but then they died, and the summer's Demerol-like languor came flooding back.

"That's a specious thing to say," she said serenely. "Anybody who hurts for any reason has to be taken seriously. Do you think that pain has to be somehow worthy and noble before it's valid? Is there trivial pain and important pain? Remember in the end of *Death of a Salesman*, when what's-her-name . . . the wife . . . looks out at the audience and cries, 'Attention must be paid'? I've always loved that line. I believe that."

"Oh, Christ," he said wearily. "You're not equating yourself with Willy Loman, surely. One of the great tragic figures in literature. A fossil, a dinosaur, doomed by his very nature."

Nell was silent. He rose on one elbow and looked at her. His eyes were very bright, his pointed nose almost quivered with interest and malice.

"Maybe you're right, at that," he said. "I thought at first, a thousand years ago when I married you, that you could still climb out of that tar pit on Church Street; I really thought you had it in you to pull yourself up out of

331

the primordial ooze, as it were. But to tell you God's truth, Nell, I don't think you ever will now. A million years from now they'll dig and find your mummy perfectly preserved amid the broken columns of dear old Fox's Earth, and they'll ship you off to a museum, the most perfect specimen of your kind in existence. *Vulpes fulva,* vixen, circa 19-whatever, in her native habitat. Thought to have become extinct through inability to abandon a hostile environment."

Nell rose silently and went into the dressing room and dressed and drove home. She thought of the day of their wedding; that bright, lost, sun-jeweled Christmas Day. It lay far away in another country. Had it been cold? She could not remember. Perhaps it had not been bright, after all, for sometimes southern Christmases were not, but were soft and gray and opalescent with rain.

"What a long way we've come," she thought. "What a very long way."

27

TOWARD THE END of that September, classes began again, and the annual reception to welcome new faculty members was held at the president's home. Of all the rituals that attended the slow turning of the academic year, Nell loathed this one the most. The overdressed young newcomers and the ostentatiously casual . . . some would have said fusty . . . tenured veterans circled each other like stiff-legged dogs ("it would liven things up considerably if they'd go ahead and sniff asses," Phillips had said in better days); the heat in the old house atop its bare hill was invariably stifling; and the president and his marginally senile, blue-blooded old wife served nothing but Coca-Colas, persimmon-sweet iced tea, and a cloying punch with a base of blond Dubonnet. But the reception was absolutely *de rigueur* and so they went every year.

This year would be the first that Phillips could be introduced as chairman of the English Department, and though he grumbled as peevishly as ever at the president and the heat and the punch, he dressed with elaborate care in summer-weight gray trousers and his blue summer blazer, and brought out his club tie and white bucks. His fair hair shone with cleanliness and the tracks of the summer's sun; his sharp face was tanned gold and his eyes against the tan were an arresting deep-water blue; his body was still erect, though with the soft beginnings of a paunch. Watching him dress, Nell thought how much more elegant and compelling Phillips would look than the hot, wilting throng he would move in, how eastern. He still wore the faintly exotic air of ivied quadrangles and white sloops on northern summer seas that he had had about him when she first saw him, nearly twenty years ago, and it still kept him the center of a chirruping flock of undergraduate women. He enjoyed this, Nell knew, but Phillips had always avoided the casual intimacies with individual female graduate students that his position might legitimately have involved him in. She did not know if this had been by choice, out of affection for her, or out of his fastidious need for emotional space around him. She assumed the latter.

"You look nice," she said. Her own words surprised her. They had spoken very little since the night of the swimming party at the country club. Nell, bumping dreamily at the glass of her bell jar like a swimmer in a tank, did not feel particularly unhappy about this, or anything else. She thought she could live a long time as a swimmer in a tank.

"Well, thank you very much, my dear," he said, raising a sardonic blond eyebrow at her. "I shall bask in the glow of your approval this evening and not mind the punch at all."

She met Lewis Wolfe in the library of the president's home, a high-ceilinged, dust-smelling room that always reminded her of the library at Fox's Earth. Nell had fled from the crowd around the punch bowl in the dining room, where the conversation was edging dangerously toward contemporary southern fiction and one of the new assistant professors was looking at her with a dawning now-I-know-who-you-are expression on his pale sheep's face. She banged her rented punch cup down on a leather drum table beside the deep wing chair into which she had sunk so hard that the pale, viscous fluid slopped out and onto the tabletop.

"Oh, shit," Nell said crossly to no one at all, for the room appeared to be empty, and rummaged in her purse for a tissue to mop up the spill.

"Indeed, it would probably be better for the table if it were," said a soft, deep, disembodied voice, and a man came around the wing of her chair holding out a handkerchief. "That stuff will probably eat clear through to the carpet."

Nell stared at him, speechless with embarrassment and surprise. She did not know who he was; she had never seen him before. He was rather short, no taller than Phillips, but heavier by twenty pounds, and stocky; he had dark hair and a pale face and very bright brown eyes behind round aviator's glasses, and he wore huge, clumping running shoes with no socks and a pale-blue sweatshirt that said "Agnes Scott College" on it. He smiled, an ingenuous smile of mingled sweetness and unrepentant mischief. The effect was totally charming. The word "puckish" leapt into Nell's mind, but it was too contrived and precious a word, and she discarded it. She smiled back.

He bent over her and mopped up the spill with his handkerchief, sniffed it, and shuddered.

"Swine before pearls," he said. Nell laughed aloud.

"I'm sorry you blundered into my temper tantrum," she said. "But I didn't know you were here. It's what you get for lurking in dark libraries. I'm Nell Jay. My husband is the chairman of the English Department."

"I know who you are," he said. "I recognized you from the picture on your book jacket. I've been following you all evening waiting for a chance to get you alone. And I think I would have said that Mr. Jay is the husband of Nell Geiger Jay, the novelist. Your book was one of the happiest experiences of this year for me, and it's more than a little responsible for my being here at all. I wanted to meet you the minute I opened it, and I was determined to do so when I saw your picture on the jacket. I came here with the clear intention of acquiring you for myself, and the fact that you have an impeccable husband who is the chairman of the English Department and undoubtedly have one or more exemplary children to round out the set means not a holy hoot in hell to me. Be warned."

He beamed agreeably at her.

Nell laughed again and tossed the heat-damp mop of her curls off her forehead with a quick, pretty, and entirely spontaneous gesture. She heard her own laughter in her ears; it might have been that of a young girl at a dance, a girl who knows she is invincible in her youth and prettiness and uniqueness. "I'm actually *flirting* with this ridiculous man in this ridiculous sweatshirt," she thought in pleasurable astonishment, and looked up at him through her lashes.

"Who on earth are you?" Nell said. "Do you have a name?"

"I'm Lewis Wolfe," he said. "And you should be feeling a definite *frisson* right now, as the French say. The name should be ringing in your head like a bell."

"No *frisson*," Nell said. "But great admiration for your sweat shirt. It's very becoming. My daughter would love it. She collects sweat shirts . . . though I don't think she'd be caught dead at Agnes Scott."

"My daughter gave it to me," he said. "And she wouldn't either. It's her idea of a joke. She gave it to me when she heard I was coming to Georgia . . . she knows some girls at home who go to Scott, and she thinks it stands for everything quaint and cornpone and anachronistic that she hates about the South. At sixteen Leah is an accomplished hater."

"I know the syndrome," Nell said wryly. She felt obscurely deflated at the mention of a daughter. "But Agnes Scott is a very good school. A lot of people think it's just as good as any of your Seven Sisters. Has your daughter ever been south?"

"No," he said. "Leah gets all her ideas about the South from *Gone With the Wind*. The movie, not the book. I don't think she can read. I'm not an easterner, by the way."

"What are you, then? An alien? Come to think of it, I didn't see you come into this room. You just . . . materialized."

"I'm an Illinoisan by birth and an Iowan in my last incarnation. I teach English literature at the university. I'm the Byrd Satterthwaite visiting professor this year. The Victorians. I'm surprised your husband the chairman hasn't told you about me. I made quite an impression on him at MLA last year. I'm also a Jew, and I don't think there are any more of us in the department."

"He didn't mention you, but I don't think it was because you're Jewish. We aren't talking a lot right now," Nell said, and then stopped. What was there about this elfin, clever-faced man that made her babble like a teenager? She smiled again, ruefully.

"So much the better for my seduction, then," he said, and his V-shaped smile deepened, showing incongruous dimples. But his eyes were warm and interested.

"You said your daughter," Nell said quickly. "Has your family joined you yet? My daughter Abby is fifteen; maybe she could show your . . . Leah, did you say? . . . around some; get her situated. And if I could help with any house hunting or anything . . ."

"I'm alone," he said neutrally, pleasantly. "I'm divorced. My family is in Iowa. I've rented a farmhouse out from town, near the river. But thanks anyway."

"I'm . . . sorry."

"Yes. So am I. Now, tell me about your new book. Because there must be one."

"No. I'm not working on anything now."

"God, why ever not?" he said in real concern. "It would be an act of criminal negligence if you didn't do another one as soon as you can."

Nell looked with great interest at the whitening ring on the table where her punch cup had stood. She felt a long-dead prickle of tears in her nose; her throat ached with them. Oh, God, *surely* she wasn't going to cry, not now, not in this horrible house at this horrible party, in front of this nonplusing chipmunk of a stranger.

"I wonder what he'd say if I told him I couldn't write because I didn't know who I was and my head is in a thousand pieces and terrible things happen when I do write and my marriage is coming apart in my hands and my husband can't even stand to talk to me?" she thought.

"Your husband is a goddamned fool," Lewis Wolfe said suddenly, catching her thought.

Nell put her face into her hands and began to cry. "You were right, Rip," she thought. "I did find him. It took a long time, but here he is, in this stupid library at this stupid faculty reception, of all places in the world . . . he's short, and Jewish, and he's going bald, I think,

336

and he's from *Illinois,* of all silly places in the whole world to be from . . . and he's the other end of me."

"Come on," said Lewis Wolfe. "Let's get out of here."

He steered her out the open French doors and onto the terrace, where the red dots of cigarettes in the fast-gathering hot September dusk were farther apart, and the soft babble of voices was not so pronounced. He paused, scanning the terrace and drought-browned formal rose garden, said "Ah," softly, under his breath, and drew Nell across the terrace and down the shallow fan of brick steps and along a flagstone path to a small gazebo veiled with willows at the far edge of the garden. Blinded with tears and refusing to look to her left or right, lest she see someone at whom it would be mandatory to nod and speak, Nell followed stiffly after him. Twice she stumbled on her unaccustomed high heels; his hand was under her elbow instantly. He dusted off a portion of the gazebo's circular bench seat with the punch-dampened handkerchief and sat her down, and sat down beside her, but he did not touch her.

"You'd better let it out," he said, "or you'll get lockjaw from carrying it around."

And then it came; it all came out, on a breathless, hiccuping flood of tears and words. It came flowing up from the deepest wells of Nell's hurt and anger and hopelessness, pumping out through her lips and over them, as though something terrible and malignant and core-deep inside her had been lanced and must seek to spew free even if it burst her apart in the escaping. It was out of context and out of sequence and made no real sense for long minutes at a time. She did not know, and would never remember, how far back she started, but she did remember struggling through choking gasps to tell him about the cage under the back steps, and about the terror and outrage of the banishment of Paul and Yancey, the anguish of Paul's death, of Yancey's breakdown. All of it . . . the anger and bewilderment and guilt, always the guilt; the erosions of trust and closeness in her marriage, the small stabs and sabotages; the pain and disappointment surrounding her book; the baffling and bone-deep hurt of her estrangement from her child . . . and Gamma. Always, eternally, under and above and through and beyond everything, the beautiful, smiling, incomprehensible menace of Gamma. Through it all, as she cried, as she talked, Nell was thinking quite clearly and coolly, "I am, of course, totally insane. It is absolutely unthinkable that I am behaving like this in front of a total stranger. I have never done anything even remotely like this in my entire life. In a few minutes he is going to go and get Phillips, and he will take me someplace for insane people. He will put me in a home. It will be terrible for his career."

The stream of wild words slowed finally, and died, but she could not stop crying.

He let her cry in silence. He still did not touch her, and he did not cluck or murmur or fidget uncomfortably, or make as to go and fetch Phillips or a woman friend. He simply sat beside her in the now-darkened gazebo and waited. Finally the crying began to spend itself, and bumped and shuddered to a stop, and Nell sat in silence inside the greater silence of the night, with only the last of the summer's cicadas whispering brassily off in the dark, her hands dangling helplessly in her lap, as emptied out and hollow-light as a maypop or a martin gourd. He fished in his pocket and pulled out the crumpled handkerchief and handed it to her, and she mopped at her ravaged face with it, feeling the stickiness of the drying punch on her puffed eyelids and lips. It was not an unpleasant feeling.

In fact, Nell realized, she did not feel bad at all. She did not feel like a woman whose life was like a ball of snakes cupped in her hands; whose husband scorned and baited her and whose daughter ridiculed and defied her. She did not feel like a writer whose wavering fountain had dried to mocking dust. Above all, she did not feel like a hysterical middle-aged woman who had just come unraveled in the most unattractive manner possible in front of a kind stranger whom she had met barely thirty minutes before. She felt, all in all, rather pleasantly washed and scooped out and . . . the words flickered through her mind . . . readied for something that might possibly be very agreeable. She raised her head and waited for sensation to flood in; she examined the void where it would pour, tentatively and shyly. Was it possible that in a moment, or a day, or a week . . . that in a short time she might feel centered and whole again? Even happy?

"If you say you're sorry and you don't know what on earth came over you," Lewis Wolfe said in his warm, low voice, "I am going out there and tell the assembled academicians that the Big Enchilada's wife just flipped out all over the new hired help. They'll still be whispering about it seventeen years from now."

"I wasn't going to say that," Nell said. Her voice worked fine, and the cooling air felt wonderful on her tear-dampened face and neck. There was a new smell in the air, of rain and freshness and October to come. "I'm not sorry at all. But I really don't know what came over me. This isn't a thing I do very much of."

"I gathered that," he said.

They sat in silence for a small space of time, and then she said, "Why are you here?"

"It seemed the gallant thing to do."

"No, I mean in Sparta. How did you come to be here?"

"To carry you off. Like I said."

"Please don't tease me," Nell said. "I really want to know."

He paused, his face still in the willow shadows. Then he said, "Well, I heard about the chair here a couple of years ago, at the MLA meeting in St. Louis. That it wasn't filled for this year. And I thought I'd like to see what the South was all about. It's one of the few places in the world I haven't been. The Deep South mystique has always intrigued me. But in the main I think regretfully that, for me, it's going to prove to be a bunch of bullshit. So far, nothing here seems quite real. I am very fond of real things. Your book was real. To wring reality out of unreality must be a great satisfaction to a writer."

Nell said nothing. She had not considered this; it was one more satisfaction she might have derived from the book but had not. She thought, too, looking at his face in the whitening light of the great, bleached moon that was rising through the willow branches, that he would know about real things. She thought that he was the realest thing she had ever seen.

"Where else have you been?" she said. "Where did you start out from? Tell all."

"I was born in Apple River, Illinois. Really. It's in Jo Daviess County, up in the northwest corner, just across the Mississippi from Dubuque and just across the state line from Wisconsin. Within spitting distance of Charles Mound, our highest mountain. Soars a dizzying thousand feet or so above Apple River. I was the only kid in town who never climbed it and stuck up a flag. I think it must have been because I was a Jew. Everybody in Apple River knows that Jews don't climb mountains."

"Were you sensitive about that? Being Jewish?" Nell said.

"God, no." He chuckled and the dimples flared. "I was in college, practically, before I knew we were. We didn't practice it. I didn't play the violin or want to be a plastic surgeon, and my mother couldn't make chicken soup to save her life. Dad didn't keep a store or a tailor shop; he was the county agricultural extension agent, and as blond and hawk-eyed as a Viking. Mother was tall and skinny and redheaded and freckled. I must take after some Uncle Moishe or somebody, back in Russia. I think that's where we come from, but nobody in the family really knows. No, the reason I never climbed Charles Mound was that I was a fat little only kid with my nose in a book all the time, and I didn't care about anything else besides books but animals. I loved animals. Still do. There are raccoons and possums out on my rented doorstep every night, and I brought my two cats with me. Hilton and Sheraton. You must meet them. And there are horses in the pasture just across the river."

"We have something else in common beside teenage daughters, then," Nell said. "I was alone most of my childhood, too, with my nose in a book. I was the despair of my grandmother. She thought I would grow up to be the spinster town librarian."

"For once, I think I agree with your famous Gamma . . . who sounds like Grendel's Mother, by the way. Much easier for me to carry you off across my saddle if you were the spinster town librarian."

Nell was suddenly uncomfortable with this line. "Where else have you been?" she said.

He chuckled gently in the dark. "Well, I've been to the University of Iowa in Iowa City. That's near Cedar Rapids, in case you're interested. And then to graduate school . . . Oh, hell, who am I to be modest? I'll never win your favors by hiding my light under a bushel. I was a Rhodes Scholar, and from there I bummed around Europe, saw most of the cities I wanted to see there. And finished graduate school at New Haven. And took off again for Greece and the Near East and then the Far East . . . broke all the time, of course, but those were good days to be broke in. It was considered romantic.

340

And if you hung around any American Express office, a little Bennington or Sweet Briar tootsie who was picking up her stash from Daddy back home would take pity on you and feed you. I stretched it out for an indecent length of time, until I finally came back to Iowa City and started teaching English. Full circle. And that's where I've been ever since."

"I really am impressed," Nell said. She was. "Oxford, and Yale, and all that traveling . . . have you published? Forget I said that, it was the goddamn academic in me. It doesn't deserve an answer. I *hate* people who ask that before they've even shaken your hand."

He laughed again. "Well, considering the fact that you've done considerably more than shake my hand, I'll answer it. Yes, I have published. Several very scholarly and esoteric slim volumes on the Victorians, none of which you will ever be required to read, but all of which have earned me indecent renown in very small circles. Any more questions, madam?"

"I really don't understand why you came here," Nell said seriously. "I mean, it's a good university, and all, and the English Department is well thought of . . . I'd have to say that, wouldn't I . . . but, my God, with your credentials you could have gone anywhere in the country. Maybe what I don't understand is why you wanted to leave Iowa City."

"I told you. I came here to seduce you."

"Lewis . . ."

"I needed to leave there, Nell. I couldn't stay any longer. This chair came up, and I grabbed it."

His voice was remote and devoid of expression, but Nell's face flamed red in the dark. Of course, the divorce. It must have been more recent than she had thought from the way he had first spoken of it, and obviously very painful.

"I'm sorry," she whispered.

"Don't be."

A small dark woman in print silk and harlequin glasses parted the curtain of willow fronds and peered into the gazebo.

"Hey, Nell, I thought I heard your voice out here," she said. "Phillips is looking for you. He wants you to meet the new guy who's taking survey of American. He's read your book and asked to meet you."

Nell jumped guiltily; she had forgotten about Phillips and everything else in this last hour. She was glad of the dark and the enshrouding willow fronds. Her eyes must be a total wreck.

"Thanks, Millicent," she said. "Dr. Wolfe and I were fleeing the long arm of that punch. If you're going back, tell Phillips I'm on my way."

They walked into the circle of light from the terrace, and Nell stopped and fished her compact out of her bag. She reapplied makeup, and scowled at her swollen eyes.

"I look like I've been on a two-day bender," she said.

"Blame the ragweed," said Lewis Wolfe. "And take a deep breath. Here comes your fan club."

Phillips and the president walked across the terrace and met them at the foot of the brick steps. Behind them loomed the archetypal figure that Nell had long come to recognize as the classic Assistant Professor: tall, thin to gangling, stooped, leaning forward in eagerness, peering myopically about him, nervously fidgeting with his bow tie, his bony elbows protruding from the short sleeves of his polyester shirt. Nell could not see his feet, but would have bet much that he had on Hush Puppies. He beamed nearsightedly at her as she and Lewis Wolfe stopped before the small party.

"Ah, so you've met Wolfe, the star in my crown this year," Phillips said to her, taking her hand and turning her to the young man. His hand was cool and dry, not sticky, like her own. He withdrew his fingers quickly. "Hello, Lewis. Nell, this is Curtis Culpepper, who comes to us fresh from the wilds of Madison Wisconsin, and will be taking the survey of Americans for me this year. He's a great fan of your suthren mellerdrammer, and wishes to kneel at your feet."

The president tittered politely, and the young man giggled nervously. Lewis Wolfe, behind her, made a small sound in his throat. It sounded ridiculously like the low, gentle snarl of a carnivore. Nell felt the color rising in her face and glared at Phillips, who smiled back enigmatically.

The young man's face was as red as her own. "I loved your book, Mrs. Jay," he said. His voice was a clear treble. "It was one of the reasons I was eager to come south. I was encouraged to think that there was, perhaps, a renaissance going on here . . . not that I ever felt the South was *backward*, I didn't mean to imply . . ."

"I should hope not, Culpepper, or I would be forced to trade you to Georgia Tech for a graduate assistant in structural engineering and an undisclosed amount of cash," Phillips said in even tones, but Nell could hear the annoyance in his voice and ached for the clumsy, silly young man. She searched for something graceful to say, but her emptied mind could find no propitiatory chatter. The men laughed, all but Lewis Wolfe.

"That makes two of us, then, Mr. Culpepper," he said, smiling warmly at the hapless young man. "Mrs. Jay's book was also a carrot for me. You have fine taste. It's a wonderful book."

"Enough, or Nell will be flown with herself and I'll get no breakfast tomorrow," Phillips said, and Nell felt a slight, brushing touch on her bare elbow. Lewis.

"Let's go into the library," the president said. "Just between us, this punch of Isabel's has glued my tongue to the roof of my mouth. I've got a small but impeccable private stock hidden behind Mr. Bulwer-Lytton. We'll toast the auspicious arrivals of Mr. Culpepper and Dr. Wolfe with some vintage Wild Turkey."

"I'd love to," the young man breathed gratefully. The president turned to lead the way across the terrace and through the lighted French doors. Phillips stood still, looking fixedly at Lewis Wolfe.

"I think Nell and I will pass, thanks," he said. "I've got an early meeting with the graduate counselors in the morning."

"I have to get going myself," Lewis Wolfe said. "I have to see to the livestock. Good night, gentlemen. Good night, Mrs. Jay. It really was an . . . unexpected pleasure."

He beamed impishly at her, and was gone across the terrace and into the thinning crowd around the buffet table.

"Good night, Dr. Wolfe," Nell said after him. She and Phillips left soon after that.

On the way home in the car, she said, "I like your Lewis Wolfe. He ought to be a good addition to the staff." Saying his name aloud felt strange and heady, like caressing a small object you have shoplifted and secreted in your pocket.

"Apparently it's mutual," Phillips said. "Millicent Atkins

343

said you two were hidden off in the dark in the gazebo for the longest time. What were you talking about, the future of southern literature?"

Nell looked sideways at him. His profile was calm and full-looking, as if his first social evening as department head had pleased him.

"We were talking about running off together," Nell said. "He came down here to seduce me away from you."

"He aims high." Phillips chuckled. "Especially for somebody who's lucky to have a teaching job at all."

Nell slewed around on the seat to face him. "He told me some of his background. I'd say you're damned lucky to have him, Phillips," she snapped. "I'd say anybody was."

"Did he also tell you he's an alcoholic?" he said. He did not turn his eyes from the road, but Nell could tell there was a small flicker of self-satisfaction in them. Phillips was naturally abstemious, and felt little but contempt for excess of any kind. "Did he happen to mention that he was such a bad drunk that he half-killed his wife and daughter in an automobile accident before the woman had the sense to divorce him, or that he screwed up his classes so bad that his university wasn't going to give him another chance? He swore on his mother's grave that he'd been sober for a year when I interviewed him, and so far as I know he has . . . God, I thought we were in for it to-night when Dr. Abercrombie offered to break out the hard stuff, but he saw me looking at him, and he had the sense to take himself home before the temptation arose. But I know and he knows that I'm taking a big chance on him. I wouldn't have done it if it hadn't been for his background, but you're right about one thing . . . he's got the credentials, all right. I'm going to have to watch him very closely, though. One bender . . . one drink, even, one whiff on his breath . . . and out he goes. I've told him that. He knows I'm serious, too. It's a big risk for a new department chairman to take. I hope he remembers that."

"I feel sure that he is sufficiently grateful," Nell said. She could hardly speak for the fury boiling in her chest. She wanted to take his face in her hands and claw the self-satisfaction out of his eyes until they hung from their sockets; her fingers curled with the wanting of it. She thought of Lewis Wolfe's soft, flat voice in the darkness:

344

"I needed to leave there, Nell. I couldn't stay any longer."
Her heart squeezed with pain for him.

All that week the viscous heat of early autumn held,
and the life on the streets and campus of Sparta had a
heavy, underwater languor to its comings and goings. Heat
eddied and shimmered, cobralike, from the sidewalks, and
swayed in the gusts of stale-chill air from the air condi-
tioning when doors to stores and shops were opened. It had
not rained in weeks, and soft pink dust lay thick and
tickling over everything. Trees were going yellow and
red and bronze and brown, early this year because of the
drought, but instead of looking rich and valiant and
glorious, as they usually did in Sparta's slow bronze au-
tumns, they looked dead and painted. New fall wools in
shop windows looked nauseating, and pale, dispirited summer cottons stuck damply to backs and legs, and tempers
flared.

Then, on Friday, the heat broke, and the morning came
in almost cold and pearled with ground mist and so clear
and blue-edged that each separate leaf on the painted
dead trees leapt into life and shouted like clarion trum-
pets. Nell awoke brimming and humming with simple joy;
she dressed in tweed pants and a heavy, cream-colored
Irish sweater and made a totally unnecessary trip to the
supermarket. When she came out, pushing her cart into
the stinging blue of the morning, she looked up directly
into the eyes of Lewis Wolfe.

"What a coincidence," she said, laughing with a free
and leaping young joy at the sight of his fine smile. He
wore faded, paint-spattered blue jeans this morning, and
a plaid flannel shirt that smelt of mothballs and looked as
though he had slept in it. He was beard-shadowed and
square and rumpled and his glasses were mended with
cellophane tape, and he was, there in the October light,
such a swarthy and earthbound antithesis of Phillips that
Nell doubted, for a moment, that she herself was Nell.

"No coincidence at all," he said. "I've been haunting
grocery stores for a week. The Phantom of the Produce
Aisle they know me as. I figured you had to shop somewhere sometime."

"Well . . . here I am," Nell said, feeling tongue-tied
and stupid and fourteen years old and about to burst with
secret glee, and on the brink of something enormous and
never before imagined.

"Here you are indeed," said Lewis Wolfe. "And not a second too soon, either. I've got a bottle of ghastly Blue Nun straight out of the refrigerator case going warm in the back of the car, and some iced tea in a jug, and some Brie melting rapidly, and a loaf of plastic French bread, and I'm going to take you out to my house and we're going to have a picnic and we'll probably make love on a blanket. I have the blanket in the car, too."

He said it mildly and affably, and Nell began to laugh, and she laughed all the way to his car, which turned out to be a battered Porsche badly in need of painting, and she laughed all the way out the old road toward Atlanta to the turnoff to Lewis's farmhouse, and she laughed all the way down the goldenrod-bordered, pebbled road that led to an old white clapboard house, gabled and elled and porched and gingerbreaded and vaulted over with great, blazing hickories and poplars and surrounded with leaning outbuildings and pastures and pens and coops. It was ot the thin, nervous laughter of near-hysteria that had been Nell's laugh for a long time now, when she did laugh, but the laugh of a usually obedient child who has participated in some undignified and covert small mischief in church, under the very noses of the stern grown-ups, and cannot stop the fountain of incandescent laughter that starts forth from the very marrow. He looked at her often, smiling, and sometimes he laughed with her, but mainly he smiled and drove, steadily and one-handedly and well, and he whistled as he drove.

He came to a stop on the circular turnaround in front of the porch, and vaulted himself over the car's door and came around to her side and opened the door. She got out and looked around her.

"I know this place," she said. "It's the old Turnipseed place. They used to raise horses. And they sold cider; they had wonderful orchards. Gamma and Mama brought me out once with Robert to get some cider. One fall. I remember now; the air smelled like apples and sun. And somebody . . . I guess it was Mr. Turnipseed; he was very tall, and had on overalls, and smelled like sweat and apples . . . held me in front of him and rode me around the yard on a great, huge horse."

"Did you like that?" Lewis Wolfe asked.

"No. I was afraid. I was afraid of almost everything when I was little. I was even afraid of the pony I inherited from Paul, and he was old as Methuselah when I got him. But I told Mama and Gamma that I loved it. I remember that. And then I was terrified for weeks that they'd buy that monstrous animal for me, and I'd have to ride him. I had a very strong sense of sin and punishment as a child, a real little prig. And a liar. You'd have hated me."

"I doubt that. I've always been partial to liars. They are, I find, the last pure moralists. Most people lie to avoid pain, either for themselves or other people, and the avoidance of pain is a number-one moral priority of mine. I think the uses of adversity stink. But why on earth did you say you loved it if it scared you so?"

"I don't think you must ever let on if you're scared," Nell said seriously, looking at him. "It leaves you wide open, when people know you're frightened. Anything can come in. I spent most of my life being afraid of something or other, and the rest of it trying to hide it. I'm not proud of the scared part, but I am sort of proud of the not showing it part. It seems to me that there's real courage in that. That was one of the few things about myself I could ever feel really proud of."

"God help you, then, and God pity the child you must have been, Nell," he said, and his voice was very soft. "Because that's bullshit. Poor little girl, what kind of a house is this Fox's Earth, what kind of people are they, that they did that to you?"

"Nobody did anything to me on purpose, of course," Nell said, but she was not sure of this even as she said it. Some enormous, soft mass of time and days past seemed to swim into her mind, shimmering and pulsing as it came, as if seeking focus, trembling with the effort to become clear. Some great unthinkable thing was struggling to become thought.

"They're just Mama and Gamma. Two women. By themselves most of their lives, so they have to be strong, or Gamma does. Mama is . . . Mama is sort of a joke, even though she's a dear and I love her. But neither one is a . . . a . . . tormentor of children."

"From what you told me the other night about your brother and sister and how they went away, I wouldn't be too sure about that," he said. "Come on, Nell. Bring that sack. It's apples for the horses; there are some of them still here, in the pasture down by the river where I plan to take you and ravish you. A very pleasant village-idiot type comes out every morning and feeds them, and I feed them in the afternoons, in return for part of the rent being knocked off. It's the only way I could have afforded all this space. In addition to all my other sterling qualities, I am dirt poor. Do you mind?"

"No," said Nell, her heart pounding high in her throat. "Not that you're poor, and not feeding apples to horses, either. I'm more their size now. It's different."

They walked side by side through tall grass and weeds, the blue-edged morning going hot and gold on their eyelids, the smell of summer dust and autumn leaves and leaf mold and drying manure rising sweet and thick in their nostrils, the rich, smoky smell of old apple trees coiling out to meet them from the beginnings of the orchard that lay along the river. They ducked under the rusting wire of the last corral, and walked through a pasture gone to waist-high goldenrod, a sea of pure yellow feathers, down to the dark line of old trees, and into them. Under the tangled web of the ruined orchard the grass was deep green and still pearled with the last of the morning's dew, and the spilt globes of fruit underfoot gave off a scent of incense when they stepped on them. The trees overhead had few apples, and the ones that hung along the gnarled black branches were wizened and flinty-hard. But the smell was glorious, intoxicating.

"I'm drunk from just breathing air," Nell said, throwing her head back and inhaling deeply. Then she remembered what Phillips had told her in the car going home, and she said, "Oh," involuntarily.

"That's okay," he said, not turning his head to her. "I knew he'd have told you about that immediately. I was going to myself, this afternoon. It's no big deal, Nell."

They came out of the dark grove onto the lip of a small, low cliff that hung over the slow, dark-brown Oconee. It was narrow and shallow at this point, hardly wider than a creek, and the water ran slow and thick with golden ragweed pollen, hardly breaking over the sandy ford where, judging from the welter of damp and dried hoofprints, the horses crossed and recrossed. Nell had seen no horses on the walk down. Behind them the dark bulk of the orchard was like a solid wall, and before them, across the creek, more pastureland climbed gently up toward the top of a hill where a little wood, lighted now to wildfire, stood silhouetted against the ringing cobalt of the sky. It was past noon.

Nell drew her breath in pleasure.

"It's a beautiful spot, Lewis."

"I'm glad you like it," he said. "I found it the first day I was here. And when I met you, I knew this was the place I'd bring you for the first time. That's now, Nell. You know that, don't you?"

"Yes," she said. "I know that."

"Is this going to be difficult for you?"

"No," she said wonderingly, filled with a sly, creeping joy. She could feel her nipples standing up, brushing feather tips against the fabric of her bra; the spreading tingle ran down her stomach and spine, tickled between her legs, forced her breath high and shallow in her throat. She looked at him in the clean sunlight. They were the same height; their eyes were perfectly level. His were dark and soft and shone with pleasure and surety and wanting and something else . . . "Why," Nell thought, "it's kindness. Besides all the other, there is kindness in his eyes. I have never seen that in a man's eyes before."

"Oh, no, oh, no," she murmured, reaching her arms out to him. "It isn't going to be difficult at all!"

It was not difficult. At first it was clumsy, and fumbling, and inept, and adolescently awkward; Nell stumbled stepping out of her underpants, and caromed into him as he stood on one leg struggling out of his tight blue jeans, and they went down together in a tangle of long, tanned legs and short, muscular, black-thatched ones, their bare white buttocks imprinted with the red stigmata of short, tough, horse-cropped grass and small, sharp, white river flintstones. After they had disentangled themselves, laughing helplessly, she had gotten her head stuck in the tight, handknit turtleneck of her sweater, and he had had to yank it ruthlessly over her head, finally, as she yelped with laughter and gasped for breath, inside the smothering shroud. Her hands and wrists, by then, were so weak with laughter and desire and nervousness that he had had to reach around her and unhook her bra, and this had taken another three or four minutes, there in the mercilessly blazing sun and the slow, oily river sounds and the casual calls of the field birds.

"I've never felt so teenaged or so naked in my life," she gasped, when he finally conquered the brassiere's hook and tossed it aside and knelt astride her, looking down at her. His face was flushed with the effort and the laughter, and his eyes, without the glasses, were brilliant and sun-warmed to a pure, good chestnut, softer and larger than they seemed behind the panes of glass, and somehow terribly vulnerable. His black hair wisped into his face, and his smile was calm and sweet and steady.

"I think you are the most beautiful thing I have ever seen," he said. And Nell raised her arms to him and drew him down upon her, and it began.

Their lovemaking was like Lewis himself, she reflected later, slow and sweet and strong and infinitely tender, so that for a long time after he entered her, she felt only a sort of primal, rocking peace, a great, ocean-deep, rhythmic sense of being connected to the very earth at its core, a musky sweetness as of spreading wild honey from her loins. The sun-hot earth beneath the blanket, and the near-cold little wind off the river on her legs and buttocks as they clenched with him and around him, and the relentless bronze weight of the sun on her eyelids and the crown of her head, and the smell of earth and apples and river and horses and wild muscadines somewhere in the distance, and the great, windy blue bowl of sky overhead—they all seemed part of a separate, elemental entity that merged with him, sliding in and out of the entity that was Lewis himself. It was as if she were being taken by the very spirit of the place, a virile October god. And then the slow-spreading honey turned abruptly to thick, sweet fire, and the core of her swelled and burst and ran with a sharp nectar too keen to bear, and she heard his cry of "Nell, I love you!" mingle with her own wordless shout, and October's god became Lewis and Lewis only, Lewis always, and it was truly, for her, the first time, and maybe the first time in the world. Above them on the khaki blanket, high in the dome of the bowl, a red-tailed hawk soared and dipped, rode the October thermals straight up into a dizzying parabola, and was lost into the sun.

Later, still naked and as unself-conscious now as children in a bathtub or puppies in the sun, they dipped the store-stale French bread into the gamy, melted pool of the Brie, and ate greedily, licking the good, smelly coating from

350

their fingers. He reached for the sack that held the wine and the plastic jug of iced tea.

"What will it be, Eleanor my love? Wine or tea?" he said.

"Wine. By all means. Oh, no. Wait. I'd rather have tea. Really. Do you have enough?"

"Nell," Lewis said, setting the paper bag down and sitting up straight, "we're going to have to talk about this booze business right now. It's a little ridiculous at this stage of the game for you to go skating around it like a dowager entertaining a wino off the mission steps. Mr. Chairman has undoubtedly told you that I am an alcoholic, and that because I am, my wife and daughter were both injured in an automobile accident in which I was at fault. And that my wife subsequently divorced me, and my daughter is with her now. That is all true. Fortunately, I was not driving the car, or I would now be under some Iowa jail with very little chance of getting out soon, but I was arguing violently with Harriet, who was driving, and I was very, very drunk, and I shoved her, and the car went off the road and into a drainage ditch, and it was as surely my fault as if I had been at the wheel. Harriet had a broken collarbone and a badly cut face, and Leah lost a couple of her front teeth and broke her wrist . . . she was in the back seat . . . and I was not hurt at all, beyond a few bruises and a black eye. Drunks bounce like India rubber."

"You don't have to tell me this, Lewis . . ." Nell began unhappily.

"I do have to tell you this. I'm not going to have it crawling between us every time we make love or have a fight or see a movie or scratch our behinds. All right?"

"All right," Nell said.

"I always drank too much," he said. "From the very first drink I ever had, in college, I loved the taste and I loved the effect. I don't recall feeling that drinking ever gave me courage or the ability to sparkle in front of people, because I was never afraid and I was never shy. I just loved the . . . specialness that booze gave everything. The ritual, the festival quality. And it seemed that everybody drank in those days. It was what you did when you weren't studying. And so, when I met Harriet in New Haven, we spent a lot of time drinking with my crowd, and she

351

seemed to like it. Poor Harriet, I think she was truly convinced that she had her hands on a future Nobel laureate, and I didn't do anything to disabuse her of the notion. My crowd must have seemed like cadet Einsteins to her after that country-club crowd she ran around with in White Plains, and she wasn't a stupid girl herself . . . just astoundingly unformed. As for me, I couldn't believe any girl as rich and pretty as Harriet could be seriously interested in me, the fat little kid from Apple River, who never even climbed Charles Mound, and one night when we'd all been drinking more than usual we just drove all night down to Elkton, Maryland, and got married. Or rather, my ego married her expectations."

"God," Nell breathed softly, "Phillips and I ran away and got married, too. And so did my mama and daddy. It's like a curse, or an omen."

"The former in my case," he said. "It only took us about three months to realize that neither of us was going to be any good for the other, but by then Leah was on the way, and in those days and in that world you just did not divorce, especially with a baby coming. And to make a long, dull tale shorter, I stayed at Iowa and became more and more eminent and drunker and drunker, and finally the embarrassing behavior and the missed classes and the arguments and tears and passing out on the couch night after night outweighed the eminence, and by the time of the accident, the university had had it with me and so had Harriet, and they both threw me out. I don't blame either of them. I was lucky neither happened long before. Or maybe not so lucky, after all. I had nothing to give Harriet anymore, God knows, nor she me, but I had no wish to hurt her, and the fact that I hurt my daughter will haunt me for the rest of my life. That almost killed me; fortunately, it also stopped me. I probably won't see much of Leah anymore . . . Harriet won't have it, and she is within her rights . . . but neither will I drink anymore."

"Oh, Lewis, I am so very sorry," Nell said. Pain for him was heavy and searing in her chest. "Leah will come back when she's old enough to make her own decisions; she knows you love her, surely. Give her time . . ."

"She may and she may not," he said. "Don't start to cry, Nell. It's easily lived with. I have not been an unhappy man. Now I will be a very happy one."

"But, Lewis, surely when she's grown herself, she'll see what a desperately unhappy marriage can do to a person. No wonder you drank a little too much . . ."

"No," he said. "I didn't drink a little too much. I was a drunk. There wasn't a reason; there isn't a reason for a drunk. Don't romanticize it. It's a devil inside you, and for it you will lie, and cheat, and steal, and betray the people you love best over and over again; you will do that, and finally you will stop or you will die. I stopped."

"All right," she said. "Thank you for telling me."

"You're welcome," he said. "Now how about that tea?"

"I'll fix it," Nell said, reaching for the jug and the paper cups. She rummaged in the sack. "Do you take lemon and sugar?"

He threw back his head and laughed, and the sun, moved now across the softening sky so that it shone through the fringes of the wood on the opposite hill, dappled him with pagan coins, so that he looked, in his black-pelted, muscular nakedness and his easy supine slouch, like something half wild, something of both flesh and forest.

"God, if you aren't the very essence of the Old South sometimes! You've just been fucked six ways to Sunday out in the woods on a blanket by a hairy ex-drunk you've known exactly six days, and you sit there with your legs all which way and your bare ass shining and ask me if I take sugar or lemon in my tea!"

Nell crossed her legs hastily. "Maybe you'd prefer hemlock," she said.

He laughed again, and reached over and ran a finger lightly across her full breasts, dappled also with gold. The nipples rose again, and goose flesh stood up on her breasts and arms.

"What I'd really prefer is seconds," he said. "But I'd probably better get you back or your family will think you've come to no good. Which is true. What about it, Nell? Are you going to be able to handle this? It's going to be one hell of an affair, at the very least, and God knows where it will lead. Anywhere you say. You're the one who's going to have to come to terms with Herr Professor, not to mention with your Abby and yourself. *And* the legendary ladies of Fox's Earth. I'll give you all the support I can; I'll always be there when you need me. But you'll have to carry the ball yourself. Is it going to scare you to death?

Can you take the guilt? Because you're the world's original guilt collector, you know."

Nell leaned back and stretched, catching the sun on her face and breasts, wriggling her buttocks voluptuously into the sun-warmed blanket. She felt washed and free and strong and young.

"I will probably feel all those things," she said, her eyes still closed beneath the weight of the sun. "And I have no idea what will become of us, of this. But right now, Lewis, I do not feel one teeny, tiny crumb of a shred of guilt or fear."

She opened her eyes and smiled at him, and then looked beyond him at a massive deep-gold shape moving in the shallows of the slow river. A whistling wet snort broke the bee-droning silence of the afternoon. A sorrel horse stood there, slow, dark water breaking around his fetlocks; his white muzzle, as he looked gravely at them, dripped river water.

"I'll show you just how afraid I am, Lewis Wolfe," Nell said, laughter breaking in her voice, and she leapt to her feet and ran down the bank and, with one sure hand on the sorrel's withers, vaulted onto his back and wrapped her long legs around his sides. Startled, the horse nickered and broke into a clumsy, stumbling trot, and scrambled up the opposite bank and out into the field with Nell, naked in the great green-gold day, fastened like a burr to his back, hands wrapped in his rough mane. With her bare heels she urged him on; she leaned close over his neck and slapped his flank with her hand. The horse broke into a canter and moved easily off through the field, up the slope toward the wood, which stood in deep shadow now. Lewis Wolfe sat straight and still as a statue, watching them. The goldenrod was flank-high on the sorrel, and Nell's feet hung down in it as in some fantastic sea. Her silver-brown curls flew free and her head was tipped back in joy and triumph, and she looked, sitting the running horse in the golden field halfway between the darkling wood and the light-struck river, like some mythic Hippolyta strayed out of antiquity into that queer, enchanted October Friday.

She turned the flying horse at the fringe of the wood, and they started back down the hill toward the river and the man on the blanket, and he could hear her laughter, jubilant, exultant, invincible; then her voice, curling toward him as out of more than distance; out of time: "Lewis! Lewis! Look at me! I AM NOT AFRAID!"

When she finally let the horse slow to an ambling trot and then a walk and slid down off him to come splashing across the little creek and stand before Lewis Wolfe, sun and sweat glistening on the long, white, pagan nakedness of her, she saw that he was crying.

28

BUT SHE WAS AFRAID, after all. The affair . . . for it was that; even Nell, flinching away from the word when it crept into her consciousness, could not call it anything else . . . ran through the winter and into the following spring, and as often as she was scourged, freed, exalted, transported, airborne, Nell was smashed and hollowed with guilt and fear. As often as she shouted and crowed with great, gut-springing laughter, she wept with utter misery, and the caroming plunges of her spirit often left her mortally, perilously vulnerable.

But she could not end it; hopelessly, in the depths of her blackest moments of sucking guilt, she knew that she had not the power even to contemplate breaking it off. She could only talk of it, compulsively, endlessly, to Lewis Wolfe; could only cry until the tears became laughter and then swooped back up to one of her Olympian crags. He did not chide her and he did not attempt to assuage the guilt and fear, and he did not become impatient with her. Rather, as she sobbed of betrayed trust and what the affair would do to her child and her husband and the two old women at Fox's Earth if they should find out about it, he replied briefly, in gentle tones of infinite reason.

"What would it do to them if they found out, Nell? Your mother and grandmother, I mean. It would fatten them up like leeches, is all. Your extraordinary Gamma would love it."

But mostly he listened, and she tried to make him see,

355

make him understand. With every fiber of her being, she tried.

"I want to be like you. I want to be strong and free; I want to get totally free of the stupid college, the town, the whole South, if that's what it takes. Maybe my marriage, too, God help me; maybe even that, although I'm not sure . . . it was so good at first with Phillips, so good, so sure, so *safe,* and oh, Lewis, I want that safety, I need that safety! I am so terribly afraid of not being safe! And it was me, my writing that did it, that blew it all apart . . . and Abby. My God, what about Abby? I'm losing Abby right now, right this minute, because I've done everything wrong. Listen, Lewis, listen to me: More than anything else in the whole world, I have to be good and right, I have to know that I am a good little girl. That's sick, and it's crazy, but it's absolutely vital if I am going to live in this world, because it's all I know how to be. And if I should walk away from it all, from them all, then I would never again in this life have a chance to be good . . ."

"But," he said, honestly puzzled, "you're bleeding to death, *you,* not them, and who is it helping?"

"I don't know. God, maybe."

"Bullshit."

Once, in misery and exasperation, she lashed out at him: "Don't you ever feel guilty about this? Just the slightest bit?"

"Nope," he said. "I feel terrific. Hear this, Nell: If you have to hurt, go on and do it. I'll do whatever can help you not hurt so much. But at least see that you wove your own whips. They may have handed you the rawhide a thousand times over, bushels of it, whoever *they* are, but it took your hands to weave them, and your arms to flog yourself with them. I will love you and listen to you and cry with you and laugh with you and live with you always, if you'll let me, but I will not suffer with you. I'm having too good a time."

And she had to laugh. It really did feel better than crying. Soon she was not crying so often.

It often seemed a miracle to her that the affair went undiscovered, for Nell knew viscerally and from birth the quivering radar of the town and its insatiable appetite for gossip. They were discreet, but in a perfunctory sort of way; Lewis would not, for instance, let her ride in his car with him so that she might have to duck down below window level at the approach of a familiar figure or vehicle, and he would not ride in hers.

"I will not become a crouching toad for you or any other woman," he said cheerfully, "and I will not have you squatting in the bottom of my car. I'll do the obvious things, like not calling you at home, and like not touching you when we meet in public, and like not dropping your monogrammed underpants out of my raincoat pocket in the faculty club, and all, but beyond that I will not go. I'm at the farm every afternoon after three. Every afternoon. I will have no other people there, ever. That's where we will meet, when we meet. You don't have to call me. Just come when you can. I'll be there."

It worked better than Nell might have thought. Abby had long been badgering Nell to let her ride into Atlanta for her twice-weekly piano lessons with a school friend who was old enough to drive; the girl had horrific acne and went for treatments at a clinic on Abby's lesson days, and could easily drop Abby at the Memorial Arts Center and pick her up. The girl was flighty and overdeveloped and smoked cigarettes from the moment she left the Sparta city limits to the moment she stepped from the car in Atlanta, as Abby readily admitted to Nell when she was questioned about the lingering smell on her clothes and hair after these trips.

"Is that all she smokes, Abby?" Nell had asked, worrying about pot-induced accidents and death and guilt. "Otherwise you know what my answer is. It would be out of the question."

"Don't be stupid," Abby said coldly. "She doesn't do dope. It makes acne a hundred times worse. And I'm not going to smoke anything. I couldn't play if I did. You ought to know that by now."

Nell believed her and let her go with the girl. There was no reason not to, she told herself. "Lewis has nothing to do with it, really. I would have anyway." But she knew she would not have, had Lewis Wolfe not been waiting for her. Nevertheless, her afternoons were now her own as they had not been for the past three years, and she went at least twice a week out the old Atlanta road to the cutoff toward Lewis's farm. She did not vary her route and she did not wear dark glasses or consider somehow obtaining a car no one knew. She nodded and waved to friends on the streets and in cars within Sparta proper, as she had always done, and, incredibly, saw no vehicles she knew once she was outside the bounds of the town, where she might have been noticed.

In the afternoons, in the high old farm bed beneath the wedding-ring quilt that the apple farmer's wife had left for Lewis, or on the hearth rug before the bedroom fire, or in the chipped bulbous white clawfoot bathtub of the great, stark, clumsy farmhouse bathroom, they coupled and rolled and splashed and laughed, and for the two hours of Lewis, anyway, she was a woman who was not Nell Geiger Jay but a creature of dark, flaming blood and shameless loins and high, savage appetite. But even in the mindless, highest spiral of transport, she knew somehow that she would be Nell Jay again in less than an hour, and often, as they lay watching the winter dark lower through the wavy old panes of thick glass in the bedroom's high windows, she would wonder, honestly and humbly, what he had ever found in her that he should love her. For he did love her. In the darkest of the dark times, even, Nell did not doubt this, only wondered why.

"I am so totally different," she thought. "I am not free and honest and open as he is. I never was, I don't think I ever can be. What can he see?"

"You," he said briefly, when she asked him once. "I can see you plain."

Nell grew humming and beautiful with the surety of him. Her cheeks flew the hectic flags of the storms that blew and died and blew again within her; her eyes glowed with satiety and excitement and guilt. Phillips seemed to notice nothing, but Abby, she thought sometimes in terror, Abby noticed. Could it be that Abby somehow knew? She would look long and levelly at her mother, a veiled look, pure female and old as the world, and Nell would shrink inside with unease and dread. She had seen that look before, on Ruth Fox's face. It pierced deep and held its images long; Nell feared and hated it, and dropped her own eyes before it. Abby responded by moving in on her mother on soft, inexorable young predator's feet: "You never even ask me about my music anymore. You don't even mention it. You're all wrapped up inside yourself these days, and you don't care about me. I can tell you don't. It's horrible of you to keep me here when you don't care, when I could be with Yancey in New York. If you keep on saying no, I'll hate you for the rest of my life.

And I'll leave here the minute I can, and I'll never see you again as long as I live. Only daddy. Not you."

Angry and wounded, Nell nevertheless saw it clearly: "She is blackmailing me. She doesn't know, she can't possibly. But she smells the blood, and she knows there is a weakness somewhere, a wound, an opening in me. Will I let her do this to me? God help us both if I do. But if I don't . . ."

She grew truly angry with Abby for the first time in her life, deeply and coldly angry, and the anger did not go away, and the resulting guilt burnt her worse than any she had felt before. She lavished more attention on her daughter, and on Phillips, too, who acknowledged it with a rusty, grudging gallantry that touched her in an abstract sort of way, but even as she fussed over her husband and child, she was with Lewis in her essential core. She felt that she could live this way indefinitely; forever, perhaps. Phillips and Abby had all of her that they wanted or needed. At her core, Lewis was there. There was a crazy peace to it, under the great, careening plunges of that winter.

Inside Fox's Earth, the changes in Nell did not go unremarked. Ruth Fox was quick to scent this new threat to her hold on Nell, and though she could not name it, it fed her faltering strength and will as nothing else had in many years. She blossomed with the nourishment of the new challenge; she took sustenance from it, until she grew as flame-licked and beautiful as she had been in the early days of her powers.

"I declare, Ruth," her contemporaries would marvel, "you look twenty years younger all of a sudden. I'm gon' haunt you till you tell me what you're doing; are you sneakin' off to one of those goat-gland doctors?"

And Ruth would smile archly and say, "I'm sneaking off to meet a beau. It does wonders for a girl. You all should try it." And they would laugh, and cluck, and say among themselves that she was the most remarkably beautiful woman for eighty-five years . . . or any age, for that matter . . . that they had ever seen. And Rip, overhearing, would watch Ruth Fox even more closely.

For she *was* sneaking off. There was no other word for it. At least twice a week, she would wait until Hebe was sleeping in her room and Rip herself was resting in the tiny attic cubicle that had become hers again, and she would go quietly down the stairs and out to the garage, and coast the big Chrysler down to the street before starting the engine. She did not mention the trips, and Rip did not know how many of them she had made before she became aware that Ruth was slipping out in the darkening winter afternoons. When she did discover it, a great fear took her, and the danger that had come into Fox's Earth with the nameless new man whose image she had seen lately superimposed upon Nell's face stirred and breathed through the house, and she rose up to go and meet it.

After that, she set out to follow on foot old Ruth Fox in the car. It was not so difficult a task as it might have seemed, for Ruth did not go far, and she drove slowly and deliberately, nodding as in a royal passage to passersby and stopping long at intersections on the quiet streets around the university, to look up this one and down that one for Rip knew not what. Rip would fling her woolen shawl over her head and wrap the warm, dark coat that Nell had given her closely about her slender figure, and her long legs would eat up the small distances behind the creeping Chrysler. People on the streets saw only Ruth Fox's Rip, out on some errand for one of the Fox women, and if they thought anything at all it was, "How on earth do they do it in that house? Old Rip is as straight as a two-by-four and moves like a racehorse still, and she's not much younger than Ruth."

It was not until nearly Christmas that Rip realized what it was that Ruth Fox sought when she took the Chrysler out, though later she realized that she had always known. Pausing on a windy intersection to fix the Chrysler more firmly in her view, Rip saw the familiar dark-blue length of Nell's Volvo station wagon inch its way out of a parking spot before the supermarket and swing out onto the main street of town, and watched as the Chrysler nosed after it like a great bloodhound. The two cars were soon blocked in the cheerful Christmas traffic; Rip had no trouble at all following until she saw that Nell was turning off onto the road that led only to the subdivision out by the river where she lived. Then she turned and came home; she was safely ensconced in her bedroom once again when she heard the Chrysler slide into the garage.

It was very important that she beat Ruth Fox home from these trips. She must not know that Rip followed in the winter afternoons. Rip thought long about whether or not she should tell Nell that old Ruth was following her, but in the end she considered that the time was not yet. So far, Ruth had found nothing. If she got too close, then Rip would tell. Let Nell keep this good new love she had found clean and unsullied for as long as she could. In the shrinking days, Rip watched. In the nights, she prayed that she would know when she must move.

And in the days also, Ruth Yancey Fox watched Rip for any sign that she knew of the clandestine afternoon trips in the Chrysler, and in the nights she planned and charted Rip's probable next-day movements so that she might circumvent them, and though she saw as yet no sign of knowing in Rip's dark face, still she watched, she watched. And under the great flat roof of Fox's Earth the two beautiful old women stalked each other like two fabulous wild things out of the morning of the world.

At Christmastime, Lewis Wolfe gave Nell a small golden apple, convex and charmingly detailed on one side, flat and polished on the other. On the back was engraved "P.F.G.&V.V." He fastened the thin gold chain around her neck and let the apple slip down into the still-sweated hollow at the base of her throat. They were naked in the farm bed; rain was turning to fine, needling sleet outside, and the apple log fire snickered behind its screen, and Nell stretched with the heavy, aching limbs of love and sighed with the imminence of her departure. She touched the apple.

"I love it! It's beautiful; and an apple is perfect. I'll never forget that first time, in the apple orchard . . . What does this mean on the back here? Lewis, I'm sorry; I haven't had time to get anything for you yet . . ."

"It doesn't matter. Listen. This stands for something I want you to remember, starting right now. Memorize it. It's got to become as automatic and familiar to you as your own name. It stands for 'Pretty fucking good and vice versa.'"

She laughed, delighted, and rolled over and hugged him, and buried her face into the hollow of his throat.

"Oh, God, you fool! It couldn't be more perfect. I need to hear it fifty times a day, and now I can see it whenever I want to. It will be like you're there saying it to me whenever I start getting stupid and whiny again. I do love you, Lewis. Nobody else in the whole world would ever think of giving me a thing like that."

"I should hope not."

He put her away from him slightly, and looked intently at her. "Okay, Nell, there's a reason for it, besides the fact that you *are* pretty fucking good and vice versa. There are some things I want you to start doing now. You're ready for them. It's time. This will help you do them. This will stand in for me when I can't be there to prop you up and keep you going."

Nell looked at him doubtfully. "What things?"

"Number one, I want you to start writing again. Now. When you get home tonight. And a little bit all through Christmas, when you can, and then really get down to it the first of the year. I want you to promise me you'll do that. Promise me on this apple."

"Oh, Lewis . . ."

"Nell?"

"Do you really think I could? Do another book? Oh, God, after the last one I didn't think I ever could again. I still don't know if I'm up to it; I don't even know if I'm any good anymore . . ."

He flipped the apple so that it bounced sharply against her throat. "If you ever doubt that you're any good, at writing or anything else, just remember that you're so damned good they gave you a medal for it."

She did it. It was frightening and terrible; her heart jolted in her throat as she pulled out a fresh legal pad from her long-locked desk and got into bed with it and a new felt-tip pen. She was afraid to use her typewriter; they must not know. Not yet, and maybe not ever. She felt none of the leaping freshet of electricity that had sometimes borne her fingers along on pads of air, but only staleness and stunted, lumpy little words. But she wrote. At the end of an hour, she went to the door of her bedroom . . . for Phillips slept regularly in the guest room now, making it his own . . . and looked for a telltale crack of light beneath his door. There was none. She padded into the den and locked the scrawled pages away in the bottom desk drawer, and took the key back into her bedroom and put it in her black satin evening purse on the top shelf. She slipped the apple around her neck and fished in her lingerie drawer for a nightgown high enough at the neck to conceal it, and from that night on, she wrote in her bed

362

at night and she wore the apple on the chain beneath her clothes.

In March, she had three chapters of a new novel, and she brought them to him. He took them away into the farmhouse kitchen to read them, and she sat alone on the porch in a whistling green wind, thinking nothing at all, feeling the weak new sun of another spring on her face.

He came back out an hour later, and his face was strange . . . set, stern to austerity. He did not like it, then. She sat, simply, and waited to hear what he would say.

"It's wonderful," he said. "I am astounded at you. Another woman entirely wrote this. It's grown-up, and mean, and tough, and funny, and fine, just fine. You've got to go on with it now. And, Nell . . ." He sat down beside her on the top step, and took both her hands in his and peered nearsightedly into her face through the aviator glasses.

"You've got to tell him you're writing. It's essential; it cannot wait. Otherwise you are going to lose your power over this book. And you've got to do more. If he gives you any shit, any shit at all about it, you've got to tell him you're leaving him . . . and then you've got to do it. Right away. If you can tell him about us while you're at it, fine; do it and come straight to me. It will be the real start of us. Bring Abby if you wish; I'm good with girls. I'd love another crack at one. But if you can't tell him about us, at least tell him about the writing and then get the hell out of there."

Nell jerked her hands away; she began to shake her head from side to side, silently, and to form the word "Please" with her mouth, but no sound came out. He captured her hands again.

"Listen, listen," he said softly, insistently. "Don't even think about me, then. Do it for yourself. Don't see me for a while, for as long as it takes, if the guilt of us is too much for you on top of the leaving. If it takes it, Nell, don't ever see me again. Just swish your ass out of there with your novel and don't look back at him or me. But *do it. Leave him. Write.* It's time; it's past time; you're ready."

She was crying. "I can't, I can't, don't ask me to do this, I can't leave them, and I can't leave you, ah, God, never you . . ."

"Look, Nell, it won't kill me. I've learned to be content

with very little because I've had to, but you don't. As the man says on the telly, baby, go for the gold."

"No, NO! You're going to kill me, Lewis, you're going to kill me and this poor goddamned book . . ."

He sighed, and pulled her close, and kissed the top of her head. It was as damp with sweat as if she had been running miles on an August day.

"Okay. I'm sorry. Okay. Then at least promise me this: that you'll keep writing. That's all. That you'll keep writing. And promise that if . . . when . . . you find that you're able, you *will* tell him and you'll at least try to leave him. It's the rest of your life, Nell."

"I'll promise that. Yes. I can promise you that I'll try."

Two weeks later she called Lewis at his office in the English Department. She had never done so before.

"I think I can do it, now. I'm taking these three chapters to the Copy Shop to be Xeroxed, right now, before I lose my nerve. I'm on my way out to the car. And then I'm going to mail a copy to my editor. And when I hear from him, I'm going to tell Phillips."

"Tell him what, Nell?" His voice was casual.

"That I'm writing another book. And . . . that I'm going to leave him. At least, I think I am. I'm going to try . . ."

"That's good," he said simply.

Nell replaced the receiver and went out of the house and got into the car, placing the thick manila envelope carefully on the seat beside her.

Inside Fox's Earth, in the dark nook beneath the right-hand spiral of the curving stair, Rip took off her coat and dropped it onto the faded old Chinese Chippendale chair that had served the foyer as a telephone chair since Alicia Fox had come south, and lifted the receiver off the telephone. Her heart was hammering so hard in her throat that she could hear it in her ears and feel it in her neck and temples, and it was not just from the exertion of the flying trip home. Rip had seen the Chrysler slide into a parking space in front of that place where people took important papers to be made into copies—she herself had delivered and picked up house documents there for Ruth Yancey Fox in days gone by, and she knew the place for what it was, even though she could not read the sign— and she had seen Nell's Volvo leave just before the Chrysler arrived. Rip knew with certainty that Nell's errand in the copy place had something to do with a new book, and that Ruth Fox would go inside and learn about the book, and she knew that this was a terrible new weapon to be used against Nell. She had nearly run home, in terror that she would see the Chrysler parked primly in the driveway when she got there. But the raked white gravel drive was empty, and her slamming old heart lurched with gratitude. Her long finger shook as she dialed the telephone; her heart sank again when Abby's light voice answered.

"Hello?"

"Where yo' mama, Miss Abby?"

"Well, hello to you, too, Rip," Abby said petulantly. Even in her haste, Rip noted the mingled tones of Phillips Jay and Ruth Fox in Abby's voice.

"I ain't got time to fiddle now, Miss Abby. I got to talk to yo' mama . . ."

"Well, she's not here. She went off in the car about an hour ago, and I don't know when she'll be back."

"Where she go?"

"*I* don't know, for God's sake, Rip. She never tells anybody where she's going anymore."

"Lissen, Miss Abby, you tell her when she come in to call me right then. Tell her not to bother Miss Ruth nor Miss Hebe, jus' call me . . ."

"Excuse me, Rip," said a new voice, "but could I speak with you just a second? No, don't hang up, I won't take long . . ."

Ruth Yancey Fox stood behind her, all gilt and white in a smart wrap coat and tiny, teetering high-heeled pumps. Her eyes were ringed with white also; she was a dazzle of light in the gloom. Rip's thin, straight shoulders slumped imperceptibly, but her eyes, as she turned them to old Ruth, were still and calm. She covered the receiver with her palm.

"Yes'm?"

"Why are you calling Nell?"

"Thought maybe she might pick up them strawberries you ordered down to McKinnon's on her way over here this afternoon, did she be comin'. My feets is actin' up some . . ."

"The strawberries came an hour ago. The boy brought them. They've been sitting on the kitchen table big as life."

"Yes'm."

Ruth Fox came closer. "Rip, a long time ago . . . a very, very long time ago . . . we talked, the two of us did, about what was most likely to happen if you ever forgot your place. I wouldn't like to think that you've forgotten your place, Rip." Her voice was very soft and quiet, but it carried, Rip thought, clear up into the ceiling of the foyer. She met the blue eyes levelly.

"I know what my place be, Miss Ruth."

"Good. Now hand the phone to me."

"This ain't Miss Nell; it Miss Abby . . ."

"Hand the phone to me."

Rip did. Ice formed in her throat as she passed the instrument to old Ruth Fox. Winter whistled in her heart.

"Hi, chickie," Ruth Yancey Fox chirped gaily into the telephone. "Tell your mama for me when she comes in that I sure do wish she'd come see us, and bring you for a change. It's been ages. Oh, and tell her congratulations on the new book she's writing. Tell her I'm on to her little secret . . . a little bird told me . . . but I won't tell a soul till she's ready. Of course, I'm sure you and your daddy know about it, but I bet she was saving it for a surprise for your Grandma Hebe and me . . ."

On the other end of the phone, Rip heard Abby begin to shriek, a piping glissando of pure rage: "What do you mean, she's writing a new book?" Ruth replaced the receiver and went away into the upper regions of Fox's Earth.

They found Abby two hours later at the Trailways bus station downtown. Phillips found her, at least; Nell had not returned from Lewis's farmhouse, where she had driven in trembling triumph after leaving the post office. The stationmaster had been summoned to deal with a young woman with a suitcase who was attempting to purchase a ticket to New York and did not have enough money; when the agent refused to take a check, she became hysterical and then collapsed on the floor, the center of a crowd of fascinated and horrified passengers. The stationmaster was a local young man and recognized Abby Jay instantly . . . only he thought of her as the little Fox girl, the youngest one. He called Fox's Earth immediately, and Ruth Fox, with remarkable calm and restraint, managed to reach Phillips at his office and dispatch him to the station. By the time Nell came home, flushed and burning with resolve and a sort of gallows gaiety, the doctor had been there, and given Abby a sedative by injection, and left a supply of Valium, and gone again, promising to see her in his office first thing in the morning. She was sleeping heavily in her room, and Phillips was sitting in the living room nursing a Scotch and waiting for Nell.

"I hear you're writing a book," he said pleasantly. "It will undoubtedly be a best-seller. It's already caused a stunning sensation right here in the bosom of your own little family."

She turned cold. "What are you talking about?"

"Go in and look at Abby. And when you come out, I'll tell you what I'm talking about."

At the end of that long evening, Nell gathered up her new manuscript and fed the pages one by one into the fire that Phillips had left burning in the den when he went to bed. The next morning, she called her editor and asked him to return the package she had just sent him without opening it. She removed the apple from around her neck and put it away in the back of her jewelry drawer. Abby went back to school and about her routine of weekly trips to Atlanta, Phillips went back to his classes, and no one mentioned the book again to Nell. Not even Lewis Wolfe, after she had told him what had happened. He just smiled his quirky, charming smile at her and said, "No sweat. There'll be another book in another time. You want some of this pizza, here, or shall I make glad the hearts of these gobblegut cats?"

After that, the glass bell that had enveloped Nell all through the painful spring and summer before she met Lewis snapped back into place around her, and things drifted. She continued to go in the late winter and spring afternoons to the farmhouse, for Lewis was all she could see from inside the bell; everything else outside it blurred and ran as in rain. But it was not a real perceiving, only a seeing. He did not seem to mind.

On an afternoon in May, Ruth Yancey Fox came into the foyer of Fox's Earth out of a diffused brilliance of mingled sun and rain and silhouetted her small figure like some uncanny aura. "The Devil's beating his wife," southerners all over Sparta would say on that day, seeing the sun shining through the spring rain. Rip would remember this about the day, that mingling of water and light, and much else. The women of Fox's Earth would all remember.

Rip had been dozing in the kitchen rocking chair; the whole night before she had paced and moaned with the arthritis in her long feet. Now she stood in the shadowy dining room and watched Ruth cross the foyer. She wore the silk raincoat she had ordered from Hong Kong the year before, and on her feet were the ridiculous, fragile, four-inch-heeled Charles Jourdan sandals that she had just had Yancey dispatch to her from New York. Her stride on the black-and-white marble was that of a sleepwalker, steady and measured and not quite connected to the floor. Rip saw her face and knew with pain that she had been set to watch and had failed, betrayed, finally, not by her staunch heart but by her treacherous bones. Ruth Yancey Fox was a tiny, terrible burning bush in a dead wilderness. She smiled, a great, radiant, unfocused smile, and she talked softly as she crossed the foyer and started up the stairs. Rip knew that she talked once again to dead Pearl Yancey. And she talked of a new man, a man who had come to storm the very doors of Fox's Earth and take from it, finally and forever, the final Fox woman for whom it waited.

"She done catch up with 'em, then," Rip thought. "She know about Miss Nell an' her man, an' I ain't git there in time." A swimming dizziness took her, started at the ends of her fingers and swarmed up them, up and up, until she spun with it toward the pale nap of the dining-room rug, and she could only cling to the back of the massive chair where Mr. Claudius Fox had sat when she first came to Fox's Earth as a girl, where now old Ruth sat in the evenings. She clawed at the chair and fought against the close-pressing, buzzing darkness, and when at last it cleared and she could lift her head again, she straightened her spine and walked softly out of the dining room and into the foyer and up the stairs.

At the top of the stairs, where the upstairs telephone nook was, Rip heard the click of the receiver being replaced, and she heard Ruth Yancey Fox cry aloud for the final time in her life, "Mama! Mama! Wait for me!"

Rip mounted the stairs one by one, noiselessly, her aching feet light as on green mountain earth, her small head on the long, slender neck held as high as if, upon it, the crown of the old queens of her faraway ancestral Futa Jallon lay light and fitting and sweet.

"You will have two weeks," Phillips Jay said to Nell, across town in the long, low Colonial house by the river with the pierced-brick patio walls to let in the little water winds that were so sweet on this May day of singing rain and shying sun. He still held the telephone in his hand; he had not replaced it. Nell did not know who had called him. She was dead, incurious. It did not matter. All that mattered to her was that Abby should not hear this. Catching her apprehensive look about her, he said with stiff lips, "She isn't home from school yet. Do you think I would let this slime touch her?"

He was cold, incandescent. Nell realized, dimly, that he was capable of anything at this moment; capable of murdering her. This did not matter, either. She looked at him; behind the glass of the bell, he looked like a goldfish, mouthing.

"In those two weeks," Phillips Jay continued, "you will decide whether or not you will come back to Abby and me. If you do, you will live in this house as we have always lived and this . . . escapade . . . will not be mentioned again. You will not pursue your writing. Never again. You will not see Wolfe again. He will be gone at the end of this term; he will not teach again anywhere in this country. I can see to that, and I will. Your name will not be spoken to him nor to anyone else in connection with him. But he will know why.

"If you do *not* return, I will send Abby to Yancey at the beginning of the summer, and she will stay there, and I will file for a divorce. You will not gain custody of Abby and you will not see her again until she is old enough to decide for herself whether she wants to see you. I think you know how she will decide. I will not give you one penny, and no court in the country will make me do so. If you think you and your . . . lover . . . can live on the fruits of your pen, try it with my blessing. In addition, I will tell your mother and every living soul in your precious Old Sparta about this, and I will then tell the entire campus everything, including the identity of the man whose pants you have been crawling into for God knows how long. Go to your grandmother's house now. Pack enough clothes so you don't have to come back or call me. She will undoubtedly be delighted to take you in. If

369

you do not return to me, you will certainly never leave that house again. Call me when you have decided."

Nell was in the big sun-and-rain-lighted bedroom that had been hers and Phillips's, packing a bag, when the call came from Rip that Ruth Yancey Fox had tripped in her new four-inch Jourdan heels and fallen headlong down the curving stairs of Fox's Earth and broken her neck. She had died instantly.

On the way to Fox's Earth, Nell stopped at a pay phone and called Lewis Wolfe out of class. It seemed ludicrous to her, as she waited for the young graduate student who tended his phone when he was teaching to answer, that she had ever been afraid to do this.

"Tell him it's Mrs. Jay," she said. "Nell Jay. And please tell him that it's an emergency."

"Yes'm," said the young woman. "How are you, Mrs. Jay? It's been a long time since we've seen you. When are you coming to see us?"

"One day soon now," Nell said. "Could you get Dr. Wolfe, please?"

"Yes'm."

"Then it's settled," Lewis said. "Do what you have to do there . . . I'm sorry about your grandmother, Nell, but not very, and you shouldn't be, either . . . and then come out to the farm. We'll start from here and now, I'm glad, love. In fact, I think I'm probably the happiest man in North America, and that's not an exaggeration."

"No," she said.

"What do you mean, no? You can't mean you're going back to him. God, Nell . . . do you want me to come there? To Fox's Earth?"

"No. No, I don't. Don't come here, Lewis. Don't call me. I can't live with this anymore. I can't cause any more destruction. I was a fool to even begin to think I was free to choose. I've never been free."

"You're free now."

"No."

"I'll wait to hear from you."

"Don't wait."

"I'll wait."

When she drove up the circular drive of Fox's Earth, Abby was waiting for her on the veranda.

370

29

THE MORNING BEFORE Ruth Fox's funeral was sullen and cottony with undescended rain. Nell waked late to a silent house. She had slept heavily and without dreams, and she was stiff and sore deep in the long muscles of her legs and arms, as though from a mild case of flu. She lay for a moment, pushing her weighted legs against the damp sheet, trying to remember what lay so heavily over this already heavy day. Of course, the quarrel. She remembered the fountaining rage at Yancey, the hateful and delicious words she had flung at Abby. Oh, God. And today would be spent sitting in the drawing room with Gamma's body, nodding and cooing sweetly at every sniveling old trout in town. So many hours to get through before she could sleep again . . .

She looked across at the ormolu clock on the mantel-piece of her old room. Nine o'clock. She scrambled from the bed so quickly that her head spun and light motes danced before her eyes.

In the bathroom mirror, as she brushed the sour skin of fatigue and old rage from her teeth, Nell studied her face. She looked no different. Her father's long, sherry-colored eyes were ringed with shadows and Hebe's fine bones were sharper under her skin, but the shadows and the sharpened mask of bone had been there for a long time now. Nothing had changed since last night. Nell grimaced at herself with her foam-mustached mouth. Why should anything be different?

"Because," the thought came clearly, "people cannot say such things to each other and be the same people they were before they said them."

It had been a terrible day yesterday; she thought it only fitting that it culminate with a near-mortally savage quarrel with her sister and daughter. The quarrel had, she thought now, been building since Abby's birth, and it had

had fifteen years in which to acquire its killing momentum. In actuality, she reflected, it had begun germinating long before that. Paul's death had left in Yancey a desperate hunger that she had sought to fill with a succession of men in her life and bed for the past twenty years; when Abby, so like Paul as an infant, came along, Yancey's insatiable passion had focused on her, and the remaining years had been spent in a concerted effort, conscious or unconscious, to recapture her fiercely loved brother in the small effigy of him that was Abby. Not that the men vanished from her bed; they had merely become more numerous and shorter of tenure. Yancey's current man was an internationally famous fashion photographer, a fact which she used shamelessly and constantly to further mesmerize the infatuated Abby.

Since Yancey had stepped off the plane in the Atlanta airport yesterday, rumpled and careless in severe silk and linen but still as golden and sinuous as Nell remembered her, Nell had been at war with her and Abby. It had begun on the drive over to Atlanta. Nell had not asked Abby to come along, but when she went out to the Volvo the girl had been sitting in the front seat, looking straight ahead, her eyes shielded by enormous, opaque sunglasses. Nell did not know why her daughter was there, any more than she knew why Abby had been waiting for her on the front veranda of Fox's Earth when she arrived yesterday.

"Are you sure you want to come?" she said neutrally to her daughter. "It's a long, hot drive, and you didn't get much sleep last night."

"Yancey would never forgive me if I wasn't at the airport to meet her," Abby drawled, and Nell wondered when that fluting, dying note had crept into her voice. It was the voice of old Ruth. "She said so when she called back last night. She said she couldn't wait to see me because we had lots to talk about. I know she means the Juilliard thing."

"She *is* punishing me," Nell thought wearily. "I think she does know about Lewis, after all. She's terribly angry at me for some reason, but I don't know if it's because she thinks I'm going to go away with him and leave her, or because I've made such an ignominious damned fool of myself. Probably the latter. I just can't go into it with her now."

Aloud she said, "I imagine your Aunt Yancey can survive the drive from the airport quite nicely without the pleasure of your company. Especially in your present mood."

"Well, I sure didn't want to hang around Gamma's with Grandmama going bananas and all those creepy old women prowling around, practically crawling into the casket," Abby said. "Besides, I don't like to be there with Gamma. She looks icky. She looks like she ought to be hanging over the fireplace." She giggled.

"She looks dead, which is what she is," Nell said crisply. "And you don't have to be at Gamma's if it upsets you so. You can go home and stay with Dad any time you want to."

"Which is more than you can do, isn't it?"

Nell looked at her in dull hurt. So she did know. Abby stared straight ahead, her mouth formless with the enormity of her own words. They were silent. Then Nell said, "I see that you know about . . . me and Mr. Wolfe. Lewis Wolfe. I assume that you overheard your father and me yesterday . . . I'm sorry that you heard it that way. If you heard that much, you must know the . . . terms that your father laid down. I wouldn't leave you alone, Abby. Things might not be so good between your father and me, but that had nothing to do with you. I love you. Your welfare is the most important thing in my life."

Abby slewed around on the seat furiously. "You really give a huge, enormous shit about my welfare, don't you, Mother? My welfare was obviously numero uno in your mind when you wrote your precious book, because it made everything just so *wonderful* for all of us. My welfare was obviously numero uno when you crawled in the sack with old what's-his-name . . ."

"That is enough, Abby," Nell said. Something in her voice silenced the girl. She gave a great, rattling sniff and turned her face to the flying May morning outside. But the first thing she said to Yancey, after she had hugged her and been hugged and they were walking along the crowded concourse toward the baggage claim was, "Mother and Dad have had an awful fight over a man Mother has been having an affair with, and Dad's thrown her out of the house and told her not to come back for two weeks and maybe ever." She said it roundly and clearly, her eyes fastened on her aunt's thin, handsome face.

"Not funny, Abby," Yancey said coolly. "Badly done.

Gauche." But she was looking at Nell. Abby's face flamed and she moved swiftly ahead of them, her back ostentatiously straight.

"What's going on, Nell?" Yancey said.

"Just what my loving daughter told you so graphically," Nell said. "With a few toothsome details missing. I don't want to talk about it now, Yancey."

Her sister seemed not to have heard her. She laughed sharply.

"That awful house," she said. "That house without men. We're not lucky, Nell, you know, we Fox women . . . because that's what we are, Fox women, no matter what our last names are. Men don't stay with us. Daddy didn't, Paul didn't, and now Phillips. It's the curse of the Foxes."

"Yancey . . ."

"I'm sorry, Nell," Yancey said. "I really am. If you want to talk about it later, or if I can do anything to help, I will. I want to."

"Thanks," Nell said. She meant it.

But after all, Yancey did nothing to help. Instead, from the moment she entered the foyer of Fox's Earth, she grew more and more perverse, more sharp-tongued, and it seemed to Nell that she went out of her way to wound. Wherever she looked in the old house, Yancey found something to mock. Nell reacted with a slowly mounting anger whose strength truly shocked her. She could not sense its limits.

Hebe had been prostrate with pale grief when Nell left her earlier, the grief of a favored, sheltered young girl who has lost her mother and is now open to the terrible winds of God. But by the time they returned, Rip had gotten her up and dressed, and she was sitting in the little parlor behind the Sheffield tea service. She was brightly pleased to see Yancey, but it was the pleasure of one child greeting another who has been away briefly.

"Why, hey, there, Yancey," she chirped.

"Hello, Mama," Yancey said, kissing the soft cheek. "I'm terribly sorry about Gamma."

"Mama is dead," Hebe said in a clear, surprised voice. "Mama died yesterday. Did you know that? Mama fell down the stairs and twisted her neck, and Rip wouldn't let me look at her in the hall, but after she came back from Cromartie's I looked at her. She's in the drawing room. We can go look at her now, if you'd like to."

"We've seen her, Mama," Nell said gently. Yancey was silent. Rip took Hebe back to her room then, and they heard the television set go on.

"Christ," Yancey said. "She's crazy as a loon, isn't she?"

"She's no more crazy than you are," Nell said shortly. "This is the way she always is when there's something she doesn't want to deal with. You wouldn't know that; it's been a long time since you've been here when there was a crisis going on."

Yancey looked at her narrowly, through smoke.

"Meaning that I should have sacrificed my precious all on the altar of family responsibility, like my baby sister did? No way. But she is crazy, and somebody is going to have to take care of her from here on out, and it sure as hell isn't going to be me."

"I wouldn't dream of asking you," Nell said tightly.

Later that afternoon Nell drove downtown to Cromartie's to pick up the clothes Ruth had been wearing when she was taken there. When she returned home and pulled into the driveway, Abby was pushing Yancey in the old rope swing in the back yard that Johnny Geiger had hung on the oak limb on the day of Nell's birth, those long years before. Yancey swung high, head tipped far back, her long body in linen slacks arched like a bow. She was laughing, and Abby laughed, too, standing behind her aunt, pushing her when she swung back. It was her own laugh, infectiously deep and guttural and free, not the unnerving fluting she had recently developed.

Yancey saw Nell and slowed and stopped herself with one foot, and got out of the swing. She went to Abby and stood behind her, resting her chin on Abby's head. She rocked back and forth contentedly, and Abby rocked with her. Both smiled winsomely at Nell, and the sight hurt her heart and dashed the smoldering anger higher.

"Go in and put on a dress, Abby," she said briefly to her daughter. "People will be coming by, and you can't meet them like that."

"I'm not going to meet them, period," Abby said, looking up at Yancey. "Yancey and I are going into Atlanta. Yancey says there's a Ralph Lauren at Saks that would be terrific on me, perfect to audition in. I don't have anything that even vaguely looks like New York."

She stared at Nell, mulishly defiant.

Nell turned away and started for the house.

"I will expect you downstairs and dressed in one hour, Abby," she said, her voice trembling. "I'll pay you back for this, Yancey," she thought.

"I will *not*," she heard Abby shriek shrilly, and then she heard Yancey say lightly, conspiratorially, "Don't make her mad. Go ahead and do what she says. We'll sneak away tomorrow after the damned receiving. Maybe we'll stay overnight at the Peachtree Plaza and have dinner somewhere fancy. Would you like that, love?"

Abby's muttered reply was lost to Nell. She climbed the shallow steps to the veranda and walked around the side of the house to the wisteria bower. She sat down in an old-fashioned glider and put her face into her hands and wept. For a small space of time, the anger eased. Soon afterward, Yancey and Abby came out of the house and got into Gamma's Chrysler.

"We're going uptown for a little while," Yancey called gaily. "Want anything?"

Nell did not answer.

They came back from town late, and the full force and fury of the quarrel came with them.

Rip was laying the table in the dining room and Nell, mindlessly tired, was in her mother's room trying to coax her to eat some of the light supper Rip had brought up on a tray. Their laughter preceded their footsteps, dancing up the stairs. Nell felt new rage run through her veins. What right had they, they who had done nothing at all to help, but only to hinder, to laugh like irresponsible children when there was so much to be done, coped with, borne? They had ignored the dead old woman downstairs and the living one up in this musty, frozen bower; taken as their due endless services and solicitude from Rip; gone their own ways in search of diversion. Nell's hand twitched with fury, and Hebe whined at the spoonful of bouillon Nell was trying to slip between her lips, and it dribbled down her chin. The fury swelled like a Japanese water flower.

They clattered into the room without knocking. Hebe started violently and shrank back against the pile of ruffled pillows. The white wicker tray lurched, and toast and bouillon flew from it to puddle on the eggshell-satin comforter. Butter glistened fattily on the perfectly ironed organdy ruffles. Yancey and Abby stopped still, glancing guiltily at the ruined comforter and then at Nell. Hebe began to cry her thin kitten's wail. There was no other sound but Nell's sharp indrawn breath, and then Abby giggled. She rolled her eyes up at Yancey in a parody of sophisticated amusement and disgust.

"How gross," she drawled. It was Yancey's drawl.

For a long, buzzing moment, Nell looked at her daughter. Abby stood in the center of the room, her young body drawn without shadow or softness through the sleazy jersey of her dress, her long feet bare and awkward and somehow immensely sensual in teetering, stiletto-heeled sandals. The sandals were new; she had not had them on when she left the house with Yancey. Nell knew that Yancey had bought them for her in town. She looked at Abby's newly lipsticked mouth, drawn artfully around the dreadful false laugh; at her face, a conscious, glittering-hard parody of Yancey's. Abby's eyes were closed theatrically. She stood hipshot and slack-thighed, as Yancey often did. On Yancey the stance was natural and somehow rakishly elegant. Abby looked about to open her thin child's thighs to receive a man. Nell walked across the room to where Abby stood and slapped her ringingly across the face.

There was no sound, and then a long wail of hurt and outrage from Abby, and louder weeping from Hebe on the bed. Nell's ears rang and rang. She felt nothing but an animal-simple sense of release, and then the familiar beginnings of a grinding, weary old guilt. Before she clamped the thought off surgically in her mind, Nell realized that it had felt very good to slap her daughter.

"You are absolutely *monstrous*," Yancey began in her crystal voice, and Nell's rage burst.

"You shut up," she screamed into Yancey's face. Yancey flinched involuntarily. Nell turned to Abby, whose wails had stopped, forgotten, at the alien sound of her mother's voice soaring out of control.

"Get out of here right now," Nell screamed into Abby's blank face. "Go straight to your room and take off those shoes and that dress, and wash your face while you're at it. If you could just see yourself standing there simpering like an idiot, *laughing* at the mess you caused your grandmother to make . . . you look like a little hooker . . ."

"Yeah, well, I guess you're not the only one in the family with a lock on that," Abby shot back, frightened and furious, emboldened by Yancey's protective arm around her shoulders.

"GET OUT OF HERE BEFORE I SLAP YOUR HEAD OFF YOUR SHOULDERS! YOU AREN'T MY DAUGHTER: I DON'T EVEN KNOW YOU ANYMORE!"

Nell could hear her own voice squalling through the vast silence of the house. "How funny if there should be people downstairs," she thought mildly, somewhere under the noise. "I really don't often do this."

Abby began to cry in earnest. She whirled and fled from the room. They heard her door slam, and then silence. Yancey swung around to face Nell, her face blanched white.

"Good, Nell," she spat, her words low and venomous. "Wonderful. You're a model American mommy, you are. That's the best thing you could have done for Abby at this point. She's just found out her sainted model mommy is fucking the visiting fireman from old Ioway six ways to Sunday, and her father has thrown said mommy out of the house, and her great-granny has done a swan dive down the stairs and broken her neck, and her grandmother has come over queer as a three-dollar bill, and she has to spend a whole day shut up with a goddamn corpse and a parade of slobbering old ladies, and then you slap her face and call her a whore. Perfect."

"Yancey, you keep your . . ."

"Shut up! What do you know about whores? What do you know about fucking, for all that you think you've been doing it with the famous professor for the past year? You know nothing! I'll bet it's as dry as a bone with you, your famous fucking! You're scared to death of real sex; I've always thought you were. Look at you! You still look like a fourteen-year-old Barbara Bel Geddes, with your little denim skirts and your button-down shirts. The perennial virgin. There's nothing in your face, there's no juice in your eyes or mouth. And look at Abby. She doesn't look like a little whore; she looks like a little boy. You've done that to her. If you have your way, she'll be forty years old before any man ever touches her. What's the matter, Nell? Are you afraid she'll find out it's good, this fucking?"

"I don't need any lectures on how to run my life or raise my daughter from you of all people, Yancey."

Nell's voice was clear and even. Each word hung rich

and sumptuous as a pearl in the thick, buzzing air. From somewhere far apart from the white-faced, cord-necked woman who stood facing her sister on a synthetic fur rug in their mother's sickroom, Nell caressed and admired each word that she spoke. "Clever me," she thought. "Especially when I cannot breathe."

"Oh, don't you though! Since when could you ever manage . . ."

"You have no right to criticize me," Nell's exemplary voice cut across Yancey's. "You dropped out years ago. You wigged right on out when Paul died and left the rest of us to carry all that, and you've done absolutely nothing for this family since, nothing. You've never cared about anything but your own wonderful, perfect career and your string of alley-cat men; you never gave a damn about any of us left here at home, nobody but yourself. Always you, always Yancey first. What I couldn't have done with your chances . . ."

Yancey's voice rose above Nell's, shattering the pretty pearls of words.

"My chances? My *chances*? God, that's funny! It's you who've done nothing! Nothing, Nell! You've always taken everything, everything in the world but a chance. Christ, you've had everything in the world done for you; you never had to lift your finger! It wasn't you they sent away from here; you were the pick of the litter, the only one they kept. And if you're stuck now, it's nobody's fault but your own. You don't have an ounce of gumption, you never fought one minute for the precious career you so woefully bemoan, you never made one move to leave this house and these awful old women. You've never even tried to resolve things in your own family! You can't keep a husband or a lover either, and you won't let go of your daughter. I could do *wonderful* things for Abby in New York, I could give her a *real* life, music, Juilliard, but no . . . You gripe about Mama and Gamma, but when did you ever try to get away from them, when did you ever try to get out of this damned house or this damned soft, wet, stinking South, where nobody can breathe? You've let your own potential die right down to the ground, and now you're killing Abby's as surely as if you'd taken a hoe to the roots. You think you never had my famous chances? You've had *everything!* What the hell more do you want, Nell?"

Yancey's face blurred before Nell's eyes and she saw instead a series of Yanceys, in a row, as on a classical frieze, through a gauze of red-black.

"I want you to shut up," she screamed. "I want you to leave my daughter alone! You can't have her, Yancey; you can't ever have her! She's not Paul. You can't make her Paul. Not any way, not ever. Do you hear me? *Paul is dead!*"

There was a long, vibrating space of time when both were silent, chests heaving, blood pounding in ears. And then Hebe began to scream, shrilly, like a mill whistle. Still they stood there on the rug, unable to look away from each other. Hebe was still screaming and they were still standing there when Rip came silently and swiftly into the room, her face eloquent with disapproval, and went to bend over Hebe. As if by signal, they dropped their eyes and went out of Hebe's room to their own rooms.

Nell, deafened and lightheaded, lay down on her bed. She was not, she realized with mild astonishment, angry with Yancey any longer, nor with Abby. Neither did she feel remorse. Lying in the darkness of the narrow tester bed of her childhood, she tested the air around her, touching it compulsively, as one does a sore tooth. The quarrel had not cleared it; the air of Fox's Earth felt only static, dead.

"Yancey said yesterday, before the fight, that she felt almost hopeful about coming home after so long," Nell thought. "Almost as if there was some sort of resolution for her here, some kind of answer she'd been waiting a long time to find. But I don't feel any answers for any of us. I don't feel anything ahead for us. We've come to the end of things here. All of us, every one of us under this roof except maybe Rip is crippled and hurting and in pain and trouble. I don't know what is left for any of us."

Surprisingly, she slept.

Now she stepped back from the bathroom mirror and went to look at herself in the pier glass against the wall of her room. "Barbara Bel Geddes? Virgin? Do I really?" she thought. Her brown silk shirtwaist did seem austere, chaste, somehow neuter. She went to her suitcase and rummaged out a long strand of pearls and held them up to the dress. She winced. Barbara Bel Geddes did indeed

380

look back at her. She paused a moment, and then dug into a zippered side pouch of the suitcase and pulled out the gold apple charm. She slipped it around her neck and looked into the pier glass. The charm slid into the tender hollow of her throat and nestled there as though it had been poured to fit while molten.

When she had taken it off in despair last winter, he had said, "You'll wear it again. When you really need it, you'll put it back on. And when you take it off after that, it will be because you won't need it anymore."

"I need it now, Lewis," she said aloud, and fastened the chain behind her neck. The apple gleamed in the cup of her throat as if spotlit, and she saw that it had come to rest with the flat side up, so that the engraved P.F.G.& V.V. stood out in the weak morning light. But she did not pull her collar over it, or tie on a scarf. She brushed her drying hair and smoothed her skirt and went, lightly and in dread, down the great curving stair of Fox's Earth to attend Ruth Yancey Fox in her last rites.

She lay now, enthroned in mahogany and silver, in front of the southernmost of the twin white marble mantelpieces, directly under the massive chandelier that Wade Howell Fox had had shipped from Venice in 1817, when Fox's Earth was rising from the grove of water oaks on Church Street. Outside, rain threatened but did not fall. The French doors on either side of the fireplace were open, but the air was heavy and still, clotted with the decaying sweetness of the flowers banking the coffin. Nell automatically murmured the right things to the blue-rinsed, hatted and gloved old women who had been her grandmother's contemporaries. They seemed frailer than usual, stained by the death of this tiny, perfect, seemingly invincible doll; how much more vulnerable were they, with their crawling worms of veins and arthritis-warped limbs and melted faces? Nell felt their fear and the bright, vicious, bird-eyed curiosity that overrode it. They leaned close to Ruth Fox to price her dress, and they said how extraordinarily lovely she looked, and how unbelievable it was that she wouldn't just sit right up and take charge like she always had. Several wept and were borne off on the arms of aging children or old servants. One old woman whispered loudly, like a hoarse night bird, "She's wearing every one of the Fox diamonds. You don't think they're going to put her in the ground in them, do you?"

"Shhhh, Mama," her daughter hissed, and led her from the drawing room into the dining room, where a funeral feast was spread out on old damask on the Hepplewhite table. Rip's work.

"I'm sorry, Nell," Yancey said presently from across the coffin, where she had come to sit along with Nell. Her voice was subdued. Nell looked at her.

"It's okay, I am, too," she said, and smiled. They both knew that it was not okay.

"I keep hurting you," Yancey said bleakly. "I always did. I really am sorry about last night, and so is Abby, in case she hasn't gotten up the courage to tell you yet."

Nell looked away from Yancey and into the dining room, where Rip had stationed Abby behind the Sheffield coffee service. Abby wore a long-sleeved shirtwaist dress and low-heeled pumps; she slouched, and slopped the coffee, but she stayed at her post. Feeling her mother's eyes on her, Abby looked up, and then bent her head so that her thick bell of fair hair swung forward to obscure her eyes. But Nell had seen the closed, sullen face and knew that Abby had not forgiven her.

"You don't love me . . ." she had shrieked. "You never did love me . . ."

"Love," Nell thought. "I don't want to hear that word ever again. What a great lot of pain there has been in this house in the name of love. Yancey withered and blasted with it. Abby mean and old from it, scared to death of it. Mama upstairs sedated out of her mind, stunted into a monstrous old baby by it. Phillips and me, now, cold and sick and finished with it. And Paul, dead of it . . ."

She saw him plain and totally then, her long-dead brother, in a sort of supranormal focus, a flash of summation and knowing. Paul, his brief life, his history, the wholeness of him, seemed drawn on the air before her, armature and mass, bones and modeling, vivid and finished. The wholeness was as good as earth and air, light and clean, an X-ray of essential decency. She was consumed for a moment with pain and loss and love for him.

"Miss Nell."

Rip stood before her, her face thunderous, her brows knit together.

"What is it, Rip?"

"Boy here to see Miss Yancey," Rip said. "Wouldn't tell me what he want, say he got to speak direct to Miss Yancey. I say she in here settin' with Miss Ruth, but he say he wait . . ."

"What boy? I don't know anybody here anymore," Yancey said.

The boy, a reedy teenager in Adidas, indistinguishable from a dozen other Sparta boys, materialized in the arch of the drawing room and Nell rose and went to meet him. Yancey followed.

"I tol' you Miss Yancey busy right now," Rip began indignantly, but Yancey lifted her hand. Rip fell silent.

"Are you Miss Yancey Geiger?" the boy said. Yancey nodded. The boy looked down at the bulky paper-wrapped parcel that he carried.

"Miss Yancey Fox Geiger?"

"Yes."

"I'm Beau Howell, Miss Geiger," the boy said. "I'm doing summer work for Crum, Hurlbert and Hill. Mr. Stuart Hill, Senior, asked me to bring this to you and put it directly into your hands and bring a receipt back to him. I have a form right here for you to sign."

He began to rummage through his pockets, encumbered by his tight blue jeans and the bulky package. They waited.

"What is it?" Yancey said finally.

"We don't know, ma'am," Beau Howell said importantly. "Mr. Hill, Senior, says it's a bit of a mystery. All he knows is that your grandmother, Mrs. . . . Ruth Yancey Fox?"

Yancey nodded again, mesmerized.

"Mrs. Ruth Yancey Fox brought it to him, wrapped and sealed like this, just three days ago, with instructions that he keep it in the safe until her . . . er, death . . . and then it was to be put directly into your hands on the day before the funeral. Mr. Hill, Senior, said that little did he know when he accepted the package that it would be the last time he looked upon Mrs. Fox alive . . ."

"Thank you," Yancey said in her clipped voice. "Tell Mr. Hill, Senior, that I appreciate his meticulous attention to my grandmother's instructions. I'll take it . . ."

The boy moved back slightly, gripping the package.

"Mr. Hill, Senior, said for me to get you to sign this form first, Miss Geiger."

"Oh, for . . ." Yancey breathed. She signed. The boy

relinquished the package and padded out of the foyer as silently as he had come. Nell looked at Yancey, and then at the package in her hands.

"Now what on earth," she said, puzzled.

"I think I'll take it into Granddaddy's study and open it," said Yancey. "Gamma obviously meant it to be private or she'd have told the famous Mr. Hill, Senior, what's in it. It's wrapped up like she was going to mail it to Madagascar. Maybe it's my inheritance . . . a box of cobras or something. Can you hold the fort without me for a little while, Nell?"

"Sure," Nell said. She turned back toward the drawing room, but stopped when she saw Rip's face. The old woman . . . for she was old now, old for the first time in Nell's remembrance, old, old . . . stood looking after Yancey with a face as distorted as though killing winds or furious gravitational forces dragged at it; a face rigid with what, on any other face, would look to be terror. Her long body stooped; she leaned heavily on the gate-legged table with one hand, and there was an iridescent wash in the webbed and pouched eyes that seemed, incredibly, to be tears.

"Rip?" Nell said. It came out lightly and breathlessly.

Rip turned and was Rip again, impassive, erect, no longer deathly old.

"Catch in my back," she muttered, not looking at Nell. She walked silently out of the foyer and through the dining room into the kitchen. Nell stared after her for a moment, and then went back to her seat beside the coffin of her grandmother, and the endless afternoon wore on.

At four thirty, with the rain light slanting lower through the French windows and only a handful of Ruth Yancey Fox's closest friends left in the drawing room, Yancey came out of her grandfather's study across the foyer of Fox's Earth and walked into the drawing room. Nell sat up straighter on her aching spine, grateful to be spelled at last in the litany of hand pressings and cheek peckings. The remaining friends of Ruth Fox saw Yancey, too, and stopped their decorously mournful chatter and fell silent. The drawing room was silent; the afternoon sang with silence.

In a pool of thrumming silence, Yancey walked across the carpet to the coffin and looked down at her grandmother. Her narrow Fox head and neck and back were very straight, and her face looked rapt and chaste in the fading light, like a carved effigy on a Crusader's tomb. Her heavy flaxen hair seemed to snap and burn in the dimness. She was smiling, a soft, dreaming, terrible smile.

She stood looking down at her grandmother, dead and still more beautiful than any of her living progeny, for a long moment, and then she reached down and slipped her left hand gently under the frail, diamond-laden neck, and lifted the small head with its coiled gilt hair off the satin pillow, and raised it so that it drooped sweetly down upon the white-powdered breast like a flower on a too-tender stalk. Small murmurs rose from the remaining mourners, who anticipated, not without doleful relish, a tender, grieving scene.

Slowly Yancey drew her right hand back and slapped the dead white face so hard that the sleek little head bounced wildly on the satin pillow and flopped antically to rest at a roguish angle on the shoulder. The shining hair spilled forward and slid seductively down over one closed eye. The painted mouth slackened and opened archly.

By the time Yancey had turned on her heel and drifted like a sleepwalker out of the drawing room and up the curving, twilit stair, the thin old squalls of shock had faded once more into silence. And by the time Nell's frozen muscles released her so she could move to the side of the coffin, the stinging red imprint of Yancey's hand had faded from the cheek of her grandmother.

It was only much later that Nell realized, with the sense of something nigglingly awry slipping finally into place, that of course there could have been no handprint, for Ruth Fox had no blood.

30

NELL DID ALL the right things.

While old Ruth Fox's broken neck still lolled upon her breast and her eyelids opened slowly over violet eyes that were ever so slightly crossed, Nell went to each of the appalled and terrified old people, some of whom were beginning to cry loudly, and hugged them gently, and led them tenderly to the front door.

"You must forgive Yancey. You can see that she's not herself," she murmured to first one and then the other. "Gamma would not want any of us to condemn her. You go on home and rest some, now."

And finally they were gone. Nell shut the great door behind the last of them herself. The dining room and the little parlor were empty; Rip and Abby had not seen Yancey's terrible somnambulist's act, then. Good. Maybe they would not have to know. Nell went into the drawing room and straightened her grandmother's head until it rested once more on the satin pillow. She smoothed back the gilt hair. She could not close the eyelids, so she closed the lid of the coffin.

She climbed the stairs and looked into her mother's room; Hebe's drugged snores rattled peacefully in the dim room. She paused before Yancey's room, then knocked softly. There was no answer. She pushed the door open hesitantly. Yancey lay on her bed, her back to Nell. She was still. "Well," Nell thought, "let her sleep. Better I don't have to talk to her about it yet. It had to be that package; I'll go see for myself." Abby's door was closed, but music throbbed from behind it. Nell walked on and back down the stairs.

She went out into the kitchen where Rip sat in her rocker, her hands flashing with the mending of Hebe's eternal ruffles. Rip looked ill and diminished. Nell thought,

"I must see that she gets a complete vacation from us when this is all over."

"Ever'body done gone?" Rip said, glancing up at Nell.

"Yes. I want you to go rest some, too, Rip. I don't need you anymore for now. I'll get us some dinner later."

Rip's head came up square and high, and she looked hard at Nell.

"What the matter, Miss Nell? Where Miss Yancey?"

"Yancey's upstairs lying down. Mama's still asleep, too. And so is Abby, I guess. It's a perfect time for you to curl up. I want you to go on and do it, Rip."

"No'm. I ain't goin' nowhere. There somethin' bad the matter, an' I ain't gon' leave this here chair till you tells me what. Do it be them papers that old boy brought Miss Yancey?"

"How did you know they were papers?" Nell said, mildly curious. Fatigue and the draining residue of shock had dulled her mind, not unpleasantly.

"Look lak papers to me. Miss Nell, if they's trouble . . ."

"There is no trouble," Nell said coldly, gathering herself together. "I want you to go to your room now, Rip. I need to be by myself for a while."

"I'll make that up to her somehow," she thought inside her wrapper of frigid calm.

Rip looked at her for a long time, but there was no rancor in her eyes. Finally she rose stiffly.

"Yes'm," she said, and walked silently out of the room.

Nell went to the door of her grandfather's study and opened it and entered. The room was as it had always been, musty and dim and somehow still male-smelling, comforting. And then she saw the package lying neatly in the middle of the desk on the fresh blotter that Rip had placed there before the afternoon's receiving began. It was the tautly wrapped bundle that Yancey had brought here to open earlier in the afternoon; Nell had known she would find it here. She sat down in her grandfather's leather desk chair, as her sister had done before her, and prodded the package with her index finger, and the brown wrapping paper fell away. She saw that it was a loose pile of papers covered with fine, faded, cursive handwriting: Gamma's.

Nell leaned forward over the sheets. She riffled through them. The ink was fresher as she neared the bottom of the stack. The letters on the last pages were blue-black and still crisp. She recognized the thick, creamy bond sheets that Gamma used for business correspondence, and the pen was undoubtedly the one in the old-fashioned desk set she had always kept in her bedroom desk drawer. What was this?

Nell bent closer to the first sheet. It was dated something, 1949 . . . Nell could not make out the month . . . and it seemed to be a letter. It began, "Yancey, my dear firstborn grandchild . . ."

She frowned slightly. "1949 . . . Let's see. I was what? Seven? And Paul was nine or ten, and Yancey would have been thirteen or maybe fourteen. Why on earth would Gamma be writing her a letter that she only had delivered to her now?"

She riffled rapidly to the last page. It was dated four days previously. Her frown deepened. Just four days ago . . . "Why, this must have been written the day before she died," Nell thought stupidly. Her brain could not get a purchase on the thought. She stared, unseeing, at the sheet of paper. And then her own name leapt out at her, as if it were alive and wriggling and poised to sting furiously.

". . . and I know where Nell goes now. Tomorrow I will follow her and see for myself who he is. After that she will stay here with us at Fox's Earth, and everything will be all right again. She won't be going away with that home-wrecking beast, whoever he is, after all. We'll all be safe, finally. Don't you think I've been a smart girl, chickie? Mama couldn't have done it better herself. I'm sorry you never knew Mama. In many ways you're very like her. Goodbye now, Yancey. You know just what you need to know, and I'm sure you're going to be a better little girl for it. I have complete faith that you'll react the way I mean for you to. See, I still know my little Yancey better than she knows herself, no matter how long she's stayed away."

It was signed, simply, "Gamma."

The air around Nell began to chill and shimmer. Warmth and feeling receded from her hands and arms, slowly, from her fingertips first. Her lips felt numb and her breath came fast and shallow. Gamma. It was Gamma, then, who made the telephone call to Phillips telling him about Lewis. And then the call had come that she had fallen . . .

With fingers that felt nothing Nell pulled the first sheet forward and began to read. She read for a very long time.

It was all there. What they had sought and flinched away from, what they had felt but could not name, what had waited, unseen and unchanging, in the old house: The why of all their lives, hers, Yancey's, and Paul's, in that great house of women.

And the how. In a graceful copperplate hand that was not the hand of the white-radiant mill child Ruth, but of another woman entirely, Ruth Yancey Fox had spelled it all out for them in her letters to Yancey.

The seeing of the great white house by the strange, ragged child of the mad preacher Cater Yancey; the dark-blooded women's words that passed between that child and her stunted mother, Pearl; the blind need for the land and the house and the bitter blood wisdom that lighted the child's way toward it. The terrible thing that had gained her the house of the Foxes and cost the madman his life: the poisoned knowing in the nights of his own small daughter.

The coldly obscene getting of a daughter, Hebe, for Fox's Earth, and the sure and polished deaths of Ruth's mother-in-law and, later, her husband.

The molding of the toy woman who was her daughter; the paying off of the outlander Johnny Geiger, and the final cementing of the useless but necessary daughter into the mortar of Fox's Earth.

The discovery, on the date of the first letter, that the house for which she had fought and schemed and killed was not, after all, her own, to lay into the hands of the unbroken line of Yancey-Fox women she envisioned, but would go at her death to the small, innocuous boy child she had suffered to be raised at Fox's Earth . . . her grandson, Paul. Paul, the enemy for whom all that followed was fashioned, whose fate was fact before it was even dreamed of, like an exploded star whose death-light reaches the sight of men only eons later.

The deliberate throwing together of Paul and Jacob Lee; the simple, roughhouse embrace that she used as a lever to get Paul out of Fox's Earth forever, and into the Virginia boys' school where, as she had hoped, the seed took root.

The growing realization that Yancey was coming dangerously close to seeing her plain and true, and the necessity of ripping her, too, from the fabric of Fox's Earth.

The nonexistent embrace, that final Christmas of Yancey's, between her and the already disgraced Jacob Lee, that had so satisfactorily resulted in the banishment of the black boy to Detroit and the golden girl to wherever she might land.

And then: Nell. The careful shaping and molding of Nell, who must be the chosen one, who must remain to tend the temple. The fear and repression that kept the small child malleable and obedient. The careful thwarting of the writing talent; the so-nearly-successful attempts to break her, fade her, subjugate her, keep her forever in the house of women, yet another Yancey-Fox woman for the nourishment of Fox's Earth.

The frail, helpless leanings and twitterings and frettings, the constant summonses that kept her close, kept her tied to the great, consuming husk of the house on Church Street. The bludgeoning shame heaped upon her at the publication of her novel, the harvest of guilt laid at her feet.

And, during the last year, in response to the new and threatening buoyancy and strength in Nell, the careful trailing of her movements, the discovery of the new novel, and the final, fatal certainty of the affair with Lewis Wolfe.

The evil lay clear and living on the dead pages. Ruth Yancey Fox had indeed kept her house a house of women.

Nell laid the papers down carefully and lifted sightless eyes into the room.

"She was mad," she said aloud into the empty air. "Gamma was completely and totally mad from the time she was a small child, and we never even suspected it."

She rose from the desk and laid the bundle of papers on its polished surface, edges precisely squared. "Yancey, poor Yancey," Nell thought, simply and dreamily. "I must go to her." To find, these long, bitter years later, that you had been driven from your home by a mad-woman's malice, to find that your sentencer and executioner was blood of your blood, bone of your bone . . .

Something rolled and crackled under her foot, and she stooped and picked it up, mindlessly smoothing it out. She must keep things tidy. Nothing must trail, tag, flutter, sag awry. Everything must be neatened and trued. It was a yellowed newspaper clipping; Nell stared stupidly at the headline, reading but not comprehending the small black
390

letters. They made the words: "Miss Longshore to wed Mr. Geiger." Nell shook her head to clear it. Paul never . . . Frowning obtusely, she peered at the clipping: it announced the June wedding of Miss Molly Elizabeth Longshore of Sparta to Mr. Paul Fox Geiger of New York City, formerly of 15 Church Street, Sparta.

"The wedding will be held, following a long tradition in the groom's family, at Fox's Earth, the home of Mr. Geiger's maternal grandmother, Mrs. Horatio Paul Fox," the clipping concluded. It was dated January 2, 1958.

Five days before Paul had died by the hand of an anguished professor of French at Columbia University, a man none of them ever saw because he himself died only seconds later, but who Yancey had said was "very, very pretty."

A man who, Nell saw with a leap of knowing that was as clear and unshakable as it was agonizing, had held in his hands an anonymous letter from a small town in the South, and had opened it, and had found the twin to this malignant clipping.

The one that Yancey had found and flung to the floor only hours before, along with the exultant letter explaining how it had been done. That letter lay still on the carpet, crumpled at Nell's feet; she did not pick it up. Far back in her head, drowning in the great red surf of blood that was pounding at her temples, she could hear Gamma's voice, clear and amused, coiling out of her childhood: "I'm in no hurry to collect from Thomas Roundtree. I figure that debt is a good investment. You never know when you're going to need a little favor on the q.t. from a newspaperman, and they're just as . . . easily persuaded, let's say . . . as the rest of us mortals if they think there's any threat to their silly old paper."

"Oh, my brother," Nell whispered.

The glass bell dropped. Nell picked up the bundle of papers and began to walk Fox's Earth.

She walked as the afternoon rain light faded from the day and the mothy gray of evening slid in from the west; she walked as the gray drained into black. She walked up and down the curving stairs, first one side and then the other. She walked through the empty caverns of downstairs: foyer, drawing room, little parlor, dining room, breakfast room, back porch, veranda, back again. She did not slow her stride, or pause. In all of Fox's Earth, no living creature stirred but the littlest Fox, alone again in this place where once gods strode. Where now only malice and death had substance. She walked in perfect, airless calm. She knew that she was very near to being demented. It did not matter, as long as she could keep walking.

At eight thirty, as if in response to a signal, Nell went up the stairs to the third floor and knocked at Rip's door. When she entered the bare little cell of a room in response to Rip's soft "Come in," she saw that there were the silver snail tracks of tears on the carved black face. Rip was sitting in the old rocking chair that was one of the first things in her life that Nell remembered, rocking to and fro, to and fro. Waiting. Nell sat down on the edge of the narrow iron cot and looked at Rip.

"Something terrible has happened, Rip . . . or rather it happened a long time ago, and we've just found out about it," Nell said. Her voice sounded strange and canted and bell-like in her ears; the madness that lived still in the thick pile of pages in her arms came curling at them like a mist, like a flung shawl.

"Yes'm," Rip said.

"I need you to tell Mama for me," Nell said. "You can use your own judgment about how much to tell her, but she'll have to know some of it. Otherwise she's going to hear what happened this afternoon downstairs . . . that Yancey walked in and slapped Gamma's face almost off her neck in front of half the town . . . and she's going to go even crazier than she is now, and before God, I cannot bear another crazy woman in this house."

Rip waited silently, looking at her.

"Gamma sent Jean . . . that man, you know, Paul's roommate . . . a clipping that said Paul was getting married," Nell said. "It was a phony clipping, a fake. She had something on the editor of the newspaper and she used it to get him to print her up a couple of copies of it. She sent it up there to New York without signing it, and when he opened it, he shot Paul and then he shot himself."

"Do it say that in them papers there?" Rip said. There was nothing in her rich voice; she might have been talking to small Nell Geiger in the warm kitchen of Fox's Earth, over tea cakes and the good peaty fragrance of Irish breakfast tea.

"Yes," Nell said. "That and a lot more. I'll tell you all

of it, but, Rip, can you possibly tell Mama for me? You'll have to do it tonight. I'm not going to be able to do that."

"Miss Nell," Rip said, and Nell saw again on the leathered, scraped-to-bone old face the terror she had seen that morning when Yancey went into her grandfather's study with the wrapped package, "did Miss Yancey read that there clipping?"

"Yes. I'm afraid she did, Rip. But she's all right; I looked in on her before I . . . read it. She was lying real still. She was asleep. Let her rest . . ."

"Lord God, Miss Nell!" It was almost a scream. "Go in there and see 'bout her quick! She gon' go outen her head agin . . ."

"No, Rip, I told you, she's sleeping . . ."

"No'm! No'm! You ain't see her that other time! I seen her! She lie so still you think she dead; she ain't move, she ain't talk . . . go on down there an' ten' to her, Miss Nell, or fo' the Lord is God, Miss Ruth gon' be done kill her too . . ."

"But Mama . . ." Nell said witlessly.

"I'll take care of yo' mama! Ain't I always? Go, Nell!"

And Nell flew on hobbled, leaden feet toward an inevitability too terrible to dwell upon, thinking only that for the first time since she married Phillips Jay, Rip had not called her "Miss Nell."

Yancey's room was flooded with light; every lamp in the room was on, and the old crystal chandelier overhead blazed. At first Nell saw no one, nothing but Yancey's clothes, piled tidily in the center of the old red-and-gold Persian carpet. Dress, shoes, stockings, panties, bra. Even her jewelry was there, the gold shell earrings that she always wore, and the heavy gold cuff from Cartier's that some former lover had given her. Yancey herself sometimes could not remember who.

And then she saw Yancey, and the bell lifted finally and forever from Nell's shoulders, and fear turned her bones to rotten stumpwater. She sagged against the foot of Yancey's bed, loose and sick with fear. Her sister was crouched naked in the small space between the other side of the bed and the wall, crouched on her knees with her fingertips brushing the floor like a naked runner awaiting the starting gun, and her mouth and chin were covered with pink foam. It was a long moment before Nell realized that Yancey had chewed her lips and tongue to a bloody

393

pulp, and was humming and singing softly to herself through the blood and foam.

Nell stood in the middle of the floor and the fear left her and a great red fury took her.

"No, you will not," Nell said clearly to her dead grandmother. She wedged herself into the small space between bed and wall and knelt before her naked sister, and she took Yancey's thin shoulders in her hands. She could feel the bones clearly, as once, long before, she remembered feeling the larger bones of her brother when he hugged her, during his last Christmas at Fox's Earth and on earth. Living bones, then.

Nell thrust her face into Yancey's blind one, and she shook her sister, and she shouted over the roaring in her blood: "Goddamn you, Yancey, you come back here! Don't you *dare* let her get you, too! You can lick her, Yancey; you can lick a goddamned dead woman, you can lick a dead sack of bones, you can lick a bag of dust and *rot*, for God's sake! You can! You can!"

Yancey smiled terribly through the bloody foam.

"Paul couldn't," she giggled.

"You're not Paul! Paul is dead, too; Paul is bones, too! Paul is dust and rot and . . . Yancey, listen; you can lick Paul, too, yes, even Paul! You must! Because Yancey, listen, *they are dead!* Paul and Gamma are dead and they are death and *you are alive!* You are in life. Christ, I never thought I'd see the day that Yancey Fox Geiger let a dead bag of bones lick her! She is *bones* and *dust* and *shit* and . . . Yancey, listen. Listen! Yancey . . . *she dyed her hair!*"

Yancey drew in a long, sobbing breath that seemed to go on and on until it rattled in the very marrow of Nell, crouching there in the angle of the bed. And then she began to laugh, and then to cry, and she pitched over into Nell's arms and they fell together to the floor in the small dusty space between the wall and the bed that had been the childhood bed of Yancey Geiger, and they wept for the first time in more than twenty years for the golden brother who had died.

They cried for a long time, until Hebe came pittering fretfully into the room, beginning the mewling kitten's keening that presaged a major spell, one that would last, Nell thought wearily through the scalding, loosening tears, all through the night and perhaps into the day ahead.

"Mother," Nell said over her shoulder, without turning, "shut up."

"You know," said Hebe Fox Geiger, "I believe I will."

Much later, when Hebe had been taken away into her room again and Rip had at last gone up to her small cell, eased; as Nell's aching arms were numbing with the slackening weight of her sister's body and Yancey, tears softening into hiccups, was just beginning the long slide into sleep, Nell felt two arms creep around her neck from behind. Reaching up, she felt the shy, spatulate pianist's fingers: Abby. Loosening her arms from Yancey's body, Nell reached up and covered her daughter's hands with her own.

Part Four

Part Four

AFTERWARD

31

A WEEK LATER Nell and Yancey sat in the stale chill of the Delta Airlines terminal in the Atlanta airport, in a flood of sunshine. The boarding call was late, and the throng of New York–bound passengers jostled impatiently in the boarding line. Nell shaded her eyes against the white glare and looked at her sister.

"Yancey, was he really gay?" she said. They had not been speaking of Paul, but he had been with them for a week, closer than at any time since his death.

"I don't know," Yancey said. "I don't think even he knew, really. Even after all those years in that awful school, and all the years after that, I don't believe he could ever be sure. Which means, of course, that he wasn't really . . . anything. Not even fully gay, so he could at least make peace with that. And he could have, Nell; it could have been a good, dignified life for him. In the end, it didn't matter, because he died a gay death, didn't he? I think I'll always hate her most for that . . . that with all he had and was and could have been, he died thinking that he wasn't . . . anything at all."

"It all goes back to Paul, doesn't it?" Nell said painfully. "For instance, if it hadn't been for me . . . for his wanting to help me get away to Columbia, and her overhearing it . . . he might still . . . oh, I don't know. The worst, the very *worst* thing is, I keep thinking that maybe she did it out of some kind of terrible *love* for me . . . sick, warped, awful, but real love, anyway . . . to keep me with her. That's going to haunt me, Yancey."

"Well, don't let it," Yancey said sharply. "She never loved you or any of the rest of us. She may have *needed* some of us . . . Mama, and certainly you, but she needed you for Fox's Earth, not for herself. She never loved anything in her life but that house and the land it sits on. That was Gamma's great love, that house. God, how it must have galled her to leave it, how she must have *hated* the thought of leaving it. I bet it was her last thought before her neck cracked . . ." They paused and fell silent, both hearing that dreadful, brittle snapping in their heads.

"You know what my nightmare is going to be for the rest of my life?" Yancey said. "That that streak of craziness in me could be hereditary. Her father, and her, and then me . . . that my madness could be her madness. She had to know I'd crack up again when I found out she'd . . . killed him. Somehow she knew. That's why she sent me those goddamned letters. How could she *know* that?"

Her voice was edging upward, and Nell looked hard at her.

"She didn't know," she said firmly. "It was her last long shot, don't you see? So the house could come to me. In a way that's my fault, too. You wouldn't come home so she could . . . get at you directly, so she took the next surest way. It didn't take a genius to recognize your breaking point, Yancey. But the thing is . . . you didn't break, did you? And Fox's Earth is yours now, whenever and if ever you want it. You're free to come home now."

"*God,* no," Yancey said, and laughed. It was a strong, whole laugh, and Nell's shoulders relaxed.

"I don't want it. I don't ever even want to see it again. I'm going to sign it over to you the minute the will's probated. It should be yours, Nell. You earned it . . . you loved it in spite of her, of them; you stayed. And it fits you, somehow. I need to think of you there, in Fox's Earth, no matter how far away I am. It makes an anchor for me."

Nell smiled at her, then her face shadowed again.

"I don't know. It would be hard; there's been too much pain there. It would be so easy just to go. But still, Fox's Earth . . . You know, I *may* stay."

"Not because of Phillips, surely?"

"No. Not because of Phillips. Poor Phillips; with Abby in New York with you, and Gamma gone, and the worst that could happen to me over and done with, he must know he can't get to me anymore. He's got no teeth left. We haven't been good for Phillips; not the South, not the Foxes. He'd probably be delighted to see me go. I wish I cared more than I do. No, if the house could *really* be mine, I might be able to stay. And who knows, Mama may really mean it when she says she never wants to see the place again either. If she can go to the Greenhouse by herself after all these years, and then to Neiman-Marcus and *then* to Sea Island for a month, she can do anything . . . leave Fox's Earth, even. I think I might like to see what Fox's Earth is like on *my* terms."

"That *would* mean she's won, though, Nell," Yancey said. "Have you thought of that? The one she chose, the one she groomed, and schemed for, and destroyed us all for, right back where she meant you to be all along."

"No," Nell said. "She didn't win, Yancey. We did. We won because I could walk away from it in a minute and never look back, and you could come back to it in a minute and never give it a thought. *If* you chose to. The thing is, Yancey, we can choose now. And so she didn't win, after all."

"Well, if you should stay there," Yancey said, "what about your man? Your Lewis? Will you marry him? Would you live there with him, at Fox's Earth?" She grinned. "I like that, Nell. A Yankee Jew at Fox's Earth. Gamma would spin for all eternity, and that's even better than burning."

"I don't know," Nell said. "I told him I wouldn't see him again, and I'm still not at all sure . . . Phillips could make things bad for him at the university, if he wanted to. Somehow, though, I don't think he will. It just seems that we've gotten past and beyond so much this week. I'm meeting Lewis for lunch today . . . at the club, in broad daylight, in front of God and everybody. Maybe we'll talk about it. And maybe we won't talk about anything much at all. I'm sick unto mortal death of talking."

"I know. Me too. Have you told Phillips any of this?"

"No, but I will." Nell grinned suddenly. "My two weeks aren't up yet."

Abby came hurrying through the crowd with an armful of new magazines. Her long stride was strong and easy and her gilt hair bounced on her shoulders with it, all of a piece, like a shining sheaf of wheat. She looked more than ever like a medieval court painting in the lambent morning light . . . and, for a heart-stopping moment, like Paul. They smiled involuntarily at her youth and light and at Paul in her. Behind her, in the crowd, a teenaged boy made a loud, fervent comment, and Abby giggled. It was her old giggle, throaty and free and slightly bawdy. It was infectious; several of the impatient, sharp New York–

pointing faces smiled at the sound and turned to look. They stared at the three women, beautiful women, so obviously of the same blood and bone, caught in this moment of parting.

"Oh," Nell said. Suddenly to her daughter, "I forgot. I have something for you."

"What?"

Abby smiled at her mother, but the pull of the white jet waiting to lift her into the sun toward New York was almost palpable. Nell's heart twisted once again, but she thought. "I've never had so much of her as now, when I'm letting her go. I know now that I will not lose her."

She fished in her purse and pulled out the golden apple. "Turn around," she said, "and let me fasten it for you."

Abby lifted the sheaf of pale hair off her neck and Nell fastened the fine chain. The charm bounced against Abby's fragile collarbone and slid into the loose neck of her dress. She pulled it out and turned it over and read the engraving on the back.

"It's pretty, Mom," she said. "What does this mean? 'P.F.G.&V.V.'?"

"I'll tell you soon, I think," Nell said. "Maybe next time you're home, or when I come up. I don't think it will be long before you're ready to know. We'll see."

"I'm afraid it's too big, though."

Nell took her daughter in her arms and hugged her, a long, hard hug that started a fresh rainbow wash of tears across her eyes. Abby's young body seemed forever imprinted against her own. Nell held her away and smiled at her.

"You'll grow to it," she said.

The boarding call came. Yancey put her hands on either side of Nell's face and looked closely at her younger sister. For a moment she was beautiful, invincible, sixteen-year-old Yancey Geiger of Fox's Earth, her just-brushed silk hair snapping about her proud young face.

"Thank you," she whispered.

"What for?" Tears scalded Nell's eyes and throat.

"For giving me back my life."

They turned, Yancey and Abby, and were gone into the sun.

When she came into the foyer of Fox's Earth out of the blinding noon, Rip stood there waiting for her.

402

"Sorry I'm late, Rip," Nell said. "The plane was late leaving. Let's see, here's your money for the last two weeks, and a little something extra for Detroit. No . . ." for Rip had started to shake her head and hand the bills back. "A month is a long time, and you never know what will come up. We'll settle up when you get back. Take it. Enjoy. Take everybody to supper. Buy Jacob Lee the biggest steak in Detroit. Oh, Rip . . . do tell him hello for me. For Yancey and me. It's been so long, but I *have* thought of him . . ."

Rip looked down at the black-and-white-marble tiles of the foyer. "Jacob Lee kilt fifteen years ago robbin' a liquor sto' in Detroit," she said. "It just my sister now."

The grief that had begun to draw back, like a freezing tide, crashed down over Nell again. Shock hollowed her chest.

"Oh, Rip," she breathed, "we didn't know. Oh, God, we never knew! You just said he was all right; you never told us . . . Rip, why didn't you *tell* us?"

"One of you knowed," Rip said. "The call come here. One of you knowed all along."

Nell stared at her. "Gamma," she said slowly. "Gamma . . ."

"I been know yo' Gamma ever since I come here, Miss Nell, an' I just a young'un then myself. I knowed her ways. Maybe I cain't read, but I knowed what was in them papers she left for Miss Yancey 'thouten you tellin' me. I've knowed that all along, too. All of it 'cepten 'bout Mr. Paul. 'Fo' God I never knowed that . . ."

"Oh, Rip, in the name of almighty God, why didn't you tell us?"

"Who here gon' believe me, Miss Nell?"

"Nobody would have," Nell thought. "Mother couldn't have. I couldn't have. Paul and Yancey, they would have . . . but they weren't here."

"But, Rip," she said, "Jacob Lee . . . he didn't . . . he never . . . you know what she did to him, don't you? How could you stay after that?"

"Seem to me somebody got to look after you an' Miss Hebe, Miss Nell," Rip said simply.

Tears started again in Nell's eyes. Comprehension came, too, slowly, slowly.

"You knew Gamma called Phillips and told him about

me and Lewis Wolfe, then?'' she said, looking at Rip's bowed head.

''Yes'm. I knowed that.''

''And she never in this world tripped on those stairs, did she?''

Rip's head came up. She looked Nell full in the eyes.

''No'm.''

Nell held out her arms and Rip came into them, and they hugged, silently, for a long time. The last of the Fox women, saying good-bye.

Outside, the sun swung free of the great, shrouding trees of Church Street and burst in a flood over the flat roof of Fox's Earth.

More bestsellers by
Anne Rivers Siddons

FOX'S EARTH
"You are special." Ruth Yancey's worn-out mother told her this every day. Indeed, Ruth was beautiful, with a fiery splendor that rose above her squalid Georgia mill town roots. She used her looks and a cold, calculating intelligence to wrench open the doors of Fox's Earth, the most exquisite mansion in town. Ruth became its mistress for three generations, and she ruled with an absolute evil that destroyed the minds and souls of her family. Finally, the only woman in the house with the strength to confront Ruth decides the time has come to put an end to the madness and evil.

"A splendid book...Absolutely mesmerizing!"
—*Chicago Tribune Book World*

HOMEPLACE
Micah (Mike) Winship is a sophisticated New York journalist who is called home to Georgia after twenty years of bitter exile. In 1963, her father cast her out, but now he's dying and he's asking for her. Confronting a past that includes an old lover, an overindulged sister, and a plot to seize her family's homestead, Mike begins to learn about love and loss and the inexplicable pull of a place called home.

"Siddons is a fine teller of tales."
—*The Washington Post Bookworld*

More bestsellers by
Anne Rivers Siddons

THE HOUSE NEXT DOOR

Colquitt and Walter Kennedy live a peaceful and sheltered existence in an affluent Southern neighborhood surrounded by a congenial group of friends. Colquitt is a rational, intelligent woman, but how could she know her peace of mind would be shattered forever when construction begins on the McIntyre lot next door? It was as if the house knew how to destroy its inhabitants, driving them to scandal, madness, and even murder.

"Spellbinding...You will not be able to put down this book!"
—*Dallas Times Herald*

PEACHTREE ROAD

Lucy Bondurant Chastain Venable is a beautiful woman of great passion and terrible need. Into the eye of this storm steps Sheppard Gibbs Bondurant III, her cousin and lifelong confidant, who is nearly destroyed by his own fatal feelings. Their mesmerizing story begins on the childhood day when Lucy goes to live with Shep's family in the great house on Peachtree Road. Set in an Atlanta suffering from growing pains, this is the unforgettable story of the astonishing love and hate between one man and one woman.

"Every bit as fascinating as the story of Scarlett and Rhett..."
—*Detroit Free Press*

Rare & Wonderful Books

by

Anne Rivers Siddons